PRAISE FOR
ALYSSA PALOMBO

THE SPELLBOOK OF KATRINA VAN TASSEL

"An enthralling lovers' tale woven from 'The Legend of Sleepy Hollow,' Alyssa Palombo's captivating story, told through the eyes and heart of Katrina Van Tassel, is like visiting a treasured childhood friend and finding out all her secrets."

—Gwendolyn Womack, award-winning author
of *The Memory Painter* and *The Fortune Teller*

"Palombo has conjured up a dark, sexy twist on Washington Irving's classic tale. *The Spellbook of Katrina Van Tassel* will satisfy romance fans who crave a dash of spine-tingling horror."

—Cat Winters, award-winning author of
The Uninvited and *In the Shadow of Blackbirds*

THE MOST BEAUTIFUL WOMAN IN FLORENCE

"This captivating, beautifully written novel may be more fiction than fact, but readers will be entranced and will feel they are an integral part of the unfolding story. Palombo joins the ranks of Tracy Chevalier, Rosalind Laker, and those who perfectly merge history and reality." —*RT Book Reviews*

"Alyssa Palombo follows up her outstanding debut, *The Violinist of Venice*, with this stunning novel . . . a reflection on beauty and how it can be a curse." —Historical Novel Society, Editor's Choice pick

ALSO BY ALYSSA PALOMBO

THE
SPELLBOOK
OF

KATRINA
VAN TASSEL

Alyssa
Palombo

St. Martin's Griffin ❧ New York

THE SPELLBOOK OF KATRINA VAN TASSEL. Copyright © 2018 by Alyssa Palombo. All rights reserved. Printed in the United States of America. For information, address St. Martin's Press, 175 Fifth Avenue, New York, N.Y. 10010.

www.stmartins.com

The Library of Congress Cataloging-in-Publication Data is available upon request.

ISBN 978-1-250-12761-7 (trade paperback)
ISBN 978-1-250-20266-6 (hardcover)
ISBN 978-1-250-12768-6 (ebook)

Our books may be purchased in bulk for promotional, educational, or business use. Please contact your local bookseller or the Macmillan Corporate and Premium Sales Department at 1-800-221-7945, extension 5442, or by email at MacmillanSpecialMarkets@macmillan.com.

First Edition: October 2018

D   11

For Jen Hark-Hameister, the Katrina to my Charlotte, the Lafayette to my Hamilton, my partner in crime for all fun fall activities and all things Halloween-related. We always sort of hoped the Headless Horseman was real. I did my best to bring him to life.

. . . This sequestered glen has long been known by the name of Sleepy Hollow . . . Certain it is, the place still continues under the sway of some witching power, that holds a spell over the minds of the good people, causing them to walk in a continual reverie. They are given to all kinds of marvelous beliefs; are subject to trances and visions, and frequently see strange sights, and hear music and voices in the air.

—WASHINGTON IRVING, "The Legend of Sleepy Hollow"

THE
SPELLBOOK
OF
KATRINA
VAN TASSEL

Prologue

Washington Irving got it wrong. I don't know what secondhand version of Katrina Van Tassel's story he heard, but it was all wrong. Oh, he got the names right: Ichabod Crane. Brom Bones. The Headless Horseman. But he left out the important parts of the story—the parts that matter most.

When I was a young woman, if you had told me that the man I loved and I, and the men who loved me, would one day be as much a part of Sleepy Hollow's lore as the Horseman himself, I would have laughed. I had no concept, then, of how deeply my actions affected those around me. I was selfish. I could not see beyond my own life, my own struggles, beyond the tale I was trying so desperately to write for myself. But isn't it so for everyone?

Charlotte knew, I think, even back then. In some corner of her mind, she recognized that our story would last and grow beyond us, taking on a life of its own. It is a story that forgot her entirely, forgot the enormous part she played in everything that happened, though often I think that that is how she wished it. She made sure her part would be forgotten.

The appeal of this legend should not surprise me. After all, why should the story—my story—not be one for the ages? It has everything that a grand, epic tale should have, even if the details have been lost: a romance between a handsome hero and a beautiful heroine, a jealous rival, loyal friendship, music, ghosts and demons, magic, and murder most foul.

I have let the wounds from that long-ago time heal, letting the ghosts die and lie in their graves. I had to. It was the only way I could go on.

And yet I will tell the tale all the same, because I would have the true story known at last. For all these years, the truth has been known only to two souls living. But I have kept it inside long enough. Now you, too, will know the truth.

1

The Schoolmaster

It was in early summer of my eighteenth year that my destiny arrived, and despite my fancy for premonitions he took me quite by surprise.

"Katrina!" my mother's voice called, summoning me from downstairs. "We've a guest! Do come down, dear!"

I rolled my eyes and put my book aside. We always had a guest, or nearly so. My father was the most prosperous farmer for miles around, making him Sleepy Hollow's unofficial lead citizen, and as such we often entertained our fellow townsfolk, in addition to travelers passing through: our home was the largest for many miles, situated conveniently along the Albany Post Road, and therefore the first place they would stop to pay their respects, usually in hopes of a handout. Word had long since traveled far and wide that the esteemed Baltus Van Tassel could not turn anyone away.

I should not be so uncharitable, I knew; but it wearied me, a girl who preferred the company of her books and her dog and of nature, to have to entertain strangers so often. That these travelers and visitors were usually men who seemed to find it their right to openly ogle the heiress of so wealthy an estate only meant I had grown quite tired indeed of assisting my mother in playing hostess.

Perhaps, I mused, smoothing my hair before my mirror, I had better give some consideration to these bachelors, before I wake up someday soon to find myself betrothed to Brom Van Brunt.

But I would not think on that now.

Satisfied I looked as respectable as could reasonably be expected on such short notice, I left my bedroom and went down the stairs, my dog, Nox, uncurling from his nap on my bed and following after me. I stepped into the kitchen at the rear of the house, where my mother was issuing instructions to Cook. She nodded for me to pick up the tray that held two silver mugs, filled with the pale wheat beer made in the brewery my father owned, and take it out onto the portico. The large porch was situated at the back of the house and framed gorgeous, sweeping views of the Hudson. I took the tray without comment, Nox trotting at my side. It was a routine we had long since perfected.

"Ah, and here is my lovely daughter, Katrina," my father's booming, jovial voice said as I entered the parlor. He spoke English, I noticed, rather than the Dutch we used in casual company. I had grown up speaking both languages, as did most local families of wealth and property. Our guest must be from a different region of the country. "So nice of you to join us, my dear. Pray, set that down and meet our guest."

I placed the tray on the low table between my father and the other man, then straightened to see that the stranger had risen on my entrance. "Miss Van Tassel," he said, taking my hand and bending to kiss it. His speech was clear, crisp. "A pleasure to make your acquaintance."

I was taken aback by his courtly manner, and even more so by his appearance—but agreeably so.

He was young, that much was certain—likely only in his early twenties. He was tall and gangly, with long arms and legs; he nearly towered over me. Were my father to stand, his own considerable height would be no match for this man. His brown hair, which he had tied back at his nape with a simple black ribbon, was shot through with gold. Wide eyes stared back at me, a startling deep green, like the moss that grew at the banks of the stream in the woods. His ears, I noted, were unfortunately large, yet somehow made his already pleasant face even more endearing. He was handsome, but not too much so.

"The pleasure is mine, sir," I said, not untruthfully.

"Katrina, my dove, this is Mr. Ichabod Crane, our new schoolmaster, just come from Connecticut," my father said. "He has come to visit with us in the hopes that we may smooth his way as he joins our fair community."

The schoolmaster turned to me. "I have heard tales of your father, miss, and his exceeding kindness and generosity. Therefore I had hoped I might prevail upon him on my arrival, seeing as I know no one here."

"You have certainly made the best choice available to you, Mr. Crane," I said, my words coming out in an unexpectedly low, throaty pitch. "My father is indeed a pillar of our community, worthy of all the praise you have heard, and more."

"And who is this distinguished-looking gentleman?" Mr. Crane asked, his attention turning to Nox at my side. He extended a hand slowly, and Nox stepped forward, sniffing him thoroughly. His large, bushy tale began to wag, indicating his approval. Mr. Crane took it as such and reached out to scratch Nox behind his ears, something the big dog enjoyed immensely.

"This is my dog, Nox," I said. "He was born into a litter of herding dogs my father raised, and I could not resist taking him into the house as a puppy and spoiling him." He was also an excellent judge of character, and if he liked this Mr. Crane, my initial favorable reaction to the schoolmaster was justified.

"Nox," Mr. Crane mused, as the dog shifted closer, giving him better access to the spot behind his ears. "Latin for night, is it not?"

I smiled, delighted. "Indeed. He was black as night when he was a puppy, though now that coloring remains only on his face and ears, as you see." The rest of Nox's coat was a magnificent gray and brown brindle.

"And do you speak Latin, Miss Van Tassel?"

"Just a bit. I expressed an interest, and so my tutor in my younger years taught me a little."

My father chuckled, patting my hand. "Katrina is my delight, Mr. Crane," he said. "She is the only child the Good Lord saw fit to send to my wife and me, and yet I hardly think any other daughter—or son, for that matter—could be her equal."

"I am certain that is true," Ichabod Crane said, smiling at me.

"Indeed, indeed," my father said. He reached for his mug of beer. "And now, a toast." At this, our guest hastily picked up his own mug. "To you, sir, and to your future endeavors in our fair town. May you succeed in amply educating our young ones."

"Hear, hear," I murmured as the two men clinked their mugs together. More education would hardly go amiss in this town, for the adults as well as the children; perhaps then the old Dutch farm-wives would not look at me quite so askance whenever they saw me with a book, nor would the foolish young men—like Brom Van Brunt—tease me that my face was far too pretty to be hidden behind its pages. "At least my fair face conceals a far more beautiful mind, something I would not expect you to understand," I had snapped at Brom not long ago in the churchyard. He had stormed away, brow furrowed, as he tried to work out how, precisely, he had been insulted.

"Do they speak much Dutch in Connecticut, Mr. Crane?" I inquired. "For you will find that most of your prospective students—especially from the farther-flung farms—have no more than a passing familiarity with English."

"I know a bit, Miss Van Tassel, though not as much as I should like," the schoolmaster confessed. "But as part of my duty here will be to teach my students English, I am sure between the two languages we shall get along well enough."

"No doubt," my father agreed. "We are fond of our Dutch language and Dutch food and Dutch ways here, Mr. Crane, as you will soon find, but English is the language of this new nation of ours, so we do not teach it to our children at our peril."

"Very wise words, sir."

"Even so, Mr. Crane, should you like to practice your Dutch, you may certainly seek me out," I said, giving him a quick, coquettish smile. It did no harm to flirt with the handsome newcomer, after all.

"And, Katrina," my father added, after the two men had drunk of their beer, "Mr. Crane also brings us some news which I think will be agreeable to you. He is a musician, and in addition to his duties at the schoolhouse, he will be taking on students for singing lessons. I took the liberty of engaging his services for you."

I could feel my face brighten as I considered this Ichabod Crane anew. "This is most agreeable news indeed," I said, and this time my smile had nothing of the coquette in it—it was only genuine. "As my father may have told you, Mr. Crane, outside of books nothing delights me so much as music."

"Indeed?" Mr. Crane said, meeting my eyes. "We will have much to talk of, then."

My father chuckled. "Katrina is wont to wander in the woods and sing to the birds," he said. "I fancy her voice is even finer than theirs, but I am no musician, only a doting father. I shall entrust her to your expert tutelage, Mr. Crane."

"I look forward to it," he said, having never taken his eyes from mine.

"And when may I expect my first lesson?" I asked.

"My dear, the boy has been several days on the road," my father said. "Perhaps we had best allow him time to rest first."

"If I may be so bold as to contradict you, sir," Mr. Crane said, "I find nothing so rejuvenates me as music." He glanced over at me again. "Your father, Miss Van Tassel, has been kind enough to invite me to stay for a time, so I may get settled and determine which of my student's families may host me next. As such, I am entirely at your disposal for the near future and can begin whenever you wish."

I did not look away from his green eyes. "Tomorrow, then?"

His smile widened. "Tomorrow."

2

Brom Bones

I awoke early enough the next morning to see the mist coiling low outside my window. It slithered along the fields into the small stand of woods near the farmhouse, a grayish blue in the eerie morning light. Soon the sun would rise fully and burn away the fog, taking with it my ever-present fear that I might see a ghostly rider emerging from the mist.

But that morning my fears felt far away. At first I could not remember why I felt so happy. I had never been unhappy—save of late, when such nightmares had been plaguing me—but it had been some time since I wakened with such excitement at the thought of the coming day. Then my lips perked in a smile—Mr. Ichabod Crane, the music teacher. He was in our house, and would be commencing my musical instruction that very day.

Oh, that I could tell Charlotte, my dearest friend, about this: a handsome houseguest, and he was to teach me music, as well! But she had been away for the past two months, caring for an ailing aunt near Boston.

I rang the bell to summon Nancy, my mother's and my chambermaid. She fancied herself more my meddling aunt than anything else. While I waited, I poured water from a ceramic pitcher into my small basin and quickly washed my face. I caught a glimpse of my reflection in the mirror and could not help but smile. I had never given much thought to my appearance, but suddenly I was glad that so many people considered me pretty.

When Nancy arrived, she looked down from her considerable height—she was tall for a woman, much taller than I, and had also grown stouter as she aged—and huffed at Nox. He lifted his head up and thumped his tail against the mattress at the sight of her. "I don't know why you let that dog sleep in your bed, Miss Katrina," she said to me in English. Nancy had been born a slave on a plantation in Virginia—though now she was free and paid a healthy wage by my parents—and English was still her preferred language, though she had picked up much Dutch since joining us. "Dogs are meant to be outdoors, not in a maiden's bed."

I grinned. "You say the same thing every morning, dear Nancy. And still Nox loves you." As if on cue, Nox leapt off the bed and gave a lick to Nancy's hand on his way out the door. Downstairs, Cook would let him outside so that he could do his business.

With Nancy's assistance, I commenced dressing. I had her lace me into a light summer gown I had not yet worn; it was part of a brand-new wardrobe my father had purchased for me in New York City. I had consented to go along on the trip and be measured for new clothing only because my father always allowed me to purchase whatever volumes I chose from the bookshops. But now I found myself happy and relieved I had pretty things to wear.

Nancy raised her eyebrows. "My, my, Miss Katrina," she said. "This fine dress just to spend the day at home?"

"Yes," I said coolly. "I . . . have been wanting to wear it, is all."

"I see," she said, and thankfully did not comment further. "Shall I bring you something to break your fast, Miss Katrina?" she asked. "A busy day ahead of you, what with music lessons and all."

"Yes, please," I said. "And some tea to soothe my throat."

Nancy left, and I quickly tied back the top strands of my hair with a ribbon. I frowned at myself in the mirror, twirling one long, wavy blond strand around my forefinger before letting it fall. If only this mop of straw would curl nicely, instead of insisting on this maddening in-between state, I thought. Then I broke into a laugh. Since waking I had put more thought into my appearance than I had in the rest of my life altogether, and suddenly I felt quite silly.

Nancy returned bearing a tray with a hunk of fresh cheese and some warm bread. A cup of tea stood steaming as well, and from the smell I could tell it had honey in it. "Will you be needing anything else, then, Miss Katrina?" she asked.

"No, thank you, Nancy," I said. "But pray tell," I added, unable to hold my curiosity in, "has anyone sent breakfast to our guest?" He had been put in a room just down the hall from me—only a few steps away, really—but it wouldn't be quite proper for me to knock and inquire after his comfort myself, not as the unmarried daughter of the house.

A knowing look came into her eye, and I wished, not for the first time in my life, that she did not know me quite so well. "Ahh, Mr. Crane," she said. "I believe your father has sent Henry to look after him."

"Very good," I said, taking an imperious tone that I knew Nancy would see through clear as a new window pane. "I just wish to make his stay as comfortable as possible."

Nancy chuckled and patted my shoulder. "I'll be sure to tell your mother what a fine hostess you're becoming," she said. "But mind you don't make young Mr. Crane *too* comfortable, yes?" She turned and left my room, still laughing as she went.

I scowled at her retreating back before turning my attention to my meal.

Once I finished eating, I went downstairs and peeked into my father's study. Empty. I debated briefly as to whether I ought to seek out Mr. Crane for our lesson, or wait for him to seek me out. I had just decided on the latter when my mother happened upon me. "Ah, Katrina, I was just coming to fetch you," she said. "There is a visitor whom your father wishes you to greet."

"Another visitor?" I said. "I cannot imagine that President Washington himself entertains as many guests as we do." But my mother was already gone, no doubt headed outside to check on her flocks of chickens and geese—her personal pride and joy.

I headed out to the portico, where I could hear my father's booming voice. I pinned on my charming daughter face. "Mother said you sent for me, Fa—oh." I broke off when I saw who our visitor was and switched to Dutch. "Brom. That is, Mr. Van Brunt."

Brom Van Brunt—nicknamed Brom Bones for his large frame—was the town's favorite son. The girls wanted to be his wife, and the boys wanted to be him—or at least be a part of his merry band of miscreants. Brom and his crew got into more mischief and fights than anyone else in Sleepy Hollow, yet somehow his rough charm and good looks—he was tall, muscular, and blessed with pale blond hair, blue eyes, and a perfectly sculpted face—guaranteed his punishment was never worse than good-natured tongue clucking from the farmwives and tolerant chuckles from the men. It was infuriating, especially because once, as children, there had been no closer band of mischief-makers than Brom, Charlotte, and myself. But that was before Brom had done something that could never be forgiven.

"Miss Van Tassel." Brom swept me an exaggerated bow, his cocky grin holding fast to his face as he straightened. "You are as blooming a beauty as any of the flowers in the meadow."

I rolled my eyes, my father too busy beaming his approval at Brom to notice. "Well put, young man," he said. "Katrina, what say you to such a fine compliment?"

"I would prefer one not so utterly trite," I retorted.

"Well, we can't all be that fusty old poet you read all the time," Brom said, annoyance flickering in his eyes. "What's his name, that Englishman . . . Shakeston?"

"Shakespeare," I replied through gritted teeth.

"Yes, him." Brom waved a large hand dismissively.

"Now, now, Katrina," my father said. "Brom only means to give your beauty its due, as well he might. You look quite lovely this morning, my dear—I notice you have finally seen fit to wear one of your new dresses."

The pleased look on Brom's face made me wish I had dressed in an old sack. "It is most becoming indeed, Katrina," he said. "You must have known I was coming."

I was about to sharpen my tongue on him yet again when the door behind me opened and Mr. Crane stepped out onto the portico. "Ah, Miss Van Tassel, there you are," he said. "I was just . . ." He trailed off awkwardly, having caught sight of Brom. "My apologies for the intrusion. I am Ichabod Crane," he said, extending a hand. Brom eyed him before taking it. "I am to be the new schoolteacher."

"Brom Van Brunt," Brom said, glancing at me, then back to Mr. Crane. Reluctantly he switched to English. "And you lodge here, do you?"

"Just for the time being," my father said. "Once he is more at home in Sleepy Hollow he will be lodging with his students, as is customary."

"Indeed," Brom said, releasing Mr. Crane's hand and stepping back. "An honor to meet a man of letters. We've not had need for many of your kind around here, in truth."

"High time that changed, if you ask me," I interjected, hoping Mr. Crane had not noticed Brom's barb.

"Indeed," Mr. Crane echoed, his tone cooler. He turned to me. "I would not wish to interrupt your visit," he said, "but I wondered if you might like to commence your music lesson?"

I could have kissed the man. "Yes, let us do so," I said.

Smiling faintly, Mr. Crane extended his arm to me. I took it and let him lead me back into the house. "Perhaps I shall see you again soon, Brom," I called over my shoulder to him.

But when I glanced back, he was not looking at me—did not appear even to have heard me—but was instead fixing a chilling glare on Mr. Crane's retreating back.

3

Singing Lessons

"I owe you a debt, sir," I said, as Mr. Crane and I headed toward the back room beside the parlor, which my father had determined best for our lessons. Mr. Crane had not, I noted with some pleasure, removed my hand from his arm. "You have quite rescued me from odious company."

Mr. Crane laughed, a warm, rich sound. "I had hoped I was not too bold, nor overstepping. But it did seem that you had no particular desire for that gentleman's company."

"How correct you are, Mr. Crane," I said. "Sadly, what is obvious to you is not to Brom, nor to my father."

We went inside the small room, and I saw that Mr. Crane had already been preparing: an instrument case was already inside, as well as a few books of songs.

All disagreeable thoughts of Brom Bones disappeared as Mr. Crane opened the case. "Oh! A guitar, yes?" I asked excitedly.

"Indeed it is."

"How wonderful! There is no one in Sleepy Hollow who has one. We did entertain some travelers one evening who thanked us by playing some music, and one of them had a guitar. I thought it the most delightful instrument."

"I think so, too," Mr. Crane said. "It is quite versatile in the styles for which it can be used, which has made it useful for me. And I've found I have rather a talent for it." He smiled politely at me. "You will have to tell me if I am correct, however."

"Oh, I am sure you are just splendid," I said. "Before we begin, would you play something for me?"

"I would, but . . ." He hesitated. "I am quite certain your father is not paying me to serenade you, Miss Van Tassel."

I waved a hand. "No matter," I said. "He will not know; and you would bring me such joy, truly. It is so seldom that I get to hear music."

His smile sparkled, warm and genuine. "Very well," he said. "But then I wish to hear you sing."

"I shall be happy to."

Mr. Crane placed his guitar on his knee and began to strum and pick at the strings, producing a rich, vibrant sound. Perhaps Mr. Crane's instrument was of a finer quality than the one I had heard previously, or perhaps he was a superior musician—or both—but the sound was much smoother and warmer than I had anticipated. He began to play a lovely, cascading sort of melody that called to mind a stream running peacefully through the forest. I closed my eyes, letting it wash over me, pull me in as the music played for dancing when we hosted parties never did. It seemed to tell a story and paint a picture all at once, of a leaf gently borne on a current of water, content to be always in soothing motion. Of a bird soaring over the treetops, kept aloft on a gust of wind. Of a girl wandering through the forest, content to be alone, never wondering what it might be like to have someone beside her.

As he stopped playing and I opened my eyes, I felt altered. I knew that now the girl would begin to wonder what life might be like were she not alone.

Given Mr. Crane's calm demeanor, I had expected he would be a rather relaxed and even complimentary teacher. This did not prove to be the case.

It began well enough. He had me sing a scale for him, up and back down again, with his guitar accompaniment. "Good," he said when I'd finished. "Very good. Your father is quite correct, Miss Van Tassel. You do indeed have a lovely voice, one of the finest I've heard."

I beamed at the compliment.

"A lovely voice, however," he went on, "can only take one so far. I would now like to get a sense of your ear, if I may." He plucked the first note of the scale. "Start here, if you will, with your scale again."

I began to sing once more, but this time Mr. Crane did not play along. Instead, after playing the first note, he dropped out altogether. I faltered, tried to go on, but so lost my place that I could not. "I . . . I am sorry," I said. "I do not know what happened."

"Not to worry," he said. "It is partially my fault, for I did not warn you I would not be playing along with you. Start again"—he plucked the first note of the scale twice—"and this time know I shall not be accompanying you. This is your first note; the rest is up to you."

Yet even though I was prepared to sing unaccompanied, I lost my place again. I did manage to at least find my way toward the end, landing on the correct final note, which Mr. Crane confirmed by playing for me.

"Again, if you please," he said.

If I did better this time, it was only just.

"As I thought," he said. "Your voice is lovely, Miss Van Tassel, but you must begin to employ your ear as well. Only then will you be certain you are singing the correct notes, and thus keeping the tune of the song—or in this case, the scale—as a whole."

"But this is silly," I said. "I sing all the time, when I am out of doors, or alone in my room, and it always sounds right."

"Perhaps it does, and perhaps you find it easier to keep tune within a song," he said. "Many do. Yet with no instrument of your own to allow you to check, and no trained ear to hear you, how can you be sure you are singing the correct notes?"

I remained silent.

"You see, then," he said. "There is more to singing than just a fine voice. You must have a fine ear as well. And luckily for you, a fine voice I cannot teach, but the ear I can."

"May we not try a song now?" I asked, widening my eyes in what I hoped was an innocent, fetching expression. "I am sure I will do better with a song."

"No. Not yet. First you must perfect the major scale, and then, and only then, shall we move on."

I sighed loudly, wondering what I had gotten myself into, then began the wretched scale again. This time, Mr. Crane stopped me on my first wrong note—only the third one I had sung. We continued in this manner for the rest of the lesson, by the end of which I had improved somewhat, but not enough to satisfy either of us, it seemed.

"A good start," Mr. Crane said, putting his guitar back in its case. "Perhaps by the end of the next lesson you will have mastered it."

I left the room without bidding him goodbye. For goodness' sake, it is not as though he is training me to grace the opera stages of Europe, I thought crossly as I stalked up to my room to fetch a book of poetry. I sing only for my own enjoyment, and sometimes that of our guests. And so far I do not enjoy this.

I called for Nox as I stepped outside. He came bounding around the corner of the house, panting and tongue lolling, no doubt having spent the morning in a playful tussle with his brother, who guarded my mother's geese and chicken flocks. He fell into step beside me, and I headed off the Van Tassel property, across the Albany Post Road, and into the woods, determined to shake off my unsatisfying singing lesson.

Yet later that afternoon, perched on the bank of the stream, I found myself lowering the book and singing the first notes of the scale to the trees and birds and to anyone else who might hear me.

I had no other audience that I could see, but that did not always mean much here, not in the woods of Sleepy Hollow.

I sang it again, and again, and again, until I thought I had it right. Until I thought Mr. Crane might approve.

4

Scale

"You are so close, but still not quite there, Miss Van Tassel," Mr. Crane said three days later. The lesson room suddenly felt incredibly warm and close. "The distance between those two notes is not as far as you think. Listen here." He played a series of notes on his guitar. "Do you hear it?"

I sighed for what felt like the hundredth time. Despite how well I had done practicing after my first lesson, as soon as I was standing before Mr. Crane, I felt uncertain once again. The moment I opened my mouth, my voice seemed to shrink and shrivel away to somewhere deep inside me, somewhere so deep I could not seem to reach it. The sound came out small and fragile, like a tiny bird unsure of its place in the world, unsure even if it will survive the season.

Never had I been nervous or frightened or indeed cared what any of my listeners might think, yet with Mr. Crane suddenly, somehow, it was different.

"You are far too hesitant, Miss Van Tassel," Mr. Crane said after my first attempt. "Louder, and stronger, if you please. I had rather hear a loud mistake than a nearly silent success."

I had gotten slightly louder over the course of the lesson, but not much. I could barely meet my teacher's eye as he demanded that I repeat the scale, over and over again.

"Do you hear it?" he asked again now, when I did not answer immediately. "You are going much farther than you need to in order to get to that next note."

"I think so," I said.

"Do you know, I feel as though you are not really trying, Miss Van Tassel," he said, almost conversationally. "You made such progress last lesson, and today, not much. Did you practice since then? I neglected to mention you should, but I thought it was understood—"

My head snapped up and I glared at him, his words erasing all trace of my earlier meekness. "I certainly did practice," I shot back. "It is quite different practicing on my own and trying to do it with you here shouting at me."

"Was I shouting?" he inquired mildly. "I hadn't thought so. But I shan't believe you've practiced until you can show me—"

Fixing him with a cold, haughty look, I opened my mouth and loudly, defiantly, began to sing the blasted scale again. I was barely paying attention, and yet as I reached the top I realized I had done it right. I wobbled a bit on the top note as this realization set in, but then I came down again strong.

If Mr. Crane's criticism was prickly and difficult to bear, his praise was warm and effusive and somehow worth all the difficulty. "Brava, Miss Van Tassel!" he cried, rising from his chair and applauding me. "That was wonderful! You see, your voice knew what to do all along, you had only to let it!"

I beamed at his words, though a part of me felt foolish that I should experience such a sense of accomplishment after singing just a few notes. "I suppose you are right," I said.

He clasped his hands over his heart. "Ahh," he said, "fine words to hear from so disdainful a lady."

I laughed. Slowly, realization dawned. "You did that on purpose," I said, an admiring half smile sliding onto my lips in spite of myself.

He regarded me quizzically, yet he was betrayed by his own small smile. "Did what, pray?" he asked.

"You were . . . you goaded me and made me angry, so that I would want prove you wrong and do it right," I said.

"Ah," he said, and spread his arms wide. "Guilty as charged, I am afraid."

I laughed again, at his gall, at his honesty, at his seemingly unwitting charm. "You are quite the trickster."

"No trick," he said, smiling openly now. "It worked, yes? It is one of the reasons I fancy myself a rather successful teacher. I am usually able to discern how best to coax—or provoke, if necessary—a given student into doing what I know they are capable of."

"Indeed," I said. "And what exactly did you discern from me, Mr. Crane?"

He met my gaze evenly. "You are a proud young woman, Miss Van Tassel—and rightfully so. So when our previous attempts today were unsuccessful, I thought I ought to . . . anger your pride, as it were."

"Indeed," I said again. Spontaneously I bowed from the waist, my arms held wide to the sides. "I yield, good sir. It seems I have been bested and outsmarted. Not to sound too prideful, of course, but it does not happen often."

He took my hand and kissed it, and my silly grin stilled at the touch of his lips on my hand. "I well believe it," he said.

I drew away, flushed and uneasy and not sure why. "And what task shall you set me next, Mr. Crane?" I asked after a moment. "Now that I have mastered the scale."

"One successful performance does not a mastery make," he said, chuckling when I sent a glare his way. "But we are out of time for today, I am afraid. Therefore here is what I propose: you must repeat your successful performance at the beginning of our next lesson, and if you can, I have a song we may endeavor to learn together."

"At last!" I said, heaving a mock sigh.

Mr. Crane reached out and took my hand again, but his face was quite serious. "And, Katrina," he said, his voice low. "You must never let your voice hide again. Now that I have heard its true power, I do not think I can go without it."

I froze for a moment, wondering if he was joking, but there was naught but earnestness in his eyes, green as the forest. "You . . . you quite flatter me, sir," I said, struggling to find the very voice he had so praised.

"I do not," he said. "Flattery is not an art in which I am particularly gifted." He released my hand, then turned to collect his guitar and its case. Instrument in hand, he turned back to me and bowed. "Miss Van Tassel." Then he went past me out the door.

I remained rooted to the spot, replaying his words in my head, thinking of how he had slipped, for the first time, and used my Christian name.

5

The Legend of Sleepy Hollow

The next day, I was headed out of the house, Nox at my side as usual, with a copy of one of Master Shakespeare's plays—*Macbeth*, procured on my last trip to New York—when I happened upon Mr. Crane coming down the stairs with a book of his own. "Good day, Mr. Crane," I said. "I trust you are well?"

"Indeed, Miss Van Tassel, I thank you," he said.

His tone was so polite and proper that I felt a pang of disappointment. What had become of the strange intimacy of the day before? But no doubt he had reflected upon it and found such forward speech inappropriate. Yet this logic did not serve to make me feel any better, somehow.

"Where are you off to?" I asked, trying surreptitiously to peer at the title of the volume he carried.

"To find a reading spot where I will not make too much of a nuisance of myself," he said, bending down to scratch Nox behind his ears. "The portico is lovely, but I should not want to be in the way if your father must entertain any guests. Perhaps you could recommend a place to me?"

"I should be happy to," I said. "In fact, I was just on my way to my favorite such spot. Would you care to join me?"

"So long as I am not imposing."

"Not at all. Come, follow me." I led him out the front door of the farmhouse and across the Albany Post Road to my usual path through the woods. It was a gloomy day, the sky gray and overcast, and I hoped the rain that seemed to be threatening would hold off for a time.

"Ah, into nature," Mr. Crane remarked.

I turned and smiled at him. "Indeed," I said. "There is a stream that runs through the woods just here, and eventually drains into the Hudson. On one of the banks is a small clearing that is quite my favorite place to read."

"I look forward to seeing it."

We remained silent as we walked deeper into the forest, on a path created by the first settlers of the valley—or so I always imagined. It had been here ever since I could remember.

Though I was always safe with Nox, I was glad to have some human company in these woods today.

Eventually, I stepped off the path, Nox on my heels, and Mr. Crane followed wordlessly. We had to step over some brush and fallen branches before coming upon the stream, its waters tumbling steadily through the wood.

I sat down unceremoniously on my favorite grassy spot, and when Mr. Crane did not appear beside me, I turned to find him standing a few paces away, looking around with wonder. "Beautiful," he murmured, and I could not be certain if he was talking to me or only to himself. His gaze took in the dense cover of foliage, through which the sunlight trickled on bright days and turned everything a golden green; the waters of the stream, so clear one could count every pebble on the bottom; the rise of the hill across the bank from us. "Simply beautiful. Why, this spot is pristine, virtually untouched, hidden away . . . almost an Eden." Then he looked down at where I sat and smiled at me. "Thank you for sharing it with me."

Warmth spread through me at having brought him such happiness. "Why, of course," I said. "I had thought you might appreciate it."

"More than I can say," he said, lowering himself onto the bank beside me. Nox, after drinking his fill of the cold water, flopped down onto his side next to me.

Mr. Crane's proximity made me wonder—should I have invited him? Was it not improper for us to be here alone? I bit my lip, considering. My parents had not had much occasion to lecture me on propriety and how I ought to behave around young men: I was generally only in the company of men—young or otherwise—in my parents' house, or in public. Truthfully, as an indulged only child, they had not found much occasion to lecture me on anything at all.

I shrugged such thoughts aside. We were outdoors, after all, not ensconced in a bedroom together. We were alone for my lessons, anyway. And no one ever came to this part of the wood. Should someone see us returning together, I could say we merely encountered one another along the way.

No one would know, and even if they did there would be nothing to know.

My qualms laid to rest, I glanced up and saw Mr. Crane had opened his book: *On Witchcraft* by Cotton Mather.

I had read it as well, and so longed to ask Mr. Crane for his impressions. Yet, as being interrupted while I was reading was one of my least favorite things, I decided to defer until later.

My mind now full of witches, I was delighted—and a bit spooked—to open up *Macbeth* and immediately encounter three of them, and read of their eerie, blood-soaked prediction for the Scottish warrior.

I could not measure how much time had passed, only how many pages: I found Lady Macbeth both frightening and compelling, and was both disgusted and thrilled at the couple's plot to murder the king. Absently stroking Nox's fur as I read, I held my breath in anticipation and excitement as the king arrived for the fateful banquet, bloody mayhem ensuing thereafter.

It was just the sort of tale Charlotte would love as well, the kind of dark drama that we had been wont to act out as children, roaming wild through the woods and along the river, in the days when Brom Van Brunt was still our constant companion and Nox just a puppy. I often missed those days, when the innocence of childhood protected and let no ugliness reach us.

I would have to lend the volume to Charlotte when I saw her again.

After reading the banquet scene, I closed the book and pressed it to my chest, lying back against the grass to think about everything I had read. I was desperate to read on, to see if Macbeth and his lady would succeed in their quest for mastery of Scotland, or if they would get the justice rightly owed them. But if I read too fast, soon it would be over, and I would never experience it for the first time again.

I propped myself up on my elbows and glanced over at Mr. Crane, only to find him looking right back at me. Upon being found out, his eyes quickly skittered back to the pages of his book, and the alarm on his face was so out of proportion with what had happened that I began to laugh.

The tips of his protruding ears reddened with embarrassment, yet after a moment his shoulders began to shake. He lowered his book, and our laughter echoed off of the canopy of leaves above us.

Once our mirth subsided, Mr. Crane let out a long sigh. "I find my concentration is quite broken now," he said.

"As is mine," I said, "but no matter. I have been wanting to ask you how you are finding Reverend Mather's book."

"Have you read it?" he asked.

"I have."

He smiled. "I should not be surprised, for you are possessed of a rare intellect." I barely had time to preen at his compliment before he moved on to answer me. "It is an interesting and important book. It allows us to see how witchcraft was regarded a hundred years ago, and what lessons we may apply to the world today."

"And do you believe in witchcraft, the supernatural, and the like, Mr. Crane?" I asked.

"I do," he said without hesitation. "Who does not?"

"Who indeed," I said, for I could not claim anyone among my acquaintance who did not believe in magic or the supernatural in some form. "Do you agree, then, with Reverend Mather's assessment of the women—and those few men as well—who were hanged at Salem? Were they indeed handmaidens of the devil?"

"I am of the opinion that the authorities of Salem—and Reverend Mather as well—were quite over-hasty in their findings against those accused," Mr. Crane said, his voice softer now, yet deadly serious. "The result, of course, was a most tragic loss of life. Yet I do believe there are those on this earth who wish evil upon good men and women, and no methods to which they will not stoop to bring about such evil."

I felt a chill come over me as my mind flitted to Charlotte. I had always tried never to imagine what Reverend Mather would have made of my friend Charlotte and her ways. "I quite agree," I said. "And in turn I cannot help but wonder whether Reverend Mather was over-hasty in some of his other conclusions as well."

"Interesting, and a well-reasoned point," Mr. Crane said. "But tell me, Miss Van Tassel—do you not believe in witchcraft and the supernatural yourself?"

I hesitated, selecting my words carefully. "I suppose I cannot rightly say that I don't believe," I said at last. "Yet I find I am always suspicious of accusations of witchcraft and such evildoing, and skeptical of accounts of the supernatural that I have not witnessed with my own eyes." All of magic I had ever seen was in little things, and perhaps no magic at all: the healing of a sick child, an herbal mixture that eased menstrual cramps, a remark made in passing that sometimes became an accurate predictor of the future, a strange feeling that something was about to happen.

"I applaud you, Miss Van Tassel," Mr. Crane said, a hint of admiration in his voice. "You are a most modern woman, and I think that your application of such logic and reason will serve you well in your life." He smiled wryly. "I might wish for a bit more skepticism myself. I find when it comes to frightening tales, my imagination quite runs away with me."

A mischievous smile spread across my face. "In that case, I had best not tell you the tale of Sleepy Hollow's most prominent resident spirit," I said.

He raised his eyebrows, the lines of his body suddenly taut. "Oh?" he asked.

I pretended to turn my attention back to my book. "I would not want to frighten you unduly, Mr. Crane. Perhaps it is best I say nothing."

"Now you must tell me, my dear Miss Van Tassel," he said. "My curiosity is quite unbearable. And for all that my imagination does get the better of me, I do so enjoy such tales."

"Very well," I said. As I spoke I heard the rumble of thunder in the distance. "But pray, let me tell you as we make our way back to the house. A storm is upon us."

We rose from our spot and began our trek back to the farmhouse, taking our time so that I might do the story justice.

"Sleepy Hollow has a great many tales and legends," I began, "and a great many spirits that are said to haunt these parts. But there is one specter who is considered to be the most terrifying apparition of them all," I said. I shivered, remembering my nightmares. "For you see, he is without his head."

Mr. Crane stopped short. "Without his . . . head?"

"Indeed," I said, enjoying the nervous look on his face. He started walking again and caught up to me. "And how he came to be parted from his head is quite a tale. He is said to have been a Hessian mercenary in the employ of Britain during the war for independence. Many battles took place hereabouts."

"Yes, I did know that," Mr. Crane said.

I nodded and continued. "This Hessian—whose name has since been lost to us—was known by both sides as having a penchant for violence, and for being a particularly able killer. The Americans dreaded him, and the British soldiers alongside whom he fought feared him.

"During one battle—deep in these very woods, the story goes— his head was claimed by a cannonball. The Hessian's body was laid to rest in the churchyard, an honorable burial for a dishonorable man. A local woman interceded on his behalf, for a Hessian soldier had saved her child from a burning house—though it is unlikely it was this same bloodthirsty villain—and so he was buried in an unmarked grave. Or his body was. His head, of course, was . . . beyond recovery."

Mr. Crane remained silent.

"And so," I finished, "the Hessian rides at night in search of his lost head. It is said he cannot rest without it. Some say he carries a pumpkin carved with a grotesque face in place of his own head, and some . . ." I paused for a moment—for ultimate effect, I told myself, but also to master my own sudden uneasiness, ". . . some say he takes the heads of those unfortunates he happens across." I paused again. "We call him the Headless Horseman."

We had reached the edge of the forest and were crossing the road when Mr. Crane spoke again. "You tell a marvelous and gripping tale, Miss Van Tassel."

"I thank you, sir," I said, disappointed at the continued formality of his tone. After being alone together all day, surely we might be less formal? "I pray you enjoyed it. It is a favorite legend of ours here in Sleepy Hollow."

"I can see why," he said. "It is quite chilling. I shall indeed struggle to master my imagination once darkness falls." He turned to smile at me. "The sign of a well-told tale."

"I hope you do not miss any sleep tonight, good Mr. Crane," I said.

"I hope for the same. But, tell me, Miss Van Tassel," he said, stopping. We were almost at the front door of the farmhouse again. "Have you ever seen this Headless Horseman with your own eyes?"

A chill ran through my entire body, and I knew Mr. Crane must have noticed.

For I had seen the Horseman. I saw him often enough, in my dreams.

It is always the same: he faces me through the mist of the forest that surrounds Sleepy Hollow. He never approaches, nor does he ride away; he never tries to harm me or offer me violence of any kind; never even raises his great sword—though I can see it, sheathed and strapped at his side. He never so much as moves— he only sits immobile atop his horse, turned in my direction, a hollowed out, flaming pumpkin carved with a misshapen face at his horse's feet. I cannot even say he watches me, for the collar of his heavy black coat is empty where his neck and head should be.

At many an evening gathering, as the coolness of autumn begins to leach summer from the air, my family and friends discuss him, debating whether he is mere myth, or something more. The more rational minds argue he is simply a scary tale; a legend born out of the frightened, anxious minds of those tasked with building this young nation. The rest swear he is real, though none can claim to have seen him with their own two eyes. Their only proof is a murder supposedly witnessed by some craftsman who is now dead, or stories of livestock stolen or found butchered. That such could be the work of thieves, vandals, or even wolves is, when brought up, dismissed by those who cling to the certainty of their superstitions. Tales of those who have ventured deep into the woods, only never to return, are considered by some to be proof of his existence, merely runaways or the victims of accidents by others. There can be no agreement, yet such stories and debates help to pass the increasingly dark, cold nights; the nights we do our best to ward off with the glow of candles and lanterns and roaring fires in the grate, even as the darkness encroaches on us; even as it presses in over the fields of farmland and in between the trees of those fearsome woods.

But as far as I knew, I was the only one the Horseman visited in dreams.

For a moment, it was as though Ichabod Crane and the farmhouse and the fields and the bright summer day had vanished, and I was once again standing within the landscape of my dreams, watching the Horseman linger at the edge of the forest, his attention fixed solely on me. I shook my head slightly, and soon I was back, standing before Mr. Crane, who was beginning to look rather concerned about me.

"No," I said. I reached down, twining my fingers in Nox's short fur, as if for reassurance. "I have not seen him."

Yet even as I spoke, the words tasted like a lie. And as we went inside together just as the rain began to pour, back into the safety of my house, I found myself wishing neither of us needed to be alone that night, when imagination and dreams and shadows would threaten to overtake us both.

6

The Old Dutch Church

I was awake much of the night, waiting, watching from one of my bedroom windows, the one beneath the sloping eave which faced the small patch of woods at the edge of our property. I felt as though, having spoken of the Headless Horseman, I had somehow summoned him, must have done; that now he would be waiting for me for certain, with no dream to protect me.

My uneasiness gave lie to my earlier words to Mr. Crane, about logic and skepticism and reason. Perhaps it was the darkness of the night; perhaps it was that I was weary, in spite of which I could not sleep; but all those spooky tales suddenly seemed much more probable than they ever had before.

I usually turned to books when my mind was distracted, could lose myself in the words; yet somehow I did not think that *Macbeth*, with its witches and prophecies and bloody murder, would be quite the balm for a troubled mind that I sought.

At one point I heard a heavy tread move down the hallway and descend the stairs; it had to be Mr. Crane. A part of me longed to follow, to sit in the parlor or even the kitchen with him, just to be in the company of another person—and there was no one's company I craved more than his, I realized. Yet the thought of doing so frightened me in an entirely different way than tales of goblins and spirits. Eventually I fell into a troubled sleep.

As the next morning was Sunday, we arose early, dressed, and ate a light breakfast, then piled into the cart to head to the church for services. I was pleased to see Mr. Crane was to accompany us, and my father voiced his approval as well.

"Ah, I am glad to see you are a God-fearing man as well as an erudite one, Mr. Crane," my father said, as the schoolmaster clambered somewhat awkwardly up onto the back of the cart.

"Indeed I am, sir," Mr. Crane said, once he had settled himself on one of the sideboards. "One is not a God-fearing man at his peril, it seems to me."

My father nodded his agreement before snapping the reins over the backs of the two large draft horses hitched to the cart, and with a jolt we were off.

"Sir Nox does not attend the Sunday service, Miss Van Tassel?" Mr. Crane asked me with a grin.

I returned his smile. "Indeed he does not. I do not think he would find it much to his liking, and the minister would find such a congregant even less to his."

Mr. Crane laughed aloud at this, and then we lapsed into silence.

I had hoped for further conversation with Mr. Crane on the journey—some two miles—but he was quite engrossed in the scenery, looking appreciatively over the acres of rolling farmland that alternated with the ever-present forest, sometimes encroaching directly on the road, and sometimes beaten back to make room for fields and crops and cottages. The evident delight he took in my lovely little niche of the Hudson River Valley warmed my heart to a degree I would not have expected, and so I did not wish to interrupt his reverie.

When we reached the church, my father tied up the horses to one of the hitching posts at the edge of the churchyard—just past the bridge over the Pocantico River, which skirted the edge of the church property—then helped down first me, then my mother. Mr. Crane climbed down last and, brushing off his coat, promptly offered me his arm. "May I have the honor of escorting you inside, Miss Van Tassel?" he asked.

I could feel my countenance light up at his words. "You may," I said, taking his arm. My father, with my mother's hand on his own arm, gave the schoolmaster another approving look and began to climb the hill that led up to the church. Ichabod and I followed a few paces behind.

"Did you sleep well last night, Mr. Crane?" I asked.

He glanced sideways at me. "About as well as I expected. I thank you for asking."

Our eyes held for just a moment longer. Perhaps you would sleep better with me beside you, I thought, as all sorts of unseemly things tumbled through my mind. My face began to burn, and I knew I would never be able to say such a thing, only imagine that I might.

I looked away, hoping he had not noticed my blush. "You know, there is a rather eerie tale about this church as well," I said, changing the subject.

"Is there?" he asked, a note of eagerness in his voice. "Beyond the presence of the Hessian's body in the churchyard? I assume this is the burial spot you spoke of yesterday, yes?"

"Indeed it is," I said, "though as I mentioned, he was buried in an unmarked grave, so the exact location of his remains is anybody's guess. No, the story to which I refer has to do with the building of the church."

"Then do tell it to me, Miss Van Tassel. I am most intrigued."

"The church is over a hundred years old now," I said. "It was built by Old Mr. Phillips, who owned much of this land and ran a large mill." I pointed across the road, where some buildings were just visible amongst the trees—a barn, and a manor house. "He began construction on this church for his family and their tenant farmers, but work progressed slowly. Meanwhile, the little river here"—I pointed to the Pocantico—"feeds into the millpond and helps run the mill. During the time that construction on the church was begun and abandoned and taken up again, the river flooded on several occasions, causing damage to the mill and to the flour production.

"Mr. Phillips was in despair as to what to do, when one morning one of his slaves came to him. He said the answer had come to him in a dream: once Mr. Phillips finished building the church, God would prevent the river from flooding again. Mr. Phillips heeded the slave's advice, and finished construction of the church posthaste. Since then, the river has not flooded."

Mr. Crane nodded appreciatively. "Another fine tale, and well told yet again. It is a bit eerie, as you said, though certainly not as chilling as that of the Headless Horseman."

I laughed. "I confess I do not know any tales as chilling as that of the Horseman. As for this one about the church, well, who can say if it is true or not, though most certainly do believe it."

"Kind of the slave to so help Mr. Phillips, if it is," Mr. Crane remarked, "given that he most certainly would have had reason to bear ill will against the man who claimed ownership over him."

I smiled at this remark; it made me like Mr. Crane even more than I already did. "I have often thought the same thing myself."

By this time, we were at the church door, despite our deliberately slow pace. "Where would you recommend that I, as a newcomer, sit, Miss Van Tassel?" he asked, pausing as we entered the plain yet lovely building, with its tall windows and stone walls on the outside and its whitewashed walls inside.

I placed my hand briefly over his. "Why, you shall sit with us, in our family pew, of course," I said. "Come, I shall lead the way."

I sensed his brief reluctance as I began to steer him toward the Van Tassel pew in the second row, but he followed me all the same.

I may have enjoyed a monopoly on Mr. Crane's attention on the way in to the service, but the same was not true afterward. His appearance in our sleepy little village was occasion for much talk and excitement, particularly—I noticed sourly—among the female denizens. As the villagers gathered in the churchyard after the service to visit with friends and exchange gossip, a knot of admiring young ladies gathered about Mr. Crane. "I have heard that you will be giving singing lessons, Mr. Crane," the simpering Elizabeth van der Berg said, practically hanging on his arm. "My father is agreeable, so you must come to teach me."

"It will be my pleasure, miss," Mr. Crane said. To my further annoyance, he seemed to be rather enjoying the attention.

"And me as well," added Annatje Dekker.

I rolled my eyes and turned away, casting my gaze hopefully around the churchyard for Charlotte, to see if she had perhaps returned from Massachusetts. I spotted her mother, Mevrouw Jansen, chatting with my mother, but sadly Charlotte was nowhere to be seen.

"Come, Katrina," I heard my father calling to me from the edge of the churchyard. I turned toward him only to see Brom standing beside him. I groaned inwardly and made my way over as slowly as I could. "It is high time we returned home for luncheon. I have invited Mr. Van Brunt to join us."

"Oh, good," I said, not even bothering to inject any enthusiasm or even politeness into my tone.

"Indeed, Miss Van Tassel, though for propriety's sake I must pray you not indulge in any unseemly display of emotion," Brom said.

I rolled my eyes, but my father merely chuckled. "Such a charming lad," he said. "I do not wonder that the young ladies of the village are falling over themselves for your attention, Brom."

"If that is true, then I pray you remain in the village where you are wanted," I said.

"Now, now, Katrina," my father said, of slight reproach in his voice.

"And indeed, I notice our new schoolmaster is the focus of much of the female attention today, in any case," I went on, quite ignoring my father. "I hope this does not wound your ego, Brom."

Brom scowled before quickly attempting to smooth out his features. "Yes, the music teacher," he said, a note of bitterness in his voice. "And are you learning much from this . . . what is his name?" Brom asked. "Mr. Creighton?"

"Crane," I said, annoyed. "Mr. Ichabod Crane."

"Ah," Brom said. "Strange name, that. Not from around here, is he?"

"He is from Connecticut," I said.

"Practically a foreigner!" Brom said.

"We are all Americans now," I said coolly.

"Hear, hear," my father said, interrupting our bickering. "And proud to be so!"

"Indeed," my mother said, appearing behind us. "Shall we adjourn home for luncheon, then?"

She gestured to Mr. Crane, and we all piled back into the cart, while Brom swung up into the saddle of his massive horse, Daredevil, to follow us.

7

Declarations

My mostly sleepless night in no way put me in the mood for a luncheon with Brom Van Brunt, and only the presence of Mr. Crane convinced me to attend, rather than pleading illness or exhaustion.

"Mr. Van Brunt, is it not?" Mr. Crane asked, extending his hand to Brom as we all sat down. "We were introduced recently, yes?"

"I believe so," Brom said, shaking his hand briefly before turning away to engage my father in a conversation about farming—something upon which both men could discourse for days.

I smiled warmly across the table at Mr. Crane, and he returned the smile wholeheartedly. Perhaps he enjoyed my company more than that of the village girls, I thought happily. Just then I realized Brom was watching me. My father was holding forth about the apple crop—which we expected to be very good this year—not noticing that his guest's attention had shifted. Normally I would have asked Brom loudly what he found so fascinating about my face, attempted to fluster him, but I was so flustered myself that I merely looked down at the plate Agnes, the kitchen maid, had just put in front of me. Anger began to stew within me, as though Brom had bested me somehow, as if he somehow knew a secret I had never confessed.

"Yes," Brom said loudly, causing me to start, addressing my

father though his eyes were still on me. "My father expects quite a good harvest this year as well—one of our best yet." Thankfully he looked away, focusing back on my father. "Unfortunately, though, my father has been thinking to increase our yield by purchasing some slaves, so it has fallen to me to dissuade him."

My father frowned. As many of our neighbors used slave labor to work their farms, he tried to speak of his views only in select company. It was a point of pride to him that all our Negro servants and field hands were free men and women and were paid the same wage as the white people he employed. "Why would he wish to invite that peculiar institution into his home when he already has a prosperous farm?" my father asked. "Why now?"

Brom shrugged. "He wishes to seize this chance to try to do better, to make our gains permanent, I suppose," he said. "I believe I have convinced him otherwise, though."

"Well done," my father said approvingly. "How did you manage that?"

Brom gave a hard smile. "I told him that, should he purchase any slaves, the moment the farm comes under my control I would free them all. He did not like the idea of my very publicly undoing his work. As you might imagine."

Brom glanced over at me, and for once, a knowing and sympathetic look passed between us. It felt almost as though we were children again, friends; back when Charlotte and I used to fetch Brom to come play with us and heard his father yelling at him, telling him he was a worthless idiot, a boy with a too-soft heart who would never make a man. It was no wonder Brom spent most of his childhood running wild with the two of us rather than at home.

And no wonder, perhaps, that now he strove to be a man in every way he felt defined the word.

"I applaud you, Mr. Van Brunt," Ichabod spoke up. "As contrary as it is to man's nature to court discord with one's father, on an issue of such importance there can be no other course."

Brom nodded, a look of grudging respect on his face.

Ichabod turned to my father. "I do greatly admire how you have managed to run such a successful enterprise here without any slave labor at all," he said. "Would that you might be an example to our fellow countrymen, especially those to the south."

"Slavery is a scourge," I said, "and everyone in this country must come to see that. Else how can we profess to be a nation of free men and women?"

Ichabod's eyes met mine. "I have no fonder hope than that all should come round to this way of thinking, Miss Van Tassel."

"Nor I," echoed my father.

"Nor I," said Brom.

"Nor I, certainly," added my mother.

"I wish you the best of fortune with your harvest this year, then, young Brom," my father said. "Should you need any advisement, I hope you will come to me."

"I should be honored, sir," Brom said. "For of course, our farm cannot compare to the yield of yours." He learned forward slightly in his chair, glancing between my father and me. "Imagine, though, if two such farms as ours were to combine, what profit might be reaped?"

My head came up sharply, and I glared quite openly at him, the warm feelings I had just a moment ago gone. I turned to face my father, expecting him to condemn such talk as forward and inappropriate, and was horrified to see a gleam in his eye. "Indeed," he said, leaning back in his chair, "an interesting thought, Mr. Van Brunt."

"Thank you, sir."

I dared a glance at Mr. Crane, only to find him looking—rather deliberately, it seemed—down at his plate, and away from me.

"I rather disagree," I opined to the room at large. "I do not find any interest whatever in this particular thought of Mr. Van Brunt's, though I do have many related thoughts of my own I might share." I saw a small smile on Mr. Crane's lips.

Brom's face darkened. "It is hardly seemly for a woman to have more thoughts than a man," he said, as though this were some sort of sensible defense.

"I'm afraid I must disagree with you there, Mr. Van Brunt, if I may be so bold," Mr. Crane spoke up. "Does not this new nation need all the thinkers and people of intellect it can get, man and woman alike?"

Brom scoffed and took a swig of his beer. "Men build nations, not women. I would expect a scholar such as you to be more aware of the way of the world, sir." He spat the last word scornfully.

"And any scholar of history knows that the human race would be nowhere without its women," Mr. Crane said calmly.

"Well spoken, Mr. Crane," my mother said, delighted.

"Far be it from me to disagree with so learned a fellow," my father said, raising his glass. "To women!"

"Hear, hear," I said, grinning triumphantly at Brom.

We all raised our glasses and sipped, and I glowed inwardly at the look of frustration on Brom's face. However he had imagined this afternoon going, this was certainly not it.

Still, I took a warning from his words. I had long known he considered himself a suitor for my hand, but this was the nearest he had come to openly declaring his intentions. More alarming still had been my father's reaction—it seemed plain he would entertain a proposal.

Papa is just like the rest of the village, I thought crossly, applying myself to my meal. Unable to see Brom for who he is.

Mr. Crane, though, saw Brom as he was—that much seemed certain, now. Another reason to quite like the man.

Thankfully the rest of the meal passed with no further controversial topics, and my father invited Brom to inspect the fields with him. I could only hope our guest was not mentally measuring a profit before it was turned.

"Miss Van Tassel," I heard Mr. Crane say in a low voice as the rest of us rose from the table. "If I may—"

"Katrina, do not forget you must help me with the mending and embroidery today," my mother said, clearly not having heard Mr. Crane. "You will have to leave your book for another time, I'm afraid."

I paused, glancing back at Mr. Crane, wanting very much to know what he had been about to say. "I shall bid you ladies good afternoon, then, and thank you for your company and the fine luncheon."

"You are very kind, Mr. Crane, and most welcome," my mother said. "Shall we expect you for dinner as well?"

"Not tonight, I fear, for I am to dine with the family of one of my future students," he said. "I do believe it shall be my first lodging place once I have quit your kind hospitality."

"Indeed," my mother said, "though you are welcome here for as long as you like."

He bowed to her. "You are generosity itself, madam, and as such the last thing I intend to do is overstay my welcome." With that, he left the room without looking at me again.

I remained rooted to the spot, almost aching for his gaze to fall on me again.

"Come, Katrina," my mother said, not noticing my distracted state. "The sewing pile only grows larger, I'm afraid."

Since the weather was fine, we took our sewing out onto the portico and sat in the two chairs my father had made especially for us. It was from my mother I inherited my affinity for nature, though she often lamented that, as the lady of a great farm, she no longer had the time for idle ramblings in the woods as she once did.

Nox appeared from his morning frolics and collapsed into a comfortable heap at my feet. Once we were settled and had begun our sewing, I spoke. "I quite forgot Mr. Crane will be leaving us soon," I said, hoping my tone was a casual one. For, though I felt utterly stupid, it was true. Somehow I had come to think he would remain with us forever, that I could have all the time with him I wished. "Once he no longer boards with us, will he still give me my music lessons?"

"Why, certainly," my mother said, focused on the seam she was sewing. "If you would like to continue, I am sure your father will not mind."

"I would, very much," I said.

"Then you shall." She changed the subject then, and I could not tell if the new topic was prompted by our talk of Mr. Crane or not. "What think you of Brom Van Brunt?"

My hands paused mid-stitch. "I should think my opinion of him is plain enough."

"I know well how young girls like to play the coquette, Katrina."

My head snapped up. "Surely you know me better than that, Mother. And you know the very real reason I have to dislike Brom Van Brunt."

She sighed. "I do, though I hoped I might be wrong, and you harbored more affection for him than you seem to."

I froze at this. "What are you saying?"

"Your father favors young Brom's suit," my mother told me plainly. "He likes him, and thinks he would be a logical choice for your husband and to inherit the farm after us. He can combine his father's holdings with ours, as he alluded to today."

"I . . . I didn't know Father took him so seriously," I said, struggling to keep my voice from breaking.

My mother's eyes returned to her sewing. "I thought it best that you knew, so you might act accordingly," she said. "I admit it would be a good match, but not if you would be unhappy with him." She patted my hand. "I will speak to your father. Whatever fanciful notions he has of expanding the Van Tassel holdings through your marriage will be nothing if it is not what you want."

"Do you truly think so?" I asked. I knew my father loved me dearly, but he was also ambitious and proud of the family name and reputation.

"Why, of course. Really, Katrina, when has your father ever set himself against anything you wanted? Including," she added with an indulgent smile in Nox's direction, "letting you keep that dog in the house."

I smiled. She was right; I could not rightly recall my father denying me anything. Surely he would not start now, not with something as important as my future husband. I let out a half-sigh, half-laugh, and felt Brom and his suit recede from my mind.

"But," she went on, "know that you are an heiress to extensive holdings, and so your father and I expect a good match. A man with something to bring to the marriage, and not a fortune hunter. But surely we can accomplish this and make you happy at the same time."

"Surely," I said, relieved at my mother's support. For there were plenty of men with prospects who were not Brom Van Brunt.

But as I bent over my embroidery once more, a new worry intruded. I knew very well whom I did not want as a husband, but that left the question—one my father very well might pose—of whom I did want. And what could I say then?

8

The Kitchen

That night I found myself once again restless and unable to sleep. I got out of bed and walked to the window, gazing out as if daring the Horseman to appear, to show himself to me in my wakeful state.

Before he could appear, though, and before sleep could claim me, I heard footsteps in the hallway again.

This time I did not hesitate. I whirled away from the window and pulled a dressing gown over my night shift, that I might be at least somewhat decent, and went to my door, opening it as silently as I could, leaving Nox looking at me quizzically from the bed, and followed my fellow insomniac down the stairs.

At the bottom of the staircase, I paused, listening to the footsteps move softly toward the back of the house. I moved silently down the hallway, past the parlor and music room and into the kitchen.

I opened the door to find Mr. Crane within, pouring himself a glass of milk from the pitcher Agnes always left out for us.

He started when I came in. "Miss Van Tassel," he said. "My apologies. Did I wake you?"

"Not at all," I said, stepping fully into the dim room, lit only by the single candle he had carried with him and the dim glow of the embers in the banked cooking fire. "I was awake already."

"Ah." He took a sip of his milk and did not comment further.

"And are you unable to sleep this night as well, Mr. Crane?" I inquired, when he seemed unlikely to further the conversation.

"Indeed," he said. "It is an affliction that troubles me from time to time."

Again he fell silent, and I began to feel somewhat irritated—and, I realized, nervous.

"Have I done something to offend, Mr. Crane?" I asked at last, once the silence stretching between us had grown unbearable. My heart began to pound as I spoke.

He sighed. "No. You . . . no. Not at all. I should . . . I should not take out my own disquiet upon you."

He seemed to me handsomer than ever, dressed only in his loose shirt and breeches, his hair falling about his face. I could see the muscles in his arms flex through his thin sleeves as he braced them against the high tabletop in between us, belying his scholarly life. No doubt he had grown up on a farm as well, or been trained as a craftsman of some sort. I looked at him, intent, wanting to know how he had grown up and what he had learned and whom his family was. I wanted to know everything about him.

"If there is anything troubling you, Mr. Crane, I want to assure you that you may speak freely with me," I said. I moved closer to him and covered his hand with my own, caressing it with my thumb. "I hope that we have become friends, yes?"

What madness was making me manifest these feelings that I had only begun to identify? But I could not stop myself. The talk of my marriage, as well as the reminder that Mr. Crane would soon be leaving, had spurred me into action.

When he did not move or reply, I slowly withdrew my hand from his, my face burning. I should leave. There was no good to be had in trying to force him to talk to me. I was just gathering my courage to bid him goodnight and walk out of the room with my head held high when he spoke. "I . . . it is none of my business," he said. "I should not be asking you this."

My heart quickened its pace. "You may ask me anything you like."

He hesitated briefly before continuing. "Brom," he said. "That is, Mr. Van Brunt. He is your suitor, then?"

I started. "Not if I have anything to say about it," I said, my voice cool. "He thinks himself so, but he is quite deluded if he believes I would consent to be his wife." Feeling as though my heart was beating in my throat, I forced the next words out nevertheless. "Why do you ask?"

His head came up slightly as he met my eyes. "As I said, I should not have. It is none of my affair."

"But you did ask," I pressed, "and I would know why."

"Katrina," he sighed, looking away, and a pleasurable shiver ran through me at the sound of my given name falling off his tongue. "I cannot."

"You must," I whispered, "for I must know."

"It is not that simple," he said, suddenly angry. "Not for me. You have been given everything you wanted all your life, and the world does not work that way for the rest of us. Men like me—men without power, money, land, influence—we cannot always have what we want. We must step carefully, must work for everything we can, must threaten no one."

"But . . . surely not," I protested. "This is a great new nation, now; any man has the chance to rise, to—"

He laughed shortly. "The revolution changed many things, but not everything. Who is to say this American experiment will last? I hope it does, and that it becomes everything you wish it to be, Katrina. But not enough has changed, not for poor men. Why, even now, men in Pennsylvania are beginning to rise up over the tax on whiskey."

"But the funds that taxes bring in are necessary for the running of the government, are they not?" I asked, momentarily diverted by the chance to debate. "We are no longer taxed by a foreign body that does not consult us, but by our own representatives, at least—"

Ichabod shook his head, cutting me off. "That is rather beside the point for me, right now."

"I don't understand."

"No, of course you don't," he said. "What I am saying is, even in these new United States, a man like me cannot come into the home of a wealthy, influential man, accept his food and hospitality, and then speak of love to his virgin daughter. It is not right. It is not acceptable, no matter what I may want—"

I cut him off by stepping close to him and pressing my lips to his.

He stood still, as if stunned, then began to respond, hesitantly at first, then hungrily. My mouth opened beneath his, and I moaned slightly, deep in my throat, all thought obliterated.

I had been kissed once before—Brom had stolen a kiss, in fact, when we were fifteen years old. As soon as his lips had touched mine I had drawn back and slapped him so hard my hand left an imprint on his cheek. He had (thankfully) never tried such again.

That had not been a real kiss, not like this. This kiss had passion and fire and hunger and flavors of things I had only ever read about in books, but never felt myself.

He leaned into me then, pressing my back against the edge of the table, his lean body against mine. I gasped against his mouth at the feel of him, and knew he could feel the curves of my hips and breasts in turn. Dressed as we were, in only the flimsiest of nightclothes, such contact was indecent. Yet it thrilled me even so, perhaps because of that.

Without warning, he broke away. "Katrina," he breathed, stepping back. "My God. We . . . we cannot. This is what I am saying."

I closed my eyes as if to deny his words. But I knew he was right. We had already gone far enough, could go no further. Not without terrible consequences. "Ichabod Crane," I said aloud, after I'd regained my breath. "You asked me about a man you believed to be my suitor, and I think you did so because you wanted to know what my feelings toward you might be. Now you know."

With that, I turned and left the room while I was still able, going back up to my bedchamber and closing the door behind me. I longed to know what might have happened had I stayed, yet that was precisely why I had to leave.

9

Lovelorn

The next morning I found myself both dreading and eagerly anticipating my music lesson, scheduled for two o'clock that afternoon. Like a coward, I lurked in my bedroom much of the day, avoiding Mr. Crane—or Ichabod, should it not be? It seemed ridiculous to refer to him as Mr. Crane after our kiss—even as I longed to know what he might do and say now, in the light of day.

When the appointed hour came, I approached the music room with apprehension, my stomach feeling as if I had swallowed a mass of writhing worms. Still, I would be damned if I let it show. I held my head high and went inside.

Ichabod barely glanced at me from where he sat tuning his guitar as I entered, nodding briefly. "Miss Van Tassel."

"Icha—Mr. Crane," I corrected, stumbling into following his lead.

"Shall we begin?" he asked, strumming a few chords quickly.

"I—yes," I said. "I suppose we should."

We began with scales—again—and then he began to teach me a short, simple psalm. While it was a sight more interesting than scales, it was not enough to distract my racing mind. How could he simply pretend nothing had happened?

His words from the night before—of denial, of an unpalatable truth—threatened to repeat themselves in my head, but I shoved them firmly away. Surely that could not be all there was to it, not when we both felt so for each other . . .

But felt what, exactly? There was an attraction, surely—I found him handsome, and his mind even more so. I craved his touch. But was there more than that, for either of us? What more was there?

His words forced their way into my thoughts: *A man like me cannot come into the home of a wealthy, influential man, accept his food and hospitality, and then speak of love to his virgin daughter . . .*

Love. Could he know me well enough to love me, truly? Surely love took more than a few days, a week, than even the fortnight he would be staying here? Yet the poets and playwrights spoke of love that was so powerful, so undeniable, that all it took was a single glance. I had always thought that foolish, romantic nonsense, but what if there was some truth to it?

And what did I feel for him? Love? Could I call it so? Would I marry him, should he ask for my hand?

"Miss Van Tassel," Ichabod said, exasperated. "Kindly sing the notes on the page, if you would, and not ones of your own invention."

I shook my head slightly, brought back to my somewhat uncomfortable reality by his sharp words. "My apologies," I said, my tone cool. "I am a bit tired, you see. I find I hardly slept last night."

At last he met my eyes, and I saw a flicker of something within them—but before I could determine what it might be, he looked away again.

"Be that as it may," he said, "let us try this once more, if you please, and then I think we shall end for the day."

We began again, my performance better, but certainly not what either of us considered satisfactory. Ichabod did not comment on it. "We shall revisit this next time," he said, speaking to a point on the wall over my shoulder. "Our time is up for today, I'm afraid." With that, he turned away from me to replace his guitar in its case.

I watched him, thinking he meant to say something else—to say whatever it was I was waiting for him to say—but when it became clear he was going to do no such thing, I turned and left, almost stunned.

Had he not corrected my final performance because he simply did not wish to be in the room with me any longer?

I couldn't keep the thought away. But it could not be that. Not when he had returned my kiss so enthusiastically the night before. Surely it was only the strictures of society that stood between us.

And yet . . . if he truly felt for me, should any of that matter?

You have read too many books, a vicious little voice hissed inside my mind as I hurried back up the stairs, tears stinging my eyes. You are a romantic fool, Katrina Van Tassel.

Back in my room, I vigorously brushed the tears away and opened *Macbeth* again. A tale of tragedy and blood sounded like exactly what I needed.

10

Dreams and Nightmares

I did not see Ichabod at dinner that night, for which I was fervently grateful. The more I thought about it, the more I felt it was for the best that he was leaving our house soon, and I would no longer see him as often. It would be better for both of us.

That night I tossed and turned, trying, rather futilely, to sleep. I could not leave off thinking of the moment in the kitchen, and his coldness that day. No doubt he regrets his words to me, I thought, regrets my kiss—and that he kissed me back. I could not quite bring myself to regret kissing him, however—even as recalling it caused me to flush with a heat that was at least partially shame. I must save what fond memories I had and otherwise think no more of him.

I must have fallen asleep at some point that night, for again I dreamed of the Headless Horseman. The vision that met me was different than the one that usually came. Still he faced me from the edge of the woods, astride his horse and with the burning pumpkin beside the horse's hooves. The sheathed sword remained at his hip, but this time, an axe was tucked into his belt as well. I had not seen the axe before. As always in these dreams, Nox was not beside me, though I never ventured out into—or near—the woods without him.

Strangest of all, I could see Ichabod within the woods, just behind the Horseman. He was looking in my direction, his lips moving as though speaking, calling out, but I couldn't hear him. When I tried to move toward him, the Horseman moved to block Ichabod from my view, as if to cut me off.

I awoke with a start, in the dim light of dawn.

Try though I did, I could not get back to sleep, and lay awake as the sweat from the dream cooled on my brow and chest. Why had the dream altered, after so much time? And what could it possibly mean? Or perhaps it was all moonlight and foolishness and did not mean anything. I was never so grateful to see Nancy as when she finally came in to help me dress, and I could give up the pretense of sleep.

Thankfully, I was not needed for chores that morning, so as soon as I broke my fast I took my book out into the woods, to my usual reading spot, Nox on my heels. Some time away from the house was just what I needed.

I shivered briefly as I stepped onto the forest path, the dream still fresh in my memory. Reaching down and patting Nox's head firmly, I resolved to put that confounded dream from my mind once and for all and think only of pleasant things.

I did make a success of it, if only briefly. I reached my favorite spot and settled in on the bank, opened my book, happily losing myself in *Macbeth*. All too soon, I heard the cracking of twigs that could only mean someone was approaching.

Nox, who had been dozing in the sunlight that filtered through the leaves, lifted his head and growled a warning. I lowered my book—I had never encountered anyone in my trips here, and it seemed unlikely I would do so now. Someone must be coming to seek me. My heart quickened, sending hope pounding through my body.

Indeed, it was Ichabod who stepped through the trees and into the clearing. Upon seeing a friendly face whom he recognized, Nox thumped his tail against the ground twice in greeting then lay back down, resting his head on his paws. I set my book on my lap and looked up at Ichabod, waiting for him to speak.

For a moment, doubt seized me. Perhaps he had not come to seek me at all. Perhaps he had merely returned here to read alone, and now, finding me, would turn back.

"Katrina," he said, by way of greeting. I saw that he had not brought a book with him—only himself, in his breeches and shirt-sleeves, his hair tied back at the nape of his neck in the summer heat.

"Ichabod," I replied. "What brings you here?"

"May I sit with you?" he asked after a long pause.

"Indeed," I said. "We do not stand on ceremony here."

A ghost of a smile flickered across his face and was gone, and he lowered himself to the grass—keeping, I noted with some dismay, a quite respectable distance from me.

Thus seated, he was silent for a moment more, and I felt my impatience and curiosity and hope and dread bubbling up within me like some potion created by the three witches in *Macbeth*. Just when I thought I could stand it no longer, he spoke again. "I saw you come out here, and wanted to speak with you. Privately."

"I gathered as much," I said.

He sighed. "I wanted to apologize."

"For your cold behavior yesterday? I should think so. It certainly warranted an apology."

"No," he said, frustrated. "That is, yes—you are right. It does indeed warrant an apology, one I am most willing to proffer. But that is not what I meant."

"Oh? I can think of nothing else for which you need to apologize."

He sighed again, a harder edge to the sound this time. "Katrina. Please do not do this."

"Do what?" I demanded.

"You know precisely what and are being deliberately obtuse."

"I wish to hear you say it," I shot back. "Explain to me why you think you need to ask my forgiveness. I should like to hear the words."

"Very well," he said, sounding angry now. "I wish to apologize for everything I said to you the night before last, in the kitchen. It was inappropriate. Nor should I have . . ." The tips of his ears turned slightly red. "Nor should I have returned your kiss. I should have ended it, as any gentleman must."

My own anger rose to match his. "And I tell you again that you have nothing to apologize for. I was a willing participant in our conversation, and more than that in our kiss."

"Katrina." My name came out as a half sigh, half groan. "Surely you can see why none of this can be. Why it would be better for both of us if that night had never happened."

I was silent, gathering my thoughts. Despite my earlier determination to put him from my mind, to forget about him henceforth, what I truly wanted was very different from that. I wanted him. And I could deny it no longer.

"On the night in question," I said at last, "you accused me of always getting everything I want. And you are right. I have never been denied anything, and as such have very little practice with it." I met his eyes. "I have no intention of starting now, not when I finally know what it means to truly desire something. I realize now that I have never really wanted anything before. The meanings of such words have shifted within my mind, until it feels as though my entire heart has been disassembled and put back together again, slightly different than it was before."

He did not speak. His body tensed as if trying very hard not to take me in his arms. "You speak to me in poetry," he said, his voice so soft it was almost a whisper.

"Should it not be so, between lovers?"

His head jerked up. "We are no such thing," he said. "We cannot be, no matter how much either of us would wish it otherwise."

"And why not?" I asked, the sound of my heart pounding in my ears. "If we both wish it to be so, what should stop us?"

"I can't . . . how can I ask for your hand?" he demanded. "I have nothing to offer you. I am an itinerant schoolteacher, without land or even a house of my own. Why should your father even entertain my suit? He will think me nothing but a fortune hunter."

"Who said anything about marriage?" I asked. "I am speaking of love, a different matter entirely."

"Katrina . . ." He trailed off, frustration creeping back into his voice. He got to his feet. "What are you asking of me?"

I rose as well. "I am asking you to kiss me," I said, "and what comes next can be whatever we wish it to be."

"How many times must I tell you it is not that simple?"

"How many times must I tell you it can be?"

He closed his eyes, as though struggling with himself, and I waited as one poised atop a mammoth cliff to see what the outcome would be. To see if I would fall or soar.

Suddenly, swiftly, he closed the distance between us and took me in his arms, pressing his lips to mine. It was just as glorious a kiss as our first, yet somehow sweeter, as well. One kiss may not mean anything, after all. A second kiss, though . . . surely that was no accident or mistake or moment of weakness.

His hands roamed over the curve of my waist through my dress as my lips parted beneath his. He drew my hips tightly against his own, and I felt a thrill of warmth and pleasure in the depths of my stomach, and lower. I wanted to be closer to him, to feel every inch of him, even as I thought I might drown completely in all the many sensations of this moment. It was too much, and not enough.

Finally I understood what the poets and songwriters spoke of. I knew what it was to have a man take me in his arms because he loved and desired me, what it was to feel the same for him, so that our feelings amplified each other's, and yes, I realized as his arms tightened around me, yes, this is what lovers' legends are made of. This feeling.

He drew away and caressed my cheek with his hand. "Katrina," he whispered, his eyes searching mine. I leaned forward to kiss him this time, and so we began again.

When at last we surfaced, I could not say how much time had passed—surely it had to be hours, or even days? But no, the shadows cast by the leaves above us had not changed, though the same could not be said for the two of us.

I clung to him, my head resting against his shoulder, never wanting to leave this place. I would spend my life anywhere so long as it was with him, I thought dreamily. In the end it was this thought that caused me to draw away. All the things I had read of love and passion had, too, carried a warning of the dangers to be found in falling too fast, in falling too far.

"And so what shall we do now, my Katrina?" he whispered against my hair.

Despite the sobering thoughts that lingered, I glowed at his words. *My Katrina.* "We shall do whatever we like," I replied.

He chuckled, and I could feel the sound in his chest. "I can think of one thing I would very much like to do," he murmured, "but that is no doubt the last thing we should do."

I was silent, both nervous and excited by his words. I was not so sheltered that I had not managed to glean the details of the act of love, but I had never had reason to think about it much before.

But I thought about it then, and what it might be like, and even as the thought scared me I realized I might want that, too.

I released him and stepped back. "No doubt you are right," I said.

"Katrina," he said softly, his voice deadly serious now. I looked up to meet his eyes, green as the forest we stood in. "I . . . we should not be speaking so. Not when I have not asked for your hand."

I struggled to compose myself. "Is that what you are going to do?"

He studied me carefully. "Is that what you want me to do?"

I closed my eyes. How had we gone from sharing kisses in the woods to speaking of marriage? Because Ichabod is an honorable man, I thought. He would march back up to the house and ask my father for my hand right now, if I wished it. "I . . . I do not know yet," I forced myself to say.

Oh, it was easy to daydream about it: Ichabod declaring his love for me and presenting his suit to my father; to see us becoming man and wife, perhaps taking a small cottage in town; to imagine us making love each night then waking up together; having children . . .

I swallowed. It was all too much. I wanted it all, and it scared me. How could I want so much, so soon? How could I be swept away so fast? Was falling in love always this way?

He was right; I had always gotten everything I wanted. So I must be certain I truly wanted it, and that he truly wanted it. Better men and women than us had had their heads turned by a few kisses in a wooded glen.

"Not . . . not yet," I said at last. "Let us wait, and . . . see."

He sighed. "You have kept a cooler head than I, I see," he said. "Yes. You are right. Though God knows how I shall live under the same roof as you and continue to be a gentleman."

I smiled, though it quickly faded. "You are leaving soon."

"Yes. I must."

I took his hand, for I could no longer bear not to touch him.

"And what shall we do?" he asked again, tightening his fingers around mine. "Shall we go strolling arm in arm, to let the whole world know we are courting? Shall I call for you to walk into the village with me?"

"I would like nothing better," I said.

"Nor would I," he said.

Yet we both knew it could not be. Not while he still resided with us, anyway. My parents may have been lax, but not so lax as to let their houseguest court their daughter under their own roof.

After he had gone . . . maybe then. Maybe then the time would be right. We must wait.

We went hand in hand until we reached the edge of the woods and came within sight of the house, and then forced ourselves to separate.

11

Charlotte

As if by unspoken agreement, Ichabod and I avoided each other the rest of the day. He was taking his dinner out once again, and inwardly I lamented this even as I knew it was for the best. How would we ever act normally around each other now? We would need to learn to be actors worthy of Master Shakespeare's stage, and soon.

We had a music lesson the next day, and it became nothing short of an exquisite torture. That we were alone in a room together was, suddenly, too much to bear. With my parents and the servants in the house we had, of course, to maintain a certain level of decorum, yet we took any opportunity we could to touch each other: when I leaned over his shoulder to see a sheet of music, or when he placed his hand on my abdomen to correct my breathing technique. Each touch, however fleeting, was accompanied by a swift smile, a light in our eyes, and it was all I could do to keep from giggling the entire time.

As the lesson ended and we were forced to leave our lovely little nest of a room, I contemplated what to do with the rest of my day. Should we try to escape out to the woods together?

However, as luck—if that was the correct word—had it, practically as soon as I stepped out of the music room my mother called out. "Katrina," she said, stepping into the hallway as she settled her bonnet on her head, "if you're through, come into the village with me. Mevrouw Jansen has sent word that Charlotte has returned, and I am overdue for a proper visit with her in any case."

I brightened. Charlotte was back!

Charlotte's mother was Sleepy Hollow's midwife and herb-woman, and consulted with all the women of the village—and many of the men—about medicines and childbirth, among other things. She had long been a friend of my mother's, and so Charlotte and I had become close friends as well. Charlotte was a year older than I and had learned well at her mother's knee: she would no doubt take over Mevrouw Jansen's duties one day.

"Do excuse us, Mr. Crane," my mother called to Ichabod over my shoulder. "We shall likely take our lunch in town and so may not be back 'til later."

He bowed gallantly in my mother's direction. "I am ever despondent without the company of two such beautiful ladies, but I shall be forced to make do," he said with a smile.

My mother chuckled. "Away with you, sir," she said fondly, and gestured for me to follow her.

I went quickly upstairs for my own bonnet, then rejoined my mother at the front door, from which we walked out to the Albany Post Road and set out for the village proper, leaving Nox at home. On a fine summer day such as this—warm but without the sweltering heat that had marked the previous few days—a lovely walk was just what was wanted.

"I shall be sad to see Mr. Crane go," my mother said as we began our walk. "Such a pleasant fellow. Hopefully he can be persuaded back to dine with us."

"I am sure of it, as he seems to so appreciate our hospitality," I said, fighting to hold back my glee. My mother liked Ichabod and enjoyed his company—surely this would bode well.

We chattered idly the rest of the way, soon arriving at the Jansen cottage, situated in a fairly prominent spot just off the main street.

Mevrouw Jansen's face lit up as she answered my mother's

knock. "Why, my dear Anneliese," she said, reaching out to embrace my mother, "so lovely to see you, as always!"

"And you, Sofie," mother said, returning the embrace.

"And Katrina, too," Mevrouw Jansen said, embracing me as well. "Charlotte will be delighted. She was just speaking of coming to call on you."

"She is always welcome anywhere that I am," I said.

"The feeling is mutual, dearest Katrina," a familiar smooth, low voice said. Charlotte appeared beside her mother in the doorway. "I'm so glad to see you!"

"Well, now, let us not all congregate in the doorway," Dame Jansen said. "Come in, the both of you! Charlotte, dear, do pour the tea—how fortunate you just put the kettle on."

"I made some scones this morning as well," Charlotte said, disappearing into the large kitchen—its size necessary for the work they did—and returned with a plate of pastries, which she set on the side table as our mothers were settling in.

"Let me help you with the tea," I said, following Charlotte into the kitchen. I poured four cups, and she took two into the parlor where our mothers had already launched into a fresh round of gossip. She returned to the kitchen, picking up her own cup as I took mine—as well as the two scones she'd set aside for us—and followed her out the back door into the herb garden. One of the many things Charlotte and I shared was our desire to be outdoors as much as possible.

We both sighed contentedly upon taking seats on the grass, then laughed at the similarity of our reactions. "So tell me, Katrina," Charlotte said, once our giggles had subsided. "How have you been spending this fine summer thus far?"

"With books in the outdoors, as usual," I said, pulling my bonnet from my hair.

"I hear there is a guest in the Van Tassel house of late," she said, raising her eyebrows inquisitively. She took a bite of her scone.

I felt my cheeks redden. "Mr. Ichabod Crane, lately of Connecticut. He is to be the new schoolteacher."

"No doubt you have also been busy with such a supposedly handsome guest," she teased.

I laughed. "Indeed, but not in the way you are thinking. He has been giving me music lessons, and will be providing similar instruction to others in the village."

I could not say why I did not tell Charlotte the truth. She was no gossip; anything I told her remained in the strictest confidence and always would. Even so I held back.

Charlotte eyed me curiously for a moment, as though she knew that I was not being entirely truthful. And perhaps she did. She knew me better than anyone, certainly; but, too, Charlotte had an uncanny way about her. She had a way of knowing things she ought not know and had never been told. As wonderful as her mother was with herbs and remedies, it had always seemed to me that Charlotte had a different—and far greater—gift.

A memory flashed through my mind unbidden: the day our friendship with Brom had ended; the day Brom had flung a rock at Charlotte, one that had hit her cheek—narrowly missing her eye—and drawn blood. More harmful even than the stone, though, was the word he had cast at her: *witch*.

And a mere year later, he had the nerve to steal a kiss from me.

I looked away uncomfortably from her amber-colored eyes and took a big bite of my scone to cover my lie—so big that I almost choked.

"Indeed," Charlotte said at last, and even in that one word I could hear she knew there was more I was not telling her; but, like the true friend she was, she would forgive me. "I must hear you sing again soon, then. No doubt you shall sound more beautiful than ever."

"Perhaps," I said, swallowing my scone and forcing myself to smile. "Is your aunt much improved, then? Surely she must be, since you have returned to Sleepy Hollow."

"She is, thank you," Charlotte said. "She has rebounded remarkably well, and was quite ready for me to stop hovering."

I laughed. "I am sure it was your expert care that allowed her to get well again so quickly."

"I like to think so, and I like to think that is why my mother sent me."

"Then she did right to do so, even though I have missed you."

"And I you," Charlotte said, reaching out and clasping my hands in hers. "Now come, tell me: what else have I missed while I was away?"

I rolled my eyes. "Nothing, truly. Icha—Mr. Crane coming to town has been the most interesting thing of any note."

But if Charlotte noticed my slip, she chose not to comment. "Has Brom Bones given you any peace?" she asked.

"The opposite, in fact," I said glumly. "Why, just a few days ago he came very close to declaring himself to my father."

Charlotte gasped. "No!"

"Yes. We were at luncheon besides. I almost vomited into my plate."

She laughed. "I can well imagine." She sobered almost instantly, however. "You do not think your father would betroth you to him, do you?"

"He seemed in favor of the idea, unfortunately," I said slowly, "but I cannot imagine him betrothing me to anyone against my will. Once he knows how opposed I am, I am certain he will no longer consider it. My mother told me as much, when we spoke of it."

"Your mother knows your feelings, then?" Charlotte asked. "That, at least, is a relief."

"Very much so," I said. "She said she would speak to my father about it."

"You need not worry, then, it sounds." She smiled. "And as the finest heiress in Sleepy Hollow, you may expect a parade of suitors."

This was said without bitterness, yet I could not have blamed Charlotte if she was bitter. At nearly twenty years of age, there had been no contenders for her hand, and there likely never would be. Brom had seen to that.

"Enough talk of men," she said after a moment had passed in silence. "Best not let them occupy our thoughts more than they absolutely must, I daresay. Tell me of these books you have been reading to while away the summer days."

Needing no further prompting, I launched into an explanation of the premise of *Macbeth*, promising to lend her my copy once I had finished reading it.

"Someday I should like to go to London, to the homeland of Master Shakespeare, and see such a play performed," Charlotte said wistfully. Her tea and scone gone, she lay back on the sun-warmed grass, her fiery, nearly waist-length hair spreading out about her head in a red-gold halo.

"We need not go as far as London to see a play," I said. "New York is a good deal closer, and it has theatres enough. But I would see London someday, too. And so we shall do just that, Charlotte. Just the two of us."

She glanced over, her expression apprehensive. "Do you promise, Katrina?"

Her tone seemed oddly heavy for our talk of daydreams on a summer's day. "I do," I said. "If we want it to be so, then it shall."

She smiled. "Yes. So it shall." She changed the subject again. "And what of your nightmares? Do they still visit you?"

I shivered. Charlotte was the only one to whom I had confessed my dreams of the Horseman, and how they terrified me. "Yes," I said. "More often of late, in truth."

Charlotte considered this. "I wonder what it means. That you should have these dreams at all, and that they should be increasing now."

"It does not mean anything," I said. "The people of this town are liable to discuss the Hessian at any given moment. It is no wonder he is often on my mind, and on everyone's minds, I should think."

What I didn't tell Charlotte was the dream had changed for the first time, had included Ichabod. To confess that I would no doubt need to confess several other things.

"Perhaps . . . though I think it is not so simple," she said. "I do not know as much of dream divination as I might like."

"You must not worry, I pray you," I said. "Other than some nights of interrupted sleep, the dreams do me no harm and are of no true consequence."

I could tell Charlotte did not agree, but she let the matter drop.

We chattered on for the next half hour or so, making plans to have a picnic by the river in the coming days. Charlotte inquired after Nancy, and we spent some time trading memories of our time as children together.

It felt like no time at all had passed when my mother called into the garden for me. "Come, Katrina," she said. "It is time we took our leave. We must stop at the market yet."

Reluctantly Charlotte and I rose from the sun-drenched grass. "Until next time, then," I said to my friend.

"Soon," Charlotte promised.

I turned to join my mother inside, but Charlotte grabbed my arm, detaining me. "Wait," she said, her voice low. "Be careful, Katrina."

I stared at her in confusion. "Whatever do you mean? Be careful of what?"

Her fingers tightened on my arm. "Just . . . be careful," she repeated. "I . . . I cannot say why, but . . . you should take care all the same. I think there may come a moment when you will know what I mean."

I stayed silent as she released me. I had learned long ago never to question these odd things Charlotte said, be they warnings or predictions or simply strange moments of intuition. Still, it could be frustrating. When she spoke thusly, she usually did not know the why of it any more than her listener, only that she had a feeling she must impart. And she was scrupulous only to say something in front of those she knew she could trust. She didn't dare speak of her uncanny ways in front of anyone else.

Even in the bright summer sun, I shivered, at both the earnestness in her eyes and at the memory of what she had said to Brom that day, after he had begged and cajoled and goaded her into telling him what she'd seen in his future. It was after she had finally given in that he had thrown the rock at her face and called her a witch.

"I am always careful," I said at last, trying to smile to lighten the moment. "At the very least, I can hardly be called reckless, no?"

Yet even as I spoke, I thought of kissing Ichabod, his arms around me, holding me so tightly to him that there was no space for even a breath between us. And not for the first time that day, my words tasted like a lie.

12

Ichabod's Tale

My mother and I went on to the market to procure some vegetables our farm did not grow, indulging in a lunch of fresh bread and cheese while there. The whole time, Charlotte's warning would not leave my head. Could she be referring to this new relationship with Ichabod? She had said that I would know the meaning of her words eventually . . .

If that was all it was, then she need have no further concern. I was taking the utmost care. Had not Ichabod and I both decided we must proceed slowly? That we must not let our emotions run away with us? Just thinking of him brought on the physical desire to fling myself into his arms; yet I knew upon arriving home I could do no such thing. I would go up to my room, or help my mother with some household tasks.

I did not know how to be any more careful.

Perhaps if I had told Charlotte as much, she wouldn't have felt the need to warn me.

I will tell her all, in my own time, I promised myself.

Our business in the village done, we made our way home with our purchases, as well as some remedies that my mother had procured from Dame Jansen. Upon reaching the house, I went upstairs to remove my bonnet, and found Ichabod coming toward me from his room. "Miss Van Tassel," he greeted me, his proper tone belying the fire in his eyes. "I trust you had an agreeable day?"

"Most agreeable," I said. As he made to pass me, I grasped his arm and pressed close to him. "Tomorrow after luncheon, our place in the woods," I whispered. He nodded once, then I released him, stepping into my room as though nothing had happened.

The next day it rained; and no mere drizzle, but an unrelenting, pounding rain that lasted into the night.

We'd not had much rain this summer, and while I knew I should be grateful for the farm's sake—"Thank God," my father declared at luncheon, "I was starting to worry the crops would begin to dry up!"—I could not help but take it as a personal affront. That it might have been a bad omen was something I refused to consider, but the thought returned to nibble at the edges of my mind throughout the day.

I kept an eye on the window all morning, hoping the rain would subside by the afternoon, but no such thing happened. I was confined to the house, helping my mother with further mending and the making of some preserves in the kitchen. When Ichabod's and my paths crossed, we were perfectly courteous and correct, but the frustration in his eyes was plain to me, as I'm sure mine was to him. How could two people living in the same house find it so hard to meet privately? It seemed inconceivable, yet there we were. And he would be leaving for his new lodgings in three days' time. I did not know if that would be better or worse, but I dreaded it all the same.

He passed me in the downstairs hallway as he made his way up to his room for the night. "Tomorrow," I said softly.

He nodded. "Tomorrow."

I knew we had all the time in the world—our whole lives if we wanted; infinite tomorrows. Yet knowing this could not curb the desperation I felt to be in his arms again.

———

Thankfully, by the next morning the rain had abated, though our spot in the woods would be too muddy to be hospitable. Instead we decided to take a walk along the river, and if anyone inquired or thought it unusual, I could simply say I was showing him some of the Hudson River Valley's most scenic views.

We made our way down the embankment upon which the house stood to walk right beside the river. Nox promptly ran ahead and splashed happily through the shallow waters, barking at ducks and gulls. Once we were out of view of the house and most of the farmland, Ichabod offered me his arm.

"I have been thinking," I said as we walked, the sunshine brushing our faces with warmth, "you now know much of me and my life. But I know so little of you. Of your life before you came to Sleepy Hollow."

He chuckled. "What would you wish to know?"

"Everything. About your family. Your life and home in Connecticut. Your education. How you came to be a schoolteacher. Tell me everything."

He sighed, his smile dimmed slightly. "It is not much of a story, I am afraid. The life I came from is nothing like yours here, surrounded by such plenty, with such a family."

"But it is your story, and so it is important to me."

He sighed again. "All right, then. Even though I am not half the storyteller you are, I fear." He cleared his throat and began. "My father was a carpenter. He made furniture—fine pieces, and he had many wealthy customers who bought them. He would also get work in building new houses, when such was needed."

His face darkened somewhat as he continued. "I don't doubt that my family would have been a prosperous one, had he lived. But as soon as independence from Britain was declared, he laid down his tools and went to fight for his country, with his fellow Americans. He died fighting the British at the battle of Saratoga." Ichabod paused. "I know he was proud to give his life for his country, for liberty. Yet it was bittersweet that such a decisive battle for the Americans was also a devastating blow for my family."

"Goodness," I murmured. "You must have been very young when he died."

Ichabod nodded. "I was only seven years of age. He was away fighting for a time before that, so I have only the vaguest memories of him." He smiled. "I remember being in his workshop with him. He would show me his tools and how to put together pieces of wood to become a table, or a chair."

I placed a hand lightly on his shoulder. "At least you have some memories of him."

"Yes," he agreed. "It is better than none. But the years after his death were very hard for my mother and me. My father had left us a tidy savings, but my mother wanted to hold on to it for as long as she could, so that I could continue my schooling. So she took in sewing, and laundry, and hired herself out as a cook or a servant whenever she could. As I got older, in between my schoolwork, I tried to take over some of the carpentry, but I did not have my father's gift for it, unfortunately. My mother and I grew some crops and raised some animals, enough to keep ourselves fed and make a little extra money, but it was not a comfortable existence by any means." He paused. "At times I was glad I had no siblings, so my mother need not worry about having another mouth to feed. Other times I thought it was a bit lonely, just the two of us. We had no other family, and our neighbors—kind though they were—had their own losses and struggles. We helped one another when we could, but that did not always amount to much.

"In any case, after I finished my schooling, I took a job as a clerk for a wealthy merchant in New York. I sent most of my wages back to my mother, and she was able to hire a farmhand to help keep up our tiny farm. I learned more about figures and calculations there than I ever had in the schoolhouse, and best of all, the man was possessed of an incredible library, which he generously put at my disposal. A stroke of luck, that. I read most of what he had, and he noticed. He asked me if I might tutor his young son, who was having difficulty reading. I did, and felt an enormous sense of triumph at helping the boy. My employer, recognizing this, recommended me as a tutor to others of his acquaintance, and soon I did a nice business tutoring children—boys and girls—in reading and writing and arithmetic. One of his wealthy friends, who owns much land further up the Hudson, I believe, heard of the post here and mentioned it to me, and I jumped at the chance to strike out on my own, as it were."

He smiled. "My mother, I should mention, remarried while I was in New York—to a prosperous farmer who has combined her small holdings with his and is able to keep her in comfort. So now what I do not need for food and personal effects I save like a miser."

"And what do you save for?" I asked.

"I once thought of going west and trying my hand at a homestead and farm on the frontier—they say there are fortunes to be made there, for men brave enough to try." He stopped walking and turned to face me. "But of late I think that so long as I can provide a permanent home for myself, and for a wife, that shall be enough."

I looked down and away from his earnest gaze, trying to hide my wide smile. "A most noble goal," I murmured.

"I think so," he said, his eyes never leaving my face.

We continued along the river, and our talk turned to other things: books we loved, places we both wanted to travel. We even stole a few brief kisses when we were sure no one was near enough to see us. What hung in the air around us the whole time were our hopes for a shared future, one that felt as though it might not be too far off.

13

Rendezvous

"Katrina," Ichabod groaned, frustration and desire evident in his voice. "Please. We must stop."

I drew away from him with a reluctant sigh and curled on the grass at his side. "I suppose you're right."

The day after our walk by the river was equally beautiful, so we had slipped away again that morning, returning to our spot in the woods, away from prying eyes. I had left Nox free to roam the fields, hoping no one would see him and wonder where I had gone without him.

Once alone, Ichabod and I had kissed with a fevered passion, until he lay back on the grass, I nearly atop him, our hands roaming over each other's bodies—when he cupped my breast, even over my bodice, I lost all coherent thought. My hands wandered beneath his shirt, and he stroked my bare legs beneath my light summer skirts.

But that was as far as we went. Not far enough, yet much farther than ever before. Ichabod had stopped us before we could pass the point from which there was no returning.

My body and heart cried out in protest, and I could not stop myself touching him. I wrapped an arm across his chest and held him tightly, while he let his fingers twine in my long, loose hair.

"As beautiful and radiant as the beams of the sun," he said, letting the blond strands fall through his fingers. "But such a beautiful woman as you could be adorned with no less."

I felt as though my entire body would melt into him at these words. "If you are hoping to distract me from thoughts of any further amorous activity, you are failing miserably," I murmured.

Rather than reply, he leaned over and kissed me, hungrily, deeply. I moaned against his mouth as he shifted so he was partially atop me, his hands moving downward over my body. My heart rate accelerated as I arched beneath his touch, with desire and fear and anticipation and excitement.

Yet again he pulled himself away. "By God, Katrina," he said, sitting up and running his fingers through his mussed hair. "We must stop. I am a gentleman, I swear it, though I am not behaving like one at the moment. And a gentleman does not make love to a woman who is not his wife."

I sat up, too, angry and a bit embarrassed. "Oh? And, seeing as how you're a gentleman, and unmarried, I suppose you have never made love to a woman before?"

His silence told me all I needed to know. "There is a difference between being a foolish young man and a gentleman, I'm afraid," he said, his voice somewhat cool. "Though in this instance what I should have said is that a gentleman does not make love to a woman whom he intends to make his wife, before she is so."

"And what of my intentions?" I asked.

"Yes, what of them? What are they? I should like to know."

I looked away from his steady green gaze. "I . . ."

"I would know the truth, Katrina Van Tassel. Do you wish to be my wife, or no?"

"Yes," I said, for foolish and hasty or not, it was true. Were I to be betrothed to a man from the village, as my parents no doubt had always planned, he and I would have had less acquaintance, desire, knowledge, and certainly passion between us than Ichabod and I had now, and yet it would have been considered a good match, a better match. "Yes, I do. But I . . ."

"What?" He met my troubled gaze. "You think your father will say no."

I knew he would say no. I remembered my mother's words too well: *You are an heiress to extensive holdings, and so your father and I expect a good match . . . A man with something to bring to the marriage, and not a fortune hunter.* I had no doubt both of them would categorize Ichabod Crane as the latter.

But what of what I wanted? What of the fact that I had fallen in love with this man?

"I am afraid," I whispered. "Now that you are here, I cannot bear to think of what life would be like if you were not. You were right; I am spoiled and am afraid of being disappointed for the first time. Especially when I would trade everything I have and have ever had, if only to have you."

He shook his head. "You speak so because you do not know what it would be to lose everything. To live without all your comforts in the first place."

"Do you think that I do not speak in earnest? Do you think I am a fool who does not know what she is feeling?" I demanded.

"Of course not. It is just . . ." He sighed and looked away. "Forgive me, Katrina. I, too, am afraid, that is all. Afraid I might lose you. Afraid that your life might be better for it if I did."

I moved closer, taking his face in my hands. "Never say that," I said softly. "It is not true. It cannot be."

He leaned down and kissed me once more, briefly. "Perhaps." He stepped away. "We had best return. I have a few things to see to yet before I leave tomorrow."

"I hate that you must go."

"No," he said, taking my hand in his. "Do not. It is a good thing. It is more proper this way. Once I have been gone a few weeks, I will come back and ask your father for your hand."

My heart pounded. "Truly?"

He smiled. "Truly. I must come call on you a great many times before then, however, so that my suit is not a complete surprise to the good Baltus Van Tassel."

"Yes, I suppose you must." With time, my parents—and my father especially—would come to see Ichabod for the wonderful man I knew he was, and give their blessing.

He smiled. "And what is the Dutch word for husband?"

Yet again, my pulse spiked. "*Man*."

"Ah, similar to English, when in the marriage ceremony we say, 'man and wife.' And so how do you say wife?"

I smiled. "*Vrouw*."

He returned my smile. "You will be *mijn vrouw*."

I replied in Dutch, "And you will be my husband." I prayed that in speaking the words, my doubts as to our future would be chased away.

On returning to the house, we entered through the side door into the kitchen, only to find my mother waiting for us. "Ah, there you both are," she said. Her tone was even, but her eyes held a somewhat troubled expression. "Your father asked that I send you both to his study when you return."

"I . . . the both of us?" I asked.

"Yes. He said he would speak with you and Mr. Crane."

I resisted the urge to glance at Ichabod, to suggest any sort of complicity between us. Had someone seen us? Had we been found out? My father was hardly the intimidating sort, but such a summons did not bode well, even so.

My mother smiled encouragingly. "Nothing to worry about, I'm sure."

I did not reply; merely led the way to my father's study at the front of the house.

I opened the door without knocking and found Brom Bones seated within, across from my father. Both men looked up. "Ah, Katrina, Mr. Crane," my father said.

Brom rose from his chair. "I shall be going, then, sir, as I see you've other matters to attend to." He spoke Dutch, deliberately trying to exclude Ichabod from the conversation. Brom took my hand and kissed it as he reached the door; I recoiled at the feel of his lips on my skin. "A pleasure to see you, Miss Van Tassel, as always." He tossed a triumphant glance at Ichabod as he left.

My heart pounded in my throat. If Brom was involved, whatever was happening was even worse than I'd imagined.

"Sit down, both of you," my father said, and Ichabod and I obeyed, taking the chairs across from his desk.

"What is this about, Papa?" I asked.

"Ah, well, I shall get right to the point, then. Young Brom, you see, has brought something to my attention that is most . . . interesting, I suppose you could say, and I thought I had best get to the bottom of it."

"I am quite in suspense," I said, doing my best to act nonchalant.

"Yes, well, I shall endeavor to enlighten you, then. Yesterday Brom was on his way to call on you, Katrina, and he saw you and Mr. Crane returning from . . . somewhere together. He did not think too much of it at the time, he says, but then today when he came to discuss a few farming matters with me, he claims to have seen you departing together for the woods. He thought I should know, in case there is anything, ah, untoward going on." He nodded at Ichabod. "You'll forgive me for the unseemly implication, I hope, sir. But a man with a daughter as beautiful as mine, and of marriageable age at that, cannot be too careful."

The insinuation in his words turned me to ice—I was of marriageable age, but not available to one such as Ichabod Crane.

"This is absurd," I said coldly. "What on earth does Brom think he is on about? Is he hanging about the place spying on me, then, that he knows my movements so well?"

"Of course not, Katrina. I have already explained how he came to see you on both occasions. And I am quite glad he did, for it is most unseemly for you to be spending so much time alone together, in a secluded wood, no less."

"What exactly are you accusing us of, Father?" I said. "Mr. Crane is a gentleman, I assure you." No doubt those words would have had us in fits of laughter had the situation not been so serious.

We were found out, but I'd be damned if I'd let my father—or anyone else—know it. "Mr. Crane merely expressed a desire to see our native woods, and was curious as to the species of bird that resides there. I have been showing him the paths, and also our lovely scenery along the riverbank. Nothing untoward whatsoever."

"I know that, of course, and—why, accusing is a harsh word, Katrina, very harsh indeed," my father said. "As I said, it is a bit unseemly, that is all, and I am well within my rights to speak to the both of you about it."

"Master Van Tassel, I do apologize for anything I may have done to cause offense," Ichabod said, sounding a bit nervous. "I apologize most sincerely, and humbly beg your pardon. I would never betray your fine hospitality and generosity by . . . by . . ." He stumbled about, searching, no doubt, for a word that would not give lie to our actions.

My father, luckily, seemed to think Ichabod merely wished to speak delicately in front of a lady. "Indeed, I know you would not," he interrupted. "Of course, the both of you know better. But Brom, I fear, is right—it does not look well, not at all. I will soon be entertaining offers for your hand, Katrina, as you know, and so I hope this does not become gossip for the village." He cast an apologetic glance at Ichabod. "Again, I accuse you of nothing, good sir. You have been a wonderful guest. But perhaps it is just as well you are leaving tomorrow—for appearances' sake."

"I understand completely," Ichabod said stiffly. "Again, sir, I would never damage your daughter's honor—"

"Yes, yes," my father said, waving him away. "Of course not, not at all."

I rose from my chair. "If you are quite finished with this nonsense, Father, then I shall take my leave," I said haughtily.

He sighed. "You shall understand one day, perhaps, Katrina. Yes, be off, then. I have said my piece, and truly meant no offense by it, daughter, to either of you."

I turned on my heel and marched out of his study, Ichabod

following me. Tears threatened to spill from my eyes, and I did my best to blink them furiously away as I went straight upstairs.

"Katrina, are you all right?" Ichabod asked, turning me to face him when we reached the door of my room. "Oh, my love," he whispered, wiping away my tears.

In spite of the shambles the day had become, my heart leapt at hearing him refer to me as *my love*. "It is as I feared," I said. "He . . . he will not entertain your suit. He does not think . . ."

"Shhh," Ichabod said, pulling me against his chest. "Do not worry, Katrina. Please. We shall proceed as before, yes? Only it may be a little longer before I can ask for your hand. But ask for it I will. I promise it."

"But . . . but what if . . ." I broke off. I could not even form the sentence.

"Do not worry, my love. He will see it differently when I am gone, when I am no longer under the same roof as his daughter. He is a good father, and he is concerned. I would feel the same, in his position."

I chuckled through my tears. "Someday," I said, "may we both see exactly how you will react in his position, when young men are in love with our marriageable daughter."

"Indeed," he said. "And I shall pray day and night to be so blessed as to have you bear my daughter."

This caused tears to spring to my eyes anew.

"Do not despair, I pray you," he said, releasing me. "All will be well."

Yet for a moment our eyes were honest with one another. There was worry there. A worry that everything would not be so easy as it had seemed in the forest. A worry that there was more pulling us apart than holding us together. A worry that love would not be enough.

14

Night in the Forest

I could not sleep that night, nor had I expected to. Instead I indulged in my fears and wept, then once spent lay awake, dry-eyed. Everything was slipping away from me, and as hard as I tried, I could not seem to find a better purchase with which to hold on.

After midnight, I heard a set of footsteps come from the guest rooms. They paused outside my door, then continued on down the stairs.

In the silence I seemed to hear Charlotte's voice again. *Be careful, Katrina.*

I would not heed her. I could not, anymore. For what had careful gotten me?

I leapt from my bed, prompting Nox to raise his head and look at me quizzically, and quickly changed from my nightgown into a simple, dark gray dress. I grabbed my cloak, to hide my face and keep me warm against the cool night air—and donned my boots. Moving as quietly as I could, I left my bedchamber, closed the door behind me, and tiptoed down the stairs. At the bottom, I paused, listening to see if I had roused any servants—or worse, my parents—but all was still.

I returned to the site of our first rendezvous: the kitchen. As I pushed open the door, I found Ichabod waiting within. His palms pressed down on the counter, his head bowed, as though deep in thought. He raised his head when he heard me, and a lifetime's worth of conversation passed between us as our eyes met.

Yet some things still need to be said aloud. "I cannot wait any longer," I said. Though I spoke softly, my voice rang through the dark, silent kitchen. I walked around the counter toward him. "I cannot wait any longer to be yours. I . . . I love you too much."

"Katrina," he sighed, as though part of him wanted me—and himself—to turn back. Instead, he closed the distance between us and kissed me, deeply and slowly, a promise of what was to come.

He rested his forehead against mine. "Katrina," he whispered again. "Are you certain?"

I was certain, because I was possessed of a fear that this night—perhaps a few nights—might be all that we could ever have. I could no longer speak; I only nodded. I pressed my fingers to his lips and drew him after me, through the house and out the back door. Across the road we went, and into the forest. Neither of us spoke; we made as little noise as possible as we found our way through the dark to our spot by the stream. Even then, thoughts of the Headless Horseman flickered through my mind, and I wondered if he could see us, if he knew we were there—but that night was different. I was with Ichabod, and nothing could harm me so long as I had him. And more frightening than venturing into the woods at night was the thought of who I might become if I stayed in the house, if I obeyed, bent and broke beneath such strictures as *propriety* and *what's best for you* and *a good woman*.

We reached our favorite place, our sacred place, and I removed my cloak to spread it on the ground. I turned to face him, trembling, from both chill and nerves, uncertain of what to do next.

"Katrina," he said again, as though he could never say my name enough, as though it tasted like the finest of wines on his tongue. "I never replied to you there."

"Wha . . . what do you mean?" I stammered.

He stepped closer to me, brushing my loose hair away from my face. "When you said you love me," he said. "What I meant to say was this.

"I love you as well. I love you beyond all sense and reason. I love you so much that though I know I should put a stop to this, return us to our own beds, I will not. Because I love you so much there is nothing on this earth that could compel me to refuse time with you. And I love you so much that I cannot resist the thought of becoming yours. Yours and yours alone."

Tears clung to my lashes before splashing down my face, as his beautiful words flowed over me and caressed my skin. He drew me into his arms, kissing the tears from my face. His hands worked to undo the lacings of my dress, and when his fingers fumbled I drew back.

"Let me," I said, kicking off my boots and removing the simple garment so that I stood naked before him, shivering with cold and desire and uncertainty.

His eyes took in every inch of me. Even in the dark, I knew he could see me clearly. "Do not leave me all alone," I said with a coy smile, reaching down and pulling his thin shirt off over his head. I leaned in to kiss him again, and the feel of his lean, bare chest against my naked breasts caused me to sway on my feet, lost in the forbidden sensation I had barely dared to dream of. He groaned against my mouth.

"How rude of you to remain dressed when a lady is unclothed," I teased as we broke apart.

"Rude indeed," he said with a devilish grin, and bent to remove his boots and breeches. When he straightened, I found myself blushing and averting my eyes, suddenly afraid to look at that part of a man with which I was still unfamiliar.

His grin faded as he approached me, seeming to sense everything I could not say. He pulled me to him and kissed me again, more hungrily and urgently this time, and the whole lengths of our naked bodies pressed together. I shrank away at first from the feel of his manhood against me, mentally cursing myself for acting the silly, inexperienced virgin, even if that was exactly what I was.

I drew him down upon my cloak, so that we lay side by side upon it. His hand traveled along my side, coming up to cup my breast, his long fingers gently toying with the nipple. I gasped at the sharp twinge of pleasure that shot up through me from my core.

He turned me so that I was laying on my back, and replaced his hand with his mouth. I uttered a small cry, grateful we were deep enough in the woods that no one could hear us. "Yes," I whispered.

His mouth shifted from one breast to the other, his hand sliding down between my legs. Nervous, I wanted to clamp them together, but allowed myself to relax into his touch, letting his hand move between them, stroking me in that secret place a woman was supposed to reserve only for her husband. Yet no marriage bed could have felt as sacred as that night did.

I gasped as his fingers moved gently within me, bringing forth sensations I had not thought my own body capable of. I arched my back, pressing against him, wrapping one leg around his waist, bringing him closer to me. "Yes," I whispered. "Please."

His breathing was heavy as he withdrew his hand. We were so close I could feel his heart pounding. Even so, he paused, bracing his weight on his arms so that he hovered above me. "Katrina. Katrina, my love. Are you certain?" he asked again.

"Yes," I breathed. "Oh, yes." I wrapped my arms around his neck and drew his lips down to mine, and as we kissed again I felt him lower his weight onto me, felt him at the entrance to my body, and opened my legs a bit wider. The kiss went on as he gently, slowly entered me. I jerked away and cried out at the sharp pain.

"I am sorry," he whispered. "I am sorry, my love."

I looked into his beloved eyes above mine in the dark. "I . . . I know," I said. "All is well."

With that, he began to move within me, and I became consumed by feeling, by the strange, awkward, intimate, yet pleasurable movement of his body inside mine, reveling in the feeling of our closeness, as close as two people could physically be, and felt in that moment that our hearts, our souls, were as close as they could be as well. Pleasure and happiness swept through me. I understood how desire culminated in this act, and why it was called the act of love, and I never wanted it to end.

He cried out and shuddered in his pleasure, resting his head against my shoulder, spent. I held him against me, both of us panting, the sheen of sweat on our bodies cooling in the summer night's breeze.

"God and the devil together forbid I shall ever be without you again," he murmured. "A life without you would be no life at all."

"Never stop saying such things to me," I said, pressing my lips to his. "I want nothing but you and your beautiful words for the rest of the days of my life. Never leave me."

He returned the kiss, hard. "Never," he said. "I will die first."

He lifted himself off of me and drew me against his side, his breath slowing. Tears seeped from my eyes again. I would never have expected it, but it hurt to be this happy.

15

Gunpowder

I wanted to stay in the woods all night, all week, for the rest of our lives. But we dared linger there together only an hour more—we had to make it back before the household began to stir. My father believed our innocence thus far, but if we were found returning from the woods together in the wee hours of the morning, there was no excuse that would be plausible.

Reluctantly, we rose and helped each other dress, taking the opportunity to let our hands wander over one another all over again.

"We shall never make it back in time if you do not stop that, my love," Ichabod whispered against my ear as my hands strayed below his waist.

I bit my lip, considering letting him make love to me again, and damn the consequences. I heard his breath catch in his throat and knew that he was thinking the very same thing.

Luckily—or unluckily, perhaps—reason prevailed, and we resumed dressing. I picked up my cloak from the ground—soiled and rumpled; I would need to hide it from Nancy until I could wash it—and draped it over my arm. Ichabod took my hand, lacing his fingers through mine, and together we began to make our way out of the forest, staying pressed close to one another the whole way.

We both slowed as we came out of the trees and crossed

the road, approaching the fields that surrounded my house, eyes sifting through the darkness to see if anyone was watching, then paused when we reached the side door that led into the kitchen.

Swiftly, Ichabod pressed my back up against the house and kissed me, crushing my body against his briefly before releasing me. "God help me, I wish I was not leaving in the morning," he said.

"When . . . how shall we meet again?" I asked, only now beginning to see the difficulty of the thing. "You shall be in the village, and I here . . . where can we meet safely? How will we communicate with one another? When—"

"Shhh." He pulled me close. "Do not fret, my love. We will find a way. I . . . I will borrow a horse, buy one, if I must, and ride to meet you. And I will still come to give you music lessons, if your father is agreeable, yes?"

I brightened. I had forgotten. "Yes," I said. "And then we can make . . . arrangements."

He smiled. "Indeed. Very pleasurable arrangements." He kissed me once more. "When we go inside, I shall go into the kitchen, so if anyone hears and awakens, I can say that I was simply getting myself some milk."

"And I shall go straight upstairs."

"Yes." His lips found mine again, and lingered, knowing it might be some time before we could be alone together again.

Finally, too soon, we broke apart and entered the house as quietly as possible. I moved swiftly toward the back stairs, while he remained in the kitchen. Once there, I balled up my cloak, stuffing it into the back corner of my wardrobe, then quickly removed my dress and changed back into my shift. Noticing traces of blood on my thighs, I quickly dipped a cloth into the bowl on the washstand and cleared it away. I shoved the cloth under my bed until morning, when I could dispose of it. Then, at last, I climbed into bed. Yet even then the nervous, euphoric energy of the night would not leave me, and as such, it was not until dawn was bleeding into the night sky that I finally fell asleep.

I had expected to be despondent when I awoke, knowing Ichabod was leaving, yet I was not. Though I barely slept, I rose with an enormous grin on my face, one I would be hard pressed to hide from the world.

Nancy knocked twice, then bustled in. "Good morning, Miss Katrina," she said. She paused. "And what are you so joyful about this morning?" she asked. "Is it a holiday I don't know about?"

"No," I said, trying and failing to dim my smile. "Just . . . just sweet dreams, I suppose."

"Mmmhmm." Nancy studied me for a moment. "Sweet dreams about that handsome schoolteacher, I wouldn't wonder."

"Nancy!" I shrieked, feeling my face redden. I had to fight to fend off a fit of giggles.

Luckily, she had turned away to open my wardrobe. My grin fading, I held my breath, hoping she would not notice the cloak; but she merely pulled out a clean dress and shut the door. Thankfully, she made no other teasing comments and simply helped me dress as usual. As soon as she left, I went straight downstairs, not wanting to miss a moment of Ichabod's presence.

As it happened, my parents had laid out a large breakfast in the dining room, with fresh rolls, cheese, slices of chicken and ham, and some strawberries. I walked in to find Ichabod already seated at the table with my mother and father. He and my father rose as I came in.

"Good morning, Katrina," my father said. "We decided to send young Mr. Crane off in style. Join us, won't you?"

"Of course," I said, taking a seat directly across from Ichabod. Our eyes met, and to my horror I felt my blush return, remembering in far too much detail the night before, how his skin felt against mine, how it felt to have him inside me. Quickly I looked down. By God, but it is a good thing he is leaving, I thought fervently. I could never behave normally around him after that. Never.

"Good morning, Miss Van Tassel," Ichabod said, perfectly courteous, and in glancing up, I saw he was avoiding my gaze as well.

"Good morning, Mr. Crane," I said, matching his tone. A slight, mischievous smile curved my lips. "I trust you slept well last night?"

I thought he was going to choke, but he managed to swallow the sip of tea he had just taken without incident—barely. "Indeed," he said. Ensuring my parents were both distracted, he cocked an eyebrow at me.

I looked away, fighting back laughter yet again. Oh, thank God he was leaving. We would never survive more than an hour with our secret intact.

The rest of breakfast passed without any incident. Once we were through eating, we all rose and moved toward the front door, where Henry, my father's manservant, had already brought down Ichabod's two bags and his guitar.

My father and Ichabod shook hands. "It has been a pleasure having you," my father said.

"Indeed," my mother said. "You may expect invitations to dine with us in future."

He bowed to my mother. "Nothing would please me more, madam. Truly, the pleasure has been all mine in receiving your wonderful hospitality, and I shall be forever grateful."

Apparently the talking to my father had given the both of us yesterday was to be forgotten and not spoken of again.

Ichabod turned to me, and could not entirely mask the heat in his gaze. "Miss Van Tassel," he said, taking my hand and kissing it. Even so innocent a touch of his lips caused my breath to catch in my throat. "I shall see you in two days' time in the afternoon, when we shall continue your musical education, yes?"

"Yes," I echoed, struggling to control my voice. "I shall look forward to it."

"As shall I." He turned away from me and tipped his hat to my parents. "Thank you again, dear sir and madam."

"Not at all," my father said. "And indeed, I do have a parting gift for you, if you will be so good as to accept it." He let out a sharp whistle, and Henry rounded the corner, leading one of our horses—the older gray gelding.

"This is Gunpowder," my father said. "I present him to you, sir, as a gesture of my gratitude for your work in Sleepy Hollow, and in the hopes of making your way here a bit easier."

I was speechless, and I could see that Ichabod was as well—though not only with gratitude. We had spoken of how he might somehow find a horse—and here my father was, presenting him with one. It was nearly too good to be true.

This boded well for my father's opinion of Ichabod. Perhaps things were not as dire as we'd thought.

"I . . . I do not know what to say, sir," Ichabod said. "I am quite overwhelmed with gratitude."

"You are most welcome," he said. "And now we bid you good journey, and hope to see you soon."

We waited as Henry and Ichabod attached his bags to the saddle, and once that was done, Ichabod slung his guitar over his shoulder and mounted up. He swept off his hat again. "You have my infinite thanks, all of you," he said. "May we meet again soon." His eyes locked on mine in the final instant before he wheeled Gunpowder about and turned toward the road into the village, away from our farm.

My parents went back inside, but I could not resist watching until he was completely out of sight. I felt naught but desolation as I watched him ride away.

16

Herbs and Warnings

I must confess that I moped about much of that day, like a lovesick girl—which I suppose I was. Yet after a while, even I got quite bored with myself. Ichabod had only moved to a house in the village, for heaven's sake. I would see him again, in a mere matter of days.

The following day, I awoke with a new resolve. I would go see Charlotte and tell her all.

Indeed, I was burning to tell her, had been ever since that night in the woods—was it not always so? When something so momentous had happened, did we not all wish to tell our dearest friend? I had kept it to myself for as long as I could, and I knew Charlotte would never betray me.

Yet truth be told, I had another, more practical reason for wanting to confide in Charlotte—I needed her help. There were ways a woman could go about preventing herself from conceiving a child, but I was not certain what those might be. Luckily for me, Charlotte would know. I could hardly go asking Mevrouw Jansen, as any other woman in Sleepy Hollow might.

Before lunch, I left the house and found my mother tending her geese. "I am going into the village to visit with Charlotte," I told her. "Do you need anything from Mevrouw Jansen while I am there?" I hardly needed an excuse to see Charlotte, but being a dutiful daughter would not hurt.

"No, but give her my best," my mother said, straightening up. "And invite them both to dinner Wednesday, won't you?"

"Certainly," I said, turning away. "I shall see you when I return, then."

"Have a good afternoon, dear."

I rounded the corner of the house and headed for the barn to saddle my horse, but stopped halfway down the path, grinning. Charlotte was walking toward me, a basket over her arm. "Katrina!" she called, waving.

"Why, Charlotte," I said, "I was just this moment on my way to the village to visit you."

"Were you?" she asked. "That is a happy coincidence." She winked at me. She had come because she had already known I wished to see her. Charlotte's gift could be handy that way.

She lifted her basket. "I made some more scones, and baked some fresh bread as well. I thought perhaps we could beg some cheese and wine from your cook and have that picnic by the river."

"Perfect!" I cried. And it was—along the banks of the Hudson we could talk freely, as Ichabod and I had days before. "Come inside and we shall see what Cook has for us."

Nancy was in the kitchen chatting with Cook when we went in, and we wheedled and cajoled the two women until they laughingly relented and fetched us a hunk of fresh cheese and a bottle of wine, as well as some chipped cups to drink from, and a big old cloth for us to sit on. "If either of your parents come looking for that wine, I am going to tell them you took it, Miss Katrina, make no mistake," Cook said teasingly. She was a gray-haired woman about Nancy's age whom we had all called Cook for so long that I often forgot her real name was Marie.

"Very well," I said, "but had we not, no doubt you two would have gotten to it before long!" We left them chuckling to one another as we headed out with our very full basket and clambered down the steep incline to reach the banks of the wide, glorious

Hudson. The water sparkled in the sun as if studded with diamonds, and the far bank was hazy and distant in the summer heat, as though a whole world away. Charlotte helped me spread the cloth on the grass, and then, giggling, we removed our socks and boots, lifted our skirts high, and splashed out into the water to cool off, before finally settling in and turning our attention to our food.

"You had the right idea," I said. "It is the perfect day for a picnic by the river—warm, full of sunshine, and almost too hot."

She glanced over at me, smiling. "I rather thought you might agree."

I turned toward her. "The truth is, Charlotte, I was coming to see you because I have something to tell you."

"I had a feeling."

"Yes. And this is—well, it's important, in truth. You must promise not to tell a soul."

She shifted, folding her legs beneath her. "I swear. Now, tell me!"

I took a deep breath and began, starting with the first day Ichabod and I spent reading together in the woods and ending two nights ago, when we had made love.

Her eyes grew wider and wider as I spoke, and when I confessed the last part her jaw dropped open. "Katrina!" she cried. "You didn't!"

"I did," I said. "And sin or no, I enjoyed every second of it."

"But, Katrina . . ." She closed her eyes in consternation. "How could you? You are not married! What if someone finds out?"

"No one will find out if you do not say anything," I said, annoyed and a bit hurt by her reaction. "I thought you would be happy for me. I did not think that you would be so . . . so . . ." I searched, frustrated, for the word. "So disapproving."

She sighed. "I . . . I am not, not really. I am a bit shocked, is all. You had told me that there was nothing between you and this man." Now it was her turn to look hurt. "Why didn't you tell me the truth when we first spoke of him?"

"I wanted to, but . . . it was all so strange and new, and I did not know what this relationship was, or what it would be," I said. "I was afraid to put too much stock into it yet. But . . ." I shook my head. "It all happened so fast."

Charlotte reached over and grabbed my hand. "And that is just it," she said. "It has all happened very fast, Katrina, and I am worried for you. Worried about what will happen if anyone finds out, or if, as you fear, your father does not let you marry this Ichabod Crane fellow. Worried about you having your heart broken."

"There is little chance of that," I said, recalling the words Ichabod and I had exchanged that night.

Never leave me.

Never. I will die first.

This I would not share. Some things I would keep for myself, for just Ichabod and me. "My heart you need have no fear for, that much I know," I said. "He is a good man, Charlotte, and he loves me. Very much."

She still looked troubled. "Perhaps," she said. "But oh, Katrina, how long can you go on like this? Suppose he gets you with child?"

I raised my eyebrows, and her expression hardened. "I see," she said. "You want me to help you avoid that."

"Yes," I said. "I know that you know of such things."

"I do, yes," she said. "But let me ask you this, Katrina Van Tassel—if you did not need my help in carrying on your secret love affair, would you ever have told me the truth?"

I drew back as though she had slapped me. "Charlotte! Of course!"

"Are you certain of that?"

"Yes, I am," I said. "I have been burning to tell you since it happened! I would have come to see you yesterday, but I . . ." I bit my lip. "I wanted to keep it all to myself, for just a little while longer."

Charlotte was silent for a moment, then sighed. "Forgive me, Katrina," she said. "I am sorry. Of course I will help you. Of course I know that you trust me. It is just . . . as I said, a bit surprising. It is a lot of news to take in all at once."

"I know," I said. "But you are my best friend—you are the only one I can tell." I leaned over and embraced her, and she squeezed back.

"Since that is settled," she said, grabbing the wine, "shall we enjoy our lunch?"

"Yes, let's," I said, moving to the center of the blanket. I drew out the loaf of bread and began cutting it into slices while Charlotte poured the wine. I took the knife to the cheese next, and soon we were happily eating, the momentary coldness between us gone as if it had never been.

"Contraception, then," Charlotte said. She grinned mischievously. "My mother would rather I knew nothing about this part of her business, but she has had no choice but to teach me. It is one of the most frequent requests she gets." She shrugged. "Some say it is a sin, but children cost money to feed and clothe, and that is the truth of it."

"Indeed," I said, "and a child would cost a great deal more than money for an unmarried woman."

Our eyes met, both thinking of the consequences of what I was doing. "Katrina," she said softly, "is there no way you can desist until you are safely married?"

I closed my eyes. I had asked myself this many times, both before Ichabod and I had made love, and after. I had no answer Charlotte would like, and no good reason for it. "I . . . I love him," I said. "Oh, Charlotte, one day I hope you know what this feels like. It is the most wonderful feeling, even as it hurts. Even as it frightens me."

"Sounds to me like a rather unenviable disease."

I laughed in spite of myself. "Perhaps. But I love him all the same. I cannot be without him now. I cannot go back. No matter the cost."

She sighed. "Very well. There are some herbs I can give you. Brew them into a tea and drink it after each time you are with him. And keep the herbs well hidden." She shook her head. "I do not know how much Nancy or your mother knows about herb craft, but it would not do for them to make such a discovery."

"That sounds easy enough," I said, relieved. I did not know what I had expected—something altogether messier, perhaps.

"There are other ways, of course, if you should ever be without the herbs," she said. "Sponges soaked in vinegar can do the job, as well. If properly inserted."

I frowned. "Sponges? Inserted? But how—what . . ."

Charlotte raised her eyebrows at me, and comprehension dawned. "Good Lord," I said. "That sounds altogether uncomfortable."

She giggled. "Hardly the stuff of romance! But, as I said, should you ever find yourself in a tight spot . . ."

"A tight spot indeed!" I cried, and the both of us fell over onto the picnic cloth, giggling uncontrollably.

Charlotte struggled to pull herself upright again, through her laughter. "You shall make me spill my wine!" she said, raising her glass.

"Perish the thought," I said. "Thankfully we have more!" I plucked the bottle from the basket and poured some more for both of us.

"Well, isn't this a cozy scene."

The two of us started at the familiar voice.

"Brom Van Brunt," I said, all traces of mirth gone as I shielded my eyes from the sun to look up at him. "Your family's farm must be falling into quite the state of neglect, seeing as you have been spending all your time over here."

"Hardly," he said, taking a seat beside me as though he was welcome. "Things are running along better than ever, and I have an excellent reason to visit the Van Tassel farm." He smiled at me in what he no doubt thought was a charming manner.

"Oh? And have you an excellent reason to be intruding on Charlotte's and my picnic as well?"

He spared a glance in Charlotte's direction but did not say anything to her—ever since the incident, they ignored one another whenever they could. Every inch of her was tense. "I should say I do," he said. "I keep coming to call on you, Katrina, and yet I find you are always otherwise occupied."

"That is by design."

"Come, now," he said. "You know that—"

"You are not welcome here, Brom," Charlotte said, breaking her silence at last. "You are not welcome anywhere that I am. Ever."

"Oh, yes?" he said, turning to sneer at her. "And what are you going to do about it?"

"Do you really want to find out?"

His face paled slightly. "You are nothing but a fraud," he said, a note of uncertainty in his voice.

"Is that so? I wonder, then, that you went to the trouble of accusing me of being a witch to the entire village," she shot back.

He rose quickly. "I shall not be spoken to like this!"

"Yes, being confronted with one's own sins is always an uncomfortable business," Charlotte said.

Brom's petulant expression called to mind another summer day many years ago, the three of us enjoying a picnic very similar to the one Charlotte and I now shared. Brom had brought Charlotte an apple tart from one of the village women, because it was her favorite, and he had gallantly crushed a spider that had been crawling over my skirts, causing me to scream as though the Headless Horseman himself was after me.

What happened to that boy? I wondered, studying him. Is he still inside this man, somewhere? Yet then his expression hardened, and any traces of nostalgia I had felt vanished as quickly as they had come.

"Be gone, Brom," I said. "Visit with my father if you will, for it would seem he has some desire for your company. I certainly do not."

"You will see, Katrina," he said, over his shoulder as he walked away from us. "You will come around, in time."

I rolled my eyes at his back as he clambered back up the embankment. "Honestly, why can he not take no for an answer?"

When Charlotte didn't respond, I glanced over at her. She was watching Brom with an oddly stricken look on her face. "Charlotte? Charlotte, are you all right?"

She started slightly, as though she had forgotten I was there. "Katrina," she said slowly, "you are certain Brom does not know the truth about you and this Ichabod Crane?"

"Yes," I said. "I do not see how he could."

"But he saw the two of you coming and going from the woods. Are you certain he never followed you?"

"Quite certain," I said. "We would have noticed him following us, and no doubt if he had proof of any so-called improper behavior between me and Ichabod, he would have wasted no time in telling my father."

"I suppose that's true," she said, looking visibly relieved. "Good. Make sure he does not find out."

"I shall do everything in my power to ensure that no one finds out," I said. "Why, Charlotte? What has you so worried?"

"Just a . . . a feeling I have." She reached out and grasped my arm, just as she had done in her garden. "Be careful, Katrina."

I shifted so that I faced her fully, and took her hands in mine. "But why?" I asked again. "You said the same thing a few days ago. Why all the warnings?"

She shook her head, seeming unable to speak.

"Charlotte," I whispered. "What do you see?"

"I don't know," she said, her eyes focused on something far away. "As I said, it's just a feeling I have."

17

Friends and Lovers

The next morning, I awoke to find my monthly course had come overnight. I was both relieved and disappointed: luckily, my night with Ichabod had not seen me conceive; yet this meant it would be a week's time before we could arrange to meet again.

He was coming to give me a music lesson that day, though I wondered how much music would actually be taking place. After, I would need to venture to Charlotte's house to get the herbs she had promised me.

He arrived in the afternoon, after having taught the morning classes at the schoolhouse. I had been unable to resist the temptation of waiting for him on the portico, and rose from my chair when he walked up to the house, his guitar slung across his back.

"Good morrow, Miss Van Tassel," he said. "It is an exceedingly fine day, is it not? I decided I may as well walk rather than ride, while the weather is agreeable."

This day is made all the finer now that you are here, I thought. Aloud, I said, "It is indeed, good sir. So much so I decided I may as well await you outside." This I added for the benefit of anyone inside who may have been listening.

He walked up the porch steps to me, and took my hand and kissed it. It was all perfectly proper—save the look in his eyes. "It is almost a shame we must confine ourselves indoors for a time," he said, and I grinned as I took his meaning. "But it is not truly so when there is music, yes?"

"Well spoken," I said, and we went into the house together. It was all I could do not to run with him into our music room and shut the door behind us. Once we were there, though, he immediately swept me into his arms and kissed me, hard. I returned the kiss eagerly, melting against him, feeling every inch of my skin hum like the strings of his guitar.

"I have had to remind myself that it has only been a few days, and not a lifetime," he whispered against my hair as we broke apart.

"Yes. Oh, yes."

He stepped back and went to remove his guitar from its case. "We had best engage in some music, lest anyone become suspicious."

"I suppose," I said, and he chuckled at the regret in my voice.

"Do not fear. I have brought something I think you will like. It is a duet, something for us to sing together."

"Oh?" I said. I took the music sheets from him, feeling my excitement grow as I scanned the lyrics: it was a love song, yet the words were innocent enough that no one need suspect anything. It was no different from any of the other ballads sung around an evening fire. Yet we would know the truth. I grinned. "I approve of this plan."

"I thought you might," he said, eyes twinkling. "But first, of course, you must learn your part, and learn it well."

As the lesson began, I was surprised to find him slipping back into his exacting teaching persona. Yet even as it chafed, I knew it was his way, one that would make me a better musician. He sang my part through for me once, that I might hear it, then played a phrase at a time on his guitar and had me sing it back to him, that I might learn it. As usual, it was demanding work, with his insistence on perfection, and by the end of the lesson I had only learned the first third of the song. I was frustrated, which had the strange effect of making me desire him even more.

"You have deliberately picked something difficult," I accused him as he packed away his guitar.

He glanced up at me, one eyebrow raised. "But of course. It shall take us much work and much time together to master."

A smile curled at the edges of my lips. "Yes, I suppose it will."

He rose and took my hands in his. "When shall we meet again, my Katrina?" he asked, his voice low.

I sighed. "It will not be for some days yet, my love. My monthly course is upon me."

He closed his eyes in relief. "Thank God," he said. "Do not misunderstand me; I am disappointed that we cannot meet sooner. But it is for the best, in this case."

"Yes," I said. "I wonder how many lifetimes that shall feel like."

Ichabod did not seem to have heard me. "Katrina . . . we are lucky this time. What about the next time?" He ran a hand through his hair. "I . . . I have always known this is not wise, but maybe we should reconsider. Perhaps it is best that I ask your father for your hand straightaway; surely he cannot deny us when he sees how we love each other . . ."

"No," I said, cupping his face in my hands, forcing him to meet my eyes. "Not yet. I . . . I think we had still best wait."

"But what if—"

"Do not fret," I said. "I am taking precautions to ensure I will not conceive a child. Not until we wish to, of course."

He studied me carefully. "What precautions are these?"

I waved his question aside. "There are ways," I said. "My dearest friend is Charlotte Jansen, daughter of Mevrouw Jansen, the village herbalist and midwife. She is going to help me."

"Does she . . . does she know the truth?" Ichabod asked. "About us?"

"Yes," I said. "As I said—"

"Oh, Katrina," he interrupted with a groan. "Why did you tell her? It would have been so much better if no one knew—"

"She is my best friend in the world," I repeated. "I trust her beyond anyone. She would never betray us; and what is more, I need her help."

Ichabod hesitated. "Charlotte Jansen. I have heard that name," he said at last. "There are . . . rather startling rumors about her in the village."

"Pay no attention to that slanderous drivel," I said sharply. "It was all created, every last word, by Brom Van Brunt, and it is all lies. Charlotte is the best person I know, and has never done anyone harm in her life."

Ichabod nodded. "Forgive me. I have never met her, and so was hesitant to give credence to the gossip in any case. If you trust her, then that must be enough for me."

"Indeed it must," I said, still rather piqued at him.

He looked as though he wanted to say something more, but apparently thought better of it. "Very well," he said at last. "I shall return, in three days' time for our next lesson."

"Wait," I said, an idea striking me. "I must go to the village to confer with Charlotte about . . . well . . . this." I looked up at him through my eyelashes, something I had learned men found rather fetching. "Walk with me there? You can meet her, and assure yourself that all will be well."

"Yes, of course," he said. He kissed me again, swiftly. "The longer we can delay our parting, the better."

I went into the kitchen to fetch Charlotte's basket, which I had bade her leave behind yesterday so that I would have an excuse to see her again today. I found my mother within, conferring with Cook. "I am off to return Charlotte's basket," I told her, holding it up. "Mr. Crane shall walk me there."

"Very well, dear," she said. "It is a lovely day; enjoy yourself."

And so we were on our way, free and clear. Ichabod offered me his arm as we walked toward the road—a perfectly appropriate gesture, yet one that spoke of something a bit more, perhaps. I found myself wishing my father was watching.

"And so how are you finding your teaching duties?" I asked as we walked.

He told me in detail of his first few days, of how some of the students were eager to learn and others convinced that they would never have any use for such things. "It is a struggle to reach both groups of students, to ensure that they all learn equally, whether they understand the importance of it or not," he said. "And of course there is an issue of language, as well. Some of the students speak little English."

"Indeed," I said. "And so we must improve your Dutch. But I understand the larger struggle you face. Many of the women in the village have often scoffed at me for reading so much, and for wanting to learn. They do not see a use for things that will not help run a household or raise children. Yet is not learning always worth it for its own sake?"

"That it most certainly is," he said. "And that is what I am trying to impress upon these students. Many of them plan to grow up to be farmers or laborers or craftsmen and so see no value in book learning."

"Surely they realize they must know how to read and write and count, so as to keep track of their wages and put their signature knowingly to a contract," I said. "It will make them better businessmen, better at keeping track of their money."

"That is so," Ichabod agreed. "Perhaps I must frame it in such a way."

"Of course you must," I said. "I wonder that you have not done so already."

He lifted my hand to his lips. "I needed you to show me the way, of course."

"Indeed," I scoffed. "I wonder what the good villagers of Sleepy Hollow would say should they learn just how distracted their new schoolmaster's mind is."

"I am most distracted, I confess. And if you keep looking at me like that I shall become further distracted from this road."

I laughed. "As I should not like for you to collapse in a heap upon it, pray keep your mind on the task at hand. Walking, that is."

We continued to playfully tease one another the rest of the way into the village, though we became quieter the closer we got. It would not do for anyone to overhear our flirtatious banter and make us the talk of Sleepy Hollow.

I led him to the Jansen cottage, and withdrew my arm from his as I knocked upon the door. Best not to draw any probing questions from the kind yet formidable Mevrouw Jansen.

Yet as luck would have it, it was Charlotte who opened the door. "Why, Katrina," she said. "I see you have come to return my basket," she added with a wink. "Oh, I am sorry," she said, catching sight of Ichabod. "I do not believe we have met, sir."

"Charlotte," I said, performing the introductions, "this is Ichabod Crane, Sleepy Hollow's new schoolmaster, of whom you have heard me speak. Mr. Crane, this is Charlotte Jansen, my dearest friend in all the world."

Ichabod doffed his cap. "Miss Jansen," he said. "It is a pleasure."

"A pleasure to meet you as well, Mr. Crane," she said. She threw me a mischievous yet approving look. "Indeed, Katrina has told me much of you."

Ichabod gave a nervous smile, still not entirely comfortable with Charlotte knowing our secret. He will soon see, I reassured myself. Once he gets to know her, he will see how worthy she is of our trust.

"Please, come in, the both of you," Charlotte said, stepping back so that we might come into the cottage. "My mother has run out to the market—a pity," she said to Ichabod, "for I know that she would most like to meet you, good sir."

"Kind of you to say," Ichabod said. "I look forward to making her acquaintance as well. I have heard her spoken of with naught but the utmost respect."

Once these pleasantries had been exchanged, we all looked at one another awkwardly. I could almost hear our mutual thoughts: did we speak of our shared secret? Or did we keep pretending that everything was proper and just as it should be?

Charlotte broke the silence, and the stalemate. "I believe there are some herbs that you need from me, Katrina," she said, glancing at me. Then she switched her gaze to Ichabod. "I am told they will be beneficial to you both."

Ichabod fidgeted uncomfortably. "I . . . that is, I can imagine what you must think of me, Miss . . ."

Charlotte smiled, a smile so radiant that Ichabod seemed to relax immediately. "I think no such judgmental thoughts, good sir," she said. "You make Katrina happy, and otherwise what is between you is none of my affair. Yet I would say this," she added, her voice taking on a serious note, "have the utmost care with her heart. I will not stand to see it broken."

"Nor would I," Ichabod replied. "You need not trouble yourself on that count, Miss Jansen."

"Good." Her smile returned. "We are in accord, then. I think you and I shall be friends, Mr. Crane."

"I hope so."

Charlotte turned to me, her smile wider. "Come into the herb room, then, Katrina," she said. "Mr. Crane can await us here. We women have things to discuss."

"Indeed," I said. I cast Ichabod a look over my shoulder as Charlotte led me into the herb room, where bunches of herbs hung drying from the rafters, giving the room a bold, spicy scent. Jars along the walls held liquids and dried herb mixtures alike, ready to be dispensed to whoever might have need of them.

"He is handsome indeed," Charlotte said to me in a low voice. "And he seems kind, and gentle, and sincere. I commend you on your choice."

I giggled. "Thank goodness. If you did not approve, I think I should part ways with him completely." Yet though I had spoken in jest, I realized my words were quite true. If Charlotte had distrusted or disliked Ichabod for any reason, I would have found myself with many doubts indeed.

Charlotte reached behind one of the jars on the shelf and extracted a smaller jar. "I already mixed the herbs for you," she said, handing it to me. "Pennyroyal and blue cohosh. Now, as I told you, brew these into a tea and drink it after each time you are with him. A teaspoon's worth for each cup, no more. Too much will make you ill."

I took the jar. "How soon afterward must I drink it?"

"As soon as possible. It will likely not taste very good," she added, "but a bit of honey will do no harm and should help the taste."

I nodded, tucking the small jar into a pocket of my dress. "Thank you, Charlotte. I truly cannot thank you enough."

She waved my words aside. "Of course. But, Katrina . . ." That haunted look came into her eyes again. "Do be careful, won't you? That no one discovers this secret?"

"Of course," I said. "You need not even tell me. But Charlotte, this is the third time that you have warned me to take care. What do you see?"

"It is . . . it is nothing, I think," she said, her eyes a bit unfocused. "Truly. More a feeling of apprehension, of danger, that I felt about you last week. I think I was only seeing this romantic venture of yours."

I relaxed slightly. "If it was something more, you would tell me, wouldn't you?"

"You know I would." She shook her head slightly and smiled reassuringly at me. "Truly, Katrina, do not worry. Well, you should worry, so that you do not take foolish risks, of course. But you know what I mean. All I have been foreseeing—if indeed I was foreseeing anything at all—was my own nervousness for you."

"I suppose that makes sense," I said.

"In any case," she said, returning to the business at hand. She nodded at the pocket where I had put the herbs. "If you should need any more, just tell me."

I grinned. "And what shall you think of me if I should need more in short order?"

She laughed. "Nothing I don't think already," she teased.

We returned to the front room, where Ichabod had taken a seat. He rose upon our entrance. "Everything well, ladies?" he asked.

Charlotte and I exchanged a knowing look. "Quite well," I said.

"I hope I can persuade you both to stay for a cup of tea," Charlotte said.

Ichabod withdrew a gold pocket watch from his coat and consulted it. "I wish I could," he said reluctantly, snapping the cover closed again, "but I am due back at the schoolhouse for afternoon lessons." He hesitated, then, remembering we were among friends, crossed the room to me and kissed me quickly upon the lips. "I shall see you in three days' time," he said. "For your next lesson."

I pursed my lips in a pout. "Would that it were sooner."

"Would that it could be," he said. "But I think it best we not seek each other out before then."

I sighed.

He kissed me again. "I will see you then," he said, lowering his voice, "and shall count the hours in the meantime."

"As shall I."

He put his hat upon his head and nodded to Charlotte. "Miss Jansen," he said. "It has been a pleasure making your acquaintance. And I thank you for your . . . erm . . . assistance." His face turned slightly red.

Charlotte grinned wickedly at him. "A pleasure meeting you as well, Mr. Crane."

He nodded again to the both of us, then let himself out.

As soon as he was gone, we burst into giggles. "Who would have thought Mr. Ichabod Crane was the bashful sort," Charlotte said, once she had somewhat recovered. "Did you see how red he turned?"

"I did," I said, mastering myself. "But . . . that is one of the things I love about him."

"I wonder that he managed to do the deed at all, seeing as he is so shy," Charlotte added, sending us both into a fresh fit of laughter.

"I promise you, he is much bolder when it is just us," I said once our giggles subsided. "But not . . . not too much so." I sighed, remembering. "If that makes any sense."

"It does," Charlotte said. "He does not take you for granted, and that endears him to you."

"Why, that is exactly so," I said. "I had not thought of it that way, but you are quite right."

She smiled. "What are friends for if not revelatory insights?" She made to move toward the kitchen. "I can persuade you to stay for some tea, I hope, since you are here?"

"Of course." I impulsively reached out and took her hand. "Oh, Charlotte," I said, my tone hushed. "How I wish that you could feel this way. How I wish that you had someone like Ichabod."

She drew her hand away roughly. "I do not think the chances of that happening in Sleepy Hollow are quite likely," she said coolly.

"Oh, but surely—"

"I do not need your pity, Katrina Van Tassel." With that, she swept into the kitchen, and when she returned a few minutes later with a teapot and cups on a tray, she was collected once more. I did not bring up the subject again.

18

Fear and Ecstasy

Over the next three days, I kept myself as busy as I could to pass the time until I would see Ichabod again. In addition to helping my mother with mending and with tending her flock of geese, as well as going on walks with Charlotte, I spent much time helping my father inspect the crops, something that always delighted us both.

"This summer could do with more rain," my father said one day, squinting up at the cloudless blue sky. We were mounted on our respective thoroughbreds, riding along the edge of the wheat field. "I've half a mind to begin bringing in the winter wheat now, but I've heard tell it may rain next week."

"You'd be right to bring it in now," I argued. "It is ready and perfect as is. More rain might be good, yes, but you also risk leaving the wheat another week under the sun if it does not."

He studied me from under the wide brim of his hat. "I think you are right, daughter," he said. "Very well. I'll tell George to begin the harvest tomorrow with such field hands as we have, and I'll ride into the village to secure some temporary help."

I smiled. "You will not regret it, Papa."

"You have such sound judgment in these matters, Katrina. I would be a fool not to listen."

At last Ichabod returned for another music lesson. Being in his company was wonderful, of course, but I wanted more; wanted to touch him, kiss him; wanted him to kiss and touch me.

At the end of the lesson, as he was packing away his things, I leaned in close. "Three nights hence," I whispered in his ear. My monthly courses would be over by then. "Midnight. Meet me at our spot in the woods."

He froze, before straightening to look at me. "Very well," he said. "You are sure, Katrina?"

"I can think of nothing else."

"You are certain about the risks we are taking, I mean."

"Of course," I said again. "Are you . . . you are not?"

He was silent, causing my body to grow cold, though it was quite warm in the small room. "I have been struggling with myself," he said at last. "With my selfishness, that I would put you in harm's way; risk your honor, your reputation . . ."

I took his face in my hands. "If I do not have a care for those things, my love, then neither should you."

He turned his head and kissed my palm.

"Whatever shall come—whatever pleasure or pain, whatever sorrow or misfortune—we shall meet it together," I said.

This time he kissed me on the lips. "Ah, Katrina," he said softly. "I am uncertain about many things, it is true, but never you. Never you."

And so passed another anxious three days, another three days of frantically filling them up with whatever activities I could. I could scarcely even read, for my mind wandered in a way that made me most impatient.

On the appointed night, I waited impatiently for the midnight hour to approach. At half past eleven, I could wait no longer. No one had stirred for some time, and I knew I must make my escape now, or perish of anticipation.

I donned my cloak—which I had sneaked into the laundry tub days ago—and slipped out of my bedchamber, moving down the stairs and to the kitchen as noiselessly as I could. I paused, listening to see if anyone had heard and would come to investigate. If I was caught now, I could easily say I could not sleep and wanted a bit of air. If someone awoke and found me halfway to the Albany Post Road, well, that would be harder to explain.

It felt like an eternity that I stood in the doorway, the warm night air breathing over my skin and bringing it to life; yet it was likely only two minutes. Determining that no one had heard me, I stepped out and pulled the door closed quietly behind me, setting out for the woods.

As soon as I stepped within the trees, my heart began to pound—and not just in pleasurable anticipation. I could not remember ever having ventured into the woods alone after dark—indeed, never alone at all, for I always had Nox with me. Last time, Ichabod had been with me, and his presence, coupled with the knowledge of what we had been about to do, had served to efficiently distract my mind from my fears. Without him, I had no such safeguard.

Even as I knew wild animals posed the greatest danger, my sole thought was of the Headless Horseman. Surely I was just the sort of unwitting traveler he preyed upon on his nightly rides? A foolish soul who left the safety of her house and ventured into his territory by night, and so close to the witching hour?

My eyes darted frantically through the darkness, ears alert for the sound of hooves, of a horse whinnying, of a sword being unsheathed. My breath caught in my throat, and I thought I might never regain it.

The Horseman is not real, I reminded myself as I quickened my pace, nearly running. He is a legend, a fable, naught but a tale to tell on cold nights around the fire. He is not real.

But what if he is?

When I reached the clearing, I almost wept to see that Ichabod was not there yet. I knew he would come soon, yet after my fearful trek I did not see how I could bear to wait there alone. He should be here any minute, yes? How long had it taken me to get here? It must be almost midnight . . .

I moved closer to the stream and paused, listening to the forest around me. It was not quiet, in truth: the breeze rustled the leaves of the trees; crickets played their nightly tune; and in the distance an owl let out his mournful call. I stood rooted, my every limb and muscle paralyzed, all my senses trained on listening for anything unnatural moving through the brush, a galloping horse, footsteps . . .

I thought that perhaps I may as well sit down, may as well make myself as comfortable as I could and try to relax, yet I could not bring myself to move. What if I must flee, flee for my life? I wondered. Better to stay on my feet, and be ready. My breath came faster now, and with more difficulty; it felt as though the darkness was smothering me from all sides.

Slowly, reluctantly, I turned to look at the path from which I had come, afraid to face what may be standing there. Yet there was nothing and no one; just the night.

I let out a ragged breath, but did not relax. My eyes kept flicking every which way, probing, searching. The reasonable voices of my mind had long since been overridden by this very primal fear. *Please, Ichabod, come soon. Please!*

What if he does not come? What if he has been detained, or is unwell, or is lost in the dark and cannot find his way without me to guide him? In that instant, what upset me most was not that I might not see him at all that night, but the notion of having to make my way back out of the woods alone, with fear in my every breath and terror in every step and the horrible pictures in my mind of what was surely lurking amongst the trees.

What if the Horseman had taken Ichabod?

My mind had just begun its descent into that particular hell when I heard the sound of hooves drawing near. I let out a scream of pure, bone-piercing terror.

"Katrina!" I heard a voice call, and I screamed again. I tried, in a blind panic, to run for the path, but a pair of arms caught me.

"Katrina," he said hurriedly, even as I was drawing breath to scream again. "Katrina, it is me! Ichabod!"

I collapsed against him, feeling as though all the life had drained out of me, and he staggered a bit, surprised by my sudden weight. "Oh, thank God." Tears sprang to my eyes. "Thank God."

"Katrina, what has happened?" he demanded. "Why are you in such a state?" I could feel him turning his head, scanning the clearing. "Have you seen someone? Is there someone here?"

"No," I sobbed into his shoulder. "No one . . . at least I do not think . . . oh, Ichabod." I drew back, struggling to pull myself together. "I feel quite the fool. I have worked myself into a right state, coming into the woods alone, waiting here alone . . ."

"I came as fast as I could." He released me, stepping away to tie up his horse.

"I know you did," I called to him. "I know. I have not even been waiting that long. It is just . . ." I shuddered. "I was thinking of the legend of the Horseman, and my imagination quite ran away with me."

He returned, drawing me close again. "Do not fret. All is well," he whispered against my hair. "Although I can scarcely blame you." Again he glanced around us. "There is something about these woods at night, something unsettling. Perhaps it is as you say, only the legends weighing upon us. And yet I cannot help but feel that there is more to it than that . . ."

I shivered, and he tightened his arms around me.

"Ah, Katrina," he whispered. "I am sorry. I am so sorry."

I pulled back slightly so that I could see his face. "What do you have to apologize for?"

He sighed. "All this . . . everything. That you should have to come out here into the woods alone at night, that I should bring you here . . ."

"I chose to come," I reminded him. "I fell prey to a flight of fancy, nothing more—"

He was silent. "But it is not right," he said finally. "That you—that we—should be reduced to this: sneaking off into the woods to couple like animals. That this is to what I have brought my future wife . . ."

"Ichabod, no," I whispered. "Do not think of it that way."

"Is there another way to think of it?" he asked, angry now.

"Of course there is," I said, slipping my arms around his waist. "We are doing whatever it takes to be together. We love each other too much to do otherwise. It is all very romantic, in truth." I looked up, only to find his face stony, inscrutable. "Or do I have it wrong?" I asked, stepping away from him. "Do we not love each other that much?"

He sighed again. "Katrina, please. You know it is not that. I just want to give you something better than a few hours in the woods where—"

"I appreciate that," I said. I moved back into his arms and kissed him, deeply. "Yet I only ask for comfort. And love."

He pulled away. "I should ask your father for your hand without delay," he said. "We should not go on like this."

"Shhh." I silenced him with another kiss. "All in good time."

This time, his lips sought mine, and his hands began to roam over my body. I smiled against his mouth and reached down, beginning to unlace his breeches.

"Wait," he said, and I paused, though I did not remove my hands.

"Wait?" I asked innocently. "Surely you will not try to talk me out of this again, love. For I can feel that you are most ready . . ."

He groaned slightly. "Yes. But . . . just wait a moment." He returned to where his horse was tethered and came back with a large blanket. "It is not much, but it is something," he said, spreading it on the ground. "What I would not give to be able to make love to you in a proper bed."

"All in good time," I said again. I untucked his loose shirt from his breeches and lifted it over his head.

"My turn," he said, grinning. He turned me around and pressed close against my back as he untied my cloak, letting it drop to the ground, then unlaced my dress. Once I had stepped out of it and my boots, he let his hands trail over the thin cotton of my shift, down my stomach and sides and hips. He held me tightly against him and began to kiss my neck.

I sighed, tilting my head to one side, letting his lips trail down to my collarbone. My heart was racing again, as fast as it had in my fear, yet this time each beat awoke my skin, my nerves, the tips of my breasts and between my legs. I could feel his hardness pressing against my lower back, and it only aroused me more.

I spun to face him, and he tangled his hands in my hair and kissed me, hungrily, as though he would devour me. And that was just what I wanted him to do.

Mouth working, I finished the task I had begun of unlacing his breeches, pushing them down to his ankles. He kicked them away, and returned to kissing me.

It was just as I remembered, yet more vivid because it was all happening again, and not just in my memory. Every inch of our skin was pressed together, and for a moment we did not kiss, just stood there, our arms wrapped around each other, feeling the contours of each other's body, savoring each breath and each point where our skin met, savoring the intimacy of the moment while anticipating what would come next.

His breathing quickened, and I could feel his heart begin to beat faster. It was he who broke away first, leading me to the blanket, and I pulled him down atop me. We did not speak; we did not need to. I opened my legs to him, and he thrust inside me with a soft moan. There was no pain this time; my back arched with pleasure, and I sighed aloud as he entered me. He moved within me quickly, and I bucked my hips to meet him, gasping aloud as pleasure began to build higher and higher within me. Too soon he shuddered against me, moaning my name, then dropped his head to my shoulder, spent.

I let my head fall back to the ground, breathing hard, enjoying the feel of him still inside me yet somehow disappointed. Whatever I had seemed to be waiting for had not come.

"I am sorry, my love," he said, as he lifted himself off me to lay at my side.

"And what do you apologize for now?" I asked.

"I have not been the most considerate lover," he said. He leaned over and kissed me. "Allow me to recover, and I shall make it up to you."

"I don't know what you mean."

He laughed. "I will show you. All in good time."

He tucked me into his side, and I allowed my hands to wander over his chest, the taut muscles of his arms and back. In turn he caressed the curve of my side with his long fingers, raising gooseflesh along my skin, skin too used to being under the cover of many layers of clothes. How wonderful, I was finding, to feel sensations against one's bare skin other than mere cloth, or water when washing: the flesh of a lover; the warm, fragrant night air; even the slight dampness of the ground beneath the blanket.

"Only this," he whispered, after a time. I glanced at him questioningly. "I need only this for all the rest of the days of my life, and I shall be the happiest of men."

I laughed. "You are easily pleased, I think."

"What man would not be, with the most beautiful, charming, and intelligent of women in his arms?"

"Well then, since you ask so little, you shall have your wish. You shall have me. We shall have this, all our days."

"Sometimes I fear God will not allow it, for to give us such bliss in this life will surely make the delights of heaven pale by comparison."

I gasped in mock outrage. "You blaspheme, sir."

"Not even God can alter the truth."

"I find that your words quite enflame me," I said, lightly stroking his manhood. He stiffened under my fingers. "And speaking of words, I believe you owe me an explanation of your earlier ones."

"You are quite right, madam." In one swift motion, he had me on my back again. "I do indeed."

Balancing himself on his arms, he kissed me, deeply, his tongue slowly moving against mine. I arched, gripped him tightly, wanting what came next.

He kissed his way slowly down my body, lavishing every inch of skin with attention from his mouth and hands. It may have been minutes; it may have been hours. I gasped and writhed beneath him, feeling as though I was about to be torn apart.

Finally, he kissed my lips once more, and lowered himself onto me as I eagerly wrapped my legs around his waist. Yet he was not to be rushed. Gently he slid into me, and began to move with excruciating slowness. Again my hips met his thrusts, and I heard myself moaning, gasping, begging for more in incomprehensible words.

"Ichabod . . . yes . . . please . . ."

He began to move a bit faster, just a bit, and I moaned again, in frustrated anticipation. That same sensation began to build within me, a delicious, unbearable, almost painful pressure, lifting me higher and higher. "Please . . ." I said again, wantonly pleading, not sure for what.

He thrust again, and again, a bit faster, a bit deeper, and suddenly I felt myself falling from those heights to which I had been lifted, heard my voice crying out wordlessly, felt my head fall back in ecstasy as my whole body shuddered around him. His mouth came down on mine as his own body was wracked with pleasure, and I clung to him until I landed softly, still in his arms.

I felt as though my body had turned to liquid, as though I was melting into the ground. After a few steadying breaths, I opened my eyes and met his. "Oh," I said.

"Indeed." His eyes searched mine. "Are you happy, my love?"

"In body and in spirit," I said. "You have most admirably fulfilled your promise."

"I am glad to hear it," he said. He again settled himself next to me. "I pride myself on being a man of my word, after all."

"Then I must make sure to extract many more such promises from you in the future."

He let out a hearty laugh at that and I joined him, our laughter ringing into the night. "And what," he asked, once our laughter had subsided, "is the Dutch word for lover?"

I smiled and pressed a kiss against his jaw. "*Minnaar*," I murmured.

"*Mijn minnaar*, and soon to be *mijn vrouw*."

We fell into another deep kiss. If the Horseman indeed lurked in the forest that night, surely such incandescent joy as ours chased him away.

19

Suitors

There was no fear to be found in my journey back out of the forest. I sat before Ichabod on Gunpowder's saddle as we road down the path, indulging in the feel of his body against mine for as long as I could. When we reached the edge of the Van Tassel land, he brought us to a halt.

"Much as I would like to see you safely to your door, I fear I must leave you here," he said. "You could hardly be faulted for taking a nighttime stroll on your own property; however, my presence would be far more difficult to explain."

I slid from the saddle reluctantly. "Goodnight, my love. Take care on your ride back."

He grasped my hand in his. "I shall. Do not fear for me. You, take care as well."

"I love you," I whispered. "I will see you again soon."

"Nothing could prevent it," he promised me.

The walk into the woods suddenly seemed much easier than the walk away from him. As terrified as I had been mere hours before, I now wanted to return to the darkness of the trees and never leave, if only he could always be by my side.

And yet as I glanced back at him once more, I could have sworn I saw a light in the woods behind him, a flickering, orange glow, like that of a flame. Of a flaming pumpkin borne by a ghostly rider, perhaps. My breath caught in my throat as I stared, blinking rapidly, but then it was gone, and soon Ichabod had turned and ridden away. Frozen, I stared into the distant woods, eyes probing among the dark branches, but I could see nothing. Uneasily, I turned back toward the house and quickened my pace.

I tugged open the side door and paused, listening. When I did not hear anyone within, I cautiously stepped inside. Closing the door behind me, I quietly climbed the stairs to my bedchamber, where I quickly stripped down to my shift. I wanted nothing more than to climb into bed and sink into the delicious memories of the past few hours, but I had one pressing task to attend to first.

I retrieved the jar of herbs from a large trunk that held my books—one place that Nancy would never have cause to search through. The trunk had been purchased for me in New York by my father to serve as my hope chest, and hold new linens and undergarments and the like, but those things I stored carelessly in my wardrobe so as to have more room for books.

Clutching the small jar tightly, I made my way back downstairs to the kitchen. Now, at least, if anyone should happen to awaken, I was doing nothing untoward—I certainly had a right to be in my own kitchen at any hour of the night.

I stoked the embers of the kitchen hearth into a flame, then placed the copper pot on its iron hook above the fire, filling it with water from the pitcher Cook kept on hand. I waited as the water boiled, unable to keep a silly smile from my face . . .

"Miss Katrina?"

I emitted a startled cry. "Nancy," I said, turning to see her standing in the doorway, her shawl clutched about her. "I . . . you frightened me."

"I am sorry," she said. She looked at the pot over the fire. "Tea? At this hour?"

"Yes," I said. "I awoke and could not get back to sleep, and so I thought to make myself a cup of tea."

"I see," Nancy said, glancing about with narrowed eyes. "Have you been in your room all night, Miss Katrina?"

My heart increased its pace again. Do not stop to think about why she might be asking, I told myself sternly. "Of course," I said, hoping my tone sounded suitably bewildered that she would even ask such a thing. "Where else would I have been, at this hour?"

"I'm sure I can't say," she said. "It's just I sometimes hear you tossing and turning, or pacing when you can't sleep. But I heard not a sound from in there tonight, until I woke up to hear you coming down the stairs."

"I don't know what to tell you, Nancy," I said. "I paced a bit, I suppose. You must have simply slept through it."

"Hmmm." She studied me for a second longer. It was all I could do not to squirm beneath her dark eyes. "If you say so. But seeing as I'm here now, I may as well brew your tea for you."

"No," I said, my hand instinctively tightening around the jar. I prayed she hadn't noticed. I remembered well Charlotte's warning to keep the herbs hidden: *I do not know how much Nancy or your mother knows of herb craft.* "No, there is no need. I am already awake and have gotten started; you may as well return to your rest."

"Hmmm," she said again, lingering. Then, finally, finally, she turned to leave. "Very well, then. I hope you are able to get some sleep, Miss Katrina."

"Thank you, Nancy," I said. "I am sorry to have disturbed you."

The door to the kitchen closed behind her, and I exhaled, panic subsiding.

Once the water reached a boil, I removed the pot, poured it into a cup, and added the herbs. I let them steep for several minutes, then took a sip. Instantly my face scrunched up in disgust. Well, Charlotte had warned me. I added some honey, which did much to improve the taste, but still I drank it down in a few gulps, washed the cup in some of the remaining water, and went back upstairs.

———

I was certain my racing mind would keep me awake. Yet almost as soon as my weary body touched the mattress, I fell into a deep sleep.

When I awoke, it was later than when I usually arose. I stretched my body languorously beneath the coverlet; it ached in ways it never had before, deliciously so. I closed my eyes again, allowing myself to be consumed with the memory of his mouth and hands on my body, of him inside me, of that one glorious moment . . .

I felt the heat rise between my legs. We had not planned our next tryst, and this now seemed like a very glaring omission to me.

Would that it could be tonight, today, that he could join me in my bed this very moment . . .

Soon, I promised myself, we would be man and wife, and we could make love before sleeping and again before rising each and every day, if we so chose. I still had my very reasonable fears that my father would refuse Ichabod's proposal, but it did not matter. I would run away with this man if I had to, and take the disgrace that would come along with it.

My reverie was interrupted, yet again, by Nancy, who knocked before opening the door. "Ahh, awake at last, I see," she said, coming in. "Seeing as your sleep was so disturbed last night, I told your mother I would let you sleep a bit longer."

"Thank you," I said, trying to rid my face of its no doubt dreamy expression.

Apparently I failed, for Nancy stopped to consider me, hands on her ample hips. "Seems like you must have had some sweet dreams indeed when you eventually got to sleep."

"I . . . I did," I allowed.

She went to my wardrobe and opened it, poking about for a clean day dress. "You must miss having that Mr. Crane around the house," she said casually.

I froze, startled at the change of subject—then wondered if, horror of horrors, it was no true change of subject in Nancy's mind. "I suppose," I said carefully. "He was most amiable, and I enjoyed having him as a guest."

"Heard you were walking together in the village a few days ago."

Take a deep breath, Katrina, I told myself, feeling a slight panic rise. This is what you wanted, after all. To be seen with him, in no compromising circumstance, but just enough to put the thought in Papa's head that Ichabod may ask for my hand, and that it may be a good match after all. "Indeed," I said, as though I thought it a matter of no import. "After my lesson, I went to visit Charlotte, and he graciously offered to accompany me."

"Hmmm," she said, in that same suspicious and unsettling tone she'd used the night before. "No doubt. Well, people hereabouts talk, Miss Katrina. Mind you're not giving them anything to talk about, you hear?"

Her eyes met mine for an instant, and I wondered just how much Nancy knew, or guessed. Her even gaze suggested she would keep my secret for now—but what she understood that secret to be, I could not say, and that unnerved me. Surely, though, if she knew the true extent of my and Ichabod's relationship, she would feel honor-bound to tell my parents. So she could not know all. "Of course not, Nancy," I said. "You need not even waste your breath on such words."

"I'll be the judge of what I waste my breath on, thank you," she said. "Now out of bed with you. Your mother has some mending for you, but as it's a lovely day she says you may take it out to the portico."

At least mending was a rather mindless activity; I would be free to relive the night before as many times as I chose.

"Ah, Katrina. *Goedemiddag!* How industrious you are!"

I looked up from my mending a few hours later to see my father climbing up the steps. Behind him one of the farmhands led his horse away.

I rose from my chair to kiss his cheek. "Good day, Papa," I said. "How goes the harvest?"

"Quite well," he said. "I found no shortage of help in the village and the surrounding farms, as usual. I've some of the children threshing in the barn today."

"Ahh, yes." My father could always find farmhands without their own wheat to hire for this task; though there were some white men who would not work alongside Negros who earned the same wage as them, Father always said he'd rather not hire such fools, anyway. As such, his hired hands were mostly free Negros and a few white men. And some people sent their children to be paid a few coins to do the threshing, one of the lightest tasks.

He drew up a chair beside me and sat down heavily in it. "I am getting too old to ride around in such heat as though I were a young man," he said ruefully.

"Don't say such things, Papa. You are as hale and hearty as ever."

He chortled. "You are a good daughter, Katrina. The very best, methinks."

I smiled. "I am glad you think so."

He shifted in his chair toward me. "I certainly do. And in that vein, there is something I wish to speak with you about."

I was immediately wary. I could not forget Nancy's words of warning, her knowing gaze. Her telling me of the village gossip. If the gossip is no more than what Nancy told me, there is no cause for alarm now, I assured myself. Papa cannot possibly know any more than that. "Of course, Papa," I said. "What is it?"

He sighed and paused, as though gathering his thoughts and determining how best to begin. "I have given my permission to Brom Van Brunt to pay court to you," he said at last. "And it is my wish that you shall seriously entertain his suit."

I leapt to my feet, heart thudding in anger and consternation. "What?" I demanded. Had my mother not told him of my feelings on this matter?

"Do calm down, Katrina. It is too hot for such a fuss and, may I say, it is not entirely ladylike for you to gape at me in that way."

I continued to stare at him, mouth open. "Papa, you . . . you can't mean it!"

"Why not? I like him, and his point about it being financially advantageous to eventually combine our two farms is a good one.

Besides, you and he were such close friends as children. Surely that is enough to build a good marriage on, and certainly to consider one."

"Papa," I said, "surely it has not escaped your notice that I cannot abide Brom Van Brunt, have not been able to for years now. And you well know why."

He waved this aside. "Nothing remains the same as it was when we were children, Katrina, and that is as it should be. You and he will resolve your disagreement in time."

"Disagreement?" I fairly shrieked. "He called Charlotte a witch, accused her before the whole village. In another time and place that would have cost her her life. As it is, she is still—"

"Katrina, do not be overdramatic," he said. "It is the one unfortunate result of you reading so much, I fear. No harm came to Charlotte. And do not forget that Charlotte had a part to play in that particular incident, as well. She does not always conduct herself as she ought, and fine woman though Mevrouw Jansen is, I would have thought she might have seen to such things with more care."

My mouth dropped open again. "I thought you liked Charlotte!"

"I do, and know her to be a fine young woman. My point is merely that those who do not know her as I do may, ah . . . have had cause, rather, to lend credence to young Brom's words, as impudent as they were."

"That is hardly—"

My father cut me off again. "Calm down, Katrina. I am not here to speak about Charlotte Jansen. That is not my point."

"In a way, it is exactly the point."

"Katrina, really. This was all years ago. I would have thought you could get past it by now, and settle down to the task of considering your future."

"Brom Van Brunt is not my future."

"It would be a good match," my father persisted. "For reasons I have already stated. You know I have always been fond of him, and find him to be a worthy young man. Would I so much as consider entrusting my only daughter to anyone less?"

Here I paused. In truth, my father had always been fond of Brom. For years now Brom had come to the farmhouse—regardless of his and my relationship—to speak to my father, and seek his counsel, as he had never been able to do with his own father. From the time he was a boy, Brom had admired my father a great deal and, I knew, wished that he was his own.

My father meant what he said, that he felt Brom was worthy of me. That I knew differently caused me to doubt my father's judgment, but not his heart.

"Did not Mother speak to you of this?" I asked at last. "She and I spoke of this matter once, and I let her know I was very . . . disinclined to Brom's suit."

"She did," my father allowed, "but I wish him to court you, anyway. It is my wish that you should at least formally consider him."

"I will never consider making him my husband."

"Katrina, I lose patience for this," my father said, rising from his chair. "You are of an age to marry, and then some. You must marry someone, and while I shall certainly take your wishes into account, I mean to decide on the suitor I think is best for you. That is a father's prerogative, is it not?"

I ignored this altogether. "Are there no other suitors who might come pay me court?" I asked.

"Did you have someone in mind?" he asked, studying me carefully.

This, it occurred to me, might be my moment. Perhaps now I should confess (almost) all, tell him of Ichabod's and my feelings; that we were deeply in love and wished, more than anything, to be married. Perhaps now I should ask him to at least allow Ichabod to pay court to me as well, let him at least think I was considering both men.

But I didn't. I feared too much what would happen if he refused.

If everything was going to come crumbling down around me, I could not bear for it to happen yet.

My father patted me on the shoulder. "Do not worry, Katrina. All will be well. You have nothing but good things ahead of you, I shall make sure of it."

I sank down into my chair, my mending forgotten on the wooden floor of the portico. I felt as though I were made of stone.

20

Courting

The next day, coconspirator of my father as he was, Brom appeared around midday just as we were rising from the lunch table. "Good morrow, Meneer Van Tassel, Mevrouw Van Tassel," he said as we entered the front room, where he was waiting. He bowed to me. "Juffrouw Van Tassel. *Hoe gaat het met jij?*"

I did not deign to reply. Nox, well aware of my distaste for Brom, growled low in this throat.

Unfortunately, this did not discourage him. "I have come to ask if you might take a walk with me," he asked. "Along the river, perhaps."

I remained silent for as long as I dared, until my father's face began to grow red with frustration. "Very well," I said aloud. "But Mr. Crane is coming to give me my music lesson in an hour. We must be back before then."

Brom's face lit up at my reply, as though it were not the most reluctant of acceptances. "I am honored that you should agree," he said, extending his arm to me.

I crossed the room to him as though walking to my own execution and took it. Nox followed closely at my heels.

"*Heel goed, heel goed,*" my father boomed, his good humor entirely restored by my acquiescence. He grabbed Nox by the scruff of his neck. "You stay here, boy."

At Nox's pleading amber eyes, I opened my mouth to object. I would feel better to have him with me, but in the end I did not speak. No point in arguing with my father more than I must.

"Enjoy yourselves," Papa said. "It is a fine day outside, most fine."

My mother did not say anything, but I fancied that she tossed me a sympathetic look as I went out.

Brom led me out the front door and toward the Hudson, helping me down the embankment so that we might reach the bank. I was determined to speak to him as little as possible, to give him no encouragement whatsoever; as such, I would be damned if I spoke first.

We had been strolling for a few minutes when he finally spoke. "It is an exceedingly fine day, is it not?"

"*Ja.*"

We walked along a few more feet before Brom withdrew his arm and turned to face me. "Katrina," he asked, meeting my eyes, "am I really so repugnant to you?"

"I should think the answer would be obvious by this point," I said. "And just to allay any foolish hopes you may have in regard to a betrothal between you and me: I am only going along with this because my father has insisted."

"I shall look upon wooing you as a challenge, then."

"Indeed? And are you so foolhardy as to set yourself a challenge that you have no hope of accomplishing?"

"Katrina, please," he groused. "We were friends, once. How has that changed so drastically?"

I was nearly spitting with anger. "You know how! You know what you did!"

His expression darkened. "That is still what this is about? You would turn on me so completely over Charlotte Jansen?"

"Again, the answer should be obvious. Do you have even the

slightest concept of what you did to her? Of what such slanderous lies mean for a woman, even in this day and age?"

"You were there, Katrina," Brom said, his voice low, with a dangerous edge to it now. "You heard what she said to me. What was I supposed to do, when she threatened me so?"

"I would hardly call it a threat." I sniffed. "And I was there, yes; so I also remember you begging her to tell you your future, how you pressed her even when she did not want to speak of it, and how you goaded her until she relented." I was even angrier now, remembering it all. "Like the selfish child you are, you pressed her into saying something she did not want to, and when you did not like what you heard, you made sure she suffered for it."

"You don't know anything, Katrina," he said through gritted teeth.

"Explain it to me, then. Explain to me what prompted such behavior—for Charlotte was your friend, too, Brom. If there is anyone who can rightfully be accused of turning on a friend here, it is you."

"I was scared!" he burst out. "I was just a boy, and I was frightened of what she said. Are you happy now?"

"Humanity commits its worst sins out of fear, methinks," I said. "And what on earth could you possibly have been frightened of, really? You know what she told you . . . it is impossible."

Brom glared at me. "Don't you remember how she said it? That look that comes into her eyes, like she is a . . . a sibyl, prophesying grim tidings."

In spite of the warmth of the day, I shivered. I knew exactly what he meant, had seen that look on Charlotte's face more than once. Her eyes had clouded over as she stared unblinking at Brom without really seeing him. I heard again the flatness of her voice as she'd spoken, so different from how she usually sounded.

Brom, damn him, had been watching me closely. "You remember," he said. "You know just what I mean."

I forced myself to draw my haughty air around me again, like a cloak. "And so?" I said. "That changes nothing. The Headless Horseman is not real."

"Are you so sure of that, Katrina?"

"Of course," I said, deliberately pushing aside thoughts of my dreams, of my panicked flight through the woods.

He turned his back to me and walked a few paces before returning. "I will apologize to Charlotte, if that will put everything to rights between us," he said. "It is true that I was most impudent in my speech back then."

I regarded him coldly. "Then apologize," I said, "for you owe her that much and more. But do it because it is the right thing to do, not because you seek to win any sort of favor from me." I could not resist adding, somewhat cruelly, "I will not marry you merely because you apologized to Charlotte, Brom. Know that."

He scowled. "You'll see, Katrina," he said. "I mean to have you. I'll win you over somehow, no matter what it takes."

I turned and began to walk back toward the farmhouse. It was the only way I could contain my anger at his gall, his outrageous assumption that I was his for the taking, that he was somehow entitled to me. "By all means, continue deluding yourself," I said. It took every ounce of my will not to scream in his face.

I had not gotten very far when he called after me. "Haven't you seen him, Katrina?" he asked.

I stopped walking and turned back to him. "Seen who?" I asked, though I didn't need to. I knew who he meant.

He drew closer. "The Horseman," he said, his voice low. "Haven't you ever seen him?"

I remembered, vividly, Ichabod asking me the same question. And if I would not speak the truth of my dreams, my nightmares, to him, I certainly would not speak of them to Brom. "Of course not," I said. "There is nothing to see, Brom. He is a fable, nothing more."

His eyes looked over my shoulder, scanning the river and the rise of the fields above us. "I am not so sure," he said. "I . . . I swear that I see him sometimes, out of the corner of my eye, riding toward me. But when I turn to look, there is nothing there."

I struggled not to let him see how his words chilled me. "It is your imagination, nothing more," I said, trying to sound disdainful. "You have this foolish superstition now, because of what Charlotte said all those years ago."

"Or she has bewitched me, so that I see things that are not there," he said, his voice low.

I wanted to slap him, but I settled for laughing in his face. "How ridiculous," I said. "As if she could. As if such things were possible. And to think, just moments ago you were ready to apologize for the harm you'd done her." I resumed my walk back home. "I could perhaps forgive you if I really believed you'd been young and foolish, and nothing more. But you have not changed. You still believe those lies you told about her then, and if it is possible, I like you less now than I did when you arrived at my house this morning."

Brom caught up to me, placing my hand on his arm. "And yet I have your father's approval all the same," he said through gritted teeth. "This is not how I wished this day to go, but soon everything will be different. You will see, Katrina. You will see."

I did not dignify his words with a response, even as a bud of anxiety bloomed in the pit of my stomach. What did he mean to do?

When we arrived back at the house, I was delighted—and relieved—to see Ichabod riding up earlier than expected on Gunpowder. "Miss Van Tassel," he said, pulling up the horse when he drew near enough. "Master Van Brunt."

"Good day, Mr. Crane," I said, brightening. Brom merely grunted.

Ichabod swung down from the saddle, and as he faced us his eyes lingered on my hand on Brom's arm. His jaw tightened almost imperceptibly. My discomfort returned in a rush.

"You are early for your music lesson, are you not, Mr. Crane?" Brom asked finally.

"I am," Ichabod said, "but 'tis such a fine day for riding that I find I have spurred my horse on faster than usual, and so here I am."

"I see," Brom said. "And yet *I* find that I am not through with the lady's company for the day."

I pulled away from him. "You shall have to be."

I glanced at Ichabod, but he was busy tying Gunpowder to the hitching post. "Farewell, Brom," I said loudly. A disbelieving look crossed his face. His eyes darted to Ichabod, then me. He shook his head slightly.

The blossoms of anxiety in my stomach grew into a full forest of fear. *He knows. Somehow, he knows.*

But how can he? I had done nothing to give us away. Had I? The feeling of dread would not leave me.

"Very well," he said at last. He kissed my hand, taking his time so Ichabod couldn't help but see. "But I shall visit you again soon, Katrina. And mind you do not forget what we discussed today." He spoke in English, making sure Ichabod understood every word.

Silently I turned away and went in the front door. Ichabod followed me soon after.

He did not speak until we were safely ensconced in the music room. "What was that about?" he asked.

I took a deep breath. He would not like this, but he needed to know. "Brom asked—demanded, rather—that I accompany him on a stroll today," I said. "My father has given him permission to court me."

Ichabod's face drained of color, and he clenched his jaw in anger. "And you could not refuse, I suppose."

"Obviously not. If I could have, I certainly would have." I caught sight of his face, and my anger flared. "I could not have refused," I said, my voice hard. "Whatever you are thinking, you may put it from your mind. Only under direct orders from my father would I give Brom Van Brunt a moment of my time, and even then it is grudgingly."

"And if your father orders you to marry him, Katrina?" Ichabod asked. "What will you do then?"

"I would think a man as intelligent as yourself can see the difference between a walk beside the river and a walk to the altar."

"Indeed. And yet if you can be compelled to one, why not the other?"

"You are being absurd," I said coldly. "And after what I have just endured, I do not have the patience for this."

"You have not answered my question, Katrina. What will you do if your father insists that you marry him?"

"Refuse!" I all but shouted. "He already knows of my objections. I am acquiescing in this so that I might refuse later. Can you really not see that? Are all men such jealous fools?"

Ichabod looked as if I had slapped him. Then he sighed. "You are right, Katrina. I am acting quite the fool."

Yet I was not quite so easily appeased. "That you would doubt me, after everything—"

But he cut me off by pulling me into his arms. "I am sorry, my love. I am. You are right, we men in love are jealous fools. I do not doubt you. I could never doubt you."

I remained rigid before slowly yielding, letting my body soften against his. But when I spoke again, my words were firm. "I am risking everything for this, for you," I said, looking up at him. "Just as I know you are doing the same for me. So we must trust one another to see this through."

His arms tightened around me. "You are right. Of course you are."

I sighed, letting myself relax further into his arms. "I was angry at Brom, at the whole situation, and I did not mean to take it out on you," I said. It was not an apology, exactly, for I did not feel I owed him one. Yet it was a concession I was willing to make.

"I know, my love," he said. "You are in the most difficult position of all. As God is my witness, I will extract you from it soon, no matter what it takes."

I smiled against his shoulder, the last of my anger draining away.

"Now, I suppose we must put up at least the pretense of a music lesson," Ichabod said, releasing me.

"I suppose we must," I said.

Yet I could not forget the expression on Brom's face as he looked back and forth between Ichabod and me.

Even as I struggled to focus on the music on the page in front of me, I made a decision. It was time to ask another—and far more unusual—favor of Charlotte. One I hoped I would not regret.

21

Tarot

The next day, I sent a note into town with Cook for Charlotte, asking if I might dine with her that evening. Her reply was in the affirmative, and so when the time came I set out into the warm summer evening, leaving Nox at home.

Charlotte opened the door of the cottage before I could even knock. "Come in," she said. "I've made us some beef stew, if that suits."

"That is perfect," I said, stepping inside. I glanced quickly around. "Your mother is not home?"

"No," Charlotte said, closing the door behind me. "She had to leave to attend to a birth."

"And she did not need you to come along to assist her?" I asked.

Charlotte shook her head. "She said she'd send for me if I was needed, but she expected it to be an easy birth—Mevrouw Van Buren has borne four healthy children already."

It was too easy, too convenient. I had been planning to draw Charlotte out into the garden if needed, for Mevrouw Jansen likely would not approve of the favor I intended to ask. Yet now it was unnecessary—almost as if Mevrouw Jansen, in the same uncanny way that her daughter sometimes had, somehow knew and was giving us her blessing.

Or it is a happy coincidence, and that is all, I told myself.

We served ourselves and carried our bowls and spoons out to the tiny dining room off the kitchen. Charlotte fetched some wine, and lit a few candles and lamps against the growing dark.

We chatted idly as we ate, Charlotte filling me in on the latest village gossip while I tried to think of the best way to bring up the favor I needed. Charlotte would help me in any way she could, but in this case I knew she would have reason to be reluctant.

I shouldn't have wasted a thought on it, however, for once we'd both finished eating, Charlotte laid her spoon down and looked at me seriously. "All right, Katrina. Out with it."

"Out with what?"

"You came here tonight to ask me something," Charlotte said. "So you might as well do so."

"How did you know?" I asked.

She waved a hand dismissively. "I know you better than anyone." she said. "I can tell when you've something on your mind."

I sighed, pushing my bowl away. "Very well. I do have a favor to ask of you."

"Another?" she asked. Laughter tinged her voice as she added, "You do not need more herbs already, do you?"

"No!" I said, giggling before I grew serious again. "No, it's something else."

"Well, do not keep me in suspense."

"Well . . ." I looked down and fiddled with my spoon. "My father has given Brom permission to court me, and he has already begun doing so. Or trying to."

"No!" Charlotte exclaimed. Yet then she shook her head and closed her eyes. "In truth, I am not surprised. I had expected it."

"Yes, I was not truly surprised, either," I said. "He came to call yesterday and insisted I go walking with him. It did not last long, is the best thing I can say."

"Whatever did you talk about?" she asked. "He did not try to speak to you of love, did he?"

I laughed humorlessly. "I suppose he thought that was what he was doing," I said. "In the end, we argued, and why he expected anything else I cannot say." I did not mention that we argued about her.

Charlotte shook her head in disgust. "You have my sympathies, Katrina. But what has this to do with a favor?" Her face fell slightly. "I am afraid I have already thought of poisoning him, but that is too easily traced back to me."

I laughed. "No, it is not that. It is just . . ." I sighed. "Everything seems so uncertain," I said. "With Ichabod. I tell myself that I will let nothing stand in the way of our marriage, but I know this is not what my parents would choose for me. I . . . I will defy them if I must. For him. But that path is rife with its own uncertainties, the nature of which I cannot yet know. It is difficult to bear, all this anxiousness. And so I . . ." I looked up at her and took a deep breath. "I need to know for certain. I need to know if we will be together, he and I."

"And how am I supposed to know?" Charlotte asked. Her tone had cooled slightly, as if she knew what was coming. "If I had any such assurances to give you, Katrina, you know that give them I would."

"Yes, but . . . you have ways of finding out, do you not?" When she did not answer, I lowered my voice slightly, though there was no one to overhear us. "I thought you might consult the cards for me."

She exhaled slowly, eyes closed. Only a trusted few knew that the Jansen women even possessed the tarot cards. I knew that, during the war, an injured French officer fighting on behalf of the Americans had, while recovering in the Jansen cottage, taught Mevrouw Jansen to divine the future using the beautifully painted deck of cards that he possessed—a pastime that was all the rage in France at the time. Yet whatever uncanny ability Mevrouw Jansen possessed made the reading of the tarot cards more than just a pastime, and so it was for Charlotte as well, once her mother taught her. It was not a service that Mevrouw Jansen offered to the public; even the easy-going villagers of Sleepy Hollow would be mightily unsettled if they knew the things the Jansen women could see with the help of the deck.

"Do you know what you're asking of me?" Charlotte asked finally.

"I do, Charlotte. Believe me. I would not ask if I did not have to."

"You do not have to. You could wait and see what your future holds, as everyone else must."

"This is no idle curiosity!" I cried. "This is my future, and the man I love, at stake!"

She was silent, and absolutely still, for a long time. Then she rose and picked up our bowls to take to the kitchen. "Very well," she said aloud. "I will do it this once, Katrina. And I know it goes without saying that you cannot tell anyone."

"Of course," I called after her, feeling excitement and fear coursing through my blood. "I will take it to my grave. The Headless Horseman himself could not pry it from my lips." I felt a twinge of superstitious regret as the words passed my lips, as if by invoking the Horseman's name he could now somehow hear us.

She did not reply, merely passed back through the room a moment later and climbed the staircase to the upper floor. She returned with a small bundle wrapped in a piece of dark blue silk. Moving aside some of the candles on the table, she unfurled the silk to reveal a deck of well-worn yet gorgeously illustrated cards. She spread the cloth over the table before her, leaving the cards at its center. She placed her right palm atop the deck and took a deep breath, eyes closed. I shivered slightly at the sight of her, her long, wavy red hair down about her shoulders, the candlelight casting her features into shadow. She looked mysterious and magical and otherworldly indeed. And though I would mean it as a compliment—for she looked powerful and beautiful—I could never tell her so.

She exhaled slowly, and after what seemed like several minutes she opened her eyes. "Very well," she said again. She picked up the cards and shuffled them, their edges soft and pliable from many years of use. Then she placed the deck back down, this time closer to me. "Cut the deck with your left hand," she instructed me. "And as you do so, think hard on the question you are asking. Make it a yes or no question, and ask it in your mind three times."

I cut the deck, my mind furiously reciting my question. *Will Ichabod and I wed? Will Ichabod and I wed? Will Ichabod and I wed?* Then I nodded confirmation.

"I am going to do a simple three-card spread," she said, her voice low as she picked up the cards again. "Past, present, and future. The first card is your past, what has been, and what is now behind you in regards to the question you have asked. The second card is your present, what your circumstances are now. And the third and final card is your future: what is to come, and what the ultimate answer to your question will be."

I felt my first flicker of foreboding. What if I did not like what the future holds? What if I got my answer but I could not bear what I heard? Perhaps I should not have asked.

But it was too late to go back now. Charlotte had already placed the first card down on the table between us. To me it was upside down, though I could make out the image of a man walking along his way, looking as though he were whistling a tune, while the edge of a cliff waited nearby.

Charlotte exhaled as she considered the card. "The Fool," she said. "The Fool is a naïve traveler, one who is about to embark on a great journey. He is optimistic and hopeful and unaware of the danger and risks that may await him." She pointed to the cliff. "Remember, this is your past. This is where you began with whatever is at the root of your question." She glanced up. "So in this case, your relationship with Ichabod."

"Yes," I said, my mouth strangely dry. I cleared my throat. "Yes. I fell in love and made love to him with scarcely a thought for the consequences. I did what I wanted simply because I wanted to do it. Only lately have I imagined it may not work out as I wish."

Charlotte nodded. "That is my reading of the card in this situation, as well." She placed her hand on the next card on the deck.

The room grew strangely warm and stifling, the walls seeming to shift around me. I blinked my eyes several times, trying to clear the haze that settled over them in the dimness.

Charlotte placed the next card beside The Fool. A man and a woman stood naked, their hands outstretched toward one another. An angel hovered in the sky above them.

"The Lovers," Charlotte announced, and a chill went down my spine at how appropriate the card was. "A card that signifies relationships. You have a chance for true love, and a decision you make in regards to this relationship will have long-lasting consequences for you." She glanced up at me, and our eyes locked.

"Yes," I said aloud at last. "That is certainly . . . most appropriate."

"Tonight the cards have proven themselves very accurate indeed, which is not always the case." She smiled slightly, as if to break the tension. "So far they are not telling us anything we do not know. I have found when I get an unexpected card for the past and present I must consider it more carefully, and how its meaning may apply to the situation at hand. Often I gain much greater insight into it as a result."

I scarcely heard her. Her words seemed to trail off, as though she were speaking to me from a great distance. My attention had been captured by the flickering of the candle to my left. It whispered to me as the flame danced and undulated, beckoning me to look closer, to listen more carefully . . .

I stared into the center of the flame, and I somehow *fell* into it, as though it had grown to envelop me. It expanded around me, until all I could see were images within it, like shadows cast against the great wall of a barn.

The faraway whinny of a horse. Shadows moving through the forest, one chasing the other—a man. Two men. Panting, and heavy footfalls against the dirt. The sounds of a brutal struggle, and that far off whinny yet again. And the violent, unmistakable sound of a blade being drawn from its sheath.

I screamed, and just like that the pictures vanished. The wall of flame that had become my mirror melted away and was only a candle again. I screamed again, this time from sheer shock.

"Katrina!" I heard Charlotte cry, her hands already grasping my arms. Swiftly she crouched beside my chair. "Katrina, what happened? Are you all right?"

I gasped for air. "It was him," I gasped. "I saw him. It was him."

"Who?" Charlotte asked. "Brom? Ichabod?"

"No, no." My voice wavered. "It was the Headless Horseman. I saw him."

"The Horseman?" she asked, her tone tinged with disbelief. "You . . . saw him? How?"

I pointed wildly to the candle. "There," I said. "In the flame. I was staring into it, and . . . it seemed to be calling me, somehow. And I could see . . ." I let out a sob and buried my face in my hands. "I could see all sorts of things."

Charlotte embraced me, rubbing a hand on my back. "It is all right, Katrina," she said. She drew back, frowning. "What else did you see?"

"I . . ." Suddenly the words for which I was reaching all seemed silly, overblown, dramatic. Like the words Master Shakespeare might use in one of his plays about witches. "It was nothing, I am sure," I said. "Fanciful dreams and imaginings, nothing more. I got lost in a daydream, that is all. I am overwrought and overtired and it is nothing more than that, I'm sure."

Charlotte did not look so certain. "I do not know if that is all it was," she said slowly. "Fire does not reveal its secrets lightly."

I stared at her as though she had started speaking in tongues. "What do you mean?"

She sighed. "There are those who can see visions, sometimes in water, sometimes in stone or glass, sometimes in fog or clouds, and sometimes in fire. Fire visions are rare, and always meaningful." She gave me a look heavy with significance. "Of course, one would have to have the Sight."

I shot her an incredulous look. "What nonsense is this? Visions?

The Sight? Me? That is all very well for you, Charlotte," I said. "I know you have seen things. But me? I have never—"

"I do not think that is true, Katrina," she said gently. "You have told me many times of your dreams of the Horseman. And I have always told you I thought they had meaning." She gestured toward the candle. "It would seem I am right."

"But that . . . that's . . ." I could not form the words. I had never had the kinds of visions Charlotte did, back when she would still whisper of them, before Brom's terrible deed and she became too afraid to speak of such things to anyone, even to me.

Or, at least, I had not had visions until now.

I tried to laugh, but it was a sorry imitation of the sound. "This is madness," I said, covering my face with my hands. "Madness."

"I do not think so." She squeezed my hand tightly. "Tell me what you saw."

Those fleeting shadows and images I had glimpsed, as though through a dark veil, began to come back to me. "I saw figures, one chasing the other through the woods," I said slowly. "I heard a horse's whinny, and sounds of a struggle. And I heard . . ." I recalled the sound, and a shiver went through my whole body. "I heard the sound of a blade being unsheathed. The Horseman's sword."

Charlotte was silent for a moment. "But did you see him?"

"Only his silhouette. And only quickly." I shuddered, my whole body wracked, as I remembered how I so casually invoked the Horseman earlier. He had heard, and he had responded.

She nodded, lost in thought. "I wonder what it means," she murmured.

"As do I, I assure you."

She rose from where she was crouched beside me. "Perhaps we should stop," she said, nodding toward the cards. "The reading. Maybe it is best if we do not continue."

A part of me wanted to agree, but the rest of me had to know, despite this vision that suddenly felt like a most dire omen. "No," I said. "No, we are almost finished. We must . . ." I swallowed. "I must know what is on the last card."

Charlotte hesitated. "Are you sure?"

I nodded, resigned.

Slowly she sat back down in her chair. "Very well," she said, taking a deep breath. I did the same, trying to calm my still-racing heart.

When she turned over the final card, I gasped, a scream caught in my throat.

It was plain enough what the card was without Charlotte telling me, but still she spoke. "The Devil," she said, her voice laden with sorrow and dread.

I closed my eyes, as though that would make the card, and the horrible picture of the winged beast upon it, disappear. "No," I said.

"Do you already know the meaning of this card?" she asked, as if hoping she would not have to explain it.

"No," I said. "But I can gather it means nothing good."

"No," she conceded, her tone heavy. "It does not." She paused, as though steeling herself, and when she spoke again her tone was flat. "The Devil signifies a negative state of affairs. Destruction. You cannot remedy the evil he represents; you can only hope, with good fortune, to escape it."

"No," I said, feeling as though I were gasping for breath again. "No, it cannot be. This cannot be my future."

With one swift motion, Charlotte gathered up the three cards—The Fool, The Lovers, and The Devil—and swept them back into the deck. "It does not have to be," she said, sounding unconvinced. "The cards are not foolproof. They can lie, or be meaningless, they can be misinterpreted—"

"How could we possibly have misinterpreted that?" I demanded, gesturing to the spot on the table where The Devil card had lain. "You said yourself—the first two cards were perfectly, strangely accurate. Why should they be so, but not the last one?"

"Fortune-telling of any kind is an uncertain art, Katrina," Charlotte said. "Nothing is absolute."

"Why did you read for me, then? Why did the idea of doing it scare you so much?"

She knelt beside my chair again and took my face in her hands. "You control your destiny," she told me, looking into my eyes. "You and no one else. What is on a painted bit of paper will not change that unless you let it."

I grabbed her wrists. "Even you don't believe that, Charlotte," I whispered. "Especially you. You can't. Not with the things you've seen."

She bit her lip but did not speak.

My face crumpled, and tears began to roll down my cheeks. I slid from the chair to the floor, and Charlotte wrapped her arms around me, rocking me like a child as I cried.

22

The Sight

I ended up spending the night at Charlotte's cottage; by the time I had pulled myself together somewhat it was too late for me to get home alone, and I was in no condition to make the walk, anyway. Once the fear and anguish faded, I felt drained in a way I had never experienced before; utterly hollow, as though the devil—and the Horseman, though perhaps they were one and the same—had taken everything of value within me and fled back to hell with it. I lay awake beside Charlotte in her bed for some time, trying to quiet my mind, trying to think of nothing at all. I especially tried not to think of Ichabod. It hurt too much. To imagine what I might have done—or might yet do—to bring evil upon us.

It was a long time before I slept.

By the time I awoke, Charlotte had already risen. I could hear her conversing with her mother downstairs. Mevrouw Jansen must have returned from the birth very late, for I had no recollection of hearing her come in. I pulled on my dress over my shift and wove my hair into one long, simple plait before going downstairs.

I found mother and daughter working in their herb room off

the kitchen. "Katrina!" Mevrouw Jansen said, laying down her knife. "I trust you slept well?"

"Indeed," I said, avoiding Charlotte's eyes. "I thank you for your hospitality, and I must apologize for the trouble."

"Not at all, my dear," Mevrouw Jansen said, gesturing for me to precede her back into the kitchen. "Better you stay here than venture home alone at too late an hour. Come now, we were waiting for you to break our fast. I've some fresh bread and cheese."

"That's very kind," I said. "You need not have delayed on my account."

"Again, no trouble," she said. "We had work to do that is better done in the early morning hours in any case."

"You seemed as though you needed your sleep, so I thought it best not to wake you," Charlotte added, with a significant look. I nodded gratefully, not meeting her eyes.

Mevrouw Jansen insisted Charlotte and I sit at the dining room table while she brought us some breakfast and tea. Charlotte kept casting me inquisitive looks whenever her mother was out of the room, and I nodded slightly to reassure her. We could not speak further with her mother in earshot.

In truth, though, as I let the fresh food and tea revive me, took in the sunlight spilling into the room and over my skin, the night before began to fade away, as though being dissolved by the sun's rays. In daylight the dining room table was just that, not a candlelit altar for magical cards and prophecies of devils. The cards were just painted pieces of paper, as Charlotte had so rightly named them, and my so-called vision was just the nonsensical imagining of an overwrought mind.

Charlotte was right. I controlled my own destiny. Doom is not inevitable just because a random sequence of cards says that it is so.

And so—not without some effort—I pushed last night aside and engaged in idle chatter with Charlotte and her mother. I inquired after the birth Mevrouw Jansen had attended, and she assured me all had gone well. Mevrouw Van Buren had been delivered of a healthy son.

"I trust you did not suffer over-much from the lack of Charlotte's help by leaving her here with me," I said.

"Not at all," Mevrouw Jansen said, casting significant look at her daughter. "Charlotte was just where she needed to be last night."

Goose bumps pricked along my skin. I was suddenly certain Mevrouw Jansen knew exactly what had transpired here the night before, what I had begged Charlotte to do. She knew, and we had had her tacit blessing after all.

I suppressed a shiver and changed the subject.

Once we finished eating, Charlotte and I cleaned up the breakfast dishes. "I had better return home before my mother begins to worry," I said once we were done. "I also do not wish to wear out my welcome."

Mevrouw Jansen stepped toward me and folded me into her embrace. "You could never," she said fondly. She released me, and held me at arm's length, studying me. "Take care, won't you, Katrina?" she said finally. "And do tell your mother I said hello."

I told myself her words were nothing more than courtesy. "I will," I said.

"Mama, might I walk Katrina home?" Charlotte asked. "Or do you need me to continue working with you here?"

Mevrouw Jansen smiled indulgently. "By all means. 'Tis another fine day, and you girls should be out enjoying it."

I thanked Mevrouw Jansen again, and we departed, stepping out into the warm morning and setting out onto the Albany Post Road. Normally I would be eagerly looking about me for Ichabod, hoping that we might come across him, but today I found I did not want to see him. We were due to meet in the woods that very night, but I did not think that I could face him yet, with the new knowledge I had but could never share with him. He was possessed of a far more superstitious mind than my own, and if I told him what Charlotte and I had done—let alone the outcome—he would be shocked and afraid.

No. I must carry it within myself, and never let him know the evil and destruction that haunted our future.

Yet who were the intended victims of this evil and destruction? Ichabod and myself? That certainly seemed the most likely, given the question that I had asked. Or had The Devil card signified that Ichabod and I would, through our actions, bring horror and misfortune onto others?

Enough of this drama, Katrina, I admonished. Did you not, mere minutes ago, acknowledge the whole business for the foolishness that it is?

Yet my thoughts were small and excitable birds, one moment perched firmly on the branch of reason, and the next flitting off to the branch of worry and fear. And back and forth and back again, with me unable to capture them and hold them firm.

"How are you feeling today, Katrina?" Charlotte asked, breaking into my thoughts. "Are you quite well?"

I sighed, realizing I had been wrong. I need not keep my anguish within; there was one other person with whom I could share the burden. "I don't know," I answered honestly. "At times I think you were right last night, that we control our own destinies. And others I am too afraid to be persuaded by logic. I am too afraid that two such bad omens in rapid succession can never be a coincidence."

Charlotte was silent as she considered this.

I gave her until we were out of the village proper before speaking again. "Say something, please," I begged. "I would know your true, honest thoughts, even if you think you should not tell me."

She hesitated.

I stopped and took her hand. "Please, Charlotte," I whispered. "If you are not honest with me, who will be?"

Her wide amber eyes searched mine. "Very well," she agreed, sighing as she began walking again. "The convergence of two such negative omens *is* very disquieting. The cards are not much cause for worry on their own, I don't think. As I said, the strength of the cards is that they can provide us with great insight. But one of their weaknesses is they can be misinterpreted, can be read to say whatever one most wishes them to say—or, in the same way, can reflect one's worst fears."

I nodded. That much made sense to me.

"Of much more concern to me," she said, lowering her voice, "is your vision."

I snorted. "If it was any such thing, and not merely daydreams and silliness," I said, with more bravado than I felt.

Charlotte grabbed my arm. "Katrina," she said, her voice nearly a whisper. "I have had many a vision in my life. You know this. I know what someone in the throes of such a vision looks like."

Despite the heat of the day, an ice-cold chill scuttled over my skin.

"But . . . but why now?" I asked in a hushed voice. "Why after all this time? You have had visions all your life; why would I only have one now?"

"As I said last night, I do not think that is true," she said. "I think that your dreams of the Horseman have always been of some significance, and now you have had a vision of him. So it would seem I am right, would it not?"

I bowed my head and sighed. She was right, she had to be, much as I hated to admit it. Perhaps I did have some semblance of the Sight.

Another thing I can never share with Ichabod, I realized, feeling my heart grow heavy enough to sink into my shoes. I remembered too well his uncomfortable, nervous expression when I told him Charlotte was my dearest friend. *There are rather startling rumors about her in the village*, he had said. What would he do if he knew I had the same uncanny way about me as Charlotte?

He would fear me. At least, a part of him would. There would always be a part of him, however small, that would fear and mistrust me. And that I could not bear.

But could I bear to marry him, to let him marry me, when I was keeping such a thing from him?

Yet I could never give him up. Perhaps, in time, these visions would leave me. Or more likely, Charlotte was mistaken.

"And that you saw a vision in fire," Charlotte was saying. "Even I have never done such a thing."

"So what could that mean?" I asked.

Charlotte bit her lip and glanced over at me nervously.

"Tell me, Charlotte, I pray you. I said I would have only honesty between us, and I meant it."

"It . . . it seems to me that it must have been a warning of great import," she said at last. "Of very great import, to show itself to you in fire."

"That is precisely the last thing I wished to hear."

"I know," she said. Impulsively she stopped and hugged me. "Oh, Katrina, I pray you, do not lose hope. Do not lose faith. It all may seem rather dire, but I do very much believe that whatever such visions and fortune-telling show us, we are the authors of our own fates. Else why would we see such things? Why would we be forewarned if we had no chance of changing what was to come?"

I returned her embrace, feeling heartened. "That is true," I said, my voice brighter now. "That is indeed true."

"Do not lose hope," she whispered again my ear. "Whatever may come, we shall face it together."

Late that night, when I ventured into the forest to meet Ichabod, it did not feel as terrifying as before. I had already looked the devil in the face and seen the worst of what might come. What were some shadows and darkness compared to that?

When I arrived at our spot by the stream, Ichabod was already there, a blanket spread over the ground, Gunpowder tied up a ways away. He turned as he heard me approach, and his lips parted to greet me. But I did not give him the chance. I flung myself into his arms, my lips eagerly seeking his. Surprised, it took him a moment to react. But soon enough his arms encircled me, returning my kiss, and we shed our clothes, falling to the blanket together. As we made love I held on to him as tightly as I could, as though that was all I need do to make everything turn out well.

I will never let him go, I vowed as he moved inside me. Never. Never.

And then, thankfully, blissfully, pleasure overcame us both, and I thought no more.

23

Nightmares

I stood at the edge of a clearing in the forest, a spot deep in the woods not far from the church. I knew this spot—it was rumored to be the place where the Headless Horseman had been killed in battle. Few people dared venture here, thinking it an unlucky, haunted place. Suddenly— as if by blinking I had summoned him—the Horseman was before me, sitting astride his mount. And once more, Ichabod stood behind the Horseman, his form faint in the darkness.

Yet this time I heard his voice, calling out for me.

"Katrina!" His usually warm voice rang with terror. "Katrina!"

At once I began to run to him, even though doing so meant also running toward the Horseman. I ran toward him anyway, even as every thought, every inch of muscle and skin and bone in my body screamed for me to turn and run the other way.

As I drew nearer, somehow Ichabod's voice began to fade, growing more distant as if slowly being taken from me. "Katrina! Katrina!"

Heart in my throat, I had nearly reached the Horseman when he turned away from me and galloped deeper into the woods, in pursuit of Ichabod. And in that instant I realized Ichabod had not been calling for help—he had been warning me away.

"No!" I cried, as I watched the Horseman ride toward Ichabod.

"No!" I cried, my eyes flying open as I bolted upright.

In that first hazy instant upon waking, the deep darkness of the forest surrounded me, the black outlines of the trees nearly indiscernible against the dark sky. I screamed, certain it had been no dream at all, but that the forest had swallowed me whole in my quest to find Ichabod, to save him from the Horseman. Fear flooded me as I realized I must be too late.

Ichabod's arms found me, as he sat up and drew me against him, rocking me slowly. "Shhh, Katrina," he whispered against my hair. "All is well. I am here."

"Ichabod?" I said, my voice thick and unwieldy as it forced its way up through my throat. "Is it you? You are here?"

"Yes, my love," he said soothingly.

"But . . . where . . ." I drew away from him and frantically searched the forest around us. "He must be here as well . . . the Horseman . . . I saw him, he cannot be far . . ."

"Shhh," he hushed me again, holding me tighter. "Do not fret, Katrina. I swear to you, all is well. No one else is here. You have had a nightmare, that is all."

"A nightmare . . ." I shuddered and threaded my arms around his back, burying my face in his shoulder, blocking out the darkness around us. No doubt he was right; I had dreamed of the Horseman enough times before. Yet never had I woken to find myself deep in the very forest he was said to inhabit.

As I awoke more fully, I began to recall the dream in greater detail. This dream had been different from the others. Never before had Ichabod called my name; never before had I moved, let alone run toward the Horseman. And never had I dreamt of that clearing. I shuddered again, recalling the fear in Ichabod's voice as he cried out for me, the moment of crushing uncertainty just before I woke, when I had been unsure whether he was calling for me to help him, or warning me to flee.

"Do you want to tell me what you dreamt?" Ichabod asked, stroking my hair. "The Horseman, you said it was?"

"No," I said. "I mean, yes . . . I saw him, in the dream. But . . . it is nonsense. Eerie nonsense, perhaps, but . . ."

"I am not surprised," he said, his voice hard. "When we come out into this haunted wood to meet, where anyone and anything could be watching . . ."

I shivered. "Do not say such things, I pray you."

"I am sorry. It is just . . ." He loosened his grip so he could see me, regret etched on his face. "This is not right. It is not worthy of you. How I wish I had a home of my own, a proper bed that I could take you to . . ."

"I wish it, too, but for the time we have no choice," I said. "It is either the woods, or we do not see each other alone."

He was silent, and I knew he was thinking the same thing as I: how could we bear to be apart, for any length of time? To give up such meetings, as imperfect as they were? Despite the dangers, the fears . . .

"Soon, my love," I whispered before he could ask. "Soon we will speak to my father. I must have a little time first, to convince my father that Brom and I will never make a match."

"You should not have to," Ichabod said. "Your choice should be enough. That there is a man who loves you, and whom you love, should be all that is needed."

I shook my head. "It should, but I have known Brom all my life, and my father has always fancied the two of us would wed. I *must* have time to bring him around." I suppressed another shiver as the tarot cards, and my premonition, flashed through my mind. Of these tidings, Ichabod could know nothing.

Ichabod sighed again, frustrated. "If you say so, Katrina," he said. "You know the situation and players far better than I."

I cupped his face in my hands. "We will be together, Ichabod," I said firmly. "We will be husband and wife. Do not doubt it."

He turned his head and kissed my palm. "I never have," he said.

That night, as I rode in front of Ichabod on Gunpowder's saddle, I could not seem to quiet my fears. Even with Ichabod there, solid behind me, I trembled with fear at all the shadows in which an ill-meaning spirit could hide. Ichabod wrapped an arm protectively around my waist. "There is nothing to fear," he whispered in my ear. "You are safe."

I wished that I could believe him.

He drew Gunpowder to a halt just before the road, and reluctantly I slid from the saddle. "Will you be all right the rest of the way?" he asked.

I nodded, still unsure.

"I can take you to the door, if you wish."

"And run the risk of someone hearing us, or seeing you? No," I said. "We cannot chance it."

Ichabod dismounted and took my face in his hands. "Your safety and peace of mind are the most important things by far," he said. He kissed me.

I returned his kiss, wishing he did not need to leave me. Oh, that we might both climb back onto Gunpowder's back and spur the noble old beast onward, into the night; that we might ride fast and far from Sleepy Hollow, far from the Headless Horseman and witchcraft and nightmares and ill omens. We could ride to New York City and lose ourselves in the crowds; to Boston and its Puritan churches; to the wilderness of Maine. Or we could ride west, and keep riding, until we were somewhere that no one would know us or find us, somewhere too far ever to return to this haunted place.

Reluctantly, I stepped back. "I will be fine," I said, trying to reassure him, even if I could not reassure myself. "It is not far."

"Very well," he said. "If you are sure." He swung back up into the saddle.

I nodded. "Good night, my love. I will see you soon."

With that, I turned toward my house, resisting at every step the urge to turn and look back at him. I was too afraid I might turn around only to find my nightmare come to life.

The next morning, I found myself feeling rather foolish at my nervousness the night before. As I looked out my window toward the small stand of woods at the side of the house, sunshine gilding the tree leaves, I shook my head in impatience with myself. For the first time I thought it was lucky Ichabod was of a somewhat superstitious mind; if he was not, he would think me quite mad.

The next few weeks passed unremarkably. I helped my mother and Nancy with chores, visited with Charlotte—each time, we studiously avoided talk of tarot cards or visions or the Sight—and I endured Brom's company only when I had to. I was polite, but distant at every turn. Even as he grew frustrated with me, it was plain he did not know what else to do. I felt my father frowning at my reticence on the few occasions when Brom dined with us, but I ignored him. Let him see for himself that I had no desire to marry Brom Van Brunt, no matter how he might wish it.

Ichabod came for my voice lessons, and we arranged nights to meet in the woods. I tried not to betray to him again how uneasy the forest made me, for my dreams of the Horseman had not ceased. He would put a halt to our trysts, thinking it in my best interests. So I pushed my fears aside, living for the time I spent in his arms, when nothing else mattered. And each time, I drank my herbs faithfully.

What he and I did not speak of was the fact that the end of summer was upon us. Soon the weather would cool and freeze and the woods would no longer be an option. We would need some other, hopefully permanent, arrangement. We would need to speak to my father, come what may, or endure many months apart.

I pushed away the tarot cards, and my own vision of doom, let them grow faint in my memory. I had no reason to trust in such things.

Instead I trusted the love in Ichabod's eyes, so present that I did not know how the whole village did not see it. It was there, always, visible and tangible, and I clung to it when we were apart, as I waited for the string of nights to come when he would always be beside me.

24

The Challenge

"I have a new song for you to learn," Ichabod said, one day in mid-September. Preparations for the harvest were in full swing around us, and my help could certainly have been used about the household, but my father allowed me to continue my lessons uninterrupted.

"Oh?" I asked with a smile.

"Or, rather, a new song for us to learn," Ichabod clarified.

"I can't wait," I said, as he handed me the song sheet.

I had grown much more adept at reading music under Ichabod's tutelage, and I could already hear the lovely, wistful melody in my head. The lyrics—bittersweet and beautiful—told the story of star-crossed lovers by a willow near a stream. It was so perfect for us—fitting, yet would not attract suspicion if overheard—that I began to wonder if he had written it himself.

Before I could ask, he took up his guitar. "Perhaps you'd like to warm up with a scale, and then attempt the song?" he asked.

"Yes," I said, reluctantly putting the sheets aside.

He guided me through some scales, then gestured for me to pick up the song again. "Try to sight-read the lady's part, if you would," he said.

"And you?" I asked. "Have you already learnt the gentleman's part?"

His eyes, green as spring moss, held mine. "Oh yes," he said. "I know it very well."

He played the opening bars, then nodded for me to begin. Voice hesitant, then growing in strength, I sang of how a lady waited by the banks of a stream under a willow tree for her lover to come to her. I almost could not sing past the emotion that constricted my throat, but I pushed forward, knowing Ichabod would soon stop me for corrections.

But he did not. Instead he played on, into the next verse, and began to sing himself. Somehow his voice sounded all the more rich and beautiful and resonant as he sang the gentleman's response, how he would never be far for his lady love to seek, how he would bring her a rare lotus flower to match her beauty. At the chorus, I joined in again on the melody, and his part switched to the harmony. Still we did not stop.

The third verse had us singing together, intertwining melody and harmony, passing the parts back and forth. The lovers promised their devotion, come what may. The song then ended with the chorus again, and so deep was I in the emotion of the piece that I almost didn't notice my melody change slightly at the end. I only just caught it, landing in a wobbly sort of fashion on the correct note.

Ichabod played the final measures, and then looked up and met my eyes again. Tears threatened to overflow from my eyes. "Where . . . where did you find this song?" I asked, my voice hushed as though afraid to disturb the holy forces that had come to occupy our space.

He set his guitar down and rose. "I knew you would like it," he said.

"It is perfect," I whispered.

He stepped close to me and kissed me, deeply, albeit briefly. When he drew back he stayed close, cradling my face in his hands.

"And does the teacher have any criticisms for his pupil?" I asked, trying to make my tone light, but the weight of the emotion still in it—still in me—made it waver and crack.

He kissed me again. "No," he said, his voice rough. "You were flawless. Exactly as I had dreamed."

It wasn't until later I realized that he had never answered my question about where the song had come from.

We ended our lesson early that day, though for the next few lessons all we did was sing that song together. Ichabod would have me repeat phrases here and there, under the guise of correcting. In reality we savored the repetition of each verse, each word, each note. We sang it together countless times, the duet our own secret form of lovemaking.

We continued to meet in the forest, as the weather still remained warm enough that we could brave the night air. Yet in each moment we spent at our spot by the stream, I felt the ticking of the clock. Soon we would no longer be able to meet here, and what then?

Early October favored us with a brilliantly warm and sunny day. After my lesson, I threw caution to the wind. "It is a fine day, Mr. Crane," I said as we left the music room. "Would you favor me with a stroll?"

His eyes sparked with both concern and excitement. "It would be my honor, Miss Van Tassel," he said, offering me his arm as we began to move toward the front door. "As you know, many of my students are not in classes just now for the harvest, so I find myself with an overabundance of time, something to which I am quite unaccustomed."

We left the house without anyone seeing, though we sought neither to hide nor advertise our actions. "And how is dear Miss Jansen?" Ichabod asked as we made our way, arm in arm, toward the woods. "She is well, I trust? It has been some time since I have seen her in the village."

"Well indeed, though she has been busy," I said. "She and her mother have much work to do gathering herbs at this time of the year, so they are stocked with everything they might need before winter."

"Indeed," he said. He smiled down at me. "They do good work, the both of them."

I beamed at his approval of my friend, almost as much as if he had complimented me. "That they do."

As we moved deeper into the trees, our words and actions grew less formal. Ichabod slid an arm around my waist, pulling me closer, so that our hips touched as we walked. My pulse spiked at such an intimate gesture in broad daylight. I pushed aside my uneasiness about the forest—ever-present, now, between the dreams and visions and eerie experiences of the night—and leaned into him, reveling in the simple closeness.

"Someday," Ichabod said, "we shall walk close together like this everywhere we go, and those who see us pass will know us for the most loving husband and wife that has ever been."

I stopped and kissed him, briefly. "That they will," I said. "And I do not know how you could have known it, but those were my very thoughts as well."

He smiled. "It does not surprise me that we are of one mind, my love."

We walked on to our spot by the stream, where Ichabod took me forcefully into his arms, pressing my back against a large tree and kissing me deeply, hungrily. I let out a soft moan myself in feeling.

His hands wandered down over my waist, and for a moment, I thought he meant to hike up my skirts and have me right up against the tree trunk—and I would surely have let him. But to my dismay, he paused. "We should stop," he said, his voice low in my ear as he struggled to regain his breath. "We cannot . . . it is the middle of the day. Anyone might come along."

I considered convincing him otherwise. In all the times we had come here, day or night, no one had ever happened upon us. Surely today would be no different? Yet I recognized the wisdom in his

words and sighed, mastering my desire. "Yes," I said, my voice cracking. "You are right."

He moved back and I stepped away from the tree, the two of
us brushing our clothes and hair back into order. He removed
his cloak and spread it on the ground so we could sit. I spread my
skirts around me, resting my head on his chest. I could hear his
heart was still pounding furiously as he kissed my hair.

I sighed and looked up at him. "I cannot bear any more of this,"
I said. "I know I have said it time and again, but truly I am at my
wits' end now."

His arm about my shoulders tightened. "What shall we do,
then?" he asked quietly.

I met his eyes without wavering. "You must ask my father
for my hand soon," I said. "So we need not go on like this much
longer. Do you not agree?"

He kissed me. "Oh, I agree," he said huskily. "But . . ." He leaned
back, and I could all but see his rational mind take over. "Are you
sure, Katrina? Are you sure at last? After all this time, it would not
do to misplay our hand."

I was not. I had no reason to believe my earlier concerns were
any less valid now. I only knew I could no longer abide the waiting
and uncertainty. I had to know what our future would be. And if
the worst should happen, and my father should refuse Ichabod's
suit, then we would have to decide on some other course of action.

But I had to believe he would not refuse, not when he saw
how truly we loved each other, how happy Ichabod made me. He
could not.

"Yes," I said. "We have nothing to gain by waiting much longer.
Only time together to lose, as it grows colder."

"I suppose you're right," he conceded. He squeezed me tightly.
"And when shall I speak to your father? Shall we march back up
to the house so that I may ask him now?"

"No," I said, suddenly panicked that my future might be decided within the next hour. "Not today. I . . ."

Ichabod chuckled. "I spoke only in jest, Katrina," he assured me.

"I shall need some time to prepare what to say." He kissed my fore-head. "Not that I have not already thought on it a great deal."

"Yes," I said, relieved. "Let it be . . ." I thought quickly. "Let it be the night of All Hallows' Eve."

He gave me a quizzical look. "All Hallows' Eve? Hardly an auspicious night, that."

I shook my head. "It shall be, I think. My father holds a large party on that night every year, to celebrate the harvest and lift everyone's spirits going into the dark winter. You will surely be invited. My father will be in a jolly mood, and so as the party comes to an end you shall ask for a word with him." My voice gained confidence as I spoke. "He will not refuse you. If he has doubts, I shall be there to assuage them, to make certain he knows this is what I want above all else."

I had spoken these words assuredly, yet I was no more certain than I had ever been. A traveling schoolteacher, with no home or land of his own, was not the match my parents wanted for me. But they could be made to change their minds, couldn't they?

The uncertainty on Ichabod's face melted away as I spoke. "A good plan," he said. "As good as we are likely to have, I think."

I nodded. "All shall be well, my love. We must believe only in that."

He kissed me again, and I responded hungrily. I was just re-thinking our previous decision when a most aggressive and unwelcome voice shattered the peace of our hidden sanctuary, as violent as a gunshot. "What in the name of God goes on here?" the familiar voice demanded in English.

Ichabod and I sprang apart as though our skin had burned one another, and leapt to our feet. We turned to see Brom Van Brunt within our little clearing, fists clenched and rage in his eyes. "Keep your hands off of her," he said, striding across the clearing toward Ichabod. He grabbed Ichabod's shoulders and shoved him, nearly sending him into the stream. "You lowly, no-account—"

"Brom!" I shouted. I grabbed his shirt and dragged him away, nearly tearing the fabric. Brom was a great deal larger and stronger than me, but I caught him by surprise, and he stumbled back. "Stop this, now! Do not lay another hand on Ichabod, or I swear I'll—"

Brom recovered himself and wrenched away from me. He charged at Ichabod again and landed a hard punch on his cheek. I screamed in horror, and tried to grab Brom again.

But Ichabod did not need my help. His slender frame made him much quicker than his opponent, and he easily ducked Brom's next punch and landed one on his jaw in turn, sending Brom sprawling back. He rubbed his jaw angrily. "Why, you little—"

I took advantage of this break in the action to run between them. "Stop!" I cried, holding out a hand in each direction. "For the love of God, stop it now!"

To my surprise, they obeyed me. They stayed where they were, breathing heavily as they eyed one another warily, like two wolves locked in battle for control of the pack.

I turned to face Brom, though I did not move from my peace-keeping position. "Leave, Brom," I said shortly. "Now. Your intrusion is most certainly not welcome."

Brom ignored me, addressing Ichabod. "You dare," he said through gritted teeth. "You dare come to Sleepy Hollow, a nobody from nowhere, and put your filthy hands on the woman I mean to make my wife."

"I think the lady may have something to say about that," Ichabod all but snarled, and the edge in his tone took me by surprise. I had never seen him so enraged before. "She seems to much prefer my suit to yours."

"Why you . . ." Brom made to charge Ichabod again, but I stepped in front of him protectively.

"No," I said. "If you wish to strike Ichabod, you must go through me."

Brom laughed shortly. "You hide behind a woman, then?" he taunted Ichabod, still ignoring me. "This shall not help your suit in the eyes of her father, I shouldn't think. And he is the one who matters."

Ichabod stepped around me. "I do not need you to fight my battles for me, Katrina," he said tautly.

But I would not stand aside. "How many times must you be told that I will not marry you?" I all but shouted at Brom. "And if you think my father is so enamored of you that he would wed me to you against my will, then think again."

"And yet I do not think Master Van Tassel will smile so favorably on the man who seduces Miss Van Tassel in the woods," Brom said smugly. Finally he looked at me. "Katrina, you are the wealthiest heiress for miles around; do you honestly think your father will permit your betrothal to a penniless, itinerant schoolteacher?"

I faced him squarely. "It does not matter," I said coldly. "Not to you, anyway. For I would not marry you if you were the last man in Sleepy Hollow. Not if you were the last man in all of New York."

As soon as the words left my mouth, I wished they had not. For I saw the rage ignite on Brom's face again, and I realized all too late who the target of that rage would be: not me, but Ichabod.

"Since you seem to show no shame for your dishonorable actions," Brom said to Ichabod, his anger boiling just beneath his voice, "then meet me as a gentleman. Dawn. The empty field two miles past the church."

Slowly it dawned on me what he meant. "No," I said quickly. "No. No! I will not allow it. I will never—"

Yet the two men continued their ridiculous game of honor as if I was not there. "Very well," Ichabod said. He stepped forward, past me, and shook Brom's hand. "I accept your challenge."

"No!" I shrieked at the two of them. "I forbid it! I forbid you to duel over me!" I seized the front of Ichabod's shirt. "Ichabod, listen to me! You must not do this stupid thing, do you hear me?"

Brom chuckled. "He has no choice," he observed. "He cannot be talked out of this by a woman—not if he is a man of honor." He leveled a wicked grin on me. "But as I am somewhat in doubt as to Ichabod's honor"—he spat the name like a curse—"I shall add some further motivation." He met Ichabod's eyes. "Should you fail to show tomorrow, I will tell Master Van Tassel of what I witnessed."

Ichabod's face was hard as stone as he nodded.

"And these are the words of a man of honor, then?" I growled at him, releasing Ichabod. "You will blackmail your opponent into meeting you?"

"As I said, I can't be sure he will do what's right," Brom said. He gave a mock bow. "Our business here is concluded for today, then." He sneered at Ichabod again. "I shall see you at dawn, Crane." With that, he turned and left the clearing.

As soon as he was gone, I spun to face Ichabod. "Do not do this," I said in a low voice, so that Brom might not overhear. "I beg of you, Ichabod. Do not do this foolish thing."

He looked at me as if seeing me for the first time since Brom had entered the clearing. "Oh, Katrina," he said, his voice soft. He caressed my cheek. "I have to."

Tears sprang to my eyes at the stupidity of it all. "But you don't," I said. "You don't, not really."

"Katrina, you heard him," he said, raising his voice. "Even if I were inclined to disregard my honor altogether, if I do not show, he will tell your father about us. And we cannot have that."

"But you could die," I said, tears now spilling freely from my eyes. "What is any of it next to that?"

"I will not die," he said. "I will fire into the air, and so will he, and the honor of each of us will be satisfied. That is how it is done."

"But what if he does not?" I demanded. "What if he decides to get his rival out of the way, and—" I broke off with a choked sob, unable to bear even the image in my head.

"What would you have me do, Katrina?" he demanded. "Kill him? Kill a man who was once your friend, no matter what he is to you now? It is not in me to kill a man, let alone kill one for the most commonplace crime of being a braggart and a fool. And say I could and did do it. What then? I will be the disgraced outsider who has killed the village's favorite son. That would hardly endear me to your father." He shook his head. "No, Katrina. I cannot even consider it."

"You would not consider killing a man even to save your own life?" I demanded.

"It will not come to that," he said, exasperation evident in his voice now. "As I said, we will both discharge our pistols in the air, and that will be an end to it."

"Then why bother?" I asked, trying to employ logic. "What is the point? If it does not mean anything—"

"It does mean something," he corrected me. "I have to do this, Katrina. I have no other choice."

I let out a scream of frustration. "Men are such fools!" I shouted at him. "Utter, utter fools, do you know that?"

He did not speak; he merely stepped forward and took me in his arms, holding me until I quieted. Part of me wanted to storm from the clearing, refusing his comfort.

But I could not. Not when I did not know what the dawn might bring.

25

The Duel

Our whole walk back to the farmhouse, I continued to try to persuade Ichabod not to take part in the duel. His replies were limited to a few words here and there, and as we exited the woods he stopped responding altogether. When we reached the front door of the house, he embraced me swiftly, even though anyone could have seen us. "I have to do this," he whispered against my hair. "I am sorry, Katrina. I am sorry to upset you. But I must see this through."

With that, he left and did not look back. If he had, he would have seen the silent tears streaming down my face.

I flew up to my chambers, and gathered up a nightgown and a set of clean clothes to put into a satchel. Nox, who had been lazing sleepily in the sunshine on the portico, burst into my bedchamber behind me. I paused in my frantic preparations and sank to my knees beside him, burying my face in his fur. He whined softly and nuzzled me, licking at the tears that were silently trickling down my face.

If I could not stop the duel, I at least would witness it. I would not wait quietly at home, hoping idle gossip might make its way to me to allay my fears—or, heaven forbid, confirm them.

"Come, Nox." We went down the stairs, my satchel in hand. "Mother," I called, trying my best to keep the urgency from my voice.

She emerged from the parlor. "Yes, my dear?" she said, eyeing the satchel in my hand. "Where are you off to?"

"Charlotte's," I said, hoping my tone sounded sufficiently casual. "I forgot to tell you that she invited me for dinner, and to spend the night. I will be back tomorrow morning, if that is all right with you, and I shall take Nox with me."

My mother waved a careless hand, already turning back to the kitchen. "Yes, of course, dear. And do give Dame Jansen my best."

I was out the door and toward the road almost before she had finished speaking.

Charlotte lived a great deal closer to the dueling ground than I. If I was to make it in time, better to start from her house. And, with any luck, I could persuade her to accompany me: so that I need not witness this travesty alone, and also—though it made my heart quake in my breast to even form the thought—so there was a healer present, if need be.

Once I reached the village, I knocked on the door of the Jansen cottage. I pinned a false smile to my face in case Mevrouw Jansen should answer, then nearly crumpled with relief when the door opened to reveal Charlotte. "Oh, Charlotte," was all I could muster, as she stepped back to let me in.

"What has happened?" she demanded, shutting the door behind me. "What is the matter?"

I cast my gaze furtively about the small front room. "Where is your mother?" I asked in a low voice.

"Out. Tending to a patient." She drew me over to the daybed and pressed me down, taking my hand as she sat beside me. Nox lay down atop my feet. "Whatever has happened, Katrina? Tell me. You look as though you've seen the dead arisen."

I flinched at her choice of words. "Something terrible has happened," I said, "and will happen still. I had to come right away . . ."

She moved closer and rubbed a soothing circle into the back of my hand with her fingers. "Tell me."

I related the day's events as best I could without weeping, watching her face grow more dismayed as I spoke.

"I tried my best to talk him out of it," I said, "But Ichabod is intent on meeting him at dawn tomorrow. And so the fools are going to duel."

Charlotte clasped her hand over her mouth in horror. "Oh, Katrina."

I nodded. "And I cannot persuade Ichabod of the folly of it, no matter what I say. So I . . ." I trailed off as tears sprang to my eyes again.

"So what will you do?" she asked.

"I came here hoping I could spend the night. The dueling ground is not far from here, and I must go. I could not bear waiting for news, not when I cannot even openly ask about it."

She nodded. "Yes. It may well be a horrifying sight, but I think you must go." She squeezed my hand. "I shall go with you."

I gave her a grateful smile. "I must confess I had hoped for that, too."

"And I shall bring some bandages," she said, thinking aloud, "and some herbs and poultices." She glanced at me. "If, God forbid, we should need them."

Despite our distressing topic, my smile widened. "You seem to be reading my very thoughts."

She laughed. "Sometimes I think that so long as the two of us are in accord, all will be well."

"I sometimes think so, too," I said. "I do not know how much that will help on the dueling ground, though."

Our smiles faded. "Oh, Katrina," Charlotte whispered. "What if Brom actually shoots him? What if he . . ." She hesitated. "What if he kills Ichabod?"

I shook my head, to ward off that awful possibility. "I asked Ichabod that," I said softly. "I asked what he would do if Brom sees this as a chance to eliminate him as a rival, and doesn't discharge his pistol in the air, as Ichabod expects. He . . ." I bit my lip. "Ichabod said that he cannot kill another man. But he doesn't expect Brom to shoot him."

"He does not know Brom as we do," Charlotte said, a hard note in her voice. "Brom would shoot him. He may do. And there is not a soul in Sleepy Hollow that would hold him to account."

"I know," I whispered, shutting my eyes. "I know, but I do not know what else I can do. He will not listen to me."

"Men are fools," Charlotte said succinctly. She bent down to scratch Nox's ears. "Even the intelligent ones are completely impervious to reason where their stupid honor is concerned. Aren't they, Nox? You are smarter than the lot of them, you good dog, you."

"Honor," I said bitterly. "What good will that do him—or me— if he's dead?"

It was still dark when Charlotte and I rose, dressing silently in the dark so as not to wake her mother. Outside, the air was chilly and damp, and the first frost was clearly not long in coming. We wrapped ourselves in our cloaks, hoods up, bracing ourselves for the two-mile walk out of the village, Nox padding alongside us.

Still rubbing the sleep from our eyes, we didn't talk much, still unaccustomed to the strange reality of this morning. My heart seemed to pound faster as we drew closer to the dueling ground. I found myself wishing that I could stop time before the duel ever happened, so that I would never need to deal with the consequences.

When we reached the appointed place, no one was there yet. The sky was only just beginning to lighten as the sun arose from its slumber.

"Where should we go?" Charlotte asked in a hushed voice.

I cast my gaze around and noticed a clump of trees a ways off. "There," I said, pointing. "We'll hide there. I do not want them to see us."

Charlotte hesitated. "Might it not be worth announcing yourself, and trying to persuade them again to call a halt to the whole business?"

"No. They will not be dissuaded, not at this late date. Believe me, I have tried every line of reason there is. And the last thing I want is for Ichabod to be distracted by my presence."

Charlotte did not reply, but she followed me across the field to the copse of trees.

We huddled silently behind the tree trunks, waiting. Nox hunkered down on his belly beside us. He had a happy look on his face, as if this was all a game we were playing.

I had never considered myself a woman of particularly strong faith—though I went to church every Sunday, of course—but in those fraught, cold moments I prayed as I never had before. I prayed that all would be well, no one would be hurt, and that we could move on from this folly as if it had never been.

As the sun crept higher in the sky, we heard voices approach. Brom came into the field, followed by a member of his loudmouthed gang, Pieter Van Horn. The two were joking loudly, like they were about to spend the day picking apples for the harvest, not engaging in a duel. Nox's ears pricked at the sound, but I grabbed the scruff of his neck, forcing him to stay where he was.

"Where is he, then?" Pieter asked Brom.

"Perhaps the schoolmaster has lost his nerve!" Brom declared, laughing.

I nearly snarled in my rage, clutching the bark of the tree so hard it dug into my palms. Oh, I wish that Ichabod would shoot him, I thought, in one bloodthirsty moment.

Not a minute later, Ichabod emerged onto the field as well, followed by a thin young man of similar height whom I did not know.

"Ah, you showed after all!" Brom crowed, almost sounding a bit disappointed. "The woman did not succeed in talking you out of it?"

Ichabod leveled a cool look at Brom. "I am here as we agreed, Van Brunt," he said. "To business, if you please."

Brom shrugged and turned to Pieter, who brought out a gleaming pistol. Brom took it, hefting its weight, aiming it into the sky and sighting along the barrel.

Nervously I looked at Ichabod. He, too, had a pistol in his hand now, though a sight more tarnished than Brom's. That doesn't mean anything, I told myself sternly. And, if what Ichabod had told me was true, no one would be shooting anyone.

I simply couldn't bear it, that there was to be a ritual of violence between these two men because of me. I tensed my body forward, preparing to race out onto the field and stand between them until they desisted. As though sensing what I was thinking, Charlotte reached out and gripped my arm. "No," she murmured to me. "They will not thank you for intervening now, Katrina. We can only watch and wait."

I gritted my teeth, but I stayed where I was.

"All right, Crane?" Brom called, swaggering toward the center of the field. "Let's go. If you're still man enough, that is."

Nox growled again beside me. Even when Nox was a puppy, when Brom and Charlotte and I had all been friends, he had been wary of Brom. That should have been all I needed to know, back then. I hushed him again, my fingers tightening in his fur, and he snorted slightly but stayed put. Not for the first time I was immensely grateful he was so well trained.

Ichabod refused to respond to Brom's taunts, and pride swelled in my heart. How could anyone, seeing the two of them, ever doubt Ichabod was the better man?

The seconds—Pieter and the man I didn't know—walked to the center of the field and spoke briefly, the customary last chance to negotiate a way out of the duel. Pieter made a dismissive gesture; there were no true negotiations this day.

My fingers dug harder into Nox's fur as Ichabod and Brom crossed the field and bowed to each other, Ichabod's a stiffly elegant gesture, while Brom's was exaggerated and mocking. Then they turned their backs to each other, their shoulders almost touching, and began to walk in the opposite direction.

Ten paces. Charlotte and I counted together, under our breath, eyes fixed on the two men.

"... eight ... nine ... ten ..."

I inhaled sharply as both men whirled. It all happened in an instant, though as I watched it unfold it seemed to take place painfully slowly. For a split second, Ichabod appeared to hesitate before he raised his pistol and fired harmlessly into the sky.

Brom hesitated as well—a heartbeat, a blink—and, to my horror, leveled his gun at Ichabod.

"No!" I screamed, unable to stop myself.

The gun went off with a boom, and Ichabod crumpled to the ground.

"No!" I shrieked, launching myself out from behind the trees and running toward him, Nox barking at my side, Charlotte on our heels.

Brom whirled to look at me, bewildered. "Katrina?" he asked. His eyes narrowed on Charlotte. "And the witch. What are you two doing here?"

I barely heard him. I flung myself onto the ground beside Ichabod. "Ichabod!" I screamed, lifting his head into my lap.

He opened his eyes. "Katrina?" he asked dazedly. "Where did you come from? What are you doing here?"

In my panicked, hysterical state, I was slow to realize he was clutching his shoulder, blood seeping between his fingers. "You were hit in your arm," I exclaimed. "Oh, thank God, thank God. I thought he killed you. I thought you were dead."

Ichabod gritted his teeth and raised himself slightly into a sitting position.

Charlotte knelt on the ground beside us. "He may yet be, if the wound takes an infection," she warned. "Move, Katrina. Now."

I scooted out of the way as she opened the bag of bandages and remedies she had brought. Using a pair of shears, she cut away the sleeve of his shirt so she could fully see and assess the wound.

After examining it quickly, she pulled a flask of whiskey out of the bag as well. "Here," she said, offering him a sip. "This will hurt."

He obediently took a swig and handed the flask back to her. "Go on," he said, weakly.

She poured some of the whiskey onto the wound, and a moan of pain escaped him as the alcohol scoured his raw flesh.

"I am sorry," she said, her tone businesslike as she bent her head over the wound to inspect it more closely. "But it must be done."

Ichabod nodded, eyes closed as he rode out the pain.

Out of the corner of my eye, I saw Brom moving toward me, but Nox planted himself between us and snarled, showing Brom all his teeth. Brom wisely came no further. "You should not have come here, Katrina," Brom said. "This is men's business."

"Men!" I cried. "Oh, yes, what a man you are, to shoot a defenseless opponent, to shoot someone who had already thrown away his shot!"

Fury ignited in his eyes. "How dare you speak to me so," he said. "I have won, and he has lost. He must give you up."

I laughed cruelly at him. "He will do no such thing! I will never let him! And I will tell you this, Brom Van Brunt," I swore, "This changes nothing. I would as soon shoot you myself as marry you!"

"Damn it, Katrina—"

"Leave! Now! Or I will have Nox tear out your throat!"

Brom cast a quick fearful look at the still-snarling dog, then quickly composed his face into its mask of disdain as he turned away.

"Katrina," Charlotte said, lifting her head to look at me, "the bullet is lodged in his shoulder. It will need to be removed."

"So remove it!"

"I do not have the tools here," she said, her voice low and calm, the voice of an experienced healer. "We will have to get him back to my cottage. I can remove it there. I will bandage it in the meantime, to try to slow the blood flow." She glanced down at Ichabod's pain-ravaged face. "Two miles is a long way in your condition," she said. "Can you make it?"

Ichabod grunted. "I have no desire to die in this field at the hands of Brom Van Brunt, so I suppose I will have to."

"There's a good man," Charlotte said. She began wrapping a bandage about his shoulder.

The unfamiliar man who had served as Ichabod's second spoke up. "I can help you get him back to the village," he volunteered.

I cast a brief look at him. "Who are you?"

"My cousin," Ichabod said through clenched teeth. "Giles Carpenter. He lives in White Plains."

Giles smiled quickly at me. "At your service," he said. "I suppose you are Miss Van Tassel, though I wish we could have met under better circumstances." His smile widened slightly. "A wedding, perhaps."

Ichabod's hand sought mine and squeezed it tightly. "Let us pray God that Miss Jansen here is successful," he said, as Charlotte completed the bandaging, "and we can all meet again at my and Katrina's wedding, and forget this ever took place."

"Amen," I said.

"Very well," Charlotte said. "You're going to need to stand now. Here, Mr. Carpenter, assist him. Steady, now. Don't rise too quickly."

With his cousin on one side of him and me on the other, Ichabod slowly got to his feet. He swayed violently before finding his balance under our solid hold.

"All right?" Charlotte asked. "Can you walk? Or should we return with a cart for you?"

Ichabod shook his head. "I can walk."

"Good man," Charlotte said again. "I'd rather not waste time."

We began to make our sluggish way back to the road and to the village, Nox following.

I had my arm wrapped around Ichabod's waist on the side that bore the wound, and Charlotte walked closely beside me, keeping an eye on it. Blood soon began to soak through the bandages she had wrapped around it, and I noticed her bite her lower lip with concern.

"How are you doing?" she asked, after we had gone perhaps a mile. Halfway there. Halfway still to go.

There was a sheen of sweat on Ichabod's face. "As well as can be expected, I suppose," he said.

Charlotte nodded. "Good. Is there any way we can move a little faster?"

"Charlotte, I think he is doing as much as—" I began.

She shot me a hard look. "If he loses too much blood, he will become light-headed, and it will be even more difficult for him to walk. We must get him to my cottage before that happens."

Ichabod nodded, his pale face set with determination. "I think I can."

We increased our pace, and perhaps three quarters of an hour later—though it felt much longer—the church came into view. I could have wept with relief.

Luckily, it was still early enough that not many people were up and about. It was best if we did not have to explain the circumstances of Ichabod's injury. Dueling, despite being a matter of course in terms of settling disputes, was illegal, and Ichabod was an outsider. He would be thought less of were it known he had engaged in a duel—though he would have been thought less of if he had refused to duel and that had gotten out. I shook my head, thinking of the folly of it all.

Even so, we saw a few passers-by on our way. Charlotte and I did our best to hide Ichabod's wound. We attracted a couple curious looks, but no one approached us to inquire.

Finally, we reached Charlotte's cottage—and not a moment too soon. Ichabod had started sweating profusely, his face gone waxy and his movements more pained.

"Here we are," Charlotte said soothingly. "Into the examination room, please."

I guided Ichabod and Giles into the room Charlotte and her mother used to examine patients. We helped Ichabod onto the cot within, and he immediately closed his eyes in relief and weariness.

"Charlotte?" I heard Mevrouw Jansen call. "What is happening?"

Charlotte spun around and went out. I could hear their low voices as they rapidly conversed, but I could not make out what explanation Charlotte gave to her mother—the truth, most likely. I did not care. Not so long as Ichabod emerged from this well and whole.

Charlotte returned and closed the door behind her, shutting Nox out. He whined in protest, but we ignored him. She grabbed an apron off a hook by the door and put it on, then swiftly tied back her long hair. "If either of you does not have a strong stomach, I suggest you leave now," she warned us.

Giles looked a bit green, hovering indecisively near the door. "I . . . I shall stay," he said in an uncertain tone.

"I will be fine," I said. If I had not been able to bear waiting at home for news of the duel, then I could hardly wait outside this room for word of how Charlotte's efforts had gone.

"Very well," she said, turning her attention to Ichabod. "But keep back, both of you. I can't have you in my light."

She moved about the room, working quickly and efficiently. She drew back the curtains from the high window, and lit all the lamps in the room. After washing her hands, she pulled out another bottle of whiskey. Charlotte poured a glass and handed it to Ichabod; he drank it as she assembled her tools: a pair of metal forceps, a bowl, more bandages. She motioned for me to take the glass once Ichabod had drained it, which I did, and set it on the sideboard. She drew up a chair beside the cot, as well as a small table holding her supplies, and began to unwind the now crimson-soaked bandages from the wound.

Despite her warning to stay back, I crept closer to get a better look at the wound. It was still bleeding, the edges where the bullet had gone in ragged and torn. My heart lurched at the thought of the pain Ichabod must be in, and began to pound faster with fresh anger at Brom.

Ichabod closed his eyes and Charlotte poured some more whiskey on the wound to clean it. She wiped away the liquor and blood with a soft cloth, then picked up her forceps. "I am sorry," she said briefly to Ichabod before beginning. "This will hurt a great deal."

With that, she carefully inserted the instrument into the wound, to begin digging for the bullet.

Ichabod grimaced in pain, his body twitching slightly, yet it seemed the whiskey he had consumed was having some dulling effect, at least. His face contorted as Charlotte continued to probe. She grunted a few times in frustration before making a small noise of triumph, withdrawing a bit of metal. "Got it," she said, sounding suddenly weary. She dropped the bullet into the bowl on the table beside her, and immediately set to cleaning the wound again.

Ichabod's body relaxed slightly as she rubbed an herbal paste on the wound. "Witch hazel, yarrow, and comfrey, to clean it and help it heal," she explained briefly before tightly winding a clean bandage about his arm. Rising, she washed her hands again. "I will be right back," she told me and Giles. "Make sure he doesn't fall asleep. I'm making him an herb drink that will help prevent fever from setting in. He'll need to drink it right away."

She left the room, removing her apron—now flecked with blood—as she went.

I moved to her vacated chair, taking Ichabod's hand in mine. "You must stay awake, my love," I said.

He opened his eyes slowly and took me in. "Katrina," he murmured. "You're still here. I wasn't sure."

I brushed his sweat-soaked hair off of his forehead. "And where else would I be?"

His lips twitched into the beginning of a smile. "I don't deserve you," he said.

"Of course you do," I whispered. "Why would you say such a thing?" But before he could answer, Charlotte returned.

"Can you help him to sit up?" she asked me. "It'll be just for a moment, Mr. Crane. Drink this, and I will help you to another room where you can sleep."

I helped him into a sitting position. Taking the cup from Charlotte, I put it to his lips, and he obediently drank it down. He made a face. "Not the best-tasting stuff," he remarked.

"No, but it will have the desired effect," Charlotte said. "All right, now. If you can stand—slowly—we will get you into the next room, where you can sleep. Mr. Carpenter, perhaps you can assist."

Giles Carpenter obliged and helped Ichabod to his feet, and the two men followed Charlotte into the adjoining room, furnished with a bed for patients to recover. Giles helped him into bed and drew up the covers over him, Ichabod's eyes already closed.

I moved to sit beside him, but Charlotte put a hand on my arm. "Let him rest," she said. "He should be perfectly well given some time to recover. You hovering will do neither of you any good."

Reluctantly I obeyed, and we left the examination room, causing Nox to bark joyfully at the sight of us, as though we had been gone for days. "What did you give him?" I asked.

"A tea of cinnamon, yarrow, and wormwood," she said. "It helps to cool the body and prevent a fever." She studied me carefully. "Perhaps you should rest, too," she said. "You are welcome to sleep for a bit in my room upstairs if you like. This whole ordeal has not been easy for you, either."

I realized that sleep was just what I needed right then. "Thank you," I told her, hoping my tone conveyed the depth of my gratitude, which was more than words could ever say.

"Of course," she said. And no more words were needed between us than that.

26

Healing

It was midday by the time I awoke. Nox's tail began to wag as I stirred. I had fallen into a deep sleep the moment my body touched the mattress, the stress and fear of the day—and the sleepless night before—finally earning their victory over me.

I went downstairs looking for Charlotte, and a bit nervous that I might run into Mevrouw Jansen. I did not see her, but Charlotte was in the stillroom, at work making tinctures and potions.

"You're awake," she said brightly when she saw me. "Well rested, I hope?"

"Very," I said. "How is Ichabod? Is he—"

"He is still sleeping," Charlotte said soothingly. "I have been checking on him. He has no fever, and his color is returning to normal. Rest is the best thing for him now, so I must insist you let him sleep."

I may not have liked Charlotte's admonition, but I knew she was right. And if she assured me Ichabod was well, then I could be sure it was the truth.

"You must be hungry," Charlotte said, wiping her hands on her apron. "I have some porridge and bread, if you like. We can go out into the garden."

I helped Charlotte carry the food out into the garden, and she spread a sheet over the grass, as though this were one of our carefree picnics. Nox settled in the grass beside us, sticking close. "Where is Ichabod's cousin?" I asked, once we were seated. "Mr. Carpenter?"

"He's gone back to White Plains," Charlotte informed me. "He waited a bit after you went to sleep to make sure Ichabod seemed to be well and wasn't taking a fever, then he had to return home."

I nodded. Giles had seemed an amiable sort, and no doubt he would not betray the events of the day to anyone.

"So what now?" Charlotte asked, handing me a hunk of bread.

"I must go home soon," I said. "I should like to see Ichabod before then, but if he is not awake in time—"

"No," Charlotte said, a touch of impatience in her voice. "I mean, what will you and Ichabod do now?"

I frowned, not understanding her question. "We will do exactly what we've been doing, what we plan to do," I said. "This changes nothing."

"Katrina." Charlotte sighed in frustration. "It changes everything. Brom knows about you two. The duel has not erased his knowledge, nor has it likely settled anything for him. Not when you and Ichabod are still lovers."

"He does not know that we are *lovers*, technically," I said quickly.

"That you are courting, then," Charlotte said, exasperated, "though he no doubt guessed at more than that."

"But he said if Ichabod took part in the duel, he would not tell my father," I said, my stomach sinking even as I spoke the words. "And Ichabod did, obviously. It must be settled now. That is the point of the duel."

"Surely you cannot be that naïve," Charlotte said. "Brom does not have what he wants: he does not have you. He will tell your father. He may wait, and choose his moment, but he will tell him."

"But Ichabod—"

"This is Brom we are talking about," Charlotte said. "He may bray about duels as a matter of honor, but the truth is he has none. The duel itself proved that."

I stayed silent, worry eating at me. "I do not know what else I can do," I said at last. "We can no longer meet in the woods, that is true; not now that Brom knows we have met there. But we had a plan, Ichabod and I, and we must execute it and pray that it works."

"What is this plan?" Charlotte asked.

"Ichabod is going to ask my father for my hand," I said. "On the night of the All Hallows' Eve feast. He will be in high spirits then, and more likely to say yes. We cannot wait any longer, especially with the weather growing colder so that we cannot meet out-doors . . ." I trailed off, looking away from Charlotte's thoughtful gaze. "And we cannot bear being apart anymore. We wish to live as husband and wife. It is time to face what comes next, whatever that may be."

Charlotte did not say anything for a long while. "I shall hope it all works out well, then," she said at last. "I have always hoped so. I will hope that I am wrong, for, oh, Katrina . . ." She took my hands, clutching them tightly. "I have a feeling that something yet stands in your way. I cannot help but feel Brom is not done with you."

"I am sure he is not," I said lightly, my tone belying the appre-hension I could not seem to dismiss. "I must simply hope he can do no further damage."

Ichabod was still sleeping as I prepared to take my leave. He would likely stay at the cottage for a few days, so that Charlotte might oversee his recovery. She would send word as soon as I could see him.

I was just heading out when Mevrouw Jansen came in. "Ah, Katrina," she said. "Returning home?"

"Yes," I said, swallowing down my foolish nervousness. "I must thank you yet again for your hospitality."

"You know you are welcome here anytime." Yet after she spoke, she studied me for a moment. "Charlotte told me what passed this morning," she said suddenly, and I flinched as though she had shouted at me. "I know we have young Mr. Ichabod Crane, the schoolteacher, recovering in our house. From a gunshot wound."

I stood there awkwardly, my hand on the latch of the door behind me. "Yes," I said cautiously.

"My daughter told me only what I needed to know to explain our patient's presence," she said. "I know no more than that. I certainly do not know enough to tell anything of import to your mother."

I squirmed uncomfortably.

"But, Katrina," she continued, "take care. You are a young woman, and there is much about the world and those who inhabit it that you do not know. Not everyone is as they seem."

I bristled at this. At least she would keep my secret, as much of it as she knew, anyway; which, given her second sight, was much more than she was letting on. "Thank you for the warning," I said, somewhat stiffly. "And . . . thank you."

"Of course, my dear. Get home safely, now. And give my greetings to your mother."

I left quickly after that.

27

A Night for Lovers

I spent the rest of the day and evening in a state of nervous anxiety, worrying about Ichabod and half expecting Brom to appear on our doorstep with news for my father. And I could do nothing but sit at home and stew.

The next day, thankfully, Charlotte sent a brief note letting me know Ichabod was much improved. If I wanted to come visit him, she knew he would welcome it.

With no patience to walk, I had Henry saddle my mare, Starlight, and rode quickly to the Jansens'.

"Brom Van Brunt shall not be the end of me, as I said," Ichabod said on my arrival, a crooked smile on his lips.

Overjoyed to see him looking well, I longed to embrace him where he sat in bed, but settled for holding his hand tightly. "Indeed he shall not," I said, though his choice of words had filled me with unease.

"And have you seen him since?" Ichabod asked, his expression suddenly growing worried. "He has not been to see your parents, has he?"

I shook my head. "I've seen neither hide nor hair of him, and can only hope it will stay that way."

Ichabod relaxed slightly. "Good. Good." The concern had not completely left his face. "He is still a danger to us, though."

I squeezed his hand, and tried to make my voice sound as though that very thing did not plague my every thought. "It does not matter," I said. "We shall do as we planned. You shall ask my father for my hand at the All Hallows' Eve party."

Ichabod looked away and was silent.

"If you still wish to marry me, that is," I said.

"Of course I do," he said, with gratifying speed. "I just wonder if we should wait that long."

I shook my head. "We must not let Brom make us over-hasty," I said. "In honor, after all, he cannot tell my father."

"Honor," Ichabod nearly spat. "Indeed."

"And," I went on, ignoring him, "we must wait until you are healed. No good will come from drawing his attention to your injury and its cause."

Ichabod sighed. "Very well." He leaned forward and kissed me. "I shall, as I have always done, put my trust in you."

Charlotte kept Ichabod for observation another few days, but he continued to heal wonderfully. "He has been helping us with some small tasks around the house, in fact," she informed me as we walked along the bank of the Hudson one day. "He is longing to be away, I know. He is impatient with being cooped up, and eager to get back to his students, though my mother and I have put it about the village that he has been quite ill and is recovering with us. But I told him in no uncertain terms you would never forgive me if something happened to him, and so I must watch over him like a mother wolf over her cub." Charlotte smiled. "He is the most wonderful man, Katrina. I see it now. I knew he was handsome enough, and amiable, but truly I never understood why you would risk so much for him." She paused. "But I see it now. I do."

I smiled back at her. "I knew you would, in time."

"And so I have a gift for you, in a way," she said, grinning mischievously.

I raised my eyebrows. "Oh?"

"Tomorrow night, my mother and I are off to see a friend of hers near West Point," Charlotte said. "We shall be staying the night there." She paused. "Ichabod is well enough to go home, but I have persuaded him to stay through tomorrow night, for I suggested you might join him."

"Oh, Charlotte," I whispered. "Truly?"

She nodded. "But you must take care," she warned. "Let no one see you enter or leave. The neighbors will notice Mother and I are gone, and it is known Ichabod is staying with us. My mother, of course, is not to know."

"My mother does not know you are going, does she?" I asked.

"I cannot see how she would. So you will tell her you are spending the night with me again."

I laughed aloud and threw my arms around her. "Bless you, Charlotte. You are wonderful."

She returned the embrace. "I expect to be the maid of honor at your wedding," she said. "And godmother to your first child."

"Who else?" I asked, drawing back. "Oh, Charlotte, thank you. Thank you. A thousand times!"

She left soon afterward, and I spent the afternoon and evening—and much of the night—in a haze of delicious anticipation. A whole night with Ichabod . . . just the two of us, and with a proper bed!

My lie in place with my mother, I went the next evening to the Jansen cottage. I glanced around surreptitiously to see if anyone observed me, but it was a chilly evening, and most people were inside taking their evening meal and preparing for bed.

I tried the door and, finding it unlocked, stepped inside, closing it quickly behind me.

Ichabod had come into the front room at the sound of the door, and we both froze as we caught sight of one another, drinking each other in with the satisfying knowledge that we were alone in this house for a whole night.

"Katrina," he whispered. "You are really here. When Charlotte suggested this, I almost could not believe . . ." He trailed off, still looking at me as though I were some holy vision he had never expected to behold.

"Nor I," I said. "Yet here we are."

We moved swiftly toward one another. He took me hungrily in his arms, and if his wound pained him, he did not show it. I sank into him eagerly, our mouths crashing together, as though we were starving and would devour one another.

I am not quite certain how, but eventually we made it into the room Ichabod had been staying, where the bed waited invitingly for us.

Here, everything slowed down. We took our time undressing one another, stopping to kiss and caress along the way, indulging in a way we could not in the woods. When we made it to the bed— and never before had such a narrow, lumpy mattress seemed like a soft and downy paradise—we leisurely explored one another's bodies, laughing and sighing and crying out together.

When Ichabod finally entered me, I nearly wept with the sheer joy of feeling him move inside me once more. We reached the peak of our pleasure together, feeling as familiar to each other as longtime lovers, but somehow new again to one another in this night that was unlike any other we'd spent together before.

Afterward, he wrapped me in his arms and fell asleep, and I nestled my head against his shoulder. I ran my fingers gently over his wound, still bandaged, which had once seemed like it could be the end of everything. But it had not. Secure in this knowledge, I soon drifted off as well.

———

We both woke perhaps an hour later. "I quite forgot my manners," Ichabod said, stretching his lean, naked body languidly under the coverlet. "Charlotte left us some stew and fresh bread and wine, and it never occurred to me to offer you any."

"What a barbarian you are," I teased. "You simply haul your woman off to bed and tear off her clothes without even offering her any repast."

He laughed. "Indeed. I am most base and uncivilized, we have learned."

"Well, I shall forgive you this once, for when I arrived I was not hungry in any case." I let my eyes travel over his body, grinning. "Not for food, anyway."

He laughed.

"Yet now I find I am famished," I said. "You have quite depleted my energies."

"And you mine," Ichabod said. He rose from the bed and donned his breeches, leaving his chest bare. "Shall we adjourn to the kitchen, then, my lady?"

I pulled on my petticoat and followed him, lighting the stove to warm the stew as Ichabod set to cutting the bread. I could feel myself smiling with the intimate pleasure of our domesticity: the two of us in the kitchen, readying a meal together.

This is how it shall be once we are husband and wife, I thought, happiness filling me to my core.

I got out bowls and silverware, and we set our simple but delicious feast out on the table, and sat down to dine. I poured the wine, serving Ichabod his first like a dutiful country wife. We ate by the dim candlelight, and spoke freely in a way that we had not been able to for a long time, it seemed: how he was healing, of Charlotte's generosity to us, of our plan for approaching my father. We also began to speak—for the first time in solid, definite plans—of the future that now seemed so close to our grasp.

"Once we are married, perhaps we can buy a small cottage in the village," I said, brightening at the thought. "I could ask my father for the appropriate sum as my dowry."

Ichabod leaned back in his chair, taking a moment to envision it. "A little cottage just for us," he said. "As husband and wife."

"Yes," I said. "And you can continue teaching, and I shall keep our house and read to my heart's content."

"And," he said, taking my hand, "raise our children, I should think."

"Yes, indeed," I said, my face flushing with pleasure at the thought. "And I shall teach them their letters and sums until they are old enough to be sent to your school."

"You are as skilled and wonderful an artist as any of the old masters of Europe, such is the beauty of the picture you have painted," he said. "Or perhaps you are a soothsayer, and can foresee the future."

I determined not to betray my flicker of unease at these words, at the unwitting reference to the Sight that Charlotte was sure I possessed and Ichabod knew not of. I might wish my words a foretelling, yet any visions I had had were much different, I thought uneasily. But I would not ruin the perfect oasis of happiness we had this night with such musings. "It is no foreseeing," I said lightly. "One needs no magic to know that we shall make our future what we wish it to be."

"We shall," Ichabod averred.

"And eventually, of course, we will move into my family's farmhouse, when it comes time for us to take over the farm," I said. "And we shall have everything we could possibly desire."

Ichabod sighed happily. "I will not pretend that the thought of such bounty, such financial security and even wealth, does not excite me after so many years spent struggling."

I smiled. "Soon you will never have to struggle again, nor worry more about such things," I promised.

"Simply having you as my wife shall be wealth enough; still, it will be wonderful not to have to worry," he said.

"It will be wonderful," I repeated. "Everything shall be wonderful."

Soon afterward, we cleaned up our dinner dishes and went back into the paradise of the bed. We made love again, another slow, luxurious coupling.

Yet this time we could not seem to fall asleep, and who could blame us, exhilarated and joyful as we were? Neither of us wished to waste our night together sleeping.

"Tell me a tale," Ichabod murmured in my ear, his fingers toying with my hair. "You tell the most marvelous tales, my love. Surely there are more spooky tales of ghosts and goblins that you have not yet told me."

I smiled uneasily. "Surely we've had enough darkness and terror of late." I suppressed a shiver, thinking not only of the duel and its aftermath but my fearful dreams and visions. I had no wish to inspire more of them.

"But these are just stories, yes? Legends and nothing more. We need not be afraid."

I realized that I no longer believed that, if I ever had. For all my skepticism, I knew that stories always held some truth, else why did we tell them? "So you say now," I said, "until you must ride home after dark one evening and recall all the tales of the supernatural you have ever heard."

"But no one is riding anywhere after dark tonight," he said, drawing me closer. "We shall be safe and snug in here together."

I sighed, unable to deny him, not when we were naked in bed together. "Very well. But only one tale." I sifted through all the legends in my mind, searching for just the right one. "This is the legend of the Woman in White of Raven Rock."

"Is not a woman in white a mournful, weeping sort of spirit?" Ichabod asked.

"Yes, and you shall see why in this tale." I cleared my throat and began.

"During the revolution, there was a famous battle at White Plains, as you no doubt know, and afterward British soldiers sought billet with the local folk. Two officers claimed a cottage where a young woman lived alone—her brothers were off fighting with Washington—and demanded she shelter and feed them. She obliged, having no true choice in the matter, and during the course of their stay, she fell in love with the younger of the two officers, a lieutenant.

"He returned her love, and the two planned to run away together once his service was ended, someplace where armies and loyalty could not trouble them. He promised to return for her in two months' time, when they would be married and go away. During that time, he was obliged to continue in his service under General Howe in the British army, and while she waited, she sewed her wedding dress."

Despite my initial reluctance to tell a story, I loved having Ichabod's undivided attention, and found I was quite enjoying myself. I had always loved these stories throughout my life, and they defined this place where I lived. It was a novel experience to tell these local stories to someone who had never heard them before; in a way, I was experiencing them anew myself.

"Once two months had passed, she climbed up to Raven Rock, a tall point deep within the forest. From there she could spy the waters of the Hudson, and waited for sight of her love's ship.

"All night she waited, sometimes crying out, 'My love! Have you come for me?' She would not be moved from her vigil, not even when an icy wind whipped up and brought a blizzard with it. Still she remained, waiting for her beloved.

"In the morning, two huntsmen came upon her there at Raven Rock, frozen to death in her white wedding dress. To this day, those who venture there—especially at night, and especially during a winter storm—claim they can hear her crying, 'My love! Have you come for me?'" I shivered again, at the eeriness of the tale, and in sadness for the poor woman who had died rather than give up on her love. Suddenly I understood her in a way I hadn't before. "She still keeps her vigil there, and most say she will until her beloved returns."

Ichabod's arms tightened around me silently. "And what became of her lieutenant?" he asked at last.

"No one knows. His name has been lost, so it is impossible to find out. He may have been killed in battle, or taken prisoner, or perhaps he deserted her and ran off with another woman. We shall never know."

"A sad tale," Ichabod said.

"Yes," I agreed quietly. "Very sad."

After a moment had passed, I spoke again. "Although if that was not eerie enough for you," I added, trying for a lighter tone, "I should mention that Raven Rock is not far from the infamous clearing where the Headless Horseman is said to have met his end."

Now it was Ichabod's turn to shiver. "A truly haunted place, then."

"Indeed."

"All of Sleepy Hollow, it seems to me, is a truly haunted place."

I had never thought of it in such a way before. "Perhaps," I conceded.

"And you have added to its magic," he said, "by weaving spells around me with your tales."

I smiled at him. "Surely I do not tell these tales half so well as all the old Dutch farmwives."

"I have had occasion to know many of them do spin a good yarn," he acknowledged, "but you have a true gift for storytelling, Katrina. You should write these tales down."

I laughed. "For whom? And what purpose? Everyone around here already knows them."

"For newcomers like me, then. Or perhaps they could even be published, to show the world what history and imagination the Dutch have in their river valley. Surely I could not be the only one to find such tales so fascinating."

I laughed again. "And I should write them and expect to be published? A woman author? Away with you," I said, shoving his shoulder playfully.

His face remained seriously. "Why not? This is a new country we are living in, Katrina. We, its people, can make it anything we wish it to be. What do you wish our nation to be?"

I had no answer. I lay awake for a long time after he fell asleep, pondering his words.

Later in the night, Ichabod woke me to make love to me again, and I smiled in the dark with my pure joy. And this, too, I thought, shall be a frequent occurrence once we are married. This, too, shall be how it is all the time, and we can spend each and every night in each other's arms.

Just before dawn broke, as we were drifting off once more, Ichabod whispered into my ear, *"Ik hou van je."*

Tears welled in my eyes. "I love you, too," I whispered in English.

28

Fears and Tears

I left early the next morning, albeit very reluctantly. Charlotte had assured me they did not plan to return until midday, but I did not wish to take the chance Mevrouw Jansen might choose to return early. Yet, prudent though I knew it to be, I could not imagine when I might see Ichabod again, to say nothing of when we might next be alone together.

I clung to him just inside the doorway, the front of my gown pressed against his still-bare chest. Inwardly I cursed all that separated us—society, circumstances, fabric.

"It is just over two weeks until All Hallows' Eve," Ichabod assured me. "The time will fly by, you will see."

I eyed him disbelievingly.

"Very well," he amended. "It shall pass intolerably slowly for me, as well. I was only trying to make you feel better."

Sighing, I laid my head against his chest. "All will be well," I murmured.

"All will be well," he repeated, "and it shall be worth waiting for."

I leaned up and kissed him, then turned and stepped out the door before I lost the resolve to do so.

I glanced furtively around, but it seemed that no one was about to see me leave. Relaxing slightly, I quickened my pace as I moved toward the road that led to home.

I had just arrived at the Albany Post Road when Brom seemed to materialize from nowhere. "Good morrow, Katrina," he said, his normally smug face tight with some emotion I could not quite read. "And to what does the village owe your fair presence at such an early hour?"

His words were flirtatious, but his tone was accusatory. I felt like how an American patriot carrying secret messages must have when stopped and interrogated by British soldiers. "Not that it is any of your concern," I said, hoping my tone sounded sufficiently haughty, "but I spent the night at Charlotte's, and am on my way home. So if you'll excuse me."

I moved to walk around him, but he clamped a large hand on my shoulder. "How dare you!" I exploded, all the rage I had been working so hard to conceal forcing its way out. "Take your filthy hand off me, you devil!"

"What do you take me for, Katrina?" he hissed, bringing his face close to mine. "I know the witch and her witch mother are not home. So what have you really been doing?" Realization dawned on his face, and I saw the emotion tinging his features for what it was: anger. "He is there, isn't he?" Brom demanded. "That good-for-nothing schoolteacher. Charlotte has been nursing him back to health, and you have spent the night with him!"

I wrenched away from his grasp. "How dare you!" I cried again. "How dare you make such an insinuation about a lady! I have not—"

"He is weak and worthless," Brom growled. "A nobody. And you would give yourself to him? When I . . ." He broke off, his rage seeming to choke him.

"He is a hundred times the man you are," I spat.

Brom flinched as though I had slapped him, and in the hurt look that crossed his face I saw the shadow of the boy he had been. Had I not been so violently enraged, I might have regretted my words.

"Never doubt that, Brom Van Brunt. I do not owe you any-thing, not my time, nor my body, nor my hand. Mark that well, and do not forget it." With that, I succeeded in moving past him and continuing on home, at a near run. I did not stop to consider what Brom might have taken as an admission. Or a challenge.

I spent the darkening October days reading. I finally finished *Macbeth*, and its ending seemed a bad portent to my mind—the ambition of Macbeth and his lady had come to a bloody end; a warning from Master Shakespeare, it seemed, to those who would reach for what they ought not have. But I was merely reaching for a marriage to the man I loved—a perfectly respectable and reasonable thing for a young woman to want. It was not as though I sought to murder others for power.

Yet as the days grew shorter and grayer and colder, I found that reason did not occupy so lofty a place within my mind as it once had. When it was warm enough, I found myself aimlessly wandering alone through the woods that had once seemed like a haven and now seemed a menacing, unwelcoming bastion of threat. It was as though I was daring some disaster to befall me, daring the Headless Horseman to appear and make good on his threats—or to run into Brom Bones. I did not know which I feared most.

A week later, Ichabod returned for a music lesson. He excused his long absence to my father, repeating the Jansens' story that he had fallen ill. He no longer needed a sling for his injured arm, though I fancied that I could see the outlines of a bandage beneath his shirt when he removed his coat.

Once we were alone, I fell into his arms, as though it had been months and not mere days since I saw him last. He held me word-lessly before pulling away for the business at hand.

"Shall we have another go at our song?" Ichabod asked, handing the music sheets to me. "Do you remember it well enough?"

I nodded, my eyes never leaving his. "I shall not soon forget that song," I said. "If ever."

He nodded once, and without further pleasantries strummed the delicate opening bars of the song. I started singing at my entrance, and soon he joined, and again we sang in harmony, the song about the gentleman and his lady love and all the things that stood between them but could not truly divide them. When we finished, I had tears streaming down my cheeks.

"Katrina," Ichabod said, catching sight of my face, and rising abruptly from his seat. "Why do you cry?" He gathered me against him, murmuring softly in my ear. "Do not cry. What is it that has made you cry, my love?"

Yet I could not answer him, for I did not truly know. I did not know if it was the exquisite way our voices had blended together, or the hope and sadness of the lovers in the song and my inexplicable fear for them, or that my monthly course should have come four days earlier and had yet to appear.

Perhaps it was all of those things. And so I spoke of none of them.

29

All Hallows' Eve

All Hallows' Eve dawned, somewhat incongruously, with a bright, incandescent orange sun, bringing warmth to the now empty fields. Yet of all days, the Headless Horseman would be most likely to appear on this one, when the veil between the worlds of the living and the dead was at its thinnest; but with such brilliant sunshine I did not see how a creature of death and darkness could appear.

Thankfully, my mother and Cook kept me busy much of the day, helping to bake pies and decorate the house for the party that evening. Had I been sitting around, I would have driven myself quite mad with anxiety thinking about that night, when mine and Ichabod's future would be decided. So engrossed in the tasks they set me was I that I scarcely noticed the sky cloud over, scarcely noticed the gray October afternoon that settled over Sleepy Hollow.

At four o'clock, my mother pronounced our work done, and sent me upstairs to get ready. First I took Nox out to the barn, where he would be confined with his brother during the festivities. Nancy was waiting, having already heated the metal rods to curl my hair. She spent nearly half an hour taming my long, pale hair into neat, fetching curls, and pinning the top strands away from my face, letting the rest hang freely down my back. Then she helped me into a brand-new midnight-blue gown, complete with lace trim at the sleeves and bodice. As she laced me into the gown, I could not help but let my hands rest on my stomach. My monthly course had still not arrived, and I was in a frenzy of doubt as to whether to tell Ichabod before he spoke to my father. If all went well, it would not matter. I could insist upon a quick wedding, before winter's snows came. Early babies were not uncommon, after all. Time enough to tell Ichabod once we were safely betrothed.

And yet, what if—God forbid—things did not go according to plan? What if my father refused his suit? Ichabod would need to know, so we could plan what to do next. I did not know how much time I had before my condition became obvious to all, but I knew it could be no more than a few months.

Of course, there was always the possibility that I was wrong, that my course was only inordinately delayed. Yet, whether it was the Sight or a mother's intuition or simply the knowledge a woman has of her own body, somehow I knew I was with child, and that the child had been conceived that night at Charlotte's house—in a proper bed, at least, if not the marriage bed—because I had forgotten to take my tea of herbs. I had been in the Jansen cottage, surrounded by all manner of herbs, and I had forgotten in my night of blissful, delirious happiness.

When Nancy finally pronounced me ready, I pinned on my most convincing smile and went downstairs to begin to greet the guests, playing my roles of charming hostess and fetching daughter and magnanimous heiress. Most of Sleepy Hollow would be in attendance, as my father believed in sharing his bounty with as many as possible.

When Charlotte came in with her mother, relief washed through me, and for the first time that evening my smile was genuine. While we could not speak just then, she squeezed my hand tightly and gave me a smile of reassurance.

Not long after came Brom, with his widower father. "Meneer Van Brunt, always a pleasure," my father greeted the older man. "And young Brom. A delight to offer you our hospitality, as always."

"The pleasure is mine entirely," Brom said smoothly. He turned to me, that same anger still simmering beneath his features, and my stomach contracted with unease. "Miss Van Tassel," he said, kissing my hand. "You look as radiant as ever."

"Thank you," I said stiffly. Even with my parents looking on, I could not bring myself to say more. Fear seized me. Somehow in all my planning for this night I had forgotten Ichabod and Brom would both be here. I tried to push these fears away. For what could either do or say in the rooms of a crowded party, before almost the entire village?

I did not want to find out. Excusing myself from my spot by the door, I darted into the parlor to find Charlotte. "Brom is here," I hissed in her ear, clutching her arm. "When Ichabod arrives, you must take care that they do not come into too close contact."

Charlotte nodded, casually raising her glass of mulled apple cider to her lips, as though we were talking of nothing more than village gossip. "You may rely upon me," she said. "I shall be taking pains to avoid Brom as well, so Ichabod and I can avoid him together."

Worry assuaged, I returned to the front entryway in time to see Ichabod step inside and hand his coat and hat to Henry. "Ahh, Mr. Crane," my father said, shaking his hand vigorously. "I'm so happy we have the chance to extend our hospitality to you once again."

"You are too kind, as ever, Master Van Tassel," Ichabod said. He kissed my mother's hand. "Mistress Van Tassel, both yourself and your home are exceedingly lovely this evening."

"Away with you, dear boy," my mother laughed. "And pray, eat and drink your fill, and enjoy the revels on this dark night of the year."

Ichabod scarcely seemed to hear her as his gaze fixed on me. "And Miss Van Tassel," he said, taking my hand and kissing it as well, his lips lingering a beat too long. Even here, even before my parents, and with everything I wanted at stake, the touch of his lips on my bare skin sent waves of heat through me. "You are a vision. I do not think I have ever laid eyes on a more beautiful woman."

A blush rose to my face. "You do me too much honor, sir," I said. "I speak only the truth."

My father cleared his throat rather pointedly, and my blush deepened. "I pray you enjoy the party, dear sir," I said. "I trust we shall have time later this evening to converse at more length."

"Nothing would delight me more," he said, sweeping me a bow. With another nod to my parents, he stepped through the entryway and into the receiving room. Charlotte approached him almost immediately—bless her, she must have been watching for his entrance—and led him over to the table where bottles of wine and beer and jugs of hot cider were set out.

A few more guests came after Ichabod, but the stream of arrivals had slowed to a trickle. "You are an admirable hostess, as always, my dear," my father said fondly. "Now go. Enjoy the party. I am sure you and Charlotte will have much to gossip of."

If only you knew, Father, I thought wryly. I beamed at him and went back into the parlor. Charlotte and Ichabod stood toward the back of the room, far from everyone else which, as I well knew by now, had everything to do with Charlotte. Brom was the full length of the room away, speaking to one of his friends. He was, I noticed uneasily, casting angry looks in Ichabod's direction every now and then. My stomach curdled uncomfortably.

I took a deep, calming breath, allowing myself a moment to take in the harvest-themed splendor of the room. Candles blazed from the chandelier, from wall sconces, and from candelabras, almost as though we were defying October's attempts to darken our home and our spirits. Fabric garlands of gold and crimson and orange leaves hung along the walls, and hollowed out pumpkins with faces carved into them, more candles illuminating them from within, graced every table and corner. Their faces were by turns comical or menacing, and their eyes seemed to follow me no matter where I turned.

I poured myself some warm cider, mulled with rum and spices, and went to join Charlotte and Ichabod. "Charlotte, I trust you and Mr. Crane are enjoying yourselves?" I asked in English. As more and more newcomers arrived in the village each year, it had become the language of choice at our larger gatherings.

"Indeed we are, Katrina," Charlotte said. "Though I do not presume to speak for the gentleman."

Ichabod smiled with genuine appreciation as he took in the room around him. "I am enjoying myself very much," he said. "What a lovely picture this room makes, Miss Van Tassel. My compliments."

"I shall accept them," I said, my tone more lighthearted than I felt, "for I toiled much of the day creating this very picture!"

Ichabod laughed and bowed slightly. "Then know your efforts are very much appreciated." He cast his gaze around again. "A fitting celebration of the harvest, and yet there is a touch of the eerie, too, which is only appropriate for All Hallows' Eve."

"Indeed," Brom's voice broke in. I looked up, startled, to see he had approached us unnoticed. "And do you think, Mr. Crane, that any of us might receive a visit from the legendary Headless Horseman tonight?" His eyes narrowed unpleasantly. "I wonder, how would you react were you to be faced with such a fearsome apparition?"

"Oh, indeed," Mevrouw Jansen said, coming over to interrupt— whether by accident or design I could not be sure, but I was grateful all the same. "For this is the night on which one is most likely to see him." I shivered at her words, so close an echo of my own thoughts earlier that day. "Mr. Crane, I trust someone has told you the tale of our local specter?"

"Indeed, Mistress Jansen," Ichabod said. "Katr—Miss Van Tassel was kind enough to so enlighten me early on in my stay in Sleepy Hollow."

"I did," I affirmed. "I thought it best to warn him, should he happen to encounter the ghost one night!"

"Very wise of you, my dear," Mevrouw Jansen said, smiling.

"Well I, for one, do not fancy Mr. Crane's chances were he to cross paths with the Horseman," Brom said.

My heart increased its pace. There was a threat in his voice.

"Whatever do you mean, young Mr. Van Brunt?" Mevrouw Jansen asked him coolly, leveling an icy stare on him.

He faltered slightly under her gaze; for all his fear of Charlotte, he feared her mother much more, and even he did not dare besmirch her reputation—indeed, Dame Jansen's standing in the community, particularly amongst its women, had been the only thing to protect her daughter from Brom's rumor-mongering.

"I only mean," Brom said, rallying, "Mr. Crane here is a rather bookish sort of fellow. I do not know that he has the—er—physical prowess to tangle with a supernatural soldier."

Ichabod tensed beside me, but he did not respond.

"I do not know that physical prowess would matter much against a ghost of any sort," Mevrouw Jansen said.

"Indeed," Charlotte said, speaking for the first time since Brom had joined our circle. "And do you truly fancy your own chances against one such as the Headless Horseman, Brom?"

There was a very weighty pause indeed, for Charlotte, Brom, and myself were all no doubt thinking of Charlotte's prediction for Brom the fateful day that shattered our friendship, the day when Brom had sought to master his fear and prove himself a man once and for all.

I see blood in your future, Brom Van Brunt. Blood and death. The Headless Horseman is your fate. The Headless Horseman is your end.

The rage Brom had been nurturing all night threatened to break through, and I shudder to think what may have happened were we not in a large company such as this. Thankfully others had come to join the conversation by then.

"Oh, Mr. Van Brunt, you could best even a ghost in a fight, I am sure of it!" cried Elizabeth van der Berg.

"Indeed!" exclaimed her friend, a girl whose name I thought was Sara. "Even the Headless Horseman!"

Brom glared at Charlotte a heartbeat longer before turning to his admirers with his usual smug grin.

"Wouldn't it be something to see him, though?" Mevrouw Van Buren said almost breathlessly, drawing into our circle—though not without a wary glance at Charlotte. "I don't know a soul who can claim to have truly seen him. Wouldn't it be something, only to say that you had?"

I shivered again, thinking of my dreams, my vision. "I think it would be rather terrifying."

"And most likely he is only a legend, in any case," Mevrouw Jansen interjected.

"Quite right," Ichabod said, though he did not look so certain. "I am, of course, only a newcomer to this part of the country, but I know Mistress Jansen to be a woman of the utmost wisdom, so I am inclined to agree with her on this point."

Mevrouw Jansen laughed. "Oh, but you've a silver tongue, haven't you," she said to Ichabod. "It's what comes of reading all those books, I expect."

"Ah, Mr. Crane," said one of the elderly village women, Mevrouw Douw. She joined our circle, grasping Ichabod's sleeve in her gnarled hand. "As we are trading stories, I have one for you: have you heard the tale of Major John Andre, and his haunted tree?" she asked in her heavily accented English.

"Major Andre?" Ichabod asked. "The British officer who sought to assist Benedict Arnold in his treachery?"

"The very same," Mevrouw Douw said. "He was captured with the plans for the fort at West Point secreted in his boot just up the road from here." She pointed in the general direction of the spot, perhaps halfway between my house and the village proper.

"I did know that particular episode occurred near here," he said. "I have not heard the tale of his tree as yet, though I have heard many wonderful tales since coming to Sleepy Hollow." He flashed me a quick smile.

"It is a marvelous story," Mevrouw Douw said, settling in to tell the tale. "You, boy," she barked at Brom. She handed him her goblet. "Fetch me more cider while I tell it."

Charlotte and I exchanged amused glances as Brom, looking like a chastened child, meekly went to do her bidding.

"Now, Major Andre's tree," she began. "You'll recall, of course, that he was captured by a few brave American militiamen, and turned over to General Washington and the Continental Army. He was found guilty of espionage and sentenced to hang, as is the custom for captured spies."

"He, of course, asked General Washington to have him executed by firing squad, as befits an officer," I interjected. "But since he was found on American territory in civilian clothes and not his officer's uniform, he was deemed a spy."

Mevrouw Douw nodded approvingly. "Quite right. So instead, he was hanged, one October day in, oh, what year was it?" She appealed to the gathered company.

"1781, was it not?" said Meneer Van Brunt.

"It was 1780, I am sure of it," Mevrouw Jansen said. "I remember it well."

"Yes, quite right," Meneer Van Brunt concurred.

"1780, yes," Mevrouw Douw continued. "He was hanged, and buried nearby, with only some stones as a burial marker.

"Now, as I mentioned, he was captured quite close to here, beneath a tree beside a brook, a short walk from this very house. And ever since his death, those passing by the tree claim to hear him wailing and lamenting, begging passersby to listen."

"They say he rails against his fate, against the poor luck that caused him to hang for Arnold's folly," Charlotte added.

"And some say he waits for Arnold's spirit to join him in the afterlife, so that he might finally have his revenge," I said, dramatically raising my eyebrows.

"Indeed," Mevrouw Douw said. "And mind you keep your eyes and ears out for him, Mr. Crane. You'll need to ride right past Major Andre's tree on your way home, and it would be a dreadful thing if he were to mistake you for someone else." She cackled.

Ichabod's face paled slightly at these words, though his smile stayed in place.

Just then, my father interrupted. "Please, my friends," he called. "My wife and I would like to invite you all to feast to your heart's content. Cook, if you would!"

Cook threw the door to the dining room open and motioned the guests to move inside.

The party filed in, and gasps of surprise and delight arose at the sight within. The room was decorated in similar fashion to the receiving room, though, if possible, with even more candles, garlands, and carved pumpkins. It was a lovely display, but not quite so lovely as the feast laid out on the long dining room table, which was surely groaning under the weight of its bounty.

Cook, Nancy, Mama, and I had been cooking and baking for days, and it showed. The table was laden with dish after dish to celebrate the harvest: fresh corn bread, roasted chicken and duck, mashed squash and potatoes, carrots glazed in molasses, roasted vegetables, fresh cheeses, beef stew. And the pies: savory meat pies and pumpkin pies and apple pies and cherry pies and peach pies. And, of course, Dutch *olie-koecken* and doughnuts with their hole in the middle, baked with fresh cider from the apple crop. I glanced behind me at Ichabod and saw his eyes were wide with surprise at the feast, at my family's generosity.

"Eat, drink, and be merry!" my father cried, and the guests all laughed and applauded and began helping themselves.

As it was each year, there were so many guests—and so much food—that it was not feasible for everyone to sit at one table. So, instead, the food was all set out, along with plates and cutlery, and smaller tables were arranged in rooms all over the first floor of the house. In some years, the weather had been so fine as to allow for tables out on the portico, but this year's weather made that impossible.

I hung back, allowing the rest of the guests to serve themselves first, as did my parents. In the crush, Ichabod came up alongside me. "When should I speak to him?" he murmured.

I tensed. "After dinner and dessert, and only after the brandy has been served," I whispered. "Some folks will start leaving around then."

He nodded once, then moved toward the table.

Once the guests had filled their plates, I got one for myself, though it did not contain very much food—my stomach was far too unsettled to eat much. Still, I forced myself to take a slice of roast goose—for I knew I'd need to keep my strength up—as well as some mashed potatoes (one of my favorite dishes), a slice of apple pie (another favorite, especially the way Cook made it—with extra cinnamon), and a doughnut.

I joined Charlotte and Mevrouw Jansen at a small table in the back sitting room. I did not know where Ichabod had found a seat, but I knew I could not go look for him. It was just for a short time longer that we would need to keep up such appearances, I reminded myself.

I ate as much as I could, and kept my glass filled with mulled cider. Soon enough the rum began to relax me slightly, loosening the knots in my stomach. I laughed as Mevrouw Jansen recounted a letter she'd received from her frivolous younger sister in New York, and Charlotte told me of their visit to her mother's friend a few weeks ago—and I, of course, pretended to be surprised to learn that they had visited West Point.

Soon the servants began clearing away the dirty plates and cutlery and glasses. We rose and meandered back into the receiving room, where my father now had the brandy set out.

"Ah, there she is!" he all but bellowed as I entered the room. "My Katrina! Isn't she a beauty?" he crowed to his friends.

Farmers of my father's age all, they nodded appreciatively, seeming to take my father's words as an invitation to ogle me. I smiled tightly and crossed the room to him. "You are too kind, Papa, as always," I murmured, kissing his cheek.

"She may even be the most beautiful woman in the state!" declared Meneer Stanwyck. "In all my trips to New York, I don't know as I've seen her like anywhere!"

"You may be right," my father said, eyes bright with amusement. "Why, once we were in a New York bookshop—you remember, Katrina, don't you?—and we met no less a person than Alexander Hamilton, the Secretary of the Treasury!" I rolled my eyes, but if Father saw me he was not deterred. "He was most taken with

Katrina, you know. Most taken. He's a handsome young man, and obviously rather brilliant, too—they say he is President Washington's right-hand man, and I say, better him than that puffed-up Vice President Adams, or that popinjay Jefferson, so enamored of France!" Here my father heaved a sigh. "Alas, he is married, of course, is Mr. Hamilton—but what a splendid match that would have been!"

"Oh, come now, Father," I sighed.

"That he is, and I don't think that even you, Baltus, can afford to dower your daughter as richly as old Philip Schuyler," interjected Meneer Van Brunt, naming Secretary Hamilton's father-in-law, one of the wealthiest landowners in the Hudson Valley and likely the state.

"Perhaps not," my father huffed, "but I still plan on making a splendid match for my Katrina all the same!"

Fretfully I searched the room for Ichabod, hoping that he still lingered over his meal or was in conversation with an acquaintance, and had not heard my father's pronouncements. But of course he was there, and of course he had heard. He could not hide the stricken look on his face as our eyes met, and I could read his thoughts as plainly as though he had written them down for me to read: *How can I ask for the hand of a woman whose father dreamed of marrying her to the Secretary of the Treasury?*

I bit my lip and looked away. We would go forward, no matter what, and pray my father's desire for my happiness would override his pride.

30

The Proposal

The brandy was flowing well, and guests were beginning to take their leave. I had thought the evening interminably long, yet now that our moment was here it felt as if it had arrived all too suddenly.

I moved to Ichabod's side in the parlor. "I must speak with you," I said in a low voice. "In private. Before you speak to my father."

Glancing around to see if anyone would notice, Ichabod nodded once, then left the room. I left a moment later, following him to the music room.

I closed the door behind us. "I . . . there is something you need to know," I said hurriedly. I had only just decided on this course of action, and now that I had embarked upon it, I could not go back. "I . . . I am with child."

Ichabod staggered back, as though physically struck. He stared at me in disbelief, the blood draining from his face. "You . . ."

"Of course I . . . did not mean for this to happen," I said, suddenly unable to look at him. "I had been trying to prevent it. But . . . anyway, it doesn't matter now. No matter what happens tonight . . . you needed to know."

A hesitant smile broke out on his face. "I will admit the timing is not opportune," he said. "And I would have preferred our first child be conceived in the marriage bed. But . . ." He trailed off and kissed me, deeply. "It is wonderful news all the same." He tried to smile again as we broke apart, but looked only nervous.

I could hardly blame him.

"Very well," I said. "I suppose the time has come, then."

"I suppose it has," he said. "All too soon and not soon enough."

After one last kiss, I turned and left the music room, returning to the parlor. Ichabod appeared soon after, strolling casually to my side.

"Now," I murmured to him, watching as my father bade farewell to Master Stanwyck.

Squeezing my hand once, swiftly, he crossed the room to my father. "Master Van Tassel," he intoned, somewhat formally.

My father spun around. "Ah, Mr. Crane!" he cried jovially. "A delight to see you, sir, an absolute delight. I hope you have enjoyed the party?"

"Very much, sir," Ichabod said, still sounding a bit stiff. "Your generosity truly knows no bounds."

"Not at all, my dear boy, not at all," my father said, clapping him on the back.

Ichabod spoke again, hurriedly. "I wondered if I might have a private word with you, sir."

My father looked somewhat startled, but recovered quickly. "But of course," he said. "Here, take a glass of brandy"—he motioned for Cook, who was nearby, to pour Ichabod a glass—"and come with me into my study."

Ichabod took the proffered glass and followed my father out of the room.

I felt like I might faint as I watched them go.

Charlotte materialized at my side. "Is it time already?" she whispered.

I nodded, reaching down and clutching Charlotte's hand in mine. "Oh, Charlotte," were the only words I could muster.

"Never fear," she assured me. "Do not worry. All will be well, I am sure of it."

Before I could ask whether she was speaking simply to ease my mind or had some other, more definite knowledge of what was to come, Brom was suddenly looming over us. "What is all this whispering about, ladies?" he slurred, breath reeking of drink.

"Nothing that concerns you," I said.

"Ah contrary," he said, butchering the French phrase. "I have the feeling it does concern me."

"Well, it does not," I snapped. "As shocking as it must be for you to realize, a great many things in the world do not concern you at all."

"Katrina," Brom said, and I was startled to hear a genuine note of hurt in his voice, a bit of pleading. "Why can't you—"

But I didn't want to hear whatever nonsense he had to say. "Leave us be, Brom," I said, and dragged Charlotte away, into the now empty dining room.

When he did not follow us, I whispered to Charlotte again. "I . . . I am going to wait outside the study. I cannot bear it. I . . ."

Charlotte hugged me tightly. "Do whatever you feel you need to," she said. "I shall be waiting here to congratulate you."

I flashed a thankful smile at her, then darted off to lurk outside my father's study.

And lurk I did, for quite some time, pacing nervously a ways down the hall from the door. What could be taking so long? Surely if it was good news, Ichabod would have emerged by now? Surely this meant Ichabod had been forced to reason, to persuade, perhaps to plead?

They had likely been closeted together for half an hour when Ichabod finally emerged. I froze mid-pace as he came toward me, his face ashen, stricken. "No," I whispered.

"He . . . refused me," Ichabod said. "He will not give his permission for us to wed." Every word was spoken in a stiff, solid, even tone, as though it was costing him dear.

"What?" I demanded, my voice shrill. I grabbed his hand and dragged him down the hall, into the music room again. "What did he say?" I asked, once we were both shut inside. I screwed my eyes shut. "My God, I am going to faint."

Ichabod gripped my arm tightly. "Do not faint, Katrina, I beg of you," he said. "Listen to me. Please calm down—"

"Calm?" I shrieked. "Our whole future has crumbled around us and you wish for me to be calm? How are you managing to be so calm, might I ask?"

"Because one of us has to be!" he exploded at last.

His outburst startled me. I took a deep, shuddering breath, closing my eyes. "Yes. I am sorry. You are right. Please, tell me what my father said."

He took a deep breath of his own. "He refused," he said, his tone again stark and cold. "He said that I . . . that he knew me to be a fine and upstanding fellow, and intelligent, but he was concerned I cannot provide for you. Concerned that I cannot give you the life that you most deserve." He lifted his eyes to mine, and the depth of sadness—and resignation?—I saw in them almost shattered the tenuous control I had over my emotions. "He's not wrong."

"Ichabod." His name came out in an anguished gasp. "You know that is not true. You know that does not matter to me."

"I tried to convince him otherwise," he went on. "I told him I know your heart, and that we love each other. He . . . he was unmoved. Apologetic, but unmoved. He told me it is because he has your best interests at heart that he cannot give his consent."

Tears slid down my face. "He is wrong," I whispered. "Oh, he is so wrong. Did you . . . did you tell him about the child?"

Ichabod looked thunderstruck at the very suggestion. "Of course not."

"Why not?" I demanded, frustrated even as a small bud of hope blossomed again in my heart. "If he knew . . . why, if he knew, he could not refuse! He must let us marry now!"

"I could not admit to him that we . . . that I . . . that I had dishonored his daughter," Ichabod said. "Not after he had refused me. I could not admit I had been a fool and wastrel enough to get you with my child. How could I?"

"How could you not?" I cried. "How could you not claim your

child, and the woman meant to be your wife? This child was conceived in love; there is no dishonor in that!"

"Oh, Katrina," he said, placing his hands on my shoulders.

"We . . . we must tell him!" I said, struggling to move away. "We must tell him the truth, and then he'll have to let us marry!"

"The disgrace—"

"I don't care!" I cried, weeping now. "I just want to be with you! Don't you want to be with me?"

He embraced me tightly before answering. "Yes," he said. "But, Katrina, it is not so simple as that. I wish it were."

"But it can be," I said, pulling away so that I could see his face. "If you do not wish to tell my father about the child, then let's run away together. Tonight."

"Now?"

"Tonight," I repeated. "Before anyone can know we're gone. We'll leave them all behind and start a life together, whether anyone else approves or not." I brought his hand to my mouth and kissed his palm. "Run away with me, Ichabod. Please. It is our best hope. It is our last hope."

There was a moment of terrible silence.

"No, Katrina," he said at last.

"But . . ." Tears began to well in my eyes again. "Why—"

"Hear me out," he said, grasping my shoulders again. "Please. Let us not make any rash decisions tonight. We are both upset and weary. Let us wait until morning, when we will see things more clearly. Then we can decide the best and wisest thing to do."

I wanted to rail at him, to reject his sound logic, demand that he leave with me that night, right then. But while our time was limited, we certainly had the luxury of a day or two to step back and evaluate our options.

I remained silent for a good long while, until I felt more in control. "Very well," I said. "If you insist."

"I do," he said. "It is the right course. You know that as well as I do, Katrina."

Childishly, I refused to agree.

"I love you," he whispered. He kissed me. "Never doubt that." He sighed and stepped back. "I should take my leave now."

Involuntarily, my hands tightened on his sleeves. "No, don't!"

"I must, Katrina; I certainly cannot stay here tonight," he said gently. "I will send word tomorrow, through Charlotte, to arrange a time when we might speak further." He kissed me again. "Do not despair, my love. Please, I beg you, do not despair."

I nodded, though I did not see how that was possible.

As we left the music room, I saw Brom at the opposite end of the hallway, lurking, watching us. His eyes narrowed, then he turned and was gone. But I was so shattered by the events of the evening that I could not bring myself to care.

I followed Ichabod to the front door, not caring who else might see us. He turned to look at me one last time. "All will be well," he promised me. His lips tasted like cider and brandy as he kissed me goodbye. And with that, he disappeared into the chilled All Hallows' Eve night.

31

Broken Things

I watched him go until the darkness swallowed him.

Then I turned and dashed to my father's study.

He was still seated at his desk, slowly turning his snifter of brandy in his fingers, contemplating the amber color through the crystal.

"Papa, why?" I cried, slamming the door behind me. I could not hold back my tears any longer. "Why will you not allow us to marry?"

"Oh, Katrina," he sighed.

"I love him!" I wailed. I was not making a compelling case for my maturity and ability to choose my own husband just then, but I could not help myself. I was breaking and could not stop to put myself back together. "I love him and he loves me! Why would you stand in the way of my happiness?"

"Katrina," he said, "I do not doubt that you and young Mr. Crane feel genuine affection for one another. Maybe it is truly love. But what you do not know—"

"We do love each other," I insisted.

"Perhaps you do," he allowed. "But what you do not know, nor do I expect you to know at your age, is love is not enough to sustain a marriage, nor a life together. You cannot live on love. And when he cannot provide for you as you are used to, what then?"

"I don't care about any of that!"

"So you say now," he said, "but the day will come when you will care a great deal."

"But I am to inherit the farm, anyway," I argued, trying reason now that pure emotion had failed—for the first time in my life—to move him. "We will have more than enough to live off of!"

"And in the meantime?" my father asked. "And even when you do inherit the farm, what then? Does Ichabod know how to run a farm so as to keep it profitable, let alone prosperous? He does not, Katrina. You know that. It is no easy thing."

"But I know how, Papa! You know I do—you have said as much yourself! I can help him!"

"Katrina." There was a note of pity in my father's voice. "Has it not occurred to you that perhaps his interest in you is motivated primarily—or at least in part—by his desire for your inheritance?"

In spite of myself, Ichabod's words came back to me: *I will not pretend that the thought of such bounty, such financial security and even wealth, does not excite me after so many years living on the road, and struggling.* I had thought them no more than honest, and perfectly reasonable. But could my father be right?

No, I swore to myself, as dozens of moments of love and affection and intimacy and passionate words tumbled through my mind. No. That cannot be.

But my father had seen my hesitation. "It will be better this way, Katrina, you will see," he said affably. "You may not think so now, but someday you will see the wisdom of my decision. You shall marry a man with prospects, means of his own, so that you are guaranteed a comfortable lifestyle."

"I will not marry Brom Van Brunt," I snapped. "No matter how much you desire him as a son-in-law, I will never marry him."

"There is no need for dramatics, Katrina," he said, sounding as though that rare thing was happening: his patience was wearing thin. "You need not marry Brom Van Brunt, if the idea is so odious to you. But someone of similar station and prospects. I must insist upon this."

Even in my near-addled state I recognized anything else I might say at this point would only further wound whatever chance still existed that he may change his mind. Without another word, I spun on my heel and stalked out of his study.

I found Charlotte almost immediately. "Katrina," she said, looking startled. "I was just on my way to see—why, Katrina, what is the matter?"

My eyes overflowed with tears again, and I drew her away into the front foyer, the nearest unoccupied space, so I could tell her all. The words poured out of me in a rush, like vomit, that they might be expelled as quickly as possible.

"Oh, Katrina," she said when I'd finished. "I know you were uncertain, but truly I believed your father would give his consent."

"Did you?" I flared up at her, needing to blame someone. "Or did you foresee this long ago, and not see fit to tell me? What were all those warnings about?"

She flashed a hurt look at me. "Of course I did not foresee this, Katrina," she said. "No, the warnings . . . they always had an echo of Brom about them, somehow. No doubt that was about the duel. I don't suppose he told your father anything?"

I bit my lip. I could not be sure, not after Brom had confronted me leaving the Jansen cottage. But if my father had known how far our relationship had progressed, he would have been far angrier. "There is little evidence of that," I said at last. "No, Papa's objections were no more than I had feared.

"But," I added, "Brom was skulking in the hallway when Ichabod and I left the music room, so I know not what he may now have overheard. I expect it does not matter."

Instantly Charlotte's face took on a troubled expression, but when she did not say anything right away I spoke again.

"Ichabod will be sending word through you tomorrow about meeting, so that we may discuss our options," I told her. I reached out and squeezed her hand. "This cannot be the end, Charlotte. It cannot. I won't let it be."

She still looked distracted, as though trying to see something that existed only behind a far-off fog, but she nodded. "Yes," she said. "I will be waiting for him tomorrow, then."

I hesitated, realizing that I had forgotten to tell her about the child. No matter. Quite enough had gone on for one night. I would tell her some other time, when my world had been righted again.

"Charlotte, there you are," Mevrouw Jansen said, stepping into the foyer. "It is time we took our leave."

Charlotte embraced me quickly. "We will speak tomorrow, I promise," she whispered. "Try to get some sleep, Katrina. That will be the best thing for you."

I nodded, unable to reply for fear I would start sobbing again.

Charlotte drew back and smiled at me encouragingly. "I'll see you tomorrow," she said.

I nodded again.

Mevrouw Jansen moved toward the front door, drawing her cloak around her. "Good evening, Katrina," she said, smiling. "Thank you for your family's wonderful hospitality, as always."

"Of course," I managed.

As mother and daughter stepped outside, I heard Mevrouw Jansen ask, "Is everything all right, Charlotte? You seem rather troubled." Yet then the door closed behind them, so I could not hear what reply my friend made, if any.

With Charlotte's departure, I suddenly felt weary down to my very bones. I could not bring myself to bid farewell to the few remaining guests just then. Instead, I trudged out to the barn to fetch Nox before making my way up the stairs to my room. I wriggled out of my dress, too tired to wait for Nancy, and left it in a heap on the floor. I changed into my shift and crawled into bed, pulling the covers up over my head. Despite all the turmoil in my mind, I was asleep almost instantly, Nox curled up beside me.

I do not remember the nightmares I had that night, only that they were dark and terrifying.

32

The Disappearance
of Ichabod Crane

I was awoken the next morning by Nancy's clucks of disapproval. She was shaking the wrinkles out of my gown. "What on earth possessed you to leave this beautiful dress crumpled up on the floor like rubbish?" she demanded. "You just disappeared last night, and couldn't even wait for me to help you undress, I see. Why, this might be ruined!"

"I have every faith in your pressing and laundering abilities," I mumbled.

Nancy straightened up and gave me her full attention, hands on her hips. "What's the matter with you?" she asked, eyes narrowing on me suspiciously.

"Nothing," I said automatically, like a surly child.

"Are you sure?" she asked. "Seems like something is troubling you."

"Nancy, I've said all of ten words to you," I said irritably. "Why does that lead you to believe something is troubling me?"

She sat on the edge of the bed beside me. "Because I know my girl," she said, her tone suddenly soft, softer than I'd heard it in years. "And I know when something is troubling her."

Tears sprang to my eyes, and before I could stop it I was weeping all over again.

"Oh, child." Nancy reached out her arms, and I fell into them. She rubbed my back and murmured soothing noises in my ear until I finally stopped crying. Then she helped me to get up and dress without inquiring further.

Once downstairs, I did not know what to do with myself. At some point, Charlotte would come with a message from Ichabod, or perhaps take me to an arranged meeting place. Until then, all I could do was wait.

Wait. The very last thing I felt able to do.

Unable to sit still, I wrapped myself in a cloak to ward off the chill and walked down to the river. I wandered along the bank, trying unsuccessfully to quiet my thoughts. Eventually I changed direction, making my way into the woods, just in case Ichabod was waiting at our spot by the stream. I did not truly expect him to be there, but even so, upon arriving the little clearing looked gray and cold and depressingly empty. I gave it no more than a glance before I turned and, shivering, headed back home.

The day soon trickled into afternoon, and still there was no sign of Ichabod nor Charlotte. At about three o'clock, I could bear it no longer and pulled on my cloak again. "Mother," I called, "I am walking to the village to see Charlotte."

"Have a nice time, dear," my mother said absently. She had not sought me out all morning, leading me to believe my father had not told her of Ichabod's proposal the night before. Depending on what transpired today, perhaps I could tell her myself and enlist her as an ally. She would likely be inclined to agree with my father initially, but no doubt I could bring her around, once she saw that Ichabod and I truly loved each other.

I had Henry saddle Starlight, and soon I was off, riding furiously for the village, Nox happily running alongside. When I arrived, I knocked loudly and urgently, and Charlotte answered almost immediately. "Katrina," she said, sounding unsurprised to see me. She let Nox and me in and closed the door behind us. "I was just about to come see you."

My heart leapt at her words. "You were? Ichabod has sent a message, then?"

Her forehead creased in a frown. "You don't know?"

Just as quickly as it had come, my elation was banished by the look on her face. "Know what? How could I know anything?"

"I thought someone might have come from the village to speak to your father, but I was just on my way to tell you in any case." She sighed and shook her head.

"Tell me what? For God's sake, Charlotte—"

"Mr. Crane," she said. "He is . . . he seems to be missing."

My body began to shake as if drenched in icy water as her words sank in, as they penetrated through my very skin and added weight to my bones.

"He . . . what?" I whispered. I did not feel capable of speaking louder. I reached down to pat Nox, as though reassuring myself that he, at least, was still there.

She took my hand and drew me down to the daybed, sitting beside me. "Apparently he did not return to the farm where he was lodging last night," she said quickly, as though to get the telling over with. "At first Meneer Van Ripper and his wife thought nothing of it, thinking he had elected to stay the night at your house rather than make the ride at too late an hour."

Oh, how I wished that he had. How I wished I had convinced him to do just that, in spite of everything.

"But then he never appeared at the schoolhouse for morning lessons, and some of the children went to seek him. Someone remembered seeing him leave the Van Tassel house last night, so a search party has been launched." She paused. "I thought that perhaps someone would have come to enlist your father's help, that you may have known already."

"No," I whispered. "No one came. And what . . . what of his horse? What of Gunpowder?"

Charlotte shook her head. "There has been no trace of him,

either. But surely that is a good sign, yes? He may have merely ridden off somewhere for a time." She squeezed my hand tightly.
"I am sure there is a reasonable explanation."

"And . . . the search party," I asked through my constricted
throat. "Have they found . . . anything? Any trace of him?"

Charlotte frowned. "I have not heard."

"Where are they?"

"I believe the plan was to inspect the road and its immediate
surroundings between the Van Ripper farmhouse and yours," she
said.

I rose quickly. "We must join them. We must . . . I must know
what they have found. Or what they will yet find."

Charlotte did not say a word to either agree or dissuade me; she
simply plucked her cloak from the peg on the wall, and followed
Nox and me out of the cottage.

"I did not see anything amiss on my way here, so let us go this
way and see what we find," I said, striding toward the Van Ripper
farm, which was half a mile or so past the church.

Charlotte hurried to keep up. "You did not know to be looking
for anything on your way here, and so perhaps did not notice something that—"

"One step at a time," I snapped at her. Instantly I regretted my
sharpness. I sighed. "I'm sorry. I just . . ."

"It is all right," Charlotte said, her tone even. "Let us go this
way."

We headed up the Albany Post Road, and it did not take long
before our efforts bore fruit.

As we approached the church, we could see a group of people
gathered on the bridge over the river than ran past it, the one that
had fed the mill pond of old Mr. Phillips's mill. They all gathered
at the railing of the rickety old bridge, talking and pointing at something in the water.

My knees buckled as black began to crowd the edges of my
vision. I clutched Charlotte's arm to keep myself upright. On my
other side, Nox pressed against me, as if knowing that I needed

steadying. "Charlotte . . . what . . . what are they looking at?" I gasped. "Is it . . . do you think . . . do you think they found a . . . a body?"

Charlotte slid an arm firmly around my waist and led me to the edge of the crowd. "Wait here," she murmured. "I will go see. Courage, Katrina." She slipped through the crowd until she reached the railing of the bridge.

Upon her quick return, I tried desperately to read the grim expression on her face. She drew me back a few paces from the crowd. "It is not a body," she said in a low voice. I felt faint again, this time with relief. "It is . . ." she shook her head, looking somewhat puzzled.

"What?" I demanded.

"It is . . . shards of a hollowed-out pumpkin," she said. "Littered on the bank. And . . ." She hesitated.

"What? Charlotte, for God's sake, what is it?"

"A man's hat, caught in some branches at the edge of the river," she said. "It . . . it looked like Ichabod's."

I felt as though I had been shot. I would have crumpled to the ground entirely if Charlotte had not held me up, with a strength belied by her slender frame. "It may not be his," she said quickly. "But everyone seems to think so."

"Let me see," I said, shoving her away, my resolve giving me new strength. I pushed into the crowd and to the railing.

I clutched the rail of the bridge, white-knuckled, for support. It was indeed Ichabod's hat; I was certain of it. Yet its presence in the stream was innocent enough, was it not? It may well have flown off his head as he rode over the bridge. It may mean nothing at all. Most likely it meant nothing at all.

The broken pumpkin was less easily explained. Or was it? Perhaps someone had tossed a pumpkin in the stream for whatever unknown reason. It need not mean anything at all.

The murmurings of the villagers began to break through my fog. "Aye, 'tis his hat, all right," one farmer spoke up. "I've seen it upon his head meself."

"You saw the tracks in the dirt along the road there," Mevrouw Maarten said to Mevrouw Douw, and pointed. Hoof prints dotted the muddy ground of the road behind us, imprinted with such force that the horse must have been moving at great speed. Horses, I realized, taking in the number of prints.

"Indeed," Mevrouw Douw said. "We all waste our time here. 'Tis plain for anyone to see that the Headless Horseman has carried him off."

I whirled to face her. "What did you say?" I demanded.

Mevrouw Douw cackled. "Don't tell me that you tell all the stories but don't believe them, young Miss Van Tassel," she said.

"But the Horseman is . . . he *is* just a story," I protested feebly.

"You are a fool if you believe that," she said. "And young Mr. Crane ought to have paid more heed to the stories, as well, it seems."

I spun away from her and pushed my way back to where Charlotte stood. All around me, the whispers circled. *Carried off by the Horseman, aye . . . He must have been . . . The Galloping Hessian has struck again . . . The Horseman has taken him, no doubt . . . Poor Mr. Crane.*

"Charlotte," I gasped. "It cannot be true. It . . . cannot be real."

"I shouldn't think so," she said, hesitation in her voice.

"You don't believe it, do you?"

"No," she said, though she didn't sound entirely convinced. "Do you?"

"No," I replied, the same note of uncertainty in my own response.

She gestured upstream, to where some men had set out along the bank. "They are searching the stream," she said. "In case . . ." She trailed off and bit her lip.

"In case they find a body," I finished. "We will stay until they finish searching."

Charlotte did not reply; she merely gripped my hand with her own, and we settled in to wait.

———

They did not find a body, and once the search had ended Charlotte took me back to her cottage, allowing for no protest. By then I was shivering uncontrollably, both from the cold and my own unbearable anxiety.

"Tea, I think," Charlotte said. She steered me to the daybed and disappeared into the kitchen to boil some water. I sat, huddled within my cloak until my shivering began to subside. Nox laid himself on my feet, and I took some small reassurance from his warmth and proximity.

"I know how dire this seems, Katrina," Charlotte said, after putting the kettle on. "But you must try to think objectively. There is a perfectly logical explanation for all of this. His hat might have flown off his head; the pumpkin likely means nothing; and his disappearance may be perfectly explainable, even understandable. Perhaps he has ridden off somewhere to try to clear his head after last night. He might have gone to see his cousin Giles. He may well have been in need of a friendly face and a sympathetic ear after last night. Or perhaps he is even now trying to make a plan for the two of you and wishes to finalize some arrangements before returning for you."

The rational part of my mind knew that she might well be right, but I waved her words aside even so. "Perhaps, but above all, he must know that I need to speak to him. He must. After everything. And we are running out of time. He knows that."

Charlotte's brow creased in confusion. "What do you mean? Katrina, there is plenty of time. Your father has not yet promised you to anyone else."

I groaned. She still did not know I was with child. I glanced around the cottage. "Where is your mother?" I asked, my voice low.

"Out, seeing one of the village women. She's been out all day. Katrina, you've gone quite pale. What is it?"

I took a deep breath. "We are running out of time because I . . . I am with child."

Charlotte gasped, one hand coming up to cover her mouth. "Oh, Katrina," she whispered. "Are you sure?"

"I have only missed one course so far, but yes, I am sure."

"One course need not mean anything, though," she reasoned.

"I am sure," I repeated. "I have never missed one before, but even more so than that, I . . . I am just sure. I can't explain it."

Charlotte nodded quickly, acknowledging what she of all people understood. "And so you needed to obtain your father's permission and marry quickly," she said, "so when the child is born, no one is the wiser about when it was conceived."

"Yes."

Charlotte sat back against her chair, her face ashen now as she comprehended the full extent of my predicament.

"And so Ichabod, knowing this," I continued, "knows we do not have time to lose. Whatever we are going to do, we must do it now."

"So you told him about the child, then."

"Yes, right before he spoke to my father. I deliberated about telling him, but I decided that, whatever might happen, he had a right to know."

Charlotte considered this for a long moment—too long. "Yes, I suppose that is true," she said at last. "But surely you can afford another day, if that is what he needs."

"He should know me better than that!" I exploded. "He should know that I need him with me, to reassure myself. He promised he would send word, and he has not. He is not even in Sleepy Hollow, that much seems certain. What am I to make of that?"

Charlotte had no answer to that, nor did I expect one. Instead she rose and returned with two mugs of tea. "But how did you come to be with child?" she asked once she sat down again.

I shot her an exasperated look. "Surely I do not need to explain it to you."

"That is not what I mean," she snapped. "Were you not taking the herbs I gave you?"

"Yes, I was, but one night I forgot," I retorted. "And do not think you can possibly reproach me more than I have reproached myself, Charlotte. This is a complication that I did not need."

Charlotte rubbed her forehead. "Let us not argue, Katrina,"

she said at last, though I could still hear traces of irritation in her voice. "That is something else neither of us needs at this point."

"Yes," I said shortly.

We were both silent as we sipped our tea, as neither of us trusted ourselves not to further the argument. The tea was spiced with cinnamon and cloves, and the more I drank, the more relaxed I felt. I glanced up at Charlotte in question.

"Skullcap," she said, before I could ask. "It will help calm your nerves."

Wordlessly I took another sip. It was a long time before I spoke. "Where is he, Charlotte?" Even to myself, my voice sounded like a tiny, broken thing.

"You must not fret so, not when we do not have enough information," Charlotte said. "If he has gone to see his cousin, no doubt he is riding back now, and will find all the fuss in the village to be quite ridiculous."

"Do you really think so?" I asked, desperately wanting to believe her.

"It seems most likely," Charlotte said, getting to her feet. "But we can write to Mr. Carpenter, just to be sure." She glanced at the clock. "Of course, at this hour, by the time we write and send the letter, we likely won't receive a response until tomorrow, but at least it would give us something to do. Some way of being sure, if perhaps Ichabod has decided to stay another day."

He would not stay away another day, I objected silently, for he knows that I need him. "I suppose you are right," I said, willing to go along with her plan—Charlotte was just trying to help, after all. And there was a chance, of course, that she was exactly right. Or so I tried to tell the leaden dread in my stomach.

Charlotte got a sheet of paper and pen, and I jotted a quick note to Giles Carpenter. "How will we send it to him?" I asked as I sealed it. "I do not know his direction."

"I have it," Charlotte said. "He left it for me after the duel—he asked that I write to him to let him know how Ichabod fared."

I was not so lost in my own fear and uncertainty that I did not detect the faint flush in Charlotte's cheeks, and the way her voice rose just slightly to a higher register. "Oh?" I said, raising my eyebrows. "He did, did he? And did you write to him?"

"I did as he asked," she said primly. "I let him know his cousin was quite well and would make a full recovery."

"I see." When she did not elaborate, I left it at that. If there was more to the story, Charlotte would tell me in time. Or I would drag it out of her at some other, more convenient moment.

The letter written and addressed, Charlotte and I took it to the inn, where we found a willing messenger. "Am I to wait for a reply, miss?" he asked me as I handed him a few coins.

"Yes," I said. "Do not leave without one."

"Very good, miss. I'll likely wait until morning to take the road back." He grinned widely. "There's a lass in White Plains I've been meaning to call on, anyway."

I rolled my eyes at this as we bade him farewell. He could do as he pleased, so long as he brought me my reply in the morning.

After returning to Charlotte's cottage to collect Nox and Starlight, I rode home, before it grew too dark. Yet I found I almost could not bear the thought of what awaited me: a full night of uncertainty, of having no idea where Ichabod was, or why he was there and not with me.

I arrived home in time to dine with my parents, and sat woodenly through the meal, hardly saying anything. Neither commented on my silence; no doubt my father, at least, thought I was still angry about his refusal of Ichabod's suit.

After supper I pleaded a headache and went to my room, where I allowed Nancy to undress me and see me to bed. Practically as soon as I lay down, I rose again and went to the window, looking out over the river. When I finally got into bed, I buried my face into Nox's fur and wept. He whined and craned his neck around to lick my face, and though it did nothing to fix all that was wrong, it afforded me a small measure of comfort.

33

God or the Devil

The next morning, I barely heard my excuse to my mother for why I was going to see Charlotte again. We had directed the messenger to take Giles Carpenter's reply to the Jansen cottage, so Nox and I dashed to the village once more, me riding Starlight.

When she came to the door, she had an opened letter in her hand. "The messenger's just been," she said. With no further explanation, she handed me the letter and closed the door behind me as I stepped inside.

My eyes skittered over the page so quickly I almost could not make sense of the words written upon it. I forced myself to take a deep breath, and then read the letter slowly.

My dear Miss Jansen and Miss Van Tassel—
Thank you for your letter. Unfortunately, Ichabod is not here, nor has he been to visit me of late. The last time I saw him was the day I made both of your acquaintances. I confess your inquiry has greatly unsettled me. My cousin has no other relatives or friends in the area, and so I am at a loss as to where he might have gone. I shall write to his mother in Connecticut, to see if he has perhaps gone there for some reason. I will of course relay whatever I discover, and beg you to also keep me informed

should you yourselves discover anything of his whereabouts. It is quite unlike my fastidious cousin to disappear without word to his loved ones, but nevertheless I am sure there is a satisfactory explanation to be had.

G. Carpenter

I lowered the sheet of paper with a trembling hand.

Charlotte's eyes were wide with fear she could not conceal. "I . . . I confess I had not expected this," she whispered. "I was so sure he must have gone to see his cousin. I did not even begin to think what else . . ." She trailed off.

I turned toward the door. "We . . . we could go to the Van Ripper farmhouse," I said. "See if he has returned." I no longer bothered to puzzle out why he had not come to seek me out or sent me word; all I cared about was knowing where he was.

Charlotte shook her head, and my hand froze on the doorknob. "No need," she whispered, a note of near-agony in her voice. "As soon as I read the letter, I went to the schoolhouse to find him. Many of the students were just leaving when I arrived. He has not appeared to teach, and so they were returning home."

I sank to my knees. "Charlotte," I gasped, "where . . . do you think he . . ." I could hardly speak. "What . . . what do I do?"

She knelt beside me, an arm wrapped around my shoulders. "We wait to hear what Ichabod's mother tells Giles," she said, her voice faint. "And we . . . we wait. We wait to see if he comes back."

Charlotte helped me to the daybed so I might lie down, and went to fix me some more skullcap tea. The whole while, all I could hear were her last few words.

We wait. We wait to see if he comes back.

If he comes back.

As I sipped my tea, Charlotte, good friend that she was, voiced every possible explanation for Ichabod's disappearance, however unlikely. The only one she failed to mention, the one neither of us wished to speak of, was the one voiced by all the villagers at the bridge yesterday. When I could bear her reassuring chatter no longer, I left, for she was almost as nervous and unsettled as I.

Yet as soon as I arrived home and took to my room to endlessly pace the floor, I found myself wishing I had stayed at Charlotte's. For here there was nothing to listen to but my own thoughts, and those were far, far more intolerable than Charlotte's chattering.

Ichabod had disappeared, and no one knew where he was. Part of me clung passionately to the idea that his mother must know something. Yet the rest of me could not find such a scenario plausible, no matter how much I may have wished it. Why would he have left for Connecticut in the middle of All Hallows' Eve night, on an old, broken-down horse like Gunpowder, with nary a word to anyone? Even if my father's refusal had so succeeded in scaring him off and away from me, he would not shirk his duties at the schoolhouse. Not Ichabod.

Had some ill befallen him that night? An accident with his horse? Had he fallen into the river? No body had been located, but what if he had been swept away, swept under?

Or . . . it had, after all, been All Hallows' Eve, the night when spirits and demons were said to be free to roam. Could Mevrouw Douw and the rest of the villagers be right? Could it truly have been the Headless Horseman? Had he appeared and somehow carried Ichabod off—or worse? Was such a thing really possible? I shivered, remembering how we had all spoken of the Horseman at the party, so casually invoking his name on that haunted night. And I remembered that terrible feeling all those nights Ichabod and I had spent in the woods, when I had been so sure that someone was watching us, that there was more lurking amongst the trees than nocturnal creatures.

The vision that had come to me in the candle flame came back to torment me in its every detail. Two figures in the woods, one chasing the other. The unmistakable sounds of a struggle. The whinny of a horse, and the sound of a blade—a great blade like the one the Horseman carried—being drawn from its sheath.

Charlotte had claimed I had the Sight, so what other answer could there be? I had sought answers beyond those readily available in the mortal realm. And this vision came upon me right before Charlotte drew the future card. Had I truly seen the future, and seen the truth of Ichabod's disappearance? It was the Horseman, it had to be; Ichabod had come across the Headless Horseman on All Hallows' Eve, and the specter had done him harm. That explained the broken pumpkin found beside his hat, for did the Horseman not carry a pumpkin in place of his missing head? If he . . . *oh God* . . . if he had taken a head to replace his own he would have no further need of the pumpkin, would he?

No. I must scoff at such superstitious nonsense, fit for the more simpleminded, certainly, but not someone like me; not someone educated and well-read. The Headless Horseman was a legend and nothing more; he could not appear and carry off mortal men, for such things were impossible.

But this foray into sense and reason did not bring me any solace, for all too soon I arrived at the least palatable answer of all: that Ichabod had never loved me, not truly, and after my father had refused his suit he fled, knowing he would never see a cent of my inheritance. He had taken his pleasure while he could, while I so brazenly offered myself to him, but when he saw there was no further profit to be had he left.

My stomach roiled and twisted as I recalled telling him of the child—our child—just before he spoke to my father. What if that had been the final straw? Otherwise he might have stayed, been willing to try again. But learning I was pregnant and that we were refused permission to wed had been too much for him. He had fled like a thief in the night rather than be forced to face his responsibility. Perhaps he had been recalling all the stories told at the party that night, and all the stories he had begged me to tell him; perhaps he had planted the pumpkin and his hat in the stream to fool the superstitious villagers. To fool me.

I cursed myself repeatedly as I replayed the moment I had told him of the child. If I had held my tongue, might he still be here with me now? Would withholding the news a bit longer have changed everything?

But did I want a man who would run like a coward at such an admission?

Oh, he could not have left me! Not Ichabod, not like this! I began remembering every passionate and tender moment we had shared together, the love in his touch and his eyes and his words. That was real; I would have known if it was not, would have seen it over all those months. Again and again I kept returning to his words on the night we first made love.

God and the devil together forbid that I shall ever be without you again. A life without you would be no life at all.

Never stop saying such things to me . . . never leave me.

Never. I will die first.

I will die first. Somehow I could not shake those words, despite how, more and more, logic and reason seemed to indicate Ichabod had left me. Those words had not been a lie. They could not have been.

And if those words had not been a lie . . . then had God or the devil intervened?

Maybe there truly was a Headless Horseman . . .

He could not have left me. Could he?

The next few days passed in an agonizing haze. I either paced my bedroom anxiously, or I slept, a deep sleep, the sleep of the dead. It was only in slumber that I could escape my worries and my fear. Each time I lay down a part of me wished that I might not wake. Not unless I could wake to Ichabod by my side.

I scarcely ate, despite Nancy's coaxing. My parents checked on me often but did not inquire as to the source of my distress. Likely by then my father had told my mother of Ichabod's proposal and his own denial, and they assumed I was simply heartsick and would recover given time.

And, no doubt, the rumors from the village only fueled their belief in my heartbreak.

I only left the house to go to the village and meet Charlotte, to wander through the market and listen for word of Ichabod. It was the talk of Sleepy Hollow: the disappearance of schoolmaster Ichabod Crane, last seen on All Hallows' Eve at the Van Tassels' harvest party. No one had seen hide nor hair of him since—save for the very telling evidence of the pumpkin and hat at the church bridge.

It had soon become accepted as fact that young Mr. Crane must have run afoul of the Headless Horseman, out for his midnight ride. If the schoolmaster had somehow survived the encounter with his own head still attached—unlikely, in the opinion of the farmwives—clearly he had fled the area out of fear, never to return. And who could blame him?

The worst part was I could not even be certain they were wrong.

Days passed, and soon I could hardly bring myself to leave my room, let alone the house. Finally Charlotte came, with another letter from Giles.

"Ichabod's mother has not seen nor heard from him," Charlotte reported, sitting beside my bed. Nox lay across my legs, seeking to protect and comfort me. "Her last letter from him was dated mid-October, well before All Hallows' Eve." She handed me the sheet of paper. "You may read it for yourself if you wish."

I scanned the page listlessly. Sighing, I let it drift to the floor. My last hope—flimsy as it had been—was dashed. I scarcely felt the pain of it; my heart was already in so much agony that one more wound hardly made a difference.

"He sent another note, as well," Charlotte offered. "Giles, that is. Almost as though he were unsure whether to send it when he wrote this letter."

"What did it say?"

"He asked if I thought he should come to Sleepy Hollow, if there was anything he could do here."

It took almost more energy than I had to shrug. "He needn't

bother. He knows nothing we do not already know. What would be the point?"

"He . . . well, he suggested he might ask around, inquire of the villagers if they knew or had seen anything. As Ichabod's cousin, he has cause to ask questions. We do not; not in a manner that would be appropriate."

I could not have cared any less what was appropriate or not under such circumstances. "Given the volume of gossip, we would hear straightaway if anyone knew something," I said. "They would be falling all over themselves in their haste to be the center of the gossip mill."

Charlotte narrowed her eyes at me. "Well, certainly it could not hurt to have Giles come ask a few questions," she said. "What else do you propose we do?"

I had no answer to that.

Charlotte, however, seemed to interpret my silence as hostility. "And has it occurred to you that perhaps I might wish to see Giles Carpenter?" she asked.

The selfish, merciless brat in me wanted to rail at her for finding some measure of happiness in my anguish, for using my tragedy to further her own romantic prospects. The rest of me, though—the part that was a good friend—knew no matter how hard it might be for me now, I was happy for her, happy she had found someone to take a shine to. For too long her romantic prospects in Sleepy Hollow had been nonexistent, thanks to Brom's slander. A handsome gentleman from another town was just the thing.

But I was too lost in my own pain to tell her that. "Have him come, if you wish," I said, sliding down in the bed again and turning my back to her. "You do not need my permission."

Several more days passed, and still there was no sign of Ichabod, and still the villagers could talk of little else. When it occurred to me that lying in bed brooding all day was likely not helping my state of mind, I forced myself to ride into the village again, leaving Nox at home, for even he had begun to look at me with worry in his eyes.

Luckily, I found Charlotte alone. Giles Carpenter had indeed come on her invitation, and though he was staying at the inn, I had no doubt he had called on Charlotte many a time since his arrival.

"Katrina," she said, sounding surprised when she opened the door. "Come in. I'm glad to see you up and looking . . ." She trailed off.

I gave her a wan smile as I stepped inside. I knew what I looked like; my face pale and drawn, with dark shadows under my eyes; I was thinner as well, from eating very little over the past week. "It is all right," I said softly.

She nodded and motioned for me to sit. I settled myself carefully in a chair, as though my bones were brittle and fragile now, liable to break. "Has Giles discovered anything through his inquiries?" I asked.

Charlotte reluctantly shook her head. "I'm sure you were right. If anyone knew anything they would have added it to the gossip mill long ago," she said. She covered my hand with hers. "I am so sorry, Katrina," she whispered.

I shook my head, tears springing to my eyes. Good Lord, was there an endless well of tears inside me? "I did not expect anything else," I said quietly. "He has left me, it seems. He must have. I have been over it and over it and—"

Charlotte tilted her head thoughtfully. "He may have, I suppose," she said. "But it makes no sense. If he had simply left of his own accord, why hide from Giles or his mother?"

I shrugged listlessly. "Who knows? Perhaps he did not want to admit that he impregnated the woman he claimed to love and left her." I wanted so desperately to believe that Ichabod had not left me, but what else could have happened? "And if he did not leave of his own accord, where is he?" I demanded. "If he met with some sort of accident, surely someone would have found further sign of him. If he . . ." I shuddered. "If he fell from his horse and broke his neck, they would have found him beside the road. But he has simply vanished, almost without a trace."

Charlotte was silent for a long time. "You don't think . . ." She trailed off and bit her lip. "You don't think the legends are true?"

"I can think of little else," I confessed. "One moment I am sure he has left me, and the next I think it must be true, that the Horseman is real and rides in the night." I paused. "Do you remember the vision I had?" I asked.

She nodded, sadness pooling in her eyes. "I do," she said softly. "I wondered if you did."

"As I said, I can think of little else." I put my head in my hands.

"And you . . . you actually saw the Horseman?" she asked. "In the vision?"

I lifted my head. "I did not see him, not clearly," I said. "Just shadows. But I heard the horse, and heard him draw his blade . . ." I moaned softly. "And I've dreamt of him . . . of him standing between me and Ichabod . . . oh, Charlotte, what else could it mean? I . . . I do not think I ever believed, not truly, but . . . it must all be true, mustn't it?"

She had no answer for me.

A short time later, after I had calmed down a bit and Charlotte had made us some tea, insisting I take a biscuit with mine, she brought up a subject I had been desperately trying to avoid. "And so . . . what of the child?"

I was unable to meet her eyes. "I don't know."

She stared hard at me until I had no choice but to look at her. "What do you mean, you don't know? Surely you realize that you must decide, and soon."

I rose to my feet in agitation. "What choice do I have?" I asked. "I must wait and hope Ichabod comes back, that we may marry and our child be legitimized."

Charlotte waited a long time before saying quietly, "And if he doesn't?"

I turned my face away from her.

"I am sorry, Katrina," she said firmly, "truly I am, but you must face the facts. He may never come back. And so you must protect yourself." She took a deep breath. "I can make you a potion, you know."

I stared at her, uncomprehending.

"A potion," she clarified, "to rid yourself of the child. It is easy enough to do. You will likely be sick for a few days, but better that than you are found to be with child and unwed." She frowned at me as I continued to stare at her in shock. "Why are you gaping at me like that?"

"I . . ." My mouth was dry as I attempted to speak. "I cannot. I will not. I . . ." I crossed my arms over my belly. "This is Ichabod's child. Ichabod's and mine. I . . . I cannot simply rid myself of it."

"Katrina, what choice do you have?" Charlotte demanded. "You know well what will happen if you are discovered pregnant out of wedlock. Your parents may be indulgent of you, but they are not so indulgent as to let you stay at home and raise your bastard."

"How dare you—"

"I dare because that is what this child is, and all anyone here will ever see it as," she said. "What kind of life is that, for the child or for you?"

"I just . . . I cannot," I said again.

"I do not see as you have a choice."

"Ichabod may still come back."

Charlotte looked at me, for the first time, with true pity in her eyes. "He may," she allowed. "But that seems less likely every day. And so you must make a decision before your condition becomes apparent to everyone."

"I cannot do it," I said stubbornly. "No matter what. Not his child."

"So you lied to me before."

"What? When?" I asked, confused.

"When you said you did not know what you were going to do

about the child. You lied. You do know. You mean to have it, no matter what it may cost you."

"Charlotte," I said, my voice anguished, "this child may be all I ever have of him. Can't you understand that?" My voice broke as I articulated to her what, until now, I had only felt down in my very bones.

"I can," she conceded, "to a point. Where I confess I begin to lose my understanding is why you wish to keep any pieces—let alone a child—of a man who would abandon you when you need him most."

"We do not know for certain that he abandoned me," I retorted hotly.

Charlotte met my gaze evenly. "No," she said. "That is true. We do not."

I turned away from her, the tears spilling down my cheeks now. Yet was not the idea of him leaving preferable to that of him having been murdered by a vengeful specter? At least the former would mean he still existed; that he was still out there, somewhere, alive and well.

"I . . . I cannot decide anything yet," I said at last. "I need more time."

Charlotte nodded in concession to this point. "I can well understand that," she said. "But you do not have too much time, Katrina. I know you know that, but I think it behooves you to hear the words anyway."

34

Search for Salvation

The next day, my parents, it seemed, felt I'd had more than enough time to wallow in my despair. I could not fault them, for they did not know the true extent of it, yet still I could not entirely forgive my mother for summoning me downstairs. "Katrina," she said, standing in the doorway of my bedchamber, "we have a visitor. Get dressed and come down, please." She stepped aside so Nancy could help me dress.

Perhaps playing hostess for an hour or two would not be the worst thing in the world. At the very least it would take my mind off of my incessant worrying.

Once dressed and my hair hastily pinned back, I went downstairs to the parlor. I stopped dead in the doorway when Brom Van Brunt rose to his feet upon seeing me. "Oh," I said, coldly. "It's you."

He bowed slightly. "I heard you have been unwell, and wanted to see how you fared," he said, his tone perfectly courteous. "I am glad to see you up and about."

Without another word, I turned to leave.

"Now, Katrina," my father's voice said, stopping me. Slowly I turned back into the room. "There is no need for such rudeness. Mr. Van Brunt is only asking after your health, after all."

I did not have the strength to make a battle out of this. Not today. "I thank you for your concern, Mr. Van Brunt," I said tonelessly. "I am well."

Brom smiled. "It is a fine day out," he said. "Rather warm for November. I thought you might indulge me in a stroll?"

"Very well," I said, noting the warning glance from my father. I fetched my cloak, brushed past Brom, headed out the front door and toward the river.

Brom jogged slightly to catch up. "You are moving so quickly that you must be quite recovered from your illness," he said.

I was not reassured by his courteous tone; quite the opposite, in fact. No doubt he had some fresh torment for me hidden up his sleeve. "What do you want?" I asked finally. "Why are you here?"

He looked surprised. "What do you mean?" he asked, taking my hand and threading it through the crook of his elbow. "I told you. I heard you were unwell and came to see—"

"I did not realize my health was the talk of the village," I interrupted.

"It is not," he conceded. "But I had not seen you about much, and I figured that you were upset by . . ." His gaze hardened slightly. "By the disappearance of the schoolmaster."

I wrenched away from him. "Do not you dare speak to me of him," I spat. "Do not act as though you have any sympathy for what I am going through."

He stood, motionless, watching me. "I imagine you must be in a great deal of pain," he went on, as though I had not spoken. "I know what he was to you, and for him to abandon you like that . . ."

I almost slapped him. "That is not what he has done," I retorted.

"Then what do you think has happened?" he asked, sounding genuinely curious.

I whirled away from him, unwilling to let my uncertainty show. "It could be anything," I said. "In any case, you can have no proof he abandoned me, so before you continue with such slander—"

"Oh?" Brom said, storming forward, his anger finally rising. "No? Well, the rumor in the village is he asked Baltus Van Tassel for your hand and was refused. And so he disappeared rather than face the disappointment and shame."

This time I did slap him. "Is that so?" I hissed. "My health may not be the talk of the village, but my marriage proposals are?"

"You have just confirmed it yourself," Brom said, raising a hand to where I'd struck him. "You must accept the truth, Katrina: Ichabod Crane was only after your inheritance. And when he saw he would never get his hands on it, he simply left to try his luck elsewhere."

I went to slap him again, but he grabbed my wrist. "How dare you," I said, fighting not to let Brom see me cry. "You know him not at all; you know nothing of what was between us."

"And what do you think happened, Katrina?" he asked. "I suppose the Headless Horseman came and carried poor innocent Ichabod away?" He chuckled mirthlessly and tossed my arm aside. "Believe that, then, if it makes you feel better."

"Why are you here?" I asked him again. "Did you expect now that Ichabod has vanished, I would fling myself into your arms?"

He shook his head and stepped closer to me, taking one of my hands in his. "No. Of course not. This has not gone at all how I wanted." He squeezed my hand gently. "My offer still stands, of course. I have not formally spoken to your father, but you need only say the word and I will make you my wife."

With a glare, I whirled around and stalked back up to the farmhouse. I did not know if he followed me, and I did not care.

The next day, Charlotte came to visit. "I heard Brom was here yesterday," she said, once we were alone in my room.

"Good Lord, is everything that happens here the talk of the village?"

Charlotte cast me an impatient look. "In any case," she said, "what did he have to say?"

"What you would expect," I said. "He acted as if he was full of concern for me, then informed me that Ichabod had surely left me, but he was still most willing to take me as his wife."

Charlotte shook her head in disgust.

"And yet," I said to myself, realization suddenly dawning now, "he does have a point."

"About what?" Charlotte demanded, looking alarmed. "Not that you should marry him, surely?"

"Of course not," I said. "But . . . I could get married. To someone."

Charlotte waited in shocked silence for me to explain.

"It could be my way out," I said. "My only way out. If Ichabod never returns . . ." My breath caught in my throat as I spoke the words aloud, but I soldiered on, "If he never returns, then I must protect my child, as you said. If I married soon, then everyone will assume the child is my husband's."

"Katrina . . . you cannot be serious."

"What other choice do I have?" I demanded, my voice rising sharply. "What would you have me do?"

"I already told you my suggestion," she said. "But you dismissed it out of hand."

I closed my eyes. I had considered doing as she advised, but only for a moment.

But I loved this child already, had loved it since I learned of its existence. And now, this child—son or daughter—was all I had left of Ichabod. I could not simply rid myself of it.

"I cannot, Charlotte," I said. "Do not ask me to."

"I think you are making a mistake," she said. "You would not be the first woman in the village to do so, you know. Nor would you be the last."

"I don't care. I won't."

She sighed. "And so where will you find an acceptable suitor to wed in a matter of weeks? Has any man but Brom approached your father?"

"I do not know, in truth," I said. "But I will speak to my father, and tell him I am ready to wed as he sees fit. He told me he would not force me to marry Brom against my will, so surely he must have someone else in mind."

"I do not know about this, Katrina," Charlotte said. "But you must do as you think is best, I suppose."

I took that as a sign she could not hear the sound of my heart breaking.

35

October's Legacy

Once Charlotte left, I went to see my father in his study, before I lost my nerve. After all, was I really ready to commit to marriage with a man I would barely know, if indeed I knew him at all?

And what if I did marry and then Ichabod returned for me?

That was a chance I had to take. For my child. Wasn't it?

I knocked on the door to my father's study and he called for me to come in. I entered and sat in one of the chairs before his desk. "I wanted to speak to you, Papa," I said.

"Of course, my dear," he said, setting aside the ledger he'd been examining.

I took a deep breath. "I am ready to marry, I think. And as you have said you will not force me to marry Brom if I do not choose to, I assume you have some other suitors in mind."

My father looked somewhat startled. "Why, Katrina," he said. "I knew not that you were in such a hurry."

"Not a hurry, per se," I said carefully. "I just feel it is time."

"Well, perhaps we should think on this more," he said, leaning back in his chair. "After all, you were quite disappointed at my refusal of young Mr. Crane's suit." He gave a harrumph of derision. "Of course, seeing as how he vanished into thin air right after said refusal—leaving his duties at the schoolhouse behind without a thought, I might add—I made the right decision, as you now no doubt agree."

I said nothing.

"But you may need a bit more time, my dear. There is no rush. You can marry when you are ready, and a suitable suitor has been found."

"But I am ready," I said, trying not to sound impatient. "And so I wondered if you had anyone else in mind."

"Well, no. I cannot say I had anyone in particular in mind, nor has any man approached me, save for young Mr. Van Brunt, of course. But if you are certain you are ready, I can begin to make inquiries over the coming months. I am sure we shall have no short-age of candidates, what with your fine dowry."

Yet your perception that Ichabod was interested in my dowry was what prompted you to refuse him, I thought with a spark of anger. Honestly, what sense did any of these rules make? It was to be expected when they were created by men, I supposed. "I see," I said. "No one else has approached you—no one at all?"

"No, though as I said, I will be happy to make inquiries, if you are certain that this is what you want. Yes," he said, warming to the idea, "yes, we may be able to see you married by next year at this time."

My heart sank. By this time next year? No, no, that would never do. "All right, then," I managed, rising from my seat. "Thank you, Papa."

"Of course, my dear. Whatever will make you happy."

It would have made me most happy if you had allowed me to marry Ichabod, I raged inwardly, even as I gave him a dutiful peck on the cheek.

Woodenly, I left his study and walked up to my room. I needed a husband, within the month, if there was to be any hope of my child being accepted as legitimate. My father went on about what a sought-after prize I was, that he knew of many potential and ac-ceptable suitors. But apparently not. Apparently all along there had only been Brom and Ichabod.

Of course, if I did truly need a husband, any husband, in a matter of weeks . . .

No. That was not an option. Even for my child, I could never consider it.

Gingerly, I pressed my hands against my still-flat belly. But truly, I wondered, is there anything I can afford not to consider?

The next day, I went to visit Charlotte, to tell her of my conversation with my father. She listened in silence, then shook her head when I finished. "It does seem surprising, based on things your father has said. But . . ." She bit her lip.

"What?" I asked.

"It . . . in a way, it does not surprise me," she said. "For there is talk . . ." She looked as though she wished she had not brought this up, whatever it was.

"Talk about what?" I demanded.

She sighed and gave in. "There is talk in the village—"

"Not more silly village gossip," I interrupted. "There is nothing they do not talk of in this village, it seems. It is a wonder the crops get planted and the market can run, for it seems no one in Sleepy Hollow does anything but talk."

"If you do not wish to hear such talk, I will not tell you," she said. "Indeed, it may be that you would rather not know."

That stopped me. "Very well, then, tell me."

"I mean it, Katrina. I do not say that to entice you further."

Now I had to know, in that contrary way that humans have. "Tell me, Charlotte, please."

"Very well. If you are sure." She paused before. "There is talk that Brom may have had something to do with Ichabod's disappearance. They say he learned of Ichabod's proposal and did something to scare him away, to make sure he left you and Sleepy Hollow behind and never came back. To ensure Brom had no rivals for your hand."

Somehow, I had never considered this. "And you believe this, do you?"

She shrugged. "Not particularly, no. Ichabod was—is—not a man so easily cowed, not where you are concerned. And he knew you would not marry Brom no matter what, so I do not see how Brom could have convinced him."

But it would not have surprised me in the least if Brom had tried. "And so?" I said. "Is that all? News I could have eventually put together for myself?"

"Think about what it means, Katrina," Charlotte said. "It does not matter whether we believe it, only that others do. And they are already saying it: no man will dare court Katrina Van Tassel now, for fear of crossing Brom Bones."

"But this is nonsense," I said, trying to push back a wave of despair and frustration. "Brom does not have such power. He cannot be that intimidating, surely?"

"It seems he is," she said. "Anyway, I am only telling you what people are saying. And, unfortunately, many of them are saying it."

I rode home in a daze. There was too much information to be absorbed, too many choices to make, yet not enough of them.

What was I going to do?

There was always Charlotte's option. I could rid myself of the child, and wait as my father made his inquiries, wait until he found a suitor I liked and maybe could grow to love, just as I would have done if I had never met Ichabod.

Or I could not marry and still have the child, try to carry on as best I could in the face of the scandal that would erupt. I could wait as long as I wanted—forever, if need be—for Ichabod to return.

Yet I knew that this was not a choice, not really. If I were to be found with child and unmarried, my parents would never let me keep it. The best I could hope for would be to be sent away to some secluded place to give birth, then the child sent to another family or, worse, to an orphanage.

Or they might send me away in my shame, and cut me off completely. I did not truly think they would—my parents loved me too much for that—but it was a possibility, I supposed. No one would fault them for it. And how would I support a child on my own when I had no way of supporting or even of caring for myself? I could cook, and mend, and run a house, of course, but I had never lived without servants to assist me with even the most basic of tasks.

One thing was certain: I would not be able to raise this child in any kind of comfort without a husband. And that left me with only one option.

I stabled Starlight when I returned home, but instead of going into the house I went out into the woods. I walked the familiar path alone, to Ichabod's and my favorite spot on the banks of the stream. Save for my brief visit after All Hallows' Eve to see if Ichabod awaited me, I had not been there in weeks; not since the day Brom had discovered us and challenged Ichabod to the duel. It had become spoiled, tainted, for me after that. Yet I could not bear to be anywhere else just then.

When I arrived, the clearing was so undisturbed that it seemed as if no one had set foot there since Ichabod and I had last been here—and likely no one had.

I fell to my knees on the damp ground and wept loudly in this place where no one could hear me.

That night I dreamed again, of the Horseman. It was the same as before: he stood in the fabled clearing far off in the forest, and I could glimpse Ichabod standing behind him. I started to run toward him, heedless of the Horseman's presence, words of love and relief on my lips: *You are back! I have found you! You are here!*

Yet unlike before, the Horseman did not move to block my view of Ichabod. This time, the specter allowed me to run right past him toward my lover—even as my dream-self shivered at coming so close to the Hessian. Yet then Ichabod was gone, had simply disappeared. He had not turned and run, nor faded into the shadows;

he was simply there one moment and gone the next. I tore through the forest, shoving branches out of my way, calling his name all the while. Yet I never saw another trace of him.

Far off now, I heard the loud whinny of a horse.

Then I awoke.

I lay still, unable to move, letting the tears course down my face. For I was now certain I would never see Ichabod again.

36

Star-Crossed Lovers

I stayed in bed all the next day, pleading a headache. I slept some, but mostly I tossed and turned, debating my options over and over again. Nancy brought me my meals, and I forced myself to eat, for the child's sake more than my own. It was certainly the least taxing thing I was prepared to do for my child's sake.

Time was running out.

The following day I rose as normal, and just after lunch slipped out into the gray day.

I made my way back to my and Ichabod's spot by the stream. I walked slowly, trying to take in every step. This might well be the last time I would venture there.

Once I got to the clearing I sat down, my skirts pooling around me, heedless of dirtying my dress. I closed my eyes, letting the sounds of the forest drift around me—quieter now that winter was approaching—and remembered.

I allowed myself to remember every word, every kiss, every touch. To remember every time that we had made love, in this very spot, the sensation of him inside me, of the pain that first time and the pleasure that had followed. To remember how it felt to be so wholly connected and wrapped together so that we became one person, two halves of a whole.

I remembered the promises, the plans for the future, the hopes and dreams we'd shared. I remembered the love and tenderness in his eyes when he looked at me, spoke to me, remembered the times we'd laughed together.

It was all gone now. All in the past. And I had to say goodbye to it.

I bid farewell to every memory, hoping they would not return to torment me, even as I longed to clutch them to me forever. And I wept.

Ichabod would forgive me. He would understand what I had to do, wherever he was, and he would forgive me. Even if I could not forgive him for leaving me behind, for leaving me to make this choice, however his disappearance had come about.

Goodbye, my love.

As the sunlight filtering through the branches began to weaken, and the sky faded into twilight, then darkness, I began to sing, softly at first, then louder. My voice was rough and ravaged by tears, but I did not care. I sang the song of the lotus and the willow, the star-crossed lovers who were kept apart from each other. I sang it and I cried.

Once full darkness had fallen and I had finished the song, I rose to my feet and left the clearing, forbidding myself to look back. I walked slowly back toward my house, and I did not fear the Horseman coming upon me, not that night.

Let him find me, I thought dully. Let him find me and kill me and save me from what I am about to do.

As though he knew what I planned, Brom appeared at the farmhouse again the next day.

I was ready, as ready as I could ever be. When my mother came to tell me that he was here, I brought my cloak with me and met him in the receiving room.

He bowed when I came in. "Katrina," he said. "I hope that you continue to be in good health."

"Might we walk?" I asked.

He took in the cloak I was already wearing over one of my warm dresses and nodded. This time I took the arm he offered as we made our way to the river once again.

"I am glad you have come today," I said, once we were several paces from the house.

"Oh?" he asked. "Given my usual reception, I am surprised to hear that."

"Indeed." I stopped walking and turned to face him, ready to say what I needed and set all the wheels in motion and have done with it. "I have decided I will marry you."

Surprise, and a look of triumph that he could not entirely hide, crossed Brom's face. "Oh?" he said again. "And what has led to this abrupt and rather astonishing change of heart?"

"That is none of your concern."

"Is it not?" he asked, cocking his head at me, a grin on his face. "Surely I have the right to ask the woman who has agreed to marry me why she wishes to do so?"

I shrugged half-heartedly. "I must marry someone," I said. "Better it be you than some stranger."

He eyed me suspiciously. "You will forgive my doubts, Katrina. I seem to remember several vows you made along the lines of your preference for death over marrying me."

Death was indeed something I had considered, however briefly. "And yet you persisted in your suit," I said. "It seems you do not give your charms enough credit." My God, how was I saying such things without vomiting?

Dunce that he was, he looked heartened by this. "Well, that is true."

"I do have two conditions, however."

"Ah," he said. "I was correct. There are strings attached."

"There are," I said. "But just this: the first is I wish us to be wed as soon as possible."

Brom looked torn between delight in his good fortune and wariness. Fortunately for me, his delight won out. "That can be arranged easily enough, I should think," he said. He grinned again, though this time it was more of a leer. "Eager for the marriage bed, are you, Katrina? Eager to see what it's like to have a real man in your bed?"

My face burned with both embarrassment and rage. For he was exactly right. As much as I might dread it, we must be wedded and bedded as soon as possible, so that he might believe the child I carried was his. But I would endure anything if it would mean my child would be safe. "I have never had any man whatsoever in my bed," I said. After all, Ichabod and I had never made love in *my* bed, specifically. I would need to convince Brom I was still a virgin. "So my . . . instruction in that area will fall wholly to you." God help me, but I did gag slightly, at those words, and his look of joy as I spoke them. Fortunately, he did not seem to notice.

"I am wholly in favor of this first condition," he said. "And what is the second?"

"The second is that I shall ask you a question, and you must answer me truthfully."

"Easy enough."

I took a deep breath before speaking again. It was a dangerous question, but if I was going to marry him, I needed to know. "The rumors in the village," I said. "I must know if they are true."

"And which rumors might these be? Sleepy Hollow is rife with them, as you do not need me to tell you."

"The rumors that say you somehow scared Ichabod off for asking for my hand in marriage," I said. "Did you? Did you say or do something to frighten him away, to make him leave, so you might not have a rival for my affections?"

He studied me.

"I will know," I said, "if you lie to me."

"I believe you would," he said. "But no, I did not. I did not attempt to frighten him off. I did not do or say anything to intimidate him or scare him away from Sleepy Hollow."

I searched his pale blue eyes, but saw only sincerity in them. He was telling the truth, it seemed. And though I did not know if this was the answer I had hoped to hear, I believed him.

"Very well, then," I said, turning back toward the house. "My father is in his study. You had best speak to him and secure his permission for our marriage. Let him know we wish to wed as soon as possible."

"It will be my pleasure," Brom said. "I've no doubt your father will be very pleased as well."

No doubt he would be.

"Katrina," he said with uncertainty. "This is truly what you want?"

In that moment, at the genuine concern in his tone, I softened toward him just a bit. Maybe being married to him would not be quite the nightmare I had feared.

Want, I had learned, was a very slippery word. "Yes," I said. "It is. There are many things I wish to leave in the past."

I could see from his expression that, with these words, I had erased the last of his doubts.

We walked the rest of the way to the house in silence, and Brom went to speak with my father.

37

Wedding Plans

My parents insisted Brom stay for dinner that night, and instructed Cook to prepare a celebratory feast. Many toasts were drunk, and plans for the wedding commenced immediately. The first week in December was deemed the soonest that the ceremony could take place. Meanwhile I practiced wearing the happy mask I would need to wear for the rest of my life.

When I went to bed that night, I was surprised to find myself filled more with relief than dread. It was done; we were betrothed and the wedding date was set. There was no turning back now.

Yet when I awoke the next morning, I was faced with a task that I did indeed dread. I needed to go to the village at once to tell Charlotte the news myself, before she could hear it from the village gossips—or, worse, from Brom himself.

Would Charlotte forgive me for marrying her greatest enemy, once mine as well?

I had lost so much; I could not lose Charlotte, too.

I knocked at the door to her cottage, and she answered almost immediately. "Katrina!" she said brightly. "Come in; Giles Carpenter is about to drop by, and . . ." She trailed off as she caught sight of the grave expression on my face. "What is it? Has . . . is there news of Ichabod?"

"No," I said, feeling a wrenching in my heart at his name. "But I do have something to tell you, and I would rather do it before Giles gets here, if I can."

"Come in, then; sit down." She motioned me inside, and we took our usual seats in the front room. "Whatever is the matter?"

I studied the worn carpet on the floor. Now that I was here, I did not know how to begin. "I . . . I have made a difficult decision," I said at last. "I have turned it over and over again in my mind, and I can see no other way."

"What is it? Katrina, you are frightening me."

I met her eyes. "I just . . . I hope you will forgive me."

"Katrina, what have you done?"

"I . . ." I swallowed. "I have agreed to marry Brom Van Brunt."

Silence.

Finally, she spoke. "If this is a jest, it is a very poor one."

"It is no jest. I . . . I wish it was."

"You cannot be serious."

"As the grave. Oh, Charlotte—" I rose and moved to take her hand, but she snatched it away. I flinched. "Surely you must see that I do not have another choice."

"There is always another choice," she snapped. "I myself gave you one. You cannot truly believe you have no choice other than to marry the one person I hate the most, the man who tried to ruin my life and who would have likely seen me dead if he could?"

"I do not want to marry him," I said. "It is not out of love or desire, and it is certainly not to hurt you. I truly do not have another choice that I can see. Not one that allows me to keep my child, my and Ichabod's child, and raise her in safety and comfort."

Charlotte went silent, and I realized that, for the first time, I had said her in referring to the child. A warmth spread through me at how right it felt. Hmmm, I mused to myself, my hands resting on my belly. A daughter, my and Ichabod's daughter. I could not help it; though this was hardly the time, tears sprang to my eyes.

Charlotte's face softened. "I hate that this is happening to you," she said finally. "You should not be upset on my behalf. You should be upset at what your own life is going to become, married to one such as him."

"I have thought of all of that, Charlotte. Believe me. But I can see no other way. I do not believe that Brom is any the wiser as to my motives; he never knew for certain that Ichabod and I were lovers. He will likely not doubt the child is his. It will come a bit early for it to be his child, of course, but such things happen."

"And what will you do if you marry him and Ichabod returns?"

She had hit on the one question that threatened to hold me back, even at the last. "Then I will ask him why he left me, alone and carrying his child, for so long. And I will ask him what else he would have had me do."

"But you do not think he will come back."

"No," I said, pained, even now, to admit it aloud. "No, I think that whether because he cannot or will not, he is never coming back."

She sat silently. "This will not be easy for me, seeing you marry Brom Van Brunt," she said at last. "I cannot pretend otherwise. But I know it will be much more difficult for you."

I nodded. It was the most I could hope for right then. "Thank you for understanding."

"You must do what you think is best." She rose at last from her seat. "Just promise me one thing."

"Anything."

"Promise you will still make me the child's godmother when she is born."

I smiled at Charlotte's use of *she*. "You need not even ask. I will be counting on her Aunt Charlotte to help me raise her."

"I will," Charlotte said. "I will love her to pieces. And I will tell her stories about her true father, once she is old enough to understand."

"We will both tell her such stories," I said. Then I was weeping again as Charlotte held me.

———

After that, plans for the wedding—which soon became the talk of the village—happened at a rapid pace. My mother and Cook were all too happy to handle the arrangements, and I was just as happy to let them. I did not care about any of the details; what food would be served at the wedding feast or what gown I would wear. It was all rather painful, actually, when I realized how much joy and care I would have taken in such decisions had I gotten the chance to plan my wedding to Ichabod. But as it was, I simply wanted it over and done with, the sooner the better.

In addition to the generous dowry he settled on me—and with the promise of assuming ownership of both the Van Tassel and Van Brunt farms someday—my father snapped up a cottage in the village that had recently become available as a wedding gift for Brom and me. My heart ached anew at this reminder of the life Ichabod and I had planned, and the bleak reality that I would now be living that future with another man. The only thing that gave me any solace was that the cottage was near the Jansen cottage, only a few houses down and slightly larger. Brom could hardly be thrilled by this proximity to the woman he so hated and feared, but by taking me as his wife he had assured Charlotte's presence in our house whenever I saw fit to invite her. And he would hardly say no to a house bought and paid for.

Soon after Brom and I had announced our intentions, my mother came to see me in my room one morning. "Katrina," she said, sitting beside me on the bed, "are you sure this match is what you want? I hope you are not simply acquiescing because you know it is what your father would have chosen."

I gave her my most winning smile. "I have had a change of heart, Mama. I have known Brom forever, and it is a good match, as Papa has always said. It is time I married and moved ahead with my life."

My mother had nodded, still searching my face probingly, but in the end she seemed convinced enough and was more than willing to let herself be swept up in the excitement of the wedding plans.

Maybe she did not know me as well as I had always thought.

Either that, or I was a convincing enough actress to grace the stages of Europe.

As it turned out, though I should not have been surprised, Nancy was the one who truly remained unconvinced.

The night before the wedding, she came up to help me undress and found me sitting motionless on my bed, legs crossed beneath me in a most un-ladylike fashion, staring absently as I stroked Nox's head. This was the last night I would spend in this room, something that had not occurred to me until just that moment.

"Miss Katrina," she said, coming to stand before me. "You all right, girl?"

I looked up at her blankly, unsure how to answer her.

She sat beside me. "Miss Katrina," she said, her voice soft and serious now, "you sure about this? You really want to marry him?"

I drew a deep, shuddering breath and looked down, picking at the threads of the quilt. "Yes."

"That don't sound very convincing to me."

I didn't reply.

"Look, Miss Katrina," she said, "you don't have to marry this man. You can still change your mind. Your parents might be upset, after all this fuss, but they'd forget about it soon enough. They love you." I could feel her scrutinizing me closely. "And I know you don't love Mister Brom."

Finally, I looked up at her. "What difference does it make?" I asked softly. "Love rarely enters into marriage. You know that."

"It makes a difference," she said, her voice suddenly heated, "because I know well that that isn't the kind of marriage you wanted for yourself." She paused. "And it's not what I wanted for my baby girl."

Tears sprang to my eyes, for oh so many reasons: because Nancy was right, because she had seen right through me, because she had seen what even my own mother had been unable—or unwilling—to see. "I don't have a choice," I said through my sobs.

Had she asked me, then, what I meant, I would have told her

all. I knew she wouldn't betray me. But either she already knew, or was willing to wait until I was ready to confess unprompted, for she didn't say anything. She only drew me into her warm embrace, just as she had when I was a child, letting me wring myself dry on her shoulder.

"Come with me to my new house, after I'm married," I said, when I recovered myself. "Come work for me. Please. I need you still, Nancy."

"I'd be glad to," she said. "So long as your mama can spare me, of course."

"I'm sure she can. I'm sure she will, if I ask it of her."

"And I'm thinking your husband might have something to say about what servants are hired," she added.

I rolled my eyes. "He can say whatever he likes, but it need not make a difference to me," I said. "He is making himself very rich with my father's money, and as such I shall hire whatever staff I desire."

Nancy chuckled and patted my cheek. "Now that's my girl."

38

Mistress Van Brunt

The day of the wedding dawned unexpectedly mild and sunny for early December—as if the weather was mocking me, I thought dejectedly as Nancy helped me into a bath and began the process of washing my long, thick hair. Nox was again banished to the barn, and I missed his soothing presence beside me. Once bathed, I sat in a chair by the large downstairs fire to aid with the drying of my hair. All too soon Nancy assisted me in donning my brand-new white underclothes—silk and lace, ordered special from New York—and my champagne-colored gown. It was from my last trip to New York with my father, back before I'd ever met Ichabod, long before any of this started. There hadn't been time to have a new dress made, so my mother and Nancy had added some new lace and ribbons to this one.

Then Nancy put up my hair, weaving braids and ribbons in a crown about my head and leaving the rest to hang down my back. She curled the loose strands around a poker heated in the fire. When she was finished, she had me stand to look at myself in the mirror above my dressing table. "You look absolutely beautiful, Miss Katrina," she said, taking in my reflection. "Just gorgeous."

Her words, kindly meant though they were, caused my eyes to

brim with tears. "There, there, darling," she murmured softly. "I know. This isn't an easy day."

Thankfully, she said no more, for if she had I am certain I would have broken down entirely, and all the guests would see what an unwilling, miserable bride I truly was.

My parents were waiting for me at the bottom of the stairs as I descended. My mother gasped aloud. "Oh, Katrina," she said. "You are a vision."

I smiled what I hoped was the smile a beautiful, happy bride on her wedding day would wear. "Thank you, Mama," I said.

My father kissed my cheek. "Just beautiful, my dear," he said. I was surprised to see tears shining in his eyes as he stepped back. "We are all very happy today."

I kept my smile pinned to my face. At least someone is happy today. Truly, the only unhappy ones on my wedding day were Nancy, Charlotte, and I.

"Thank you, Papa," I said. I cleared my throat, trying to steady my nerves, which had begun to mount steadily ever since I'd come down the stairs. "Shall we go?"

My parents, Nancy, and I went out to the carriage waiting outside the front door. We climbed in and Henry snapped the reins, carrying us off to the village church, where most of Sleepy Hollow's residents—and my bridegroom—were awaiting us. Awaiting me.

I took several deep breaths as the carriage rattled on, taking me closer and closer to the destiny I would not be able to escape. I chose this, I reminded myself. It is the best way. It is the only way.

I was determined not to think—yet—of what would come later that night. My skin crawled at the very thought of Brom in bed with me, of him . . . no. I must not think about it, or I would never be able to go through with the marriage vows. And for the sake of my child—Ichabod's child—I must do it all.

Perhaps it would have been better if I were a naïve virgin on my wedding night, I thought wryly. I might have less cause to dread it.

And yet if I had been a virgin, I would not be in this position. I would not be marrying Brom at all. Perhaps I should have listened to all those rules about how unmarried women should comport themselves.

"You are very quiet, Katrina," my father said, interrupting my thoughts. "And rather pale. Are you quite well?"

I very determinedly did not look at Nancy as I answered. "Yes, very well, Papa," I said.

"Just nerves, I'm sure," my mother said, smiling gently at me.

"Yes, very much so," I said.

All too quickly, we had arrived at the church, and my father was helping me down from the carriage, while my mother and Nancy went inside to take their places in the pews. We paused just outside the doors. "Are you ready, my dear?" he asked, beaming at me.

No. "Yes, Papa," I said, smiling.

He pulled open the doors, and we stepped inside.

The congregation rose as we appeared, and I could hear the gasps and appreciative murmurs as everyone took in the lovely picture I made. I tried to smile at them all, to glow and blush with the happiness they were all so sure I was feeling. None of them could know that inside, I was screaming; that in my heart I was crying and praying for someone to save me from myself and this decision I had been forced to make.

When we reached the altar, I could ignore him no longer.

Brom stood before the minister, dressed in a neatly pressed suit. The grin on his face was one part genuine happiness, one part smug triumph. And in that moment what I hated most of all was that, after everything, he had won.

Damn him. Damn him to hell and back. I shall never forgive him.

Nor, I realized, would I ever forgive myself.

Brom took my hand, his grin widening as our fingers touched. I looked down at the stone step that led to the altar so I did not have to meet his eyes as I stepped up beside him. Once we were both standing in front of the minister, I looked straight ahead. It was the only way I could endure it all.

The minister began the wedding service, and as he droned on

I caught Brom sneaking glances at me out of the corner of my eye. I kept staring determinedly forward. I would not face him, face the life I had chosen, until I had to.

When the time came for the vows, and the minister had us face each other and clasp hands, still I cast my gaze modestly down. Hopefully Brom would merely think of me as the nervous, blushing bride.

"Do you, Abraham Van Brunt, take this woman, Katrina Van Tassel, to be your wife? To have and to hold, in sickness and in health, until death do you part?"

"I do," Brom pronounced.

"And do you, Katrina Van Tassel, take this man, Abraham Van Brunt, to be your lawfully wedded husband? To have, hold, and obey, in sickness and in health, as long as you both shall live?"

I dreamed that Ichabod would fling the church doors open just then, announcing to all that he had come to claim me. He would come to save me from this choice I'd made; he would save me before it was too late.

But of course, that did not happen. Closing my eyes, I could only speak the words through clenched teeth. "I do."

We exchanged the rings, and the minister pronounced us wed, in sight of God and man. Brom leaned forward and kissed me, and I was glad that it was only a chaste kiss, here in the church before the congregation.

Hand in hand, we made our way back down the aisle. I caught Charlotte's eye as we walked, and saw that she understood my feelings completely. The unsmiling look she gave heartened me all the same, if only a little. For her, at least, I would not have to pretend.

I could not hide the tears that were streaming down my cheeks. I could only hope those watching took them for tears of joy.

We returned to my parents' house for the wedding feast. Upstairs, one of the spare bedchambers had been prepared for us, and tomorrow morning we would move into the new house my father had bought for us. But I would not—could not—think beyond the feast just then.

Brom and I sat at a table on a raised dais in the dining room, with two long tables for the rest of the guests. Cook brought out each dish and served us first, before serving the rest of the company, assisted by the other servants. As early December was the time when the pigs were slaughtered, my parents had had an entire roasted pig prepared, which caused murmurs of appreciation among the guests. Several kinds of potatoes, fresh white bread, squash, and glazed carrots were also served. Nancy gave me a wink as she passed me, carrying jugs of wine and beer, and I smiled—the only genuine smile I had given all day.

Throughout the meal, Brom would occasionally lean over to kiss me—much to the approval of the guests—and to whisper in my ear. "Are you happy, my bride?" he murmured soon after we sat down. "Are you happy to be Mistress Van Brunt?"

My stomach twisted at the name unfurling from his lips. "Of course," I lied with a smile.

The words tasted bitter in my mouth, surely poisoning me from within. Every word, every smile, felt like a betrayal: of Ichabod, of our love, of myself. Yet had I not been betrayed first? That I took no joy in my perfidy was no consolation.

The servants kept my glass filled with wine, and I imbibed liberally, for I would need it to get through what lay ahead. Brom, too, drank his first glass of wine, then called for ale; then, after dinner, my father had the brandy poured.

"To the bride and groom!" my father called, lifting his brandy glass. "To the new Meneer and Mevrouw Van Brunt, that their marriage may be long, fruitful, and happy!"

"Hear, hear!" the guests echoed, and everyone drank.

Interesting that happiness should be the last of the things I am wished in my wedding toast, I thought as the brandy burned its way down my throat. I hoped it would take me into oblivion.

———

After the feast came dancing, and then the moment I had been dreading arrived: it was time for Brom and I to retire. "Come, Miss Katrina," Nancy said, finding me in the crowd. "Time for you to come upstairs, and I'll help you out of that gown. Your husband will follow after."

Charlotte appeared at my side. "Nancy, may I steal the bride away for just a moment before you take her upstairs?" she asked sweetly.

Nancy smiled. "Of course, honey." She moved a few steps away to give us some privacy.

Charlotte took my hands in hers, quickly slipping me a small glass vial. "Chicken blood," she said.

My nose wrinkled in disgust. "Whatever for?"

"For you to sprinkle on the sheets." Her face darkened slightly. "You know . . . after." She lowered her voice until she was barely audible. "So Brom will think you were a virgin."

Finally I understood. "Thank you," I murmured, my hand closing tightly around the vial. "I would never have thought of this."

She smiled, and this time it was genuine. "I know, so that's why I did." She embraced me tightly. "Be strong," she whispered in my ear. Then she drew back, gave me a swift, tight smile, and went to return to her seat. The crowd shied away from her as she passed, and I felt a flash of anger that she should still be treated so, at my own wedding feast. That I had married the man who had made her life this way.

I pushed the guilt aside, for it would not do me any good this night. I looked around for Nancy, and she caught my eye and motioned me to the doorway.

There were some shouts and ribald cheering as Nancy led me out of the room, and I glanced back to see Brom watching me lustfully, his face red and ruddy from drink. I shuddered as we left. I chose this, I reminded myself. And I must endure what is to come next above all else if I am to protect my child. I had said it to myself a thousand times since I'd decided on this course, but it did not make me any more eager for what was to come.

In the nuptial chamber that had been prepared, and bedecked with chrysanthemums and branches of evergreen, Nancy took down my hair and helped me out of the gown. When she was not looking, I slipped the vial into the drawer of the small table that stood beside the bed, where I could easily reach it once Brom was asleep.

Once undressed, wearing only my new silk underthings, I stood motionless in the center of the room. I tried not to remember that first night in the woods, the one that had felt as sacred to me as a wedding night, and far more holy than this one would be. I tried not to remember Ichabod removing every stitch of my clothing, his hands, his mouth, the feel of his bare flesh against mine . . .

I was snapped from my reverie by Nancy placing a light hand on my shoulder. I jumped, startled. "You all right, Miss Katrina?" she asked.

I nodded, but it took me a moment to speak past the dryness of my throat. "Yes. Fine."

She pulled me into a tight hug. "It's gonna be all right," she murmured in my ear. She released me and stepped back. "I'll see you in the morning, yes?"

I nodded, unable to speak.

She gave me one last encouraging smile and then left the room, my wedding gown draped over her arm, closing the door behind her.

Slowly, I got into the bed, pulling the covers over me. And I waited, staring at the ceiling, dread slowly encroaching its way up my body to choke me. If only it could be morning and this night, at least, might be over . . .

The one night Ichabod and I had spent in a bed together came back to me. I remembered the feel of my back pressed into the mattress rather than the hard ground as he thrust deeply and hungrily into me, remembered my back arching up to meet his thrusts as I cried out, drenched with sweat and pleasure . . .

I closed my eyes and shook my head where it lay against the pillow, tears leaking out of my eyes again. No. I must not think of that. Must not compare the wonder and glory of lovemaking to what would be, for me, a wife's duty. It was strange to think the same act could take on such different meanings.

Soon I heard heavy footsteps in the hallway, and the door burst open. Brom came in, swaying slightly on his feet. "Wife," he slurred. "Already waiting to welcome me into your bed, I see."

He bent down to remove his boots and shirt. As he pulled off his breeches, I turned my gaze away.

Naked, he stumbled to the bed and got in beneath the coverlet beside me. "I have waited so long for this night," he mumbled. He pressed his lips to mine, forcing my mouth open. I tasted the drink on his breath as his tongue probed my mouth, and did not respond. In his inebriated state, he did not seem to notice.

"Ahh, yes, my sweet," he murmured. One hand moved up the inside of my thigh. I fought the urge to clamp my legs tightly together, but I forced myself to relax.

He shifted closer to me, his hands pulling up my silk shift. Apparently he did not wish to bother removing it.

Good. Let this be over with. I would not think of all the future nights when I would be expected to perform this duty again. Surely it would get easier with time; surely this first bedding would be the most difficult. Wouldn't it?

"Ahh, yes," he murmured again as his fingers reached the apex of my thighs. Made clumsy by drink, he shoved two fingers into me, probing roughly, and I did not bother to stifle my cry of pain.

He let out a small sigh, perhaps taking my exclamation for one of pleasure. He withdrew his hand, beginning to shift atop me. "Yes," he grunted, then stopped. "Damn it," he slurred. He reached down to take himself in his hand. "Come on," he growled, moving his hand quickly over himself. He leaned down and kissed me again, harder this time, moving his other hand to grasp my breast.

I glanced down to see the issue, and nearly bit off my tongue in an effort to hold back my giggles. His member was limp, even as he tried desperately to rouse himself. It would seem that too much drink had unmanned him.

No matter how he kissed or pawed at me—even biting my neck in an attempt to arouse himself—he remained flaccid. Finally he rolled off me with a groan. "Damned brandy," he murmured, closing his eyes. "Too much." Within moments he was snoring.

I let out a sound that was half laugh, half sob. I had a reprieve, it seemed, and did not know if I was more relieved or anxious at this turn of events.

I turned on my side, my back to him, and curled into a ball. It was a long time before I fell asleep.

39

Husband and Wife

For as little sleep as I managed to get, I woke quite early, just as dawn light was slipping in through the curtains. I assumed it was Brom's presence, the unfamiliarity of having someone in bed with me, that woke me. The one night I shared a bed with Ichabod I had not slept much, either, though that had very much been by design.

I squeezed my eyes shut to hold back the tears. How many times must I say goodbye to these memories before they would leave me?

Beside me, Brom stirred with a groan. I stifled a laugh again. No doubt the drink that had made him unable to perform had left behind a mighty ache in his head as well.

He caught me looking at him. "If it isn't my wife," he mumbled.

My stomach turned at the word, at how it sounded coming out of his mouth.

"My wife," he went on, becoming more alert with each word, "in name, but not yet in deed, if I recall."

I went still, not answering him.

"Drink can do that to the best of men, I'll have you know," he told me, sitting up halfway. "If I recall, I promised to show you what a real man is capable of."

Somehow I found my voice. "I shall have no basis for comparison," I said, hoping there was a flirtatious note in my voice instead of the deadness I felt, "so I shall have to take your word for it."

I had thought I would have a reprieve until that night at least, but—good. Get it over with.

Then the child will be safe, no matter what comes after.

Moving with more swiftness and purpose than I would have expected of a man in his state, Brom drew me against him, his body half covering mine as he kissed me deeply. This time, I knew with both disappointment and relief, would be much different from the night before. His mouth moved hungrily, confidently over mine, and his hands moved surely up my body. "You are overdressed, wife," he murmured against my mouth.

How rude of you to remain dressed when a lady is unclothed. The words I'd spoken to Ichabod before we'd first made love sprang unbidden to my mind, and I gasped aloud at the pain of the memory striking at that moment, like a knife slid between my ribs by a friend.

Brom mistook my gasp for one of pleasure. "Yes," he said, pulling me up into a sitting position and yanking the shift over my head. "All in good time."

His touch was foreign, alien, and every part of me wanted to recoil in shame and disgust that it was not Ichabod. And though I had no reason to feel guilt, it was present nonetheless.

Brom positioned himself above me; there would be no repeat of last night's trouble—his member, hard and erect, was pressed against my leg. He lowered himself atop me, and I tried to relax as much as I could as he pushed into me. At the last moment, recalling Charlotte's advice, I remembered to cry out as if in pain at the loss of my maidenhood.

"Oh, Katrina," he growled, his breath hot against my ear as he began to move within me, thrusting deeper each time. Jaw clenched, I waited for it to be over.

Finally he groaned as his pleasure came upon him, and I felt him shudder, then lay still against me. I opened my eyes; he was still inside me and I had to fight the urge to push him off, to get away from him as quickly as possible so that our bodies no longer touched. Tears seeped out of my eyes. *I am sorry, Ichabod. I am sorry and I hate you for leaving me behind to make this choice.*

Finally, Brom withdrew. Noticing the tears on my cheeks, he bent down to kiss them away. "Do not cry, my love," he said cheerfully. "It shall hurt less each time. And I am told some women come to enjoy it in time." His eyes hungrily took in my naked body. "God knows I shall enjoy teaching you to please me, and bringing you pleasure in return."

I turned my face away.

He rose from the bed and collected his clothes and shoes from the floor. "I shall leave you to dress, wife," he said, smiling, "and then I believe we are expected downstairs for breakfast. I shall see you soon." With that he went into the smaller, adjoining bedchamber.

Moving quickly, I took the vial of chicken blood from the drawer and, with shaking hands, removed the stopper. I tipped the vial over the area of the bed where I'd been lying and watched the viscous liquid drip out and stain the white sheets. I replaced the stopper and stowed the vial back in the drawer. I'd get rid of it later.

I retrieved my shift, pulling it back on over my head before calling out to him. "Brom!"

The door to the adjoining room opened and he stepped back in, tucking his shirt into his breeches. "Yes, wife?"

I smiled at him as sweetly as I could. "When you go downstairs, will you be so kind as to send Nancy up to help me dress?"

"Certainly," he said. His eyes caught on the bloodstained sheets, and his smile widened. "I shall tell her to come up directly."

"Thank you," I said, voice dripping with honey.

Once he left again, I let myself sag against the bedframe. God bless Charlotte and her foresight.

Minutes later, Nancy knocked. "Good morning, Miss Katrina," she said, coming in. "And how was your night?"

"As well as could be expected, I suppose," I said dully.

I saw her eyes flit to the stains on the sheets as well. "Well, let's get you dressed, then," she said. She'd brought in a fresh gown and underthings.

I saw her frown briefly as I undressed, but she quickly helped me into the clean things. "Did you wash this morning?" she asked. "I didn't know if anyone had brought you water."

"What?" I asked. "Why do you ask?"

"I figured you must've washed. Cleaned the blood off, anyway," she said, nodding toward the sheets.

There was blood on the sheets, but not on my thighs, where there would have been had I really bled. "Oh . . . yes," I said quickly. "There was water in there," I said, nodding toward a pitcher on the washstand opposite the bed. I had no idea if there was truly any water in it or not. "I . . . I wanted to clean myself up, of course. I will take a full bath later."

"I see," Nancy said. Clearly she did not believe me, but I felt no panic. I had suspected for some time that Nancy knew the truth, though how much of the truth I still was not sure. But whatever she knew or did not know, she would never betray me.

Once I was dressed, Nancy braided my hair and pinned it up. I touched the weight of it at the back of my head as I headed down-stairs. I was a married woman now, and so could no longer wear my hair about my shoulders like a girl. It was heavy, my hair, and so too was my married state.

Brom was already seated at the table with my parents. When I entered, he rose from his chair. "My bride," he said, kissing my hand. Surely I was mistaken, but was there . . . reverence in his voice, his eyes? He must be mocking me, I decided, settling into the chair beside him that he pulled out for me.

"Now then," my father said. "I trust you both enjoyed the day yesterday?"

"Very much," Brom said, taking my hand and squeezing it. I smiled tightly and nodded.

"Good, good," my father boomed, taking a sip of his tea. "I am delighted to hear it. I am indeed overjoyed at the union of our two families, so I am glad yesterday was such a wonderful celebration."

He cleared his throat. "Now, to business. My wife and I, together with your father, Brom, have taken the liberty of purchasing some new furniture for your house. It is already there, waiting for you."

"Truly, sir?" Brom asked. "That is most generous of you, and of my father as well."

"Most generous," I echoed.

"Think nothing of it, my dear boy," my father said. "All that remains to be done today is for you both to move your personal effects into the house and get settled." He took my mother's hand where she sat beside him. "I have no doubt you will soon discover all the joys of married life. Although, hopefully," he added with a grin, "it will not be just the two of you for very long."

"I confess I am excitedly anticipating grandchildren," my mother said, with a pointed look at me.

Brom chuckled. "We shall do our best to oblige you both. Indeed, we have already made a start on that task."

I blushed at his mention of such a thing in front of my parents, even as he and my father laughed jovially together. But the smile I gave my mother was not a false one. If it is a grandchild you want, I wished to say, I can promise you shall have one sooner than you might think.

After breakfast, I drew my mother aside before we went upstairs to finish packing up my things. "May I have a word, Mama?" I asked.

"Of course, dear. What is it?"

"I was hoping I might persuade you to release Nancy from your service. That she might come work for me."

My mother paused, clearly surprised by this request. "I would miss her, truth be told," she said. "But if she wishes to work for you and Brom, that is entirely her decision."

"I have spoken to her, and I believe that she does," I said. "Not that she is not content in your employ, of course," I added hurriedly. "But she was willing to come work for me."

"Very well, then," my mother said. "Yes, I think this is a fine idea. It is a big change, adjusting to married life. It will be good for you to have Nancy there with you."

My mother embraced me, and I returned the embrace wholeheartedly. "My daughter," she murmured. "It seems I looked away for but a moment, and then you were a woman."

I laughed as we separated. "It did not seem to happen quite that quickly for me."

"It never does," she said, smiling wistfully. "Someday, when you have a daughter of your own, you will understand."

I blinked back sudden tears at these words. If only I could have told her that I was at that very moment carrying a daughter.

"In any case," I said, brightly, "you can come to visit Nancy whenever you wish."

She laughed and hugged me again. "I shall come often, to see both Nancy and my daughter," she said. "And hopefully soon, my grandchild as well."

I smiled at her, already anticipating eagerly the moment I would finally be able to tell her that her wish had come true. It was the first time in a very long time that I had eagerly anticipated anything.

Brom and I loaded our belongings onto my father's farm cart, and the men drove it into the village to our new house with Mama, Nancy, Nox, and myself sitting awkwardly in the back among the trunks and bags. We brought everything inside, and then Brom and I went from room to room, exclaiming over all our new furniture. Nancy, excited and pleased at her change in employment, offered to cook us a fine dinner, and Brom went with my parents to take the cart back and to invite his father for the meal as well. When Nancy departed for the market to see what could be had fresh, suddenly I was alone in my house for the first time.

I should have begun putting away my clothes and books, no doubt, but I found quickly that silence and solitude were not what

I needed just then. So I donned my cloak and walked the—happily—short distance to the Jansen cottage.

When I knocked, Mevrouw Jansen opened the door. "Why, Katrina," she said. "Or neighbor, as I suppose I should now call you." She ushered me inside. "I am surprised to see you. I would have thought your new husband would not let you out of his reach for several days."

I forced a smile, holding back my shudder. The only thing worse than being alone would have been being alone with Brom, and sadly I had a lifetime of that ahead of me. "He has gone to invite his father to dinner tonight," I explained. "Is Charlotte home?"

"Yes, she's in the stillroom," Dame Jansen said. "Fear not, I shall not disturb you as you gossip of marriage and all related matters." She gave me a wink.

I turned away and went into the stillroom, where Charlotte was grinding up some herbs, an apron tied about her waist. "Katrina," she said, looking up. She blew a strand of red hair that had escaped her braid out of her eyes. "I did not expect to see you today."

"Oh, I . . . well, you are busy," I said, feeling awkward, as though now that I was wedded and bedded, my betrayal was somehow made manifest and corporeal between us. I turned to leave. "I can come back some other time . . ."

"No, no," Charlotte said, setting down her mortar and pestle. She wiped her hands on her apron. "I am glad to see you, it is just . . . unexpected."

"Did you think Brom would keep me in bed all day?" I asked, before I could think better of it.

She regarded me evenly. "I thought he might try," she said. "I am glad for your sake that I am wrong."

I was silent for a long time before I spoke again. "Charlotte, do you . . ." I bit my lip and looked away. "Do you truly forgive me?"

"It would do me no good to bear a grudge against you."

I glanced up, hurt at her noncommittal words, but she wore a teasing smile. "Oh, Katrina, of course I forgive you. I do not pretend to understand your decision, and my heart breaks for you, above all else. I know this was the last thing you wanted. Certainly I would be a fool to take any personal offense from any of this."

I breathed a sigh of relief, and some of the tension knotting my chest seemed to loosen. At times like this I was reminded that Charlotte was a much better person, and better friend, than I. "I . . . thank you. I was just afraid—"

"I know," she said, cutting me off. "I understand. But I will always be here for you."

"Good," I said. "Because I need you. I will always need you, but now I . . . I would ask your help again."

She met my gaze levelly. "What is it?"

"Ichabod," I said. I raised a hand at the look of surprise on her face. "I know he is never coming back. I have accepted that. Obviously. But I . . ." I took a deep breath and struggled to put into words the swirling, nebulous thoughts and decisions that had come upon me over the last few days, as memories plagued me at every turn. "I must know what happened to him. I cannot live not knowing the truth, and someday . . . someday my daughter deserves to know what became of her father. Whatever that truth may be."

Charlotte held my eyes for a long time before she finally nodded. "Very well, then," she said. "We will find out. We will find the truth. I swear it, on my very soul."

"And I swear it on mine," I said.

"And may the truth, when we find it, bring you peace."

Her words sounded part promise, part benediction, and part warning.

40

Vows

I kept up the pretense of being a happy newlywed all through dinner with my parents and Brom's father, and then again that night, after everyone had left, when we again performed the marriage act. Thankfully it was a brief affair once more, with little preamble, and soon Brom was snoring beside me. Brom had seemingly been too tired to make good on his threat to teach me to please him, in whatever odious form that might take. Soon enough I could announce that I was with child, and so all bed sport must then cease for a time.

And after the birth of this child, I would obtain more herbs from Charlotte, and not forget to take them this time. I would never bear Brom Van Brunt a child.

The next morning, Brom rose early and ate a simple breakfast of bread and cheese before leaving the house to see about hiring a manservant for himself. Without his blasted snoring to put up with, I was able to indulge in another hour or two of sleep after he left. When I finally rose, Nancy helped me bathe, and then we set about putting away all my clothes and personal effects. When we got to my books—which for now amounted to two boxes—I paused.

"We could get someone to come build you some shelves for in here, if you want them close," Nancy said, surveying the bed-chamber. "Or a bookcase for the sitting room downstairs if you'd rather."

I ran my fingers over the spines. "No," I said, almost to myself. "Let me . . ." Trailing off, I left the room and wandered down the hallway, past the bedroom that adjoined ours—already designated as a future nursery—and past the guest room, until I came to a tiny, poky room at the end of the hall. It was so small I had no idea why it had been built in the first place. All that was in it was a thickly upholstered chair—perfect for reading. I smiled as I stepped into the small room. It was plenty big enough for the chair, and two bookshelves on either side. I felt my heart grow full.

"Here," I said to Nancy, who had come up the hall behind me. "I'd like some bookshelves in here—as many and as large as will fit around the chair."

Nancy chuckled. "You and your books. But remember, you are a married lady now, Miss Katrina. You won't have time for so much reading anymore."

I turned to face her and smiled. "I shall make time."

The next few weeks saw Brom and I settle into our house, and into our marriage. Well, Brom settled into marriage; I bore it as though it were a painfully itchy cloak I could not remove for fear of freez-ing to death. In truth, though, I was delighted with the house, and set about making it my own: arranging my furniture just so; going to Beekman's shop near the church and buying new pots, dishes, cups, and mugs for the kitchen; I also chose the fabric for new cur-tains, which Nancy and I commenced sewing. I fancied taking a trip to New York City soon for new linens and candlesticks and the like, but it would have to wait until after my child was born. And, of course, the bookshelves. I hired the village carpenter, Meneer Albertsen, who came and spent two days building shelves into the tiny room at the end of the hall. They were simple wooden shelves, but served my purposes perfectly. And best of all, once I had placed my books upon them, I had more empty space than what was filled—space for so many new books, for such possibility.

Brom exerted his husbandly privilege less often than I had expected, for which I was grateful. The infrequency of the act, though, did not make it any more pleasurable or easier to bear. To my surprise—and secret delight—he found himself unable to perform on more than one occasion, though he always had some excuse: drink, or that he was especially tired that day. When he did manage to rise to action, it required some effort on his part. He touched and kissed all over my body, encouraging me to touch him in return. Once he tried to coax me to put my mouth on his member, which I outright refused. He had looked frustrated and nearly wild with denied lust, but thankfully had not forced me.

Charlotte and I did not speak of my wifely duties for perhaps the first two weeks of my marriage; we studiously avoided it. But one afternoon, she broached the subject. "And how are you faring with . . ." She hesitated, looking both embarrassed and somehow angry, as though she hated me being subjected to such a thing. "The . . . marriage act," she finished uncomfortably. "He is not . . . hurting you in any way, is he?"

I shuddered. "No, thank God," I said. "He delights in the act, of course, and seems to wish I would do the same." A wicked smile crossed my face. "When he can perform, that is."

Charlotte's mouth dropped open. "You mean he . . . he is unmanned?"

I nodded, giggles escaping me. "Sometimes, yes! He was on our wedding night, and continues to be at times."

Charlotte dissolved into laughter, and soon we were both cackling like a couple of old farmwives. "Oh, Mother Mary, how wonderful," Charlotte said, wiping tears from her eyes. "He deserves it. And so do you!"

I caught the gleam of mischief in her eye. "Charlotte," I asked curiously, more serious now, "you didn't . . . did you?"

"What?" A look of comprehension dawned as she took my meaning. "Oh, no, of course not! Although," she said, her own grin now wicked, "I could. If you wanted me to."

As appealing as the idea was, Brom was my husband, and that gave him rights to my body. I did not like it, but it was true, in the eyes of God and man and the law. And he did not use me ill, even if I hated enduring the act, my own body crying out for the pleasure I knew would always elude me. Using herbs—or whatever other means Charlotte had at her disposal—to render him impotent did not feel right. In any case, drink or ill health or whatever it was seemed to take care of that already. "No, best not," I said. "Though I shall keep it in mind." I changed the subject. "And how does an unmarried maid like you know of such things?"

She rolled her eyes. "The women of the village come to my mother and me for help with such things. Both when they wish their husbands would cease their attentions—and when they need their husbands to, ah, harden their resolve."

We both burst into laughter again.

"If only men knew how much of their lives were under the control of women," I said.

"They are blissfully ignorant, and I say we let them remain so."

"Perhaps it is best that way," I said. "But oh, imagine their faces if they knew!"

After our glee died down, Charlotte grew thoughtful.

"I confess," she said, "I am hoping that neither my virginal nor unmarried states last too much longer."

"Oh?" I asked, instantly alert. "Dare I venture a guess that Giles Carpenter has persisted in his suit?"

A rare blush colored her cheeks. "He has," she said. "And his attentions are hardly unwelcome to me."

"'Hardly unwelcome,'" I mocked. "More than that, I should think, for not a minute ago you were talking of surrendering your maidenhood to him! Tell me, Charlotte, do you love him?"

She bit her lip, looking uncertain. "I think so," she said. "But how do I know, Katrina? How do I know if this is love, and not . . . something else?"

"That is how I felt," I said softly. "I knew it was love; but I was so scared I was wrong. Scared because it meant everything to me. And that was how I knew."

She nodded slowly, considering this. "He comes to visit again in a few weeks," she said. "He always makes up a pretext for some business here. But we . . . talk, and go for walks, and spend time together."

"And so?" I asked. "When next he comes, shall I too invent a pretext and summon your mother to see me? Invite her to dine, perhaps, and my mother as well, so you might be alone with the gallant Mr. Carpenter?"

She smiled. "Perhaps. I do not know yet."

When I returned from Charlotte's house, I found Brom waiting for me, a scowl on his face. "I take it you were at the Jansen cottage?" he asked, without greeting.

"I was," I said evenly, removing my cloak and hanging it by the door.

His scowl deepened. "I'll not have you spending so much time there, Katrina."

I gave him an incredulous look. "Oh?"

"No. I'll not have it said my wife is . . . in league with that witch."

My blood boiled at the word, but I forced myself to stay calm. "Charlotte and I have been friends since we were children," I said, my tone measured. "As you well know. I doubt it is of interest to anyone in the village that we spend time together. It is hardly a new occurrence."

"Be that as it may—"

"And how do you propose to stop me?" I flared. "Will you confine me to the house, and let the village gossip about that instead? Charlotte is my dearest friend, and no one shall keep me from seeing her. Indeed, I shall invite her to this, my house, whenever I see fit."

"Now see here," Brom began, his face red.

"And how do you propose to stop me?" I asked again.

His face turned an even deeper shade of scarlet. "I am the master of this house, Katrina."

"Yes. And I am the mistress."

I held his gaze for a long time, and if he thought I would eventually back down, he was disappointed. We remained that way, eyes locked, as though we were two beasts circling each other in a wood. At last, he looked away. "Very well," he mumbled. "This is not worth creating disharmony between us. Not so soon after our wedding."

I was surprised he backed down so easily, but I did not question it. I simply turned and stalked away. *If you think there shall ever be true harmony in our marriage, then you are a sure fool, Brom Van Brunt.*

Another two weeks passed, and I knew the time had come for me to announce my pregnancy. I told Brom first, and he was so excited that he spun me about the room in his arms. "A child!" he cried. "A strong, strapping son, no doubt! And in the first month of our marriage, no less!" He set me down, grinning. "I am well pleased you should be such a fertile bride. And to know that my seed is so strong."

I almost laughed aloud. *Given your performance record in the marital bed, I have my doubts about the strength of your seed,* I thought. *But no matter. Go on thinking that you are as fertile as Zeus.*

Next I told Nancy, and she betrayed no surprise whatsoever. No doubt she had noticed that I had not bled the last couple of months, and had her own thoughts as to the identity of the father.

Then, of course, I told my parents, as we dined with them one Sunday after church. My mother wept with joy, and my father could not stop beaming. For the first time since Ichabod had disappeared, I felt a flicker of true happiness.

I would have a child. And I would love her with all my being. This, finally, was something to rejoice in.

As winter came on in force and settled in for a long stay, I found myself growing listless. The business of running the household did not occupy so much of my time as I had imagined—it was not, after all, a large household—and I had learned enough from my mother, Nancy, and Cook over the years that the tasks required of me quickly became second nature. There was the planning of meals and oversight of the kitchen, including going to the market for fresh foods whenever possible, though my parents had been good enough to share their bountiful harvest with us, as well as meat and sausages from the slaughter of the pigs. And seeing to the washing of clothes and linens—a hired girl came in twice a week to do that—and the mending, which I did myself, occasionally assisted by Nancy, if she had the time. Nancy also kept the house in good order and provided me with any advice I needed—and I needed a lot, it seemed. I also oversaw our stores of goods such as candles and firewood and would see to replacing them whenever we ran low.

Otherwise, I found myself with not much to do. Brom was not home often. He still assisted his father with matters on the Van Brunt farm as often as he could, and my father had given him a job of representing the Van Tassel business interests in New York. As such, Brom was often away in the city, taking the crops downriver to Manhattan on one of the sloops that plied the Hudson and seeing to the sale of our flour, corn, apples, and other crops and foods produced on the farm, as well as beer from my father's brewery, and negotiating the best deals on products and goods my father needed. Papa's thought was that Brom must familiarize himself with this side of the farming business if he was to inherit such an expanded holding later on. Brom enjoyed the work, though he lamented that it took him away from me so often. I could not have found a more preferable arrangement myself. He offered to procure for me whatever household goods I desired from New York, and I sent him back with a long list, knowing any desired trip to the city must be delayed on account of my pregnancy.

With so few demands on my time, I found myself reading quite a bit, of course, but all too soon I began to feel anxious for something more.

I found myself remembering the night Ichabod and I had spent at the Jansen cottage. Yet this time, instead of pain and heartache, I found the answer I had been seeking in the memory.

I recalled Ichabod's words to me after I'd told him the story of the Woman in White of Raven Rock: *You have a true gift, Katrina. A true gift for storytelling. You should write all these tales down.*

At the time, I'd not taken his words seriously. What need did anyone have for such tales to be written down? And anyway, writing was a lofty, noble endeavor for educated city men, not a farm girl—even a wealthy farm girl—from Sleepy Hollow, a tiny, haunted village on the banks of the Hudson. But as I went about my daily tasks I would think of this story or that and say to myself, *Oh, Ichabod would love that story, I must tell it to him*, only to remember that he was gone. And I would go through the pain and anger of his betrayal all over again.

And so, since I could not tell him the stories aloud, I determined that I would write them down after all. I considered the idea for a few days, and when it would not leave me alone, I finally began. I got out a small, leather-bound book of blank pages I had picked out when in New York with my father simply because I had thought it a beautiful little book, knowing that I might find some use for it, eventually. Now I had just the right use.

I started with the stories I had told Ichabod: the tale of Mr. Phillips's slave and the building of the church; the story of John Andre's tree; the Woman in White. Soon I began to write down others that had come to mind of late: the tale of the Star Maiden, and of Mother Hulda, the old witch who had lived in the woods and was reported to have cast a spell over the whole village. And many more as well.

Even if no one ever read the book of tales I was creating, I would have it, my own personal labor of love, for myself and Ichabod. And for our daughter as well. She would inherit these tales someday, would grow up hearing them as I had. Though, perhaps, I thought with a smile as I bent over my pages, one hand on my quill and the other on my swelling belly, I would save some of the scarier tales for when she was older.

41

The Haunted Clearing

I had not forgotten about my vow to discover the truth about Ichabod's disappearance. And once I was comfortable in my new house—if not in my marriage—and had made the announcement that I was with child, I felt myself ready to turn my mind fully to the task.

In late January, I brought up the topic with Charlotte again. "I have thought of a place where we might start our . . . project."

"I was wondering when you would want to begin," she said. "But I knew you would bring it up when you were ready."

Warmth washed over me, at having a friend who understood me so very well. "I am ready now," I said.

She nodded. "So where shall we begin?"

"I thought we might check the roads, or the forest, to see if there are clues that we missed." The stream where Ichabod's hat had been found had been searched, as well as the burial ground and woods immediately surrounding the area, but no further evidence had ever been found.

"Perhaps," she said slowly. "But have you considered whatever clues there might have been may well be gone by now? It has been a few months, after all."

I nodded. "I have," I said. "But it is worth a look. It is a place to start. And if we need . . . other means, we can use those as well."

Charlotte nodded at this.

In truth, I did not expect to find much in the woods or elsewhere. But it would be foolish not to look, at least. And what was more, I was hesitant to call upon Charlotte's other gifts. I could not forget the terrifying vision I had experienced when she read the cards for me, nor could I forget their horrible prediction—one that certainly seemed to have come true, however it had come about.

Can it be I do not truly wish to know? I wondered. Can it be that I avoid the means by which I am most likely to find the answer because I am afraid of what I may find? But whatever it was could not be as awful, as unbearable as not knowing.

"The weather is not too harsh today," I commented. The sun was shining, and the temperature was above freezing, a rare treat. "Perhaps we might venture into the woods today."

"Are you sure that is wise, in your condition?"

I rolled my eyes. "I am with child, not an invalid," I said. "And I am in need of some exercise. My mother and Brom do nothing but extort me to rest. I am quite tired of resting."

"I do not speak of the exercise overtaxing you," she said slowly. "For as you say, it will be good for you. But rather . . ." She hesitated. "What if we discover something that upsets you? That would not be good for the child."

I had not thought of this. After everything I had done for the child, I could not endanger her now. Yet I refused to be dissuaded. I feared if I did not start at that very moment, I might not want to start again. "As you said, we likely will not find anything," I said at last. "I just want to look, so I know we at least tried."

"If you are sure," Charlotte said. "But if at any point you begin to feel unwell, or upset, you'll tell me, won't you? You'll tell me and I'll bring you right back home."

"Of course," I said, already rising to get my cloak.

Dressing ourselves warmly against the cold, we left the cottage and began to walk toward the church, Nox trotting at our side. We made our way through the burial ground and into the woods behind the church, the portion of the forest nearest where the only traces of Ichabod had been found.

"Gunpowder was never found, either, was he?" Charlotte asked from behind me as we made our way single file along the narrow paths through the trees. Her voice sounded unnaturally loud in the hushed silence of the winter woods.

"No," I said. "So that would support the likelihood that Ichabod simply left."

Charlotte did not respond, and I knew that we were likely thinking the same thing: or the Horseman had spirited Ichabod and Gunpowder both away to the netherworld.

"Have you heard of the new schoolmaster?" Charlotte asked as we walked on, eyes peeled for anything out of the ordinary: more shards of a pumpkin, or hoof prints, or fabric caught in the branches.

"Smith is his name, is it not?" I asked. Ichabod's replacement had arrived in Sleepy Hollow a month after his disappearance. Occupied with my upcoming wedding to Brom, I had scarcely paid the talk of the new schoolmaster any attention. "He has been here for some time already. What of it?"

"He is moving the schoolhouse," she said.

I stopped and turned to face her. "What? Moving it? What do you mean?"

"Not physically moving it, of course," Charlotte said. "But the old schoolhouse—the one Ichabod taught in—is to be abandoned, and lessons will henceforth be taught in a new building nearer the Albany Post Road."

This news disturbed me more than it ought, for reasons I could not quite identify. "But why?"

Charlotte looked away uncomfortably. "They—Master Smith, the children, and some of the villagers—they say the schoolhouse is haunted."

"Haunted?" I demanded. A chill breeze swirled around us, whistling through the bare tree branches. "By whom? Surely Sleepy Hollow has more than enough ghosts to be getting on with."

"By . . . well, by the ghost of Ichabod Crane."

I spun away from her so that she might not see the look on my face and continued walking. "I thought you did not wish me to be upset," I said.

"I am sorry," she said. "I should not have brought it up. I thought you must have heard."

"I had not," I said. I sighed. "Though I suppose better that I hear it from you."

"Yes, well," Charlotte said, still sounding sheepish. "As you know, the commonly accepted explanation in the village for Ichabod's disappearance is that the Headless Horseman carried him off." A shiver went down my spine. "And so they say his ghost has returned to haunt the schoolhouse. Supposedly they hear him whistling, as he did when he would walk along the road. Other times they hear him singing."

It couldn't be true. It couldn't be. For surely if Ichabod was dead, if he had gone over to the other side and was capable of haunting the schoolhouse, why would he not haunt *me*? Why would he not bring me some message from beyond the veil?

"Anyway," Charlotte said, "that is what they say."

"Indeed," I said. "They say a great many things in the village."

Just then, Nox barked suddenly and ran ahead down the path.

"Nox, come back!" I called. We hastened after him until we arrived at the edge of a large, round clearing in the trees.

My breath caught in my throat. *This was it.* The fabled, haunted clearing where the Hessian rider was said to have met his end. Beside me, Nox growled low in his throat.

I shivered again, more violently this time. Had this been where I'd intended to go all along? Or had some other force compelled me to this Godforsaken place?

Glancing upward, I saw that dark clouds now obscured the sun. Had not the sky been clear when we'd set out from Charlotte's cottage? Surely not. I must have been mistaken. Even in winter, clouds could not come up this quickly.

I glanced over at Charlotte, who was studying the clearing with apprehension. "So this is it," she said softly, as though wary of disturbing whoever—or whatever—might be lingering here.

"Have you been here before?" I asked.

"Once," she said. "As a girl. I was wandering the woods and got lost. Then as now, I . . ." She shuddered. "I do not know if the stories are true, but something evil happened here. I can feel it. There is a power, an energy, in the ground, the very air."

Nox growled again.

"I . . . I think I know what you mean," I said uneasily.

We stayed poised uncertainly at the edge of the clearing for a moment longer before Charlotte took a step forward. "Well, now that we are here, we may as well have a look around."

"Is it safe, do you think?" I asked.

"Safe enough, I should think," she said vaguely.

I was not at all reassured by that answer, but I stepped into the clearing nonetheless. Nox followed us most reluctantly.

If I was expecting some magical wind to rise up and sweep us into its vortex as soon as we set foot into the clearing, though, I was mistaken. We wandered the perimeter, searching the ground and trees for clues, but we did not see or hear anything. There was only that same, continuous, oppressive feeling of weight, as though the air here was somehow heavier. There were no birds in the nearby trees, nor squirrels nor rabbits nor any other kind of wildlife. Many of them were no doubt hibernating for the winter, but not to hear any sort of animal at all was . . . eerie.

The ground was hard from the recent frost, and it looked disturbed, churned up in places, frozen into tiny peaks and valleys. This did not necessarily mean anything; only that a herd of deer had passed through, or a horse had ridden across the clearing. I shuddered at the thought of a horse and rider.

It felt as though we scoured every inch of the clearing but aside from the disturbed ground, did not find anything out of the ordinary. And signs of Ichabod's flight—or mishap—might be found anywhere in the woods surrounding Sleepy Hollow. Charlotte and I could not possibly search it all.

This was fruitless. As hopeful and optimistic as I was when we'd left Charlotte's cottage, so glad to be taking action, I now felt defeated. What had I expected? The apparition of the Headless Horseman himself, waiting patiently so I might inquire of him? *Excuse me, demonic specter, but did you spirit away my lover to the underworld? Of course, I understand that you cannot speak, being not possessed of a head; simply incline your torso for yes, if you would be so kind.* A peal of near hysterical laughter escaped me at the thought.

"We should go, Charlotte," I said, my voice ringing out loudly in the silence. "There is nothing for us to find here." When she didn't answer, I turned to face her. "Charlotte?"

She stood toward the center of the clearing, staring off into the empty air above her as if looking at a picture I could not see. And maybe she was. "Charlotte?" I called a little bit louder. Still she did not turn. I approached her slowly, fearfully, placing a hand on her shoulder. "Charlotte?"

She jumped. "Katrina!" she gasped, pressing a hand to her breast. "I . . . you startled me."

"I was calling your name," I said. "Are you all right, Charlotte? Did you . . . did you see something?"

"See something?" she repeated. "I . . . no. I was lost in thought, is all. I apologize." She shivered and drew her cloak more tightly around herself.

I studied her for a moment. She had appeared to be in the trancelike state I had witnessed before, when she was seeing some vision of the future. Yet surely if she had seen anything of relevance, she would tell me. Besides, it was not the future I was interested in now, but the past that had yet to reveal itself to me. But perhaps she was telling the truth. This strange clearing certainly seemed capable of casting a spell over any who dared linger. "Let's go," I said. "There is nothing to find here, and I am cold. Nox!" I called. He was at the edge of the clearing, sniffing determinedly around a tree trunk—no doubt in pursuit of some animal that had lately been there. "Nox, come away from there! Let's go."

He obeyed, and Charlotte followed me back to the path from

which we had come. "I am not so certain there is nothing to find," I thought I heard her say, but when I glanced back, she merely eyed me inquisitively. I faced forward again, certain that I had imagined it and not heard any such thing at all.

42

The Spellbook

After our trip to the clearing that day, I did not bring up the search for Ichabod again for some time. The truth was I did not know what else to do. Or, rather, I had some ideas—consulting the tarot cards again being one of them—but I did not feel ready. Every so often of a winter evening, I would find myself staring into the fire in the hearth, hoping and fearing that another vision would come to me in the flames. A part of me did not want to feel that suffocating terror again, but another part felt it would be worth it, if there was a chance it would give me answers.

Yet as my pregnancy progressed, I was often tired and irritable, and heeded Charlotte's wisdom that I not risk harming the child. That meant my search for answers was postponed until after the child's birth. This self-imposed restriction at times brought feelings of both relief and frustration.

Winter melted into spring, and I continued to run the house efficiently. When Brom was home, he slept in the guest room to ensure that the child and I benefited from a full night of rest. I was grateful for his absence from my bed, but I could not help but be touched by his obvious concern and solicitousness.

He was gone most days, in New York or occasionally Boston, and I found I did not relish being alone, not as I once had when

I was a girl. There was too much in my mind that I wanted to escape, to forget, and the empty silence of the house meant that memories could more easily find me. I did not wish for Brom's presence, but some days I could not help but feel that the more people who were in the house, the better.

Nancy was always about, of course, and she and I grew closer than ever. We dined together most nights, when she was not out visiting friends, and of many a cold evening we would sit together by the fire, gossiping and laughing.

I visited with Charlotte often, as always, and invited her to my house whenever Brom was gone. We shared many a meal together when we could, on those days and nights when she was not needed to assist her mother.

And whenever I felt as though I could not stave off the memories, I would go to my desk, seize my quill, and continue writing my stories. Some took days to write out in full, with all the detail and embellishment that I could give them. It gave me joy and purpose in a way I hadn't anticipated, and I soon found myself longing for those free, quiet moments when I could sit with only pen and paper for company. As spring ripened and the air got warmer, I would go into the woods—not far, not deep—to a new secluded spot I found where I could sit and read or write without being disturbed.

The one story I found myself unable to commit to paper, however, was the very first one I had told Ichabod: the legend of the Headless Horseman. I felt rather superstitious about writing it down. This was ridiculous, of course, and I told myself that I could not summon such a specter with my words, yet still I did not write it down.

One day, I flipped to the blank pages at the back of the book and started a new, very different entry. I wrote a date at the top of the page, then the following:

Walked with Charlotte to the clearing where the Headless Horseman is said to have lost his life in battle. Air was heavy and oppressive, somehow. We searched the whole perimeter of the clearing, but other than some disturbance of the ground did not find anything of note.

I went on to detail the fast-changing weather that day, the thoughts I'd had as we searched, Charlotte's strange moment of deep thought, before I laid down my quill, satisfied. I would record it all here, along with my stories. Everything I found—or did not find—in my quest for the truth. It would be a book of truths, stories, and spells.

For are not truths, stories, and spells all the same thing, in the end?

43

The Body in the Hudson

One fine day in early May I was at the market with Charlotte. It was my excuse to get out into the fresh air; Brom was so adamant I rest when he was home—and even Nancy was being slightly over-solicitous—such that I thought if I was forced to rest for an hour more I might scream.

"A bit of exercise is good for you, and for the babe," Charlotte told me, and I needed no further convincing.

So I wandered about the market idly, trailing behind Charlotte as she examined fruit and vegetables, and purchased a new set of glass jars for her remedies. I was simply enjoying the sun on my face when I first heard the whispers.

"Pulled him right out of the river, they did . . . they say he could have been there all winter, no telling when he was dumped in . . ."

I froze as the words entered my brain. Immediately my thoughts flashed to the small river that fed into the millpond, where Ichabod's hat had been found.

No, I told myself firmly. That river had been searched the day after he'd gone missing.

I glanced about for Charlotte, ready to put it out of my mind, when another woman joined the two who'd been whispering at the fruit stand.

"You've heard?" she said excitedly. "Not ten miles down the river, they found him. They say he was stabbed, several times."

"That's not what I heard," Mevrouw Van Buren chimed in. "I heard his throat was cut."

"I heard he was shot!" cried Mevrouw Van Ripper.

I was listening unabashedly now, could no longer pretend that I was not.

"And who is it, then?" Mevrouw Van Buren asked. "Anyone we know? Anyone from around these parts?"

The woman who'd joined the pair, whose name I thought was Mevrouw Lange, shook her head. "No one knows. Can't tell, can they? He's been in the water too long. Even with the winter cold, he's rotted too much." She pronounced these last ghastly words with relish. "All they know is he's of no little height, slender, and a man on the younger side."

I stopped breathing.

"Katrina, you are pale as ice! What . . ." Charlotte approached and clutched my arm, and I shook my head, inclining my head toward the trio. She frowned and began to listen as well.

Mevrouw Van Ripper sniffed in derision. "No doubt some young fool who got caught up in a duel or a tavern brawl or some such nonsense, and was tossed in the river so the whole affair might be hidden."

Mevrouw Van Buren had a thoughtful look on her face. "A young man, tall and slender?" she asked. She lowered her voice. "You don't think it could be the schoolteacher, do you?"

I nearly choked on the air coming into my lungs.

"I hadn't thought of that," Mevrouw Lange admitted. "I suppose it might be, mightn't it? He disappeared in what, November?"

"All Hallows' Eve, it was," supplied Mevrouw Van Buren.

"Excuse me," Charlotte broke in, stepping into their circle and pulling me with her. She smiled around at all of them; even so, they drew away ever so slightly but did not leave. "But did you say a man has been pulled from the river?"

Mevrouw Lange nodded importantly, looking wary but still

glad, in the manner of all committed gossips, to have a newcomer to whom to tell the story. "About ten miles downriver, out of the Hudson," she confirmed. "Some violence had been done to him, that's for sure, though we're all in disagreement over what kind it was."

"And did you say," I spoke up, surprising myself with my rather even voice, through every word felt about to strangle me, "you think it could be . . . Ichabod Crane?"

"Aye," Mevrouw Van Buren said.

Mevrouw Van Ripper shook her head. "It would be a terrible shame, that, if it were him. He was a good lad. Well, you know, Juffrouw Van Tassel," she said to me. "Pardon me, Mevrouw Van Brunt, that is. He stayed with you as well. He was your music teacher, was he not?"

"Yes," I managed. "Yes, I was rather fond of him."

"Indeed. Well, we shall hope it is not him," Mevrouw Van Ripper said with a shudder. "I hope he was simply spooked by all the tales and rode off, and nothing more."

"Ichabod Crane was carried off by the Headless Horseman," a scratchy voice spoke up, and they moved aside to reveal Mevrouw Douw. She grinned, the expression all sharp edges. "You'll not find him in the Hudson. You'll not find him anywhere at all."

The three women glanced warily at each other. Mevrouw Van Buren shivered. "I wouldn't doubt it," she said. "Not with the way he disappeared like that, and on All Hallows' Eve, no less. I wouldn't wonder that it was the Horseman."

"You mark my words," Mevrouw Douw said. "It was the Horseman." She looked significantly around at each of us, then nodded. "Good day, ladies," she said, and walked on.

"Charlotte," I whispered. I clutched her arm for support. Suddenly the warmth of the day, which I had been so enjoying, felt about to smother me.

But she was not done. "And what have they done with this poor, unfortunate man?" she asked, her tone light, as if this was just idle gossip.

Mevrouw Lange shrugged. "I heard they took him to New

York," she said. "Don't know why, unless they're hoping someone there will recognize him. No doubt he'll end up in a pauper's grave, poor soul."

"*Charlotte*," I muttered again, through gritted teeth. I gripped her arm harder. I had to leave; had to get out of here or I would faint.

"A terrible story, indeed," Charlotte said hurriedly. "I do think Katrina is feeling unwell; her condition, you know." The women all nodded sagely. "I must get her home. Good day!"

With that, we turned, and Charlotte began steering me back toward my house.

I began to feel slightly better as we walked, but not much. I could not rid my mind of the images that now invaded it: Ichabod, frozen and decaying with his face eaten away, pulled from the waters of the Hudson. Ichabod with his throat cut, bleeding from stab wounds with his flesh in tatters, his beautiful body torn and bleeding, blood pouring from his mouth, from the lips I once kissed . . .

I let out a sob and brought up my hand to cover my mouth. Charlotte wrapped an arm around my waist protectively.

"Do not think about it," she told me, almost harshly. "Do not think about it, Katrina. It will do you no good."

She did not speak any more until we were in my house. Nox preceded us, barking urgently. "Nancy," Charlotte called as I collapsed onto the daybed in the parlor, my swollen, ungainly body suddenly feeling much too heavy.

Nancy bustled in and stared at me in shock. "What's happened?"

"Just a bit too much excitement, and Katrina is overtired," Charlotte explained quickly. "Would you bring her some tea? That will no doubt restore her."

"Of course," Nancy said. She disappeared back into the kitchen.

"Charlotte," I moaned, once Nancy was out of earshot. "What if . . ."

"You must not think about it," Charlotte said again. "You've had a shock, Katrina, but you must not let it upset you so. Think of the child."

This did rally me somewhat. I took several deep, slow breaths, calm beginning to return to me.

Charlotte knelt on the floor and took my hands in hers. "We do not know it is him," she said, her wide amber eyes on mine. "We don't. Ruffians dispose of bodies in the Hudson all the time. They just don't always wash up, so we never hear about such things."

The certainty in her voice was such that I could not help but believe her. "But . . . what if it *is* him?" I whispered. "It might be."

Charlotte's hands tightened on mine. "It might be," she conceded, "but there is a far greater chance it is not. Remember," she added, "Gunpowder was never found. He might have been stolen, I suppose, but it is more likely Ichabod rode away under his own power. Far more likely."

I had forgotten about Gunpowder. "That . . . that is true," I admitted, the weight on my chest lifting a bit. I laughed bitterly. "Who would have guessed that the likelihood Ichabod left me would be a comfort."

Charlotte smiled. "You loved him. Love him. Of course you'd rather he was still out there in the world, healthy and whole, than that any misfortune befell him, even if it means he left you."

She was right, though I had not considered it until then. For his fate to be that of the unknown man dragged from the Hudson, whose body had been picked over and dissected by the women in the market just as much as by the rocks and the fish and the current—that was truly the worst thing I could imagine.

And so I would not imagine it. I could not. Charlotte was right; we did not know that this man was Ichabod.

Yet later that night, I turned to a new page in my book of stories and spells and wrote the day's date.

At the market with Charlotte, we heard some women talk of a body that was pulled from the Hudson. A man's body.

I recorded the details of what the farmwives had said, and at the end I wrote:

They speculated that it might be Ichabod Crane. We cannot know for certain. Yet Mevrouw Douw insists Ichabod will not be found, that he cannot be found, because he was carried off by the Headless Horseman.

Can it be?

44

The Birth

"Nancy." She did not awake at my whispered hiss, and so I reached out and shook her gently, feeling slightly guilty for waking her, but knowing I had no choice. "*Nancy*," I said, louder this time.

She jolted awake, blinking in the light of the candle I carried. "Wha . . ." Her eyes focused blearily on my face. "Miss Katrina," she said, sleep making her voice leaden. "What do you—" She broke off as she saw that my nightgown was soaked from the waist down. "Lord have mercy," she cried, leaping up out of the bed. "The baby is coming!"

"I . . . I thought so, yes," I said, my voice ragged with fear. "I woke up all wet, and . . ."

"Your water's broken," Nancy said. "Perfectly normal. Didn't Miss Charlotte tell you?"

"She said it might, but . . ."

"No matter now," Nancy said briskly. "Let's get you back upstairs."

Nancy walked behind me as I slowly made my way up the servants' staircase. My hair clung damply to me in the June heat, and I was already sweating further out of nervousness.

"Into the guest chamber with you," Nancy said, directing me.

"Good thing we've prepared this room. Now. Lie on the bed and lift your shift. I must see how far along you are."

I did as she said, feeling no shame as Nancy parted my legs and probed between them. She had helped me to bathe and dress since I was a child, so I had no sense of modesty where she was concerned. "Shouldn't you . . . shouldn't you send for Charlotte and Mevrouw Jansen?" I asked.

"When I was a slave on that plantation down in Virginia, I helped my mother birth dozens of babies before you were even thought of," she said. "And that was before I had my own. Don't you worry. I'll get the Jansen women soon enough. They know better than me what potions and medicines you should have." She peered between my legs and completed her examination. "It'll be some hours before that baby is ready to leave its nest, you mark my words."

But something Nancy said had caught my attention. "You . . . you have a child?" I stared at her, forgetting my fear and worry. How could it be that I had lived in the same house with this woman my whole life and never known about her child?

"That's a sad story, and not one you need to hear while you're bringing your first into the world."

"But . . . Nancy . . ."

"Later," she insisted. "I'll tell you later."

"Very well," I conceded. "But you will tell me?"

"I surely will. But now I need you to get up and walk."

I stared at her uncomprehendingly. "Walk?"

"Yes, walk. Pace about the room, like you're deep in thought about something. It'll help the babe shift into the proper position."

I rose from the bed and obediently began to do as she said.

"While you're doing that, I'll run down and make you some broth," she said. "You'll need to keep your strength up. Just keep walking, and if you start to feel different, holler for me."

I obeyed and kept pacing the small room as Nancy disappeared downstairs to the kitchen. I heard her let Nox, who had been whining outside the guest chamber door, into the garden.

I had yet to feel any of the pain I knew came with childbirth—the pain that was Eve's curse—but knew it was coming. That fear made me increase my steps, as though I could outrun it before it arrived.

Soon enough, Nancy reappeared with a mug of broth with shredded bits of chicken in it, as well as a thick slice of bread. She allowed me to sit as I ate. "How you doing, Miss Katrina?" she asked. "All right so far?"

I nodded.

"Good. You drink up, and I'll pop down the street to get Miss Charlotte and Mistress Jansen over here. I'll not be a minute."

"All right."

She disappeared again, and I tried not to let my nerves mount. What if I started to give birth now, when no one was here? What would I do? What if something happened, and it all went wrong?

But before I had even finished my broth, Charlotte burst into the room, Nancy behind her. "Katrina!" she cried. She took my hands. "Are you feeling well?"

"Perfectly, so far," I said, smiling at her. "Just nervous. I'm so glad you're here."

"I'm so glad to be here," she said. "Though with Nancy I don't know as I'm needed at all! My mother is off tending to an ailing neighbor," she said, "or she would be here, too."

I smiled at both of them. "I have everyone I need right here."

The night was a blur after that. Charlotte instructed me to keep walking, and as I did so the pains began to come, few and far between for the first few hours. All the walking soon began to tire me, so Charlotte and Nancy let me rest for a bit, then made me get up and start walking again.

As the pains began to come more frequently, they had me lie on the bed again so they could check my progress. "Your body has still not opened enough to expel the child," Charlotte told me, in her calm healer's voice. "It will be some time yet."

I groaned. "Do I need to walk some more?"

"Yes, for a bit."

I grumbled but obeyed. Charlotte left to fix me some tea of raspberry leaves, to aid in the birthing process and left me to do my paces under Nancy's supervision.

Once she returned I was able to sit and drink, then it was back to pacing.

After another couple of hours, the pains began coming faster. After further inspection, Nancy and Charlotte agreed it was time. "Do not be afraid, Katrina," Charlotte soothed me. "Nancy and I are right here. This is nature's way. The pain will be worth it, because it is bringing you a child."

Becoming irritable with exhaustion and pain, I wanted to snap at her, to ask her how she, a virgin with no child, could say such things. But I bit my tongue, knowing she was only trying to help.

They helped me remove my robe so that I lay on the bed in just my shift. I gritted my teeth against another wave of pain. "What . . . must I do?"

"You'll need to push soon," Nancy said. "But not quite yet."

"Push?"

"Yes," Charlotte explained. "Push with all the muscles in your lower body to help expel the child. But not yet. Wait until we tell you so."

They examined me again, and perhaps another hour passed as I lay in bed, riding each wave of pain that crested over me. Then they began to come faster still.

"All right, Katrina," Charlotte said, peering between my legs again. "When the next pain comes, you must push. Push back against it."

"How?" I cried, frustrated.

"Your body knows what to do," Nancy assured me. She stepped close to the bed. "Here, take my hand, and squeeze it when the pain gets to be too much."

I took her hand, and when the next pain came I bore down with all the strength in my lower body. While it did not lessen the pain, it felt satisfying all the same. No doubt this was what Charlotte meant.

"Yes!" Charlotte encouraged me, from the end of the bed. "Very good. Keep doing just that."

I could not say how much time passed as I pushed and pushed against the pain, so that soon I was drenched in sweat and tears as I wept in frustration.

"Why is it taking so long? Is the baby safe?" I sobbed.

"This is how long it takes," Charlotte said. Her calm, which had given me strength before, was now infuriating. "The first child always takes the longest. If you have another, it will likely go faster."

I laughed humorlessly. "That will never happen. You know that, Charlotte. I will never bear Brom a child."

Charlotte's eyes quickly skittered up to Nancy's face. I had no patience or energy for discretion just then, yet it did not matter. Nancy's face betrayed not a flicker of surprise nor concern.

"It will not be much longer now, Katrina," Charlotte said. It was early afternoon by then, or so I thought. I had quite lost all sense of time. "Just keep pushing."

I did as she said, gripping Nancy's hand all the while. "Oh, Nancy," I said, more tears leaking out as another hideous cramp passed. "I am crushing your hand." I tried to release her, but she held on firmly.

"No, you're not," she said. "It'll take more than a little thing like you to break these hard old bones, Katrina Van Tassel."

I laughed through the next pain.

"Push!" Charlotte commanded.

I was so, so tired; more exhausted than I could ever remember being. But some primal instinct urged me on, so I gathered my strength and pushed.

"Yes!" Charlotte cried. "Nearly there! I can see the babe's head!"

The pain was nearly relentless now, and I pushed back against it just as relentlessly.

"Harder!"

With a cry of anguish and frustration I felt a great flood of fluid gush from between my legs, and the child being expelled with it.

Moments later, an indignant cry split the air, a baby enraged at being pushed from its warm nest.

I collapsed back against the pillow, my head thrown back in something like ecstasy.

"Oh, Katrina," Charlotte said, and I looked up to see her cradling the squalling, wrinkled, bloody infant in her hands. "You've done it!"

I lifted my head. "Is . . . the child is well?" I asked.

Nancy chuckled. "You can hear for yourself it's got a fine set of lungs."

"Perfectly well," Charlotte said. "It's a girl, Katrina. You and—you have a daughter, just as you predicted."

I lay back again and closed my eyes, tears of relief and happiness spilling down my cheeks. "I knew it," I sobbed. "I knew it."

Charlotte cut the cord and crossed the room to a basin of water. "I shall clean her up, and then you may hold her."

While Charlotte washed the child—*my daughter*—Nancy took some damp clothes and wiped the sweat and salt from my face. "We'll get you into a bath soon," she murmured soothingly. "Get you washed so infection doesn't set in. But first you can hold your baby girl."

Charlotte brought her to me, washed and swaddled, and placed her in my arms. I scarcely noticed Nancy and Charlotte removing bloody cloths and checking my female parts, to make sure there was no dangerous tearing or bleeding. Charlotte was speaking to me again, applying an ointment between my legs that she said was to help stop the bleeding and promote healing, but I scarcely heard her. Instead I marveled at my daughter's face as she settled against me, squirming slightly in her swaddling. When she opened her eyes, they were a brilliant blue, just like mine.

And just like that, everything I had done in the last year, every decision I had made—no matter how ill-advised or how much it had pained me—was worth it.

45

Anneke

Once the baby and I were both washed, I fed her from my breast, and then Charlotte tucked her into the wooden cradle that Brom had purchased in New York, wrapping her tightly even in the summer heat. I had Charlotte bring the cradle right beside the bed and could not stop myself from craning my neck to peer into the cradle every couple minutes, to make sure she was still there, still breathing, still well.

Charlotte smiled at me. "She is not going anywhere, you know. And scarcely have I seen a newborn baby so sturdy and healthy. You have nothing to fear."

I sighed. "I know you are right, but somehow I cannot make myself stop worrying about her."

Charlotte laughed. "I know only what many new mothers have told me over the years, but I do not think that that feeling will ever fade."

It seemed exhausting to spend the rest of my life worrying about this small, perfect human being. Yet I knew I would do so gladly, would happily watch over her all the days of her life, as she grew from baby to girl and someday, into a woman.

"And you need your rest, as well," Charlotte said. "Let me go down and make you some more broth, and then you can sleep."

I nodded contentedly, my head against the pillows and my eyes on my baby.

She left to prepare the soup—Nancy we had sent off to bed so she might rest—and I passed the time staring blissfully at the sleeping face of my daughter.

"If only your father could see you," I whispered softly. Tears sprang to my eyes, tears of joy and relief and sorrow and exhaustion. "If only he might someday know what a beautiful daughter he has.

"If I could wish one thing for you, it is that you might never know sadness," I went on. "No doubt such is impossible, but I will do everything in my power to make it so that your life is filled with only happiness."

Soon Charlotte returned and handed me a bowl of soup. "Eat all that," she commanded, "and when you're finished I've a cup of tea for you as well. There are herbs in it to help prevent infection."

I greedily slurped down the soup. I was suddenly ravenous and could not remember when I'd last eaten anything of substance. Once the soup was gone, I accepted the steaming mug of tea.

"What will you name her?" Charlotte asked.

I paused and considered my baby's face again. "I do not know," I said truthfully. "I have been thinking of it often over the last few months, but have not decided on anything quite right."

"No doubt Brom will have something to say about it," Charlotte said.

I snorted into my tea. "Who knows when he shall return from New York, and when he does no doubt he will be too busy getting over his disappointment that she is not a son," I said. "I shall name her whatever I want. Though please God he shall never know it, she is my child, not his."

Charlotte smiled. "Well said." Her smile faded slightly as she studied the sleeping baby's face. "For her sake, though, I hope he is a loving father," she said quietly. "Surely it is good for a girl to have a loving father."

I looked up at Charlotte in sympathy. Charlotte's father had died of illness before she was born. A pregnant Mevrouw Jansen had reluctantly obeyed her husband's command that she not try to heal him, for fear of catching the fever and harming herself or the child she carried. He had died before the herbwife friend she had summoned could reach them. Charlotte had once confided to me that every patient her mother healed was a bittersweet triumph for her: she had saved so many, but had not been able to save the one she loved most.

"Your father loved you, Charlotte," I said softly. "He loved you so much that he put your life before his before you were even born."

She shrugged sadly. "I know. I just wish I could have met him. I wonder, sometimes, what my life would have been like, growing up with a father."

I could not imagine my life without my father, who had doted on me since I could remember. "My daughter will likely never meet her true father," I said, "but I shall pray every night Brom is good to her."

"And how could he not be?" Charlotte asked. I knew it must be difficult for her to put aside her animosity for Brom, but I was glad she did. "Who could not love such a beauty?"

I sighed as I sipped the last of my tea, my eyelids drifting closed. Charlotte reached over and took the cup from my hand. "Sleep, Katrina. Rest. You have more than earned it. I'll be right here."

I was asleep before she had even finished speaking.

When I awoke, it was morning. Charlotte was curled on a pallet on the floor, fast asleep. After a moment, I realized what had woken me: my baby was stirring fitfully, beginning to cry.

I leapt from the bed and plucked her from the cradle, then settled back against the pillows, setting her to my breast. After much squirming and mewling, she finally latched on, and I gasped aloud in both pain and relief as she suckled.

Suddenly I panicked. How had she not needed anything in the night? Should she not have awoken me at some point? But the evidence was in my arms. She was alive, and well. I had not dreamed this miracle.

And what's more, I now knew what to name her.

As she fed, Charlotte began to stir. "Katrina?" she asked drowsily. She sat up and took in the sight of my daughter and I ensconced in the bed together. "Do you need—"

I shook my head, cutting her off. "We are both perfectly well," I said. "Thank you."

She returned my smile and stretched. "She woke in the night and needed her swaddling changed," she told me around a yawn. "I took her downstairs to change her so she would not wake you. You needed your rest."

"Oh, I could have done it," I said, crestfallen Charlotte had performed this task and not me.

"It was no trouble. As I said, rest is important for you to regain your strength and maintain your health. Besides, what are god-mothers for?" She grinned as she rose and came to peer at the babe's face. "I'll go home soon, and then all such tasks will fall on you."

I laughed. "As well they should."

"But if you need any help, I am just down the street."

"Of course," I said. "I have Nancy as well. We shall be just fine." I grasped her hand, squeezing it once. "Thank you, Charlotte," I said softly. "Thank you for everything. I can never thank you enough. I can only hope that someday I may repay you for every-thing you've done for me."

"There are no debts between friends," she said.

I smiled. "But perhaps I might tell you her name."

Her face let up with excitement. "Oh! So you've decided on one?"

"Yes. Her name will be Anneke. Anneke Charlotte, after her godmother."

Tears sprang to Charlotte's eyes, and she sat down on the bed and embraced us, both me and Anneke.

My love for my daughter, my wonder at her very being, only grew, but that did not mean that there were not some difficult times as well. I had never before been responsible for another life, and at times this scared me. And save for my obligations running the household, my time had always been my own. Not so after Anneke was born. She always needed something, whether to be fed or changed or sometimes she cried for seemingly no reason. She usually woke once during the night to be fed, and I counted myself lucky it was not more than that.

Yet whenever I was exhausted and frustrated, it was as though she knew and sought to reassure me, for she would open her blue eyes and give me a beautiful smile. My heart would melt and every moment of lost sleep, every day where I had no leisure to read or write, was worth it.

Nox had still slept in my bed when Brom was away, but when he was home my poor dog was banished from our bedchamber. Yet every night since Anneke was born, Nox had taken to stretching out on the floor in front of the cradle and sleeping there. I missed his comforting presence when Brom was not home, but Anneke could have no better or more loyal protector than the big shepherd dog.

My parents came to see her right away, and were both instantly smitten. They took turns holding her, their eyes damp.

"Oh, Katrina," my mother said. "She is just beautiful. The most perfect baby girl since yourself."

I glowed. "I am sure she is far more beautiful than I was."

"Ah, how glad I am to have a granddaughter to spoil," my father said, cradling her. "No doubt Brom was hoping for a son, but there can be no disappointment with such a lovely girl. And after all, an only daughter always suited us just fine."

I hugged them both, blinking back tears of my own.

I had written a letter to Brom the morning after Anneke's birth, directed to the boardinghouse where he always stayed in New York. Part of me wanted him to stay away as long as possible so I could have my daughter all to myself, but I knew that was not acceptable wifely behavior. And so, five days after the birth—no doubt the soonest he could wrap up whatever business he had embarked upon—Brom turned up without warning.

"Katrina!" I heard him bellow from downstairs as he came in the front door. "Nancy! Where is my wife, and my daughter?"

I had been up in our bedroom, trying to rock Anneke to sleep, but at the sound of Brom's voice she began to stir fitfully again, as if she knew this man was there to disrupt her life. No, I told myself sternly. He will love her, and she him. I want them to love each other. And someday, when the time is right, I will tell her the truth. Until then the charade must be maintained.

I rose from my chair and went downstairs, Anneke in my arms, and found Brom coming toward the staircase. He stopped dead when he saw the two of us. "She is . . . that is her?" he asked, sounding dumbfounded.

I nodded, my heartbeat increasing with trepidation. He would love her, wouldn't he? Was he angry she was not a boy? Would he somehow know she was not his by blood?

He held out his arms. "Let me hold her," he said, his voice suddenly uncertain.

I obliged, coming closer and gently settling the baby in his arms. "Be sure to support her neck," I admonished him. "She cannot yet hold her head up."

Sensing she was held by someone unfamiliar, Anneke opened her eyes and seemed to be studying Brom's face.

I had been immeasurably relieved—and yet sad at the same time—that Anneke had my blue eyes and not Ichabod's distinctive, mossy green ones. But Charlotte had told me not to be so sure. "Most babies have blue eyes when they are born," she told me, "and they change color later. She may have green eyes yet."

A shy, hesitant smile crossed Brom's face as Anneke regarded him seriously. "Hello, little one," he said softly. "I am your father."

I was touched by the scene before me, and relieved. He loved her, and she and I would both be safe. Yet soon she began to cry, and he went to hand her back to me with an almost comical look of panic on his face.

I laughed and took her back. "She is just tired," I told him. "I was trying to get her to sleep when you came in. Let me take her back upstairs."

Nancy came into the hallway from the kitchen. "Let me take her up, Miss Katrina," she said. "You and your husband get caught up."

I relinquished Anneke to Nancy with a touch of reluctance, certain I would never be comfortable parting with her.

I followed Brom into the front parlor, where we sat down. "Would you like some refreshment?" I asked. "You must have been a while on the road."

He shook his head. "No. I want only to sit awhile." A grin spread across his face. "I am a father. It is difficult to comprehend."

I kept my smile even.

"I would rather she had been a son, of course," he went on, causing the smile to slide from my face, "but she is a beautiful little thing, isn't she? And we can try for a son again soon." He gave me a lustful grin.

I did not return it. "We must wait before we can engage in the marital act again, I am afraid," I said. "I would lose my milk if I fell pregnant, and so we must wait until she is weaned."

Was I imagining it, or did I see a flash of *relief* in his eyes? Surely it was only my imagination, for in the next instant he scowled and slouched down in his chair. "A man has needs, Katrina."

I bit back a retort, for I found that, for once, I did not want to fight with him. Not today, not when he had seen Anneke for the first time. "Your needs will simply have to wait, if you want your daughter to be hale and healthy," I said.

"She is healthy, is she not?" he asked. "She was born rather early, by my reckoning."

I willed myself not to betray any alarm. I had prepared for this. "Yes," I said calmly, achieving my goal other than for the racing of my heart. "Perhaps a month or so." In fact she had been nearly a week late, a small boon. "But Charlotte and Nancy and Mevrouw Jansen assured me she is perfectly well and will grow quickly." I shrugged, as though this was scarcely a matter worthy of discussion. "It happens sometimes."

"Indeed," Brom said. Was he thinking back to the blood on our sheets the morning after our wedding, assuring himself the child was his? I hope he did not doubt it, and his remark had only been out of genuine concern for her health. I had no way of knowing for certain, as he again changed the subject.

"And have you given her a name?" he inquired, almost as an afterthought.

"Yes," I said, bracing myself. "Her name is Anneke. Anneke Charlotte Van Brunt." Inwardly I winced at the surname. Her name should be Crane. *My* name should be Crane.

Brom tensed upon hearing this. "Anneke *Charlotte?*" he demanded. "After the witch?"

"Yes," I said angrily, "and were it not for 'the witch,' neither your daughter nor your wife would be in such fine health today. I do not even want to consider what may have happened had Charlotte not been able to attend the birth." Anneke and I both would have been just fine with Nancy's midwifery skills, but Brom needn't know that.

"And yet after what she said to me all those years ago? Your husband?" he demanded.

"Charlotte was my best friend long before you were my husband," I informed him. "You once told me, when you sought to woo me, you felt you had done wrong by her. Well, I call you a liar, for you hate and fear her as much as you did all those years ago. And for no reason. She has never done you any harm. She is a good, honest woman who saves lives and heals people, whether they can pay her or not, which is more Christian charity than you've ever shown in your life, I'll wager."

To my great surprise, he actually looked abashed. He opened his mouth as though to retort, then closed it again, seeming to think better of it. "Very well," he said grudgingly. "Keep the second name for our girl, if you must. But I shall name our boy, Katrina. I shall name our son when we have him and I will brook no argument about that."

"And I shall give you none," I said.

He scowled at me, as though he could not believe my agreement had been so easy, but I let it go.

Our talk turned to politics as Brom brought me the news from New York, of the return of American emissary John Jay from Britain and his treaty. Another argument ensued as I applauded the terms of the treaty Brom described, allowing us better trade with Britain and the avoidance of being pulled into a war for which our young country was woefully underprepared and might have destroyed us. Brom thought the treaty made us look weak, and scorned the decision not to assist our former allies, the French, in their own—very bloody—revolution and war against England.

"I didn't know I was married to a damned Federalist!" Brom shouted at last, rising from his chair. "Wives should keep silent on political matters, and if they must speak, take the same stance as their husbands!"

"Not if they've their own brains in their heads!" I called as he stormed away. I sighed as I heard Anneke begin to cry upstairs. In truth, I had not expected my marriage to be anything but disagreement.

46

New Beginnings

Brom stayed home from New York for a few weeks after the birth, and to my surprise it was not unpleasant to have him there. He would sit and hold Anneke for what seemed like hours on end, though as soon as she needed to be fed or changed he was quick to pass her off to me. Yet as he grew more confident in his role as father, he would take to walking her up and down the hall when she cried and would not sleep, attempting to soothe her.

We had Anneke baptized in the church while Brom was home, with Charlotte standing as her godmother and Brom's friend—and second from the duel—Pieter Van Horn as godfather. Pieter eyed Charlotte warily throughout the service, as though he expected her to suddenly begin shouting curses at him. Anneke cried loudly as she was dunked in the water, which all the village women proclaimed was a good sign.

I was surprised—and somewhat uneasy—to notice Ichabod's cousin Giles Carpenter was present for the ceremony. I cornered Charlotte briefly after the service.

"Oh—I invited him," she said, looking guiltily away from my eyes. "He is in town, and I thought it might be nice for him to see me made godmother."

"Charlotte, he does not know, does he?" I demanded. I did not believe my dearest friend would confide my secrets to her suitor, but . . .

"Oh, no!" she exclaimed. "No, of course not! I would never tell him such a thing, never! Though . . ." She lowered her voice. "He is her blood kin."

"I know," I murmured. I did not enjoy living this lie, but it was necessary for my daughter's safety. I would endure it and more.

I longed to inquire further about her relationship with Giles, but as I had other guests to see, I was forced to defer to another time.

Charlotte naturally made herself scarce when Brom was home, so the next day I went to see her. I had left Brom fondly watching Anneke sleep and Nox standing guard. Already it felt strange to go on a visit without her. Indeed it reminded me of what I already thought of as old times as Charlotte and I settled into her parlor with some tea.

"So, how are things with Giles?" I asked, raising my eyebrows.

Charlotte smiled, but it was tinged with sadness. "Well enough, I suppose. Only . . ."

"Only what?" I pressed.

"He . . . he has not proposed, but we have talked of marriage," she said.

"Oh!" I exclaimed. "How wonderful! Why should that not make you happy?"

She sighed. "I do not know," she said. "He assumes I would come to live in White Plains with him—as a husband has every right to expect that. But in truth, I do not wish to leave Sleepy Hollow. My mother is here, and our patients and clients." She looked at me. "And you and baby Anneke, of course."

"Can he not come here?"

She frowned. "I do not know that he would consider it. He owns a small but successful tavern there. He would likely not leave it."

"He could always open a tavern here."

"Perhaps. That seems like a great deal to ask of him."

"Why not? If he truly loves you?"

"Katrina, you of all people should know these things are not that easy."

I flinched at this reminder of my own thwarted romance, but pressed on nonetheless. "I want you to be happy, Charlotte. And if it would make you happy to be his wife . . ."

"It would make me happy," she said. "But would it make me happy enough to make up for everything that is making me happy *now*, here, that I would need to give up?"

Her question gave me pause. If she had a chance for a happy, loving marriage, she should take it—it was a bit selfish of her, in a way, to think of squandering such a chance. Yet I understood her predicament. Had Ichabod and I been allowed to wed, it was a foregone conclusion that we would stay in Sleepy Hollow—or if we left, it would only be temporarily—and then eventually inherit the Van Tassel farm. So I had never been faced with such a choice.

And, of course, I did not *want* her to leave, but I couldn't wish for her to stay only for my sake, and I told her so.

She sighed. "It is not solely for you that I wish to stay, though I would miss you the most." She looked off into space. "I do not know. I must think on it more. After what Brom did, I did not think such an opportunity would come my way. And so I have never had to consider all the benefits and drawbacks of marriage."

"Have you and Giles . . ." I trailed off meaningfully, and she laughed.

"No, though God knows I have wanted to, many times," she said. "I love him and desire him. I know that. But it feels wrong to lie with him when I am so undecided about marrying him."

"I understand," I said. "And have you . . ." I hesitated. "Consulted the cards, perhaps?"

She met my gaze. "No," she said. "Not yet. Though I may soon." She studied my face. "In truth, I have been expecting you to ask me to read them for you again."

I looked away uncomfortably. "Perhaps soon," I said vaguely.

She did not look away. "Whenever you are ready, Katrina. No sooner."

I kept turning her words over in my head the rest of that day. I needed to be ready soon, I knew. The late days of my pregnancy, and the birth, had sufficiently distracted me from my quest to learn Ichabod's fate. But now it was back and beginning to gnaw at me. Perhaps the time had come to find some real answers.

That night I stood beside Anneke's cradle, watching her sleep; she was bathed in the silvery moonlight that came in through the window.

Oh, Ichabod, I thought. You have a beautiful daughter. How could you have left her? How could you have left us? She is the most perfect daughter who ever was, and you are not here. Why are you not here? How could you?

His words came back to me: *I shall pray day and night to be so blessed as to have you bear my daughter.*

Were they prayers or lies, you bastard? I wanted to scream at him. For I have borne your daughter, and where are you?

I shook with silent sobs for a long, long time.

47

The Light in the Woods

The next night, Brom went out to Sleepy Hollow's only tavern—which was run by a cousin of my father's—to enjoy a rare night with his old gang. I relished the thought of a quiet evening to myself, and once Anneke was fed and settled into her cradle, I sat with a book of poetry, candles blazing on the small table beside me as the daylight faded away.

While normally I was swept away by such poetry, for some reason it was failing to hold my interest. My eyes kept wandering away from the page and roaming about the room.

I attributed my lack of focus to pure weariness, and decided to go early to bed. I had just closed the book and set it on my lap when a single candle in an iron holder snagged my attention. Suddenly I was staring into the flame, letting it envelop me as it had that night with Charlotte.

I heard the piercing whinny of a horse, again from a distance. I saw the shadow of a man running amongst the trees, heard the panting of his breath. No, there were *two* men running, for there were two sets of footsteps, and two sets of winded lungs—or was one the horse? I could not tell. One man was chasing the other, and I heard the latter scream, a sharp cry and shout for help, and my heart constricted at the sound of his voice. *Ichabod.* Then, ahead of me, I could see a glimpse of the clearing, where the Hessian had supposedly met his end.

Then, as abruptly as it had before, the vision winked out, and I seemed to fall, panting and sweating, back into my chair in the parlor.

I struggled to catch my breath as I stared hard at the candle flame, wishing it to give up more of its secrets, much as those secrets frightened me. I had seen something, but not enough. I had not seen how it ended.

Yet who was to say it was anything but my own tired, over-active imagination? What truth could there be in a vision in a candle flame? I am so tired that I am dreaming while I am awake, I admonished myself. Surely, if I could see visions, they would show me something useful, would they not?

Blowing out the rest of the candles—and shivering in spite of myself—I picked up the single candle to carry it upstairs and made for my bed. I felt no small amount of relief when I was finally settled beneath the covers and was able to blow out that candle, as well.

Given my vision, or imagining, or whatever it was, it should have come as no surprise that I fell right into a nightmare.

I was running through the woods at night, only barely able to discern the black outline of the trees against the dark night sky. Branches tore at my hair, my skin, my skirts, but I kept running.

I heard my name, echoing out amongst the trees. I could not tell what direction it came from, but it was Ichabod's voice. Yet all around his voice it seemed as though there was a second one, darker, more sinister, a somehow deafening whisper.

"Katrina! Katrina! Katrina! Katrina!"

I kept running, though whether I was running toward the voices or away from them I could not tell. Suddenly I heard the whinny of a horse and the pounding of hooves on the path behind me. Still running, I twisted my head to look behind me, and thought I could make out the shape of a figure on horseback riding straight toward me. In the darkness all I could see for certain was the fiery face of a jack-o'-lantern.

I screamed.

"Katrina," a voice mumbled. "Katrina, wake up."

I shot bolt upright in bed, panting and coated in sweat. Beside me, Brom had pulled himself into a half-sitting position. "You were screaming in your sleep," he slurred, having yet to sleep off the drink he'd consumed with his friends. I didn't know what time it was nor when he had come in; I hadn't heard him, that much was certain.

"I . . . I was?" I asked, my breath still coming heavily.

He groaned and fell back against his pillow. "Yes. And muttering and calling out words."

I froze at this. I had not been calling Ichabod's name, had I? "I . . . I am sorry to have awoken you," I said. I pushed the coverlet aside and got out of bed. I could hear Nox outside our bedchamber, whining and scratching on the door. "I may as well go and check on Anneke, now that I am awake."

Brom made an indistinct noise of assent and fell back to sleep.

Nox leapt up and placed his paws on my shoulders as I emerged, enthusiastically licking my face. With him following, I padded to the nursery next door. I was glad to see my scream had not awoken Anneke, but as I stepped into the room she began to stir. I lifted her from her cradle and sat in the chair beside it, pulling down the shoulder of my shift to bare my breast. She suckled eagerly, and nearly as soon as she finished was asleep again.

I rose, placing her back in the cradle. Feeding the baby had calmed me somewhat, but it would be some time before I was able to sleep again. Restless and still damp with sweat in the summer heat, I went downstairs, planning to step outside for a bit of fresh air. At this hour there would be no one about to see me dressed in only my shift.

I stepped out onto the stoop, stretching my arms in the cool night air and taking several long, deep breaths.

It was the light I noticed first, off in the distance, and I realized my eyes had been trained on it for several seconds before I truly registered it. I blinked several times to clear my vision, thinking it might be some trick of my eyes.

But no, in the woods that ringed the end of our lane, I saw orange light bobbing amongst the trees. I took a few steps closer, trying to make out what I was seeing, and slowly its shape seemed to solidify out of the darkness. Was it a . . . a pumpkin? A flaming pumpkin? It was high enough up that it would have been carried by . . .

Swallowing my scream, I ran inside, bolting the door behind me. I hurried to check that the back door was locked as well before hastening back upstairs, huddling beneath the covers beside a snoring Brom. I tried to block the sight of that flaming pumpkin moving through the darkness from my mind; tried not to think what it meant in light of my latest vision and latest nightmare; tried not to think that if a supernatural rider were after me, the bolts on my doors would not keep him out.

I barely slept the rest of the night; only in fitful increments of just minutes before snapping awake again, my fear preventing any true rest. As the sun rose and the light filtered in, I began to hear Nancy downstairs, lighting the kitchen fire. I climbed out of bed—Brom still dead to the world—and went downstairs again.

I went right to the front door and opened it, peering into the woods.

I saw nothing.

48

Secrets

I visited the Jansen house as early as decently possible, having asked Nancy to watch Anneke while Brom slept off the drink. Mevrouw Jansen answered my knock. "Katrina! So early," she said, surprised. "Is everything all right? Are you and baby Anneke well?"

"Yes, we are well, although there is a . . . matter I need to consult with Charlotte about," I said. "I am sorry to call so early, it's just that . . ."

Mevrouw Jansen wrapped an arm around my shoulders. "I understand completely," she said ushering my inside, Again I wondered how much she knew about my life, and Charlotte's, and the things we sought to learn together. "Charlotte is in back with a patient right now, but I will send her out as soon as she is through."

"Oh, I . . . I don't mean to impose. I can go home until she is done."

"Nonsense. Wait here, and I'll bring you a cup of tea. It is easier for you and Charlotte to speak here, I am sure."

I was nearly faint with gratitude as I sat on the daybed. "Is there anything I can help you with, while I'm here?" I asked as she brought me a cup of steaming tea—no doubt the kettle had been hot.

"You can mind the kitchen fire, if you like. I'm going out into the garden to pick some herbs and need the fire to stay hot. I've some concoctions to brew."

I did as she said, adding a small log to the fire and turning the wood over with the iron poker to keep the blaze high. I kept my eyes averted from the flames, though, afraid of some terrifying vision that I could not explain finding me once more. Still, it was hot work in the summer, even in the relative cool of the morning. By the time Mevrouw Jansen returned, beads of sweat were dripping down my face.

She smiled upon seeing me. "Why, now you'll need to bathe when you return home!" she said. "I'm sorry. It is a rather sweaty task, but necessary, I'm afraid. Go sit, and I'll send Charlotte out to you."

A few minutes later, Charlotte appeared. "Katrina! What is it? Has something happened?"

"Well . . . it . . . yes," I said. "But . . . how is your patient?"

"Oh." She glanced back over her shoulder. "Well enough. A farmhand. He is resting for a time, before I send him home. He was hit in the head with a shovel and got quite a gash. I fixed him up, but he is still a bit incoherent." She sat on the daybed with me. "What has happened, Katrina?"

Everything poured out of me, starting with my vision in the candle flame and ending with the lit pumpkin in the woods. I spoke rapidly, trying to get the words out as quickly as I could so that I did not need to live alone with them for any longer. That Charlotte could hear them, and help me.

She listened in silence until I had finished. "Dear God," she murmured. "Someone is trying to tell you something, it seems."

"Or . . . or means me harm," I suggested.

"Well, the pumpkin . . . I do not know what to make of that," she said. "But the vision and the dream . . . those mean something, Katrina. You know that, don't you? They must."

"Or it is just my overwrought mind," I said. I let out a sound that was half laugh, half sob. "Perhaps I imagined the pumpkin and light altogether, anxious as I was." It was a possibility I had considered many times, simply because nothing else made sense.

But I had seen it. I knew I had. It had been there.

Charlotte shook her head. "Believe me, I understand the urge to want such visions to be meaningless fits of fancy. It would make everything so much easier. But you cannot explain them away as such. I of anyone would know. And it may well be they hold the answers that you seek."

"But I . . . I cannot make sense of them," I protested. "They are flashes and shadows and a few frightening images, but no new information. Nothing has been revealed. And what proof do I have that there is any truth to them at all? That they are not simply coming from my own mind?"

"Such visions do not come out of nowhere, not even our own minds, not unless you are ill and hallucinating," she said. "It could be that you do not yet realize what it is that you are seeing. I can help you, Katrina. I can help you interpret them."

I met her eyes. "I . . . suppose that is why I am here. And perhaps . . ." I swallowed down the lump of fear in my throat and lowered my voice. "Perhaps you could consult the cards again? To see if there is anything further we might learn?"

Charlotte glanced at the closed door to the stillroom, where her mother was. "Yes," she said quietly. "But not tonight. Come back tomorrow night; I believe my mother will be out checking on one of our regular patients."

"Very well." I paused. "But . . . the pumpkin."

"Yes." Charlotte frowned, a trace of fear in her eyes. "Maybe it was someone playing a prank of some kind? It sounds like something Brom and his gang would get up to, honestly."

I frowned. I had not considered this, and it was plausible, at the very least. "Brom was in bed beside me when I awoke from my nightmare," I said. "But it could have been one of his friends, I suppose. But, Charlotte, pumpkins are not even in season. It is far too early. Where would they have gotten it?"

"Perhaps that part you imagined, then, just coming out of a nightmare as you were," she suggested.

Perhaps.

I returned home and tried as best I could to go about my day. Brom finally awoke and dragged himself onto his horse to ride to his father's house to help him with checking on the crops.

Late that night, when Brom and Anneke were long since fast asleep, I tried to read in the parlor, afraid to close my eyes for fear of the nightmares I might have, and of the mischief that might be wreaked as I slept. Nox rested his head on my feet, as if sensing my disquiet.

As I listlessly turned the pages of my book, Nancy came quietly into the room. Nox thumped his tail against the floor at the sight of her, his favorite giver of scraps. "Miss Katrina," she said. "Can't you sleep?"

I smiled wearily up at her. "No, Nancy, I am afraid I cannot. And you?"

"Sleep comes harder at my age," she confessed, and lowered herself into the chair beside mine. She was quiet a moment longer, then spoke again. "You remember when you were in labor, and you wanted to know the story of my daughter?"

I nodded, sitting up a bit straighter. "Yes. I'd still like to hear it, if you're willing to tell it."

She smiled sadly. "I would. I think I must, in truth. I've never told the full tale to anyone, and it gets heavier the longer I carry it."

"Then please," I said, "tell me."

After a deep breath, she began. "As you know, I was born into slavery on a tobacco plantation in Virginia," she said. "Nothing special about that; most black folks in this country are. My mother was a lot like Mistress Jansen; she knew about herbs and midwifery and helped deliver the mistress's babies. She also helped the people in the big house when they were sick, as well as the slaves. When there was no one needed tending to, she helped in the kitchen. I grew up learning many of her skills.

"Anyway, when I turned eighteen, I caught the eye of a man, a fellow slave, name of John. He caught my eye, too, and much as my mama tried to keep a weather eye on me, he and I managed to sneak around together." She gave me a pointed smile. "As young girls will do."

I blushed slightly.

"Soon I was pregnant, and John and I married. The master was delighted—he encouraged us all to marry and make babies. The more babies, the more slaves, and profit for him, of course."

I blanched at this cold view of marriage and children, though I knew that was the reality among slaveholders. Still, knowing it and hearing it from someone who had lived it was another matter entirely.

"And my daughter was born. She was the most beautiful little girl. I named her Sarah, after my mother. And I nursed her and took care of her in between my work. When I was needed to assist my mother working in the kitchen, I left her with the women who were too old to work. No matter how exhausted I was at the end of each day, Sarah always made me smile.

"When Sarah was just three, the master's sister and brother-in-law came down from New York City for a visit. They were in the market for a new cook, they said, and hadn't found one trained up enough in the slave markets of New York. Would he know of anyone? The master had several slaves working in his kitchen, so he decided he could part with me."

Her eyes grew wet with tears. "So he sold me to his sister and her husband. But not Sarah. And not John."

"Oh, Nancy," I breathed, a hitch in my voice.

"I begged him to let Sarah come with me, but he refused. She was his property, and she'd grow up to replace me in the kitchens, he said. He could find John another woman easy enough. And I hadn't conceived since Sarah was born, so I wasn't as valuable to him anymore." She nearly spat the words. "I then begged my new master and mistress to buy Sarah as well, but they had no use for a child in their small household and did not wish to spend the money, especially as my old master was of no mind to let her go." She shook her head. "So they brought me north, and my baby girl stayed in Virginia."

"Oh, Nancy," I said again, taking her hand. "I . . . I don't know what to say."

She smiled at me, but there was something hard in her eyes. "Don't know as there's anything you can say, Katrina. You live in a world where no one will ever take your baby girl from you. And that's the way it should be for us all, but reality ain't about 'should be.'"

She continued. "I missed John and especially Sarah every day. In New York, my new master and mistress would hire me out to other households in New York if they needed a cook for a big fancy event, and they let me keep some of the fee they got. It took me many years, but I eventually bought my freedom from them. They gave me my papers, and I was free.

"I had little money left after that and set about looking for work. As soon as I had some money, I wanted to find my daughter. Luckily, I met your mother and father, and your mother took a liking to me. They offered me a position for a fair wage if I was willing to move with them to their farm on the Hudson. Well, I wasn't likely to find a better offer, so I accepted.

"Not long after I started working for them, I asked your father if there was any way he might find Sarah for me. I told him her name and the name of the plantation I'd been sold from in Virginia, and the name of the master there, and he obliged me and wrote a letter. The master's son wrote back to say there were no slaves on the plantation named Sarah. It was clear that my daughter had been sold off, or was dead. And that was all we could do. I had nothing but her name, and it was a common enough one. To this day, I don't know what happened to her, whether she's alive or dead. Or if, maybe, she managed to get free."

Tears were spilling down Nancy's face. "There was nothing else

I could do. And then you were born and I looked after you and loved you. I mean that, Katrina. But there was never an hour of the day when I didn't remember you're not my own, that my daughter is out there someplace only God knows where."

I leaned over to embrace Nancy, my own tear-stained face resting against hers. We stayed like that for some time, my heart aching that there was nothing I could do, and that I, as heiress to a fortune whose daughter slept peacefully upstairs, could never truly understand. I could only listen, and let Nancy know that I had heard her.

"Well, now," Nancy said, leaning back and wiping her eyes. "You wanted to know the story, and there it is. Not a happy one. But I do feel a bit better for the telling."

"I'm glad I could do that much," I said. "That I could listen."

She smiled. "And now I think maybe you ought to tell me a story," she said. "About your own baby."

There were so many more questions I wanted to ask her, but it was clear she had told me everything she wanted to say. I would not press and ask for more. "Yes," I said. I bit my lip. "I have been wanting to tell you the truth for some time. No doubt you already suspect, but . . ." I quickly glanced at the doorway to make sure Brom was not about to appear, before dropping my voice to a whisper. "Anneke is not Brom's child. She is Ichabod Crane's."

Nancy nodded. "I figured as much."

"But Ichabod disappeared—whether of his own will or not, I do not know—and I married Brom, so everyone would believe Anneke was his. It is not what I would have preferred, obviously, but it was the best choice for her."

"I admit, I had put together that much, more or less," Nancy said. "I had a suspicion you were sneaking out to see the schoolteacher, even at night, but I didn't tell your parents. You're a smart girl; I figured you knew what you were doing. And he seemed like the type to make an honest woman of you."

Tears pricked my eyes again. "He tried. He asked my father for my hand; he knew I was with child. But my father refused, and that very night Ichabod simply . . . vanished." I looked up at her. "I do not know if he abandoned me, or if . . . something befell him. But I mean to find out, however I can."

"It may be that you are better off not knowing."

Her words had given life to one of my worst fears. "Whatever the truth is, it must be better than this."

"You be careful, Katrina," Nancy said. "I don't doubt Charlotte Jansen is helping you, and I don't doubt that she has ways of knowing things most mortals do not. But there are some powers in this world that are not to be toyed with. There were any number of wise women and what all in New York I could have consulted to try to find my Sarah—and Lord knows I thought about it. But that was a line I never crossed. One cannot cross it without paying a terrible price."

"Come, Nancy, surely that is only old superstition," I said, trying to push my unease aside.

"Maybe so. I can only hope that Charlotte Jansen knows where that line is better than anyone." She looked pointedly at me. "I assume she knows the truth about little Anneke?"

"Yes. You are the only one aside from her who knows."

Nancy rose from her chair. "And never you fear, I'll keep it that way." She bent down and kissed me on the cheek. "Thank you for trusting me with your secret."

"And thank you for trusting me with your story."

She left the room, and I could only hope she might find it easier to sleep now.

49

Death in the Cards

That night was, blessedly, free of dreams—or if I dreamt, I could not remember—and the following night I left Anneke with Brom, Nancy, and Nox, and headed to Charlotte's. I marked well the look of warning in Nancy's eyes as I left.

"Come in," Charlotte said, quickly ushering me in once I arrived. "My mother has more than one patient to check in on tonight, so we shall be alone for a few hours, at least. Let us make the most of it."

Charlotte had already prepared the table and lit numerous candles about the room. Before her chair sat the worn deck of tarot cards.

I could not suppress a shudder as I sat down across from her. Last time the cards had foretold nothing but ill fortune. Was it possible that today they would give me some measure of hope?

"I confess, I am a bit curious what you are hoping the cards will show you," Charlotte said, sitting down. "They are used to divine the future, or to give us insight into present events. I have not known them to reveal secrets from the past, which is what you are searching for."

"Indeed," I said, "but perhaps some insight into present events is just what I need. Am I on the right path? Do I have the tools I need to discover the truth? And will I ever find the truth I seek?"

Charlotte shuffled the cards. "You'll want to settle on just one of those questions for now," she told me. She set the cards in front of me. "Cut the deck with your left hand, and concentrate on the question you wish to have answered."

I narrowed all my questions down to just one, repeating it over and over: *Will I ever know the truth about what happened to Ichabod? Will I ever know the truth about what happened to Ichabod?*

Will I ever know the truth?

I finished cutting the cards and pushed them back to Charlotte. Concentrating, she closed her eyes and turned over the first card in the deck.

I gasped sharply upon seeing the face of the card, and Charlotte, when she opened her eyes, did the same.

"The Devil," Charlotte said. "Again." She glanced up at me, relieved, unlike the first time this card had revealed itself to us. "Remember, this first card signifies your past. So this means the evil is behind you."

I let out my breath. Much as I had hoped never to see that card again, if I must see it, I was glad it represented the past.

She turned over the next card, one I had not seen before: a woman seated between two pillars, dressed in flowing blue and white robes, and wearing a tall headdress.

"The High Priestess," Charlotte said. She blew out her breath in a long, slow whistle. "Interesting. Very interesting."

"What does it mean?" I demanded.

"As you know, the second card represents your present. And so to see The High Priestess . . ." She shook her head. "Very fitting indeed. But yes, the meaning. She represents hidden knowledge, and psychic abilities of some kind." Charlotte looked at me significantly. "Such things are the key to answering your question."

I sat back in my chair, surprised. But perhaps I should not have been. After all, was that not what Charlotte had been telling me all along?

"The High Priestess can also signify someone—usually a woman—who is guiding you in some way," Charlotte added.

My lips curled into a half smile. "Most fitting. For is that not what you are doing, have been doing all along?"

"I suppose I must flatter myself that, yes, I have been," she said, smiling as well. "Onward?"

When I nodded, she flipped over the next card, and I gasped again.

Facing me, right-end up, was a rider on a white horse, carrying a black banner. Below the image the word identifying the card was painted in stark black capital letters: *DEATH*.

"It does not mean literal death," Charlotte said quickly. "It almost never does. But . . . it is reversed." She tapped a finger against her lips. "Interesting," she said again.

"Please, Charlotte, just tell me what it means."

"It is not necessarily an ill omen. The Death card often means an ending of some kind, and sometimes that is a good thing. Yet because it is reversed . . ." Charlotte looked up at me and took a deep breath before continuing. "I do not mean to distress you, Katrina. Truly I don't. But I would interpret this to mean that, yes, you will reach the end of your quest, but it may not bring you any peace."

I rose quickly, jostling the table. "And can you truly tell me I will not find death at the end of my quest?" I asked, my eyes still fixed on the card.

"The cards are not absolute, Katrina. You know this. And the Death card does not foretell death. Just endings," she said firmly.

Still I had not looked away from the card. "It is a horseman," I pointed out.

Startled, Charlotte glanced down at it.

"A figure on horseback," I added. "A mounted rider."

"So it is," she said, her voice tight.

"And can you also tell me I will not find the Headless Horseman at the end of this road?" I asked.

Charlotte swept the three cards back into the deck and out of sight. She did not answer me.

50

The Secrets of the Flame

The next day, Brom returned to New York, and my whole body breathed a sigh of relief. I had, however, been genuinely touched to see the emotion on his face as he bade farewell to Anneke and promised to return soon.

I spent most of the day with my baby, pushing aside all thoughts of tarot cards and candle flames and death on horseback. I spread a blanket out in the garden for her, releasing her from her swaddlings. I fed her right there in the garden, and when her eyelids began to droop I laid curled up beside her on the blanket.

If nothing else, she deserves to know, someday, what happened to her real father. And what sort of man he truly was, I thought, before drifting off to sleep myself.

Later that day, I sat again at my desk with my quill and notebook, Anneke dozing beside me in her cradle. I wrote a brief description of my most recent nightmares and visions, and of Charlotte's cards, then I flipped back to the middle of the book and began setting down a new story, that of Van Dam, the ghostly rower on the Hudson. The story went that he had been very fond of drunken revelry, and had spent most of his Saturday nights in pursuit of such before the Sabbath. One night, he promised he would return home before the stroke of midnight, when the Sabbath began. Yet as the Sabbath bells tolled, he was still in his boat on the Hudson, rowing furiously to make it home in time to keep his promise. And so, in the early hours of Sunday mornings, many have reported seeing him rowing still, doomed to row forever for not keeping the Sabbath.

As I wrote, I heard footsteps come into the room and looked up, expecting to see Nancy. Instead, Charlotte stood there. "Why, Charlotte!" I said, rising from my chair. "Do come in and sit down."

"Nancy let me in," she said, sitting down on the daybed. "But I am sorry, I seem to have interrupted you," she said, nodding toward my notebook and quill.

"Oh, do not worry about that," I said. "My writing project, you see. I can pick it up again later."

Charlotte raised her eyebrows. "Writing project? What writing project is this?"

"Can it be that I have not told you?" Yet it seemed that I had not. The birth of Anneke, and the reordering of my life, had made me quite forget to bring it up to Charlotte.

Anneke began to stir, and I rose to pick her up. "No, please let me," she said. "I'd love to hold her." She picked Anneke up and cradled her securely in her arms. Anneke stopped fussing immediately and reached up to grasp the strands of red hair tumbling over Charlotte's shoulders, studying them with fascination.

"So, your writing," Charlotte prompted.

I told her the whole story, how Ichabod had once suggested it, and how the project had given me more purpose and pleasure than I had ever anticipated, and also how I had taken to chronicling my attempts to find Ichabod.

"What a marvelous idea, all of it," Charlotte said when I'd finished. "You must read me one of your tales!"

I laughed. "You know them all as well as I do."

"But you've always had such a gift for telling them, truly. I should like to hear how you've committed them to paper."

"Soon, then, if you wish," I asked. "But what brings you by? And I hope that I can persuade you to stay for dinner. It should be ready any moment now."

"I'm happy to accept, of course. I simply wanted to see how you were faring this morning," she said.

I sighed. "Well enough. I spent the day with Anneke and put all the rest out of my mind. But I cannot seem to forget it for long."

"I may be able to help you," she ventured.

"Oh?"

"There are certain techniques one can use to bring a vision on," she said. "If you are certain this is what you want to do. You have been resistant to such things in the past."

"Yes. Teach me whatever you can, Charlotte. I am done with half measures. Let us find the truth and have done with it, whatever it might bring."

Charlotte nodded. "Very well, then. After dinner?"

I nodded. "I will tell Nancy to set another place."

After dinner, with Anneke in bed for the night and Nox keeping watch, I led Charlotte back into the parlor. I shut the door and drew the curtains closed. A few candles were lit for our purposes, and Charlotte brought one branch to the floor, where we sat across from one another.

"Now," Charlotte said. "Fire is a difficult medium in which to see anything. On the rare occasion that I seek out such visions, I use a bowl of water or a mirror. But fire wishes to speak to you, and I think we should listen to it."

I nodded.

"Close your eyes and take several deep breaths; however many you feel are necessary to relax yourself. Keep your eyes closed," she said, her voice low and melodic. I did as she said.

"When you are ready," Charlotte murmured, "when your mind is clear and your body relaxed, open your eyes and look into the center of the flame. Ask it—silently—to show its secrets to you."

I took a few more deep breaths, then slowly flicker my eyes open, fixing my gaze on the flame. *Show me,* I thought. *Show me your secrets, show me the truth.* Somehow I felt more powerful than before, as if my intention had given me strength. *Show me your secrets, your knowledge. Reveal to me the truth.*

The flame danced lightly on the wick, flickering as our breath stirred the air in the still room. For a second it seemed like the dark center of the flame was expanding, and I leaned forward expectantly, ready to see what it had to show me, but to my disappointment nothing was revealed. The flame did not engulf me; I did not tumble into some dark world of revelations.

After a few minutes, Charlotte cleared her throat. "Let us try again," she said. "Repeat the same process—deep, slow breaths, eyes closed, clear your mind—and begin again."

I started over, entreating the flame to show me something, anything. And again, nothing.

At least show me Ichabod's face, I begged it finally. *I do not even need to see what became of him, just, please, please, let me see him one more time.*

But still the flame proved obstinate.

Tears began to trickle down my cheeks, and I squeezed my eyes shut and looked away.

"Katrina . . . ?" Charlotte said. "Please do not fret if you cannot see anything. This kind of art is very capricious and it takes time and practice. We will try again, don't worry—"

I shook my head. "It isn't that," I said through my tears. "Not really. Not only that. I just . . ." I buried my face in my hands and let out a sob. "I miss him so much."

Charlotte did not say anything; she simply slid closer to where I sat on the floor and wrapped her arms around my shaking shoulders.

51

The Woman in White

That night I dreamt that I was the Woman in White of Raven Rock, haunting the lonely forests and waiting for my love to return. In the dream, I called out Ichabod's name; called out "My love! Have you come for me?" just as the Woman in White had been heard to do, my despair growing with each unanswered call. I awoke in the early dawn light, my cheeks wet with fresh tears, and only the thought that Anneke would need feeding and changing propelled me from the comfort of my bed.

I must have looked nearly as frightful as the Woman in White, too, for as I came downstairs with Anneke to break my fast, Nancy took one look at me and asked, "You all right, Katrina?"

I smiled weakly. "As well as can be expected, Nancy. I did not sleep well last night."

She took my chin in her hand, inspecting my face. "Hmmm. You look like you've been weeping."

I met her gaze and didn't bother to deny it. "Sometimes I am sad."

"I can understand that," she said at last, and turned away to fix us both some coffee.

After we ate, I dragged myself to my desk and recorded the techniques Charlotte had outlined the night before, and our unsuccessful results. I was just getting ready to take Anneke out into the garden when Charlotte arrived, announced by excited barking from Nox.

"I just wanted to see how you were feeling," Charlotte said, stepping inside.

I shrugged. "As well as can be expected," I said yet again.

"Well, that's good enough, I suppose."

"I want to try again, Charlotte," I told her, cradling Anneke against my chest. "As soon as possible. I don't want to stop, not until we have the truth. By whatever means necessary."

Charlotte's eyes widened at my forcefulness, but she nodded. "Very well. I understand. Come to my house tonight and we will try again."

"Good. I will be there. And pray we have some success this time."

"Why do *you* not ask the fire, or your mirror or what have you?" I demanded of Charlotte that night, when I saw nothing new— only those same images I had already seen. "Why can you not see the truth for me?"

"Visions are easier to come by when they relate to the seer directly," she said. "And besides, do you not want to see it yourself? To find your answers yourself?"

"Yes," I admitted, a touch of petulance in my tone.

"I thought as much. So we try again."

Summer faded into autumn as Charlotte and I continued our quest. Our time together was somewhat limited; we preferred to have a house mostly to ourselves so as not to alert her mother or Nancy to our doings, and when Brom was home there was no question of us practicing such arts. God only knew what his reaction would be if he learned I was dabbling in witchcraft.

Perhaps a month into our endeavor, Charlotte was waiting for me one night at her cottage with a steaming mug of tea. "Here," she said. "Drink this."

I eyed it suspiciously. "What is it?"

"It's brewed with herbs that are thought to heighten the sixth sense and bring on stronger visions," she explained.

I started. "And you are just giving this to me now? Why have we not tried this before?"

Charlotte sighed. "I had hoped that you might succeed without it. Too much of this mixture can make you very sick, so it must be imbibed sparingly and only in very small doses. It becomes a bit more potent if you mix it into wine, but unfortunately we do not have any. And perhaps it is best to start with tea, in any case."

"Well, I am certainly willing to try it," I said. I took the cup from her, then hesitated. "Charlotte . . . who is to say these visions are real at all? That they are not just my own imagination? The dreams, everything . . . it could all be fantasy and illusion on my part." I knew it was not the first time I had asked these questions, but after so many failed attempts, so many shadowy visions with nothing new, I no longer trusted my own mind.

"The human mind is a very powerful thing," she conceded. "Too powerful, sometimes, for our own good. But it is also capable of things most people cannot imagine. Your dreams of the Horseman have meaning, Katrina; they are more than mere illusions or even nightmares. I think . . ." She trailed off. "I think that Ichabod's disappearance is in some way connected to the Headless Horseman, but perhaps not in the way we think."

"In what other way could it be connected?" I asked, incredulous. "I suppose the Horseman could have just ridden him off? Scared him away? But I cannot believe he would have been so scared that he would never return for me, nor send word."

Charlotte shrugged. "I cannot say. It is just a feeling I have."

I nodded in acknowledgement of all this, and without further comment drank the tea Charlotte had handed me, wincing at its bitter taste.

My heart thundered in anticipation that night, thinking these herbs would finally reveal all to me. While I was disappointed in that regard, I did manage to see something new.

"Gunpowder!" I called, and found myself thrust out of the vision again. I was breathing hard, across the table from Charlotte. "I saw Gunpowder! Ichabod's horse!"

"Where was he? Did you see Ichabod as well? Riding him?"

I frowned. "He . . . he had a rider, but I could not see who it was. I assume it was Ichabod. And he was galloping through the forest, fast. That is all I saw." I shook my head. "In all these visions, I always see the forest. But why? There would have been no need for Ichabod to ride through the forest that night. The Albany Post Road would have taken him straight home from my parents' house. And if he decided to flee, well, there was even less reason to ride through the woods. The road would have taken him north to Albany, or south to New York."

Charlotte shrugged. "He must have had a reason, for it seems certain that ride through the woods he did. Perhaps, as we've said, he went for a ride to clear his head. And either he decided to leave, or . . . something else befell him."

I remained silent. I did not believe Ichabod would have taken a leisurely ride through the woods on All Hallows' Eve of all nights, not after all the tales I'd told him, after the stories exchanged at the party that night. But for whatever reason, he had. That much we knew.

We kept it up as the months passed, and though I wanted to ask Charlotte for more herbs, I did not, nor did she offer them again. I heeded her warning about the danger of such a potion and let it alone for the time being.

I sought visions on my own as well, without Charlotte, and also tried to see in a mirror. But I had no luck. It seemed that Charlotte was right: the fire seemed to particularly wish to speak to me. Yet I only ever saw scraps of new sights—a different angle on Gunpowder, more hoof beats, and once I caught a glimpse of the church, standing dark and silent amid the tombstones of the burial ground.

All the while, I recorded everything in my book. Every attempt, whether success or failure, was written down.

As fall and the harvest wore on, we consulted the cards again one night, and afterward a part of me wished we had not. Somehow, Charlotte turned over the same three cards as the last time: The Devil, The High Priestess, and Death.

"Very strange," she said. "I do not recall ever getting the exact same reading more than once."

I stared dejectedly at the cards. "It is not telling us anything we do not already know," I said. "We are no further ahead than we were months ago."

52

Giles and Charlotte

My parents held their annual All Hallows' Eve party as usual—now a painful anniversary for me. A year had passed and I was no closer to finding the truth about Ichabod. Still, Anneke, Brom, and I were all there, as well as Nancy—attending as a guest and friend—and I pretended to be nothing more than a happy mother and wife, celebrating the harvest with my family and friends.

I was surprised when Charlotte arrived with none other than Giles Carpenter. I had not known he was in town, let alone that Charlotte would be bringing him to the party.

As always when I saw him, I felt both happiness—for Charlotte—and pain at the reminder of Ichabod. Yet I smiled and greeted him warmly. "So nice to see you, Mr. Carpenter," I said. "And I need not tell you that you could have no one more lovely accompany you."

He smiled at this. "Always a pleasure, Miss Van Tassel—forgive me, Mistress Van Brunt. I remember you as we first met, you see. But I am pleased and honored to be here. Your family's generosity is truly remarkable, and I am fortunate to be one of its recipients."

"Indeed," I said. "Well, you must enjoy, of course. I hope we will get more of a chance to converse later."

The look Charlotte tossed me over her shoulder as the pair

moved away was one alight with happiness, her cheeks flushed and her eyes bright. At least All Hallows' Eve might be a happy night for someone. And if Giles noticed the way the villagers drew back guardedly from Charlotte, or were reluctant to include her in their conversation, he surely did not comment. Indeed, he looked as though he simply could not believe his great fortune in being there at her side.

In truth, I did not speak to Charlotte and Giles again that night, and they left shortly after dinner—though Mevrouw Jansen, I noticed, remained behind, and stayed much later. I asked my parents if we might stay the night rather than make the journey home in the dark, and they readily agreed. Brom was rather drunk, so the arrangement suited him just fine. Just as well that I did not need to explain my deeply superstitious fear of riding home at night on All Hallows' Eve, and with my baby daughter. Ichabod Crane's daughter.

I passed a mercifully restful night in my old bedroom—Brom I left to sleep off the drink alone in the guest chamber where we'd spent our wedding night—with Anneke beside me. We rose the next morning and breakfasted with my parents—Brom looking somewhat worse for the wear—before journeying home.

Brom, having recovered somewhat, spent the afternoon out in the garden with Anneke, and so I was alone in the parlor when Charlotte came to call.

I took one look at her—her glowing happiness of the night before heightened—and knew.

"Oh, Katrina," she sighed, sinking down onto the daybed beside me. Her eyes sparkled. "Last night, Giles and I . . . we did it. We finally made love."

I clutched my hands in hers. "Charlotte! I confess I suspected, since you are so incandescently happy." I gave her a sly smile. "I trust it was an enjoyable experience?"

She blushed. "It was," she said. "There was pain, and I bled, which I had been prepared for. And while I did not experience the overwhelming pleasure I have heard people speak of, I . . . it was wonderful. Just being so close to him, knowing that he loves me and I love him . . ."

I nodded. "I know just what you mean." I raised my eyebrows suggestively. "And the pleasure, too, will come. With practice."

She grinned sheepishly. "I am most willing to spend time in practice, I can assure you. And Giles is only too willing to assist me."

"I suppose I need not lecture you about taking your herbs."

Her face sobered. "No, indeed. Though I would love a child of my own someday, if we wed. I have already taken them today, and will do so again tomorrow morning."

"Ah, so another assignation is planned?"

She blushed again. "Yes. He is staying at the inn, so I will slip through the crowd up to his room tonight and hope no one notices me." She sighed. "But then tomorrow he must return home. He wishes me to go with him, wishes us to marry at once. But I . . . as much as I love him and want to be his wife, I am still not ready to leave Sleepy Hollow."

"And he cannot be persuaded to move here?"

"He . . . might be," she confessed. "I do not know. There is so much to discuss."

I squeezed her hand. "You must do whatever makes you happy. And White Plains is not so far away."

"I know. And perhaps it would be worth it. Perhaps I would be this happy all the time, though I cannot imagine how that is possible."

After the harvest, winter began to set in. Brom spent most of November in New York, seeing to the sale of crops from both the Van Brunt and Van Tassel farms, then returned home in December for the feast of St. Nicholas, the New Year, and to spend the winter months.

We celebrated St. Nicholas Day with a fine feast at my parents' farmhouse after church, complete with sausage, cheese, coleslaw, mashed potatoes, and doughnuts. Brom's father, Nancy, Mevrouw Jansen, and Charlotte also attended. I noted Charlotte's aura of melancholy; Giles had not been able to visit in the past month. I knew all too well the unique pain and frustration of being separated from one's lover when he was not, in truth, that far away.

Anneke, as the only child in the family, was showered with gifts by my parents, from carved wooden toys to hand-sewn clothes and a few books that would help her to learn her letters when the time came. She was far too young as yet, but would soon grow to need them, and I felt it only right that my daughter should have her first books at a very young age.

"God willing, we will have another grandchild to spoil at our St. Nicholas feast a year from now," my father said, grinning at Anneke as she shook a new rattle in my arms. "A grandson this time, perhaps?"

Brom draped an arm around my shoulders. "We hope that it might be so," he said, grinning. "Very soon we shall continue our endeavors in that area."

I gritted my teeth behind my smile.

On New Year's Day, Brom went out to call on our neighbors, as was customary, while I stayed home with plenty of refreshments on hand to greet those who called on us. The next day it was the ladies' turn to go calling, and so I visited several houses in the village and chatted with many of the farmwives and their husbands and was offered food and drink. For whatever reason, this year I found the ritual more exhausting than ever.

After the New Year festivities had passed, Nancy and my mother pronounced it was high time Anneke be weaned, something Brom enthusiastically agreed with, as it meant that he could again exert his husbandly privilege. And so I procured the necessary herbs from Charlotte, praying his past difficulties would visit him once again.

Just after the New Year, Brom made his triumphant return to my bed. To my dismay, he had no trouble whatsoever. As soon as he removed his clothes, his member was hard and ready, and he climbed into bed and proceeded to bury himself inside me with no preliminaries. He thrust enthusiastically several times before groaning in his ecstasy, already spent. At least it was over quickly.

Once he had withdrawn and caught his breath, Brom rolled back over to face me. "I am sorry to have been so . . . brief," he said. "But it has been a long time. It is difficult for a man to wait so long."

I was surprised at the insinuation that he had not made love to a woman since before I'd announced my pregnancy—a year ago now. I had never expected him to be faithful, especially not with him spending so much time in New York, where female company was readily available for those with the coin to purchase it. Indeed, all the better for me if he exerted his energies elsewhere. I was not sure whether to believe him, but his eagerness seemed to support his words.

"I shall be sure to make it nice and slow the next time," he said, kissing me.

I did not reply. Could he really think that I longed for his touch?

It seemed he did, for the next morning, before I could go drink my herbal mixture, he awoke and drew me toward him again, kissing and caressing me.

"Do you not wish to touch me in return, Katrina?" he breathed in my ear. "Have you not missed your husband in your bed?"

I returned his kisses as best I could, even taking his member in my hand, something that caused him to gasp in pleasure. It also caused him to enter me quickly, though this time he thrust much slower, deeper, enjoying each moment. I was ashamed and horrified to feel my body responding, my breathing quickening; to find myself enjoying the physical sensations of the act, though that shattering pleasure eluded me. After Brom finished, tears leaked from my eyes at this betrayal of Ichabod. Even if I had been the one betrayed first.

Afterward, once Brom had dressed and gone out, I mixed the herbs and drank them down greedily, finding in them today a certain kind of penance. As far as I was concerned, Brom's rights to my body extended only so far. I chose to bear Ichabod's child and only his, and I would not change my mind.

With nothing else to do that day, I bundled up Anneke and walked to Charlotte's for a visit.

"I have been meaning to ask you," Charlotte said, once we were settled, Nox happily allowing Charlotte to scratch his ears, "how is your writing project coming? I still want you to read me one of your stories, you know."

"Well enough," I said. "I do not have as much time as I would like, with this little one." I gestured to Anneke with a smile. "And, in truth, I think I am running out of stories."

Charlotte smiled. "Then you must make up your own, mustn't you, so you will never run out of stories."

"Perhaps I shall," I said. The thought had occurred to me more than once. What would I write, if I could write anything?

Charlotte waved a hand at me. "Run home and get your book," she bade me. "I will stay with Anneke. Then return and read us a story."

Rising, I laughed. "Very well," I said. "I will be right back."

I dashed home, retrieved the book from its locked drawer in my desk, and returned quickly to the Jansen cottage, where Charlotte was studying Anneke carefully.

"Oh," Charlotte said, looking up at me. "I had not noticed before, but . . . her eyes. They have changed."

"Yes." I sighed. It was a source of both great joy and great anxiety to me.

"They are green," Charlotte said, unnecessarily.

"Yes," I said again. "Just like Ichabod's."

"Yes," she agreed. She studied my daughter's face again. "Very like. Has Brom noticed?"

"I'm sure he's noticed, but he has not remarked upon it," I said. "And I hope that he will never guess at the truth. I am quite sure that he is convinced I came to the marriage bed a virgin."

"Yes, perhaps you are right." She hesitated. "And in any case, I do not think he spent much time gazing into Ichabod Crane's eyes."

I laughed. "No, I daresay he did not."

"So all should be well, then," she said. "And your child resembles her father in this way at least. Whether that makes you happy or causes you pain."

"Both," I said. I opened my book and began flipping the pages to choose a story, indicating that I was ready to leave the subject.

53

Ghosts

Giles's next visit came and went, and though Charlotte was thrilled to have seen him, she had no news to report.

"And how goes the practice?" I asked, arching an eyebrow.

She laughed. "Quite well," she said. "I now know that pleasure of which so many speak."

I grinned. "I am glad to hear it, and glad to hear Giles is as skilled and considerate a lover as Ichab—as his cousin is. Was."

"I'm sorry. I know it must be difficult to speak of him," she said.

"It gets more so every day," I confessed. "Oh Charlotte, *I* am sorry. I do not wish to overshadow your happiness. That is the last thing I want."

She patted my hand. "I understand. I understand how it must be difficult for you, too, to hear me speak of his cousin in such a way."

It was, but I told myself that that mattered not, not in the face of my dearest friend's happiness.

That night Brom turned to me in bed, and I acquiesced willingly enough. Yet I was surprised when he found himself once again unable, even though he had not consumed much drink that night; just a glass of beer with our meal. Not that I was complaining.

"Damn it all," Brom swore, shoving me away as he finally gave up on his attempts to rouse himself. "Damn it all to hell." Yet he slid a hand between my legs all the same and put two fingers inside me. "Yet perhaps my wife might still know pleasure this night," he whispered in my ear, kissing my neck.

I opened my mouth to protest, but the words died in my throat as his fingers thrust and stroked. My breathing came faster, and my heartbeat increased. All thoughts were banished by the pleasure radiating up from my core, and soon I gasped aloud as it tore through me—not the almost unbearable ecstasy I had known before, but it felt good all the same.

Brom's breathing hitched as he watched me arch my back in pleasure, and this sight sufficiently roused him. Removing his hand, he thrust himself into me, and I moved with him, this time pleasure coming to both of us.

As he withdrew, the shame began again to burn me, but this time I pushed back against it. Brom had treated me well thus far, and more importantly, he was good to Anneke, loved her with all his heart. I married him out of desperation, yes, but that did not mean I must be miserable all my life, did it? My true love had left me, so was I not allowed to find some pleasure with my husband?

Surely I was, but guilt still dogged me.

"Perhaps soon we shall have a son," he said, as he lay next to me, spent. "Perhaps we have already conceived him." The hope in his voice made me feel ever guiltier as I crept downstairs while he slept and drank my herbal mixture.

Spring came, and Brom was home in Sleepy Hollow for most of it, assisting his father with the planting on the Van Brunt farm, and helping my father oversee the planting of the Van Tassel farm as well. He was quite busy, and usually left the house before dawn only to return after dark, too tired to do more than bolt down a hearty meal, give Anneke a kiss, and collapse into bed, only to rise and do it all over again the next day. The only break in his routine was

Sundays, when all work must cease and we went to church as a family, and dined with either my parents or his father or both after the service.

I continued my forays into divination, sometimes with Charlotte, sometimes without. The more time that passed, the more frustrated and upset I felt, yet there was no escaping that both of our lives had grown busier, different: mine with Anneke, who began to crawl and then walk and so needed constant watching, and Charlotte with Giles, who came to visit more and more now that they had become lovers. They continued to be happy and to delight in each other's company, yet no betrothal came to pass. Though I raged at her hesitance to take the very thing I had wanted more than anything else, I was selfishly glad that she was not planning to leave Sleepy Hollow with him.

I had little more success with my visions. Sometimes I would see a scrap of something not seen before: the coat Ichabod had been wearing that night, or the flash of a blade, a large dagger, no longer just the sound of it being pulled from its sheath. That shook me a great deal, but still it told me nothing I did not already know from that first vision, almost two years ago now.

One night in May, I finally asked Charlotte to give me the potion to help bring on visions again. She paused before rising reluctantly and heading for the stillroom. "I suppose it can't hurt," she said. "I had been wondering when you were going to ask again."

"I wanted to, but wasn't sure if it was wise," I said, following her. "But perhaps it will grant me something new, now that I have been practicing."

I watched closely as she gathered the herbs, committing to memory the labels on those jars—nightshade, nutmeg, valerian, and eyebright—as well as the amounts of each that she used. As she made the tea, I quietly excused myself and went back into the sitting room, where my book waited. Opening to a page in the back, I wrote down the recipe for the concoction.

She returned with the mug of steaming tea, and I eagerly drank down the bitter mixture. Then I positioned myself in front of the candle at her table and went through the ritual that was, by now, second nature: deep breaths, eyes closed, then opening them slowly and gazing into the heart of the flame.

At first, I saw nothing. Then, slowly, the flame seemed to expand around me, and I fell into its center, and this time the vision was different . . .

I saw Gunpowder again, with a rider astride him, and beside him—close behind him—was a rider on a dark horse. My breath caught in my throat, but I did not move or make a sound, fearful of disrupting the vision.

Then the scene flickered and changed, and I saw before me the clearing in the woods, the Horseman's clearing. The hoof beats of the two horses grew louder behind me; this was their ultimate destination.

Suddenly I was back to myself again, gasping in my chair at Charlotte's table, trying to catch my breath as though I had been keeping pace with the two horses through the woods.

"Katrina!" At once, Charlotte was on her knees beside the chair, one hand on my forehead, the other grasping one of my hands. "Breathe," she said, her voice low and soothing. "Calm yourself. All is well. You are safe.

"Tell me when you can," she said, stroking my hand. "What did you see? Did you see . . . ?"

I shook my head. "I did not see . . . everything," I said. "But I saw more." I quickly told her of the dark horse and its rider, and Ichabod and Gunpowder—how they had been heading for the clearing, for whatever reason. "Whatever happened, happened there," I said. "Oh, Charlotte, he was being chased, or driven away, or some such. He did not leave, not of his own accord."

Charlotte paused before speaking. "Perhaps," she said neutrally.

I remembered the body that had been pulled from the Hudson, the corpse that had been stabbed or shot or its throat slit or all three, and shuddered. I no longer knew what to hope for.

"You must give me some more of that herbal potion," I said. "Just a bit more. I'm sure that if you do, I'll see the rest."

Charlotte was shaking her head before I'd finished speaking. "It would be too much, Katrina, too much in one night. Too much for a week, even. I cannot."

"Charlotte, please. I'll see the rest, I can feel it, and then after tonight I won't need it ever again—"

She rose to her feet. "No, Katrina. I will not. Do not ask me again. I know this is important to you, but it is not worth your well-being."

"It has already cost me my well-being," I all but shouted, but I could see that she was not to be moved. "The not knowing. Can you not see that?"

"Do not tear yourself apart over this, Katrina," Charlotte said, an edge of iron in her voice. "You have your daughter to think of, if you will not think of yourself."

"Very well, then," I said petulantly. Suddenly, a new idea occurred to me. "If you will not give me any more of the potion, then will you do me another favor?"

Charlotte looked wary. "What is it?"

"Will you ask Giles to write to Ichabod's mother again?" I asked. "That will no doubt let us know if Ichabod simply left, at least. If he had, he would not be hiding from his mother."

Charlotte's expression cleared. "Yes, I surely can. I wonder that we didn't think of it sooner. I'll have him write as soon as he may," she promised. "You should go home and get some rest. You are no doubt very taxed by everything that has passed tonight. Best to sleep, and let the herbs pass through your body."

That night my dreams were vivid and bloody, but thankfully I did not remember much of them when I woke.

Giles worked quickly—as he no doubt did with everything Charlotte asked him to do—and two weeks later we had an answer to our query.

"Ichabod's mother has not heard from him," Charlotte said, handing me the letter as she stepped into the house. "Not a word since before All Hallows' Eve, the year before last. She has mourned him and given him up for dead, it seems."

I scanned Giles's letter; it said more or less what Charlotte had just told me. I had thought there were no intact surfaces remaining on my heart, but at this, I felt another crack splinter through it. "He is dead, then," I said, my voice emotionless as I fought back tears. How did I still have any left to cry over this man? "He is dead, or in hell. Carried there by the Headless Horseman." A tear splashed down onto the letter, blurring its ink even as it could not erase its message.

That evening, as dusk was falling, I left the house alone and walked to the old schoolhouse. Even now the villagers swore it was haunted by the ghost of Ichabod Crane. I did not know if this was true, but as I stepped into the worn-down building, the front door hanging precariously off of its hinges, I intended to find out.

"Please," I whispered into the still room. A few broken desks and chairs littered the floor, but it was otherwise empty. I walked to the center of the room and began to speak louder, my voice echoing around me. "Please, Ichabod. If you are really here—if you really haunt this place—show yourself to me. To me, of all people. Your love and the mother of your child." My voice wavered, thinking of Anneke and how she now walked so proudly, if unsteadily, on her chubby legs. "She is beautiful. And you are not here to see her. So let me know where you are. Please." I fell silent, waiting, listening for a sign. A part of me thought if Ichabod's ghost waited for me anywhere, it was surely at our clearing by the stream near the Van Tassel farmhouse. But I could not bear to go there. So I was here instead. "Please. *Please!*" I cried. I was shouting now. "Show yourself to me! *Where are you!*" I collapsed onto the rotting floorboards, sobs wracking my body.

Suddenly I thought I heard something, the strains of a familiar melody, a song perhaps. Could it be . . . ? I froze, straining my ears to better hear it.

Perhaps it was in my head, for it was less certain, less real, than any of the visions I'd had. But I thought I heard a man's voice, familiar as my own body yet hollow as an echo, singing the song of the lotus flower, the willow tree, and the star-crossed lovers.

54

Warmth

Anneke's first birthday came and went, and soon she was speaking. Her first word was "Mama," and next was "Nancy," much to that noble lady's delight, and her third was "Papa." A close fourth was "Charla," which her godmother knew undoubtedly was meant for her. Soon she had a whole slew of words at her command, both English and Dutch. Sometimes I gazed at my happy little girl with her blond ringlets and bright green eyes and couldn't believe it had been a year already since I'd borne her. At other times it seemed as if I could see the woman she would grow into one day, as full of light and hope as I'd once been, and I did not know if this was second sight or just a mother's wish.

Spring wore into summer, and Brom found more excuses to stay home with us, cutting down on his time in New York. And I found I did not mind. I had begun to like having him home; I laughed as he capered about the house on all fours with Anneke on his back and blinked back tears of tender affection as he sat beside her until she fell asleep. I even enjoyed when he would give me a quick kiss as we passed each other in the house, or before he left on some errand for the day. He carved little dolls and toys for Anneke to play with, and I found myself remembering how, even as a boy, he had been skilled enough to make such things for Charlotte and me.

I hovered much over Anneke, concerned always with her health as summer wore on—three years ago now had seen a horrible epidemic of yellow fever in many of the cities, and I scanned the news sheets from New York as often as I could for any new mention of disease. But there were none, and Anneke continued to be hale and healthy. The news was all of politics—of George Washington's decision not to seek another term as president, and what that would mean for our young nation. Debate raged even in our sleepy hamlet. How could the country go on without him, the only leader it had ever known? Who could fill his shoes? No one, it was concluded. And so everyone in the village was in one of two minds—the country would forge ahead without him, or it would crumble. There seemed to be no middle ground, or at least none anyone was willing to entertain. For myself, and for my daughter, I prayed this idealistic yet flawed nation would endure for centuries.

One night, Brom had Nancy make us up a picnic to take out into the garden, where he spread a sheet over the ground and brought out the food: chicken and bread and cheese, along with some ale. Nothing elaborate, but a lovely meal all the same. We enjoyed our food in the warm summer evening air as Anneke raced around the garden, chasing Nox, and babbling importantly to him and to her dolls.

Brom caught my eye and grinned. "Do you think she is telling them stories?"

I returned the smile, admiring his fine features—he *was* a most handsome man, after all. "Perhaps. Even at her age, she has a great deal to say."

"Just like her mother," Brom said. "You remember, do you not, how when we were children you used to make up such wonderful stories to tell us? You had no shortage of them."

In truth, I had forgotten. Long before I had learned well the folktales of the Hudson River Valley, I had made up my own, just as I had been thinking of doing again. "I have not thought about that in a long time," I said. I laughed. "Some of them were quite chilling, were they not? The air must be very haunted here in Sleepy Hollow indeed, for me to have come up with such tales as a child."

Brom shuddered. "I never told you this, but I was always terrified by your tales. Often enough I would lie awake at night after you'd told one, dreading the appearance of some specter at my window."

I laughed again, surprised. "Truly?"

"Truly. But I could not admit to being afraid, could I?" He paused, eyes filled with the truth behind what he had said: his father had never brooked any fear or weakness from his son, so Brom had never been able to confess fear to anyone. For a moment my mind flickered to Charlotte's prediction, and Brom's reaction. Perhaps the only way that he knew how to admit his fear then was to accuse her of something others would fear as well, so he would not be alone in his terror. I frowned, feeling sympathy toward him where before there had only been anger and disdain. It did not excuse what he had done to Charlotte, but it explained it.

"No," I said at last. "Though most people would believe you incapable of fear, Brom Van Brunt."

He reached out and cupped my chin in his hand. "They are wrong," he said, his voice low and urgent. "There is so much I fear." With his other hand, he gestured at Anneke, the garden, the house. "I fear losing you, and Anneke. All of this. I fear losing everything we have, everything I have wanted for so long."

This time it was I who leaned forward and kissed him—and only because I wanted to. He kissed me back, and I felt more at peace than I had in many, many months.

We were interrupted by Anneke dashing over to stand before us. "Look!" She held out her dolls for our inspection, as though we had not seen them before.

Brom drew her onto his lap and kissed her golden curls. Our eyes met over the top of her head, and suddenly I was afraid of losing all we had built together, too.

———

That night, with Anneke fast asleep, Brom and I undressed one another, and I climbed eagerly into bed, pulling him down atop me. I ran my fingers down his muscled chest, kissing him back deeply, feeling desire and happy to feel it.

He ran his hands over my body, and I sighed with the feel of it. I wrapped my legs around his waist, urging him on.

Yet nothing happened. He froze, his body tight above me, and groaned with frustration. "Damn it. *Damn it.*"

"Not again," I said. I was surprised—in a way, I had begun to think his difficulty stemmed from my reluctance to engage in the marital act. Surely now that I was eager, and freely returning his kisses and caresses, he should be more successful.

But that did not seem to be the case. "Damn it," he muttered again through gritted teeth.

I reached down and took him in my hand, stroking him lightly, trying to help. But he remained limp.

He shook his head, and I withdrew my hand, crestfallen. "It is no use," he murmured. He sighed again. "I am sorry, Katrina. So sorry."

I was about to ask how I could help, but instead he turned his attention to pleasing me with his hands, and I decided to let the matter drop.

In late August, Charlotte burst into the garden as I was helping Anneke toddle about. "Katrina!" she cried. "Oh, Katrina!"

Anneke stopped mid-stride where she had been running after Nox and clapped her hands. "Charla!" she cried.

I scooped her up in my arms. "That's Tante Charla to you," I told her fondly. "What is it, Tante Charla?"

Charlotte positively radiated happiness. "Giles," she breathed, almost unable to speak in her excitement. "He has proposed! And what's more, he is moving to Sleepy Hollow!"

My mouth dropped open, and I set Anneke down again so I could properly hug Charlotte. "Oh, this is the best news! Why did he finally decide to move here? What has happened?"

"He has been trying to convince me to move to White Plains, but I have been hesitant, as you know. To be honest, I likely would have given in soon. But now, he is going in on a venture with some other men to open a new tavern here, and he will be selling his in White Plains. Apparently, he has been working on this for a while, but everything is finally official. He did not wish to say anything before in case it did not work out, but it has! It has, and it is done, and he is moving here, and we are going to be married!" Charlotte clapped her hands and jumped up and down like a girl, more carefree than I had seen her in years.

"Oh, Charlotte!" I drew her into a tight embrace again. Tears pricked my eyes. "I am so, so happy for you," I said. "Happier than I can say. You have everything you want now!"

She beamed. "I do, everything that I have wanted and thought I would never have. We will not be able to marry for a time, of course," she said. "He will need to finalize his affairs in White Plains and get his business started here, then find a house for us. So it will be some time yet, but my mother has agreed, and his parents, and we are to be married in the church here as soon as he is settled!"

"I almost cannot believe it," I said. "It is perfect; other than the delay in the nuptials, of course."

"I almost cannot believe it, either!" she cried. "It will be worth waiting for, I know it, and worth all this time and indecision."

"Of course it will," I said. "Giles is a lucky man, and you a lucky woman, to have him. It is not any man who will leave his business and move to his wife's hometown."

"He is more rare and precious than a fine jewel," Charlotte agreed. "I can only hope to deserve him."

"Deserve who?"

"Papa!"

The two of us looked up as Brom entered the garden, Anneke

running to him. He had been in New York again and I had been expecting him back that day or the next.

In spite of the new warmth and accord between us, I was still cautious at him and Charlotte being in one another's presence. "Charlotte has just brought me the news that she is betrothed," I said, my voice even. "To Mr. Giles Carpenter, of White Plains."

"Giles Carpenter," Brom repeated slowly. "Now, why do I know that name?" I prayed he would not remember, that he would just leave us alone to our happiness. "Ha!" he laughed mockingly. "Was that not Crane's second at the duel? His . . . cousin, or some such thing?"

"Yes," Charlotte said, her voice neutral. "It was then that we met."

Brom smirked. "Then it seems you ought to be thanking me, Charlotte. This Giles perhaps not, though. What did you do, cast a spell on the poor man?"

"Brom," I said in warning, as Charlotte's face went white with rage.

"I did not," she said, her voice tight. "Nor do I have the power to do such a thing. He fell in love with me of his own accord, and I with him. I needed nothing more than that to win him. Not that you would understand such a thing."

"And what does *that* mean?" Brom demanded.

"Just that I would not expect you to know anything about winning the object of your affections through honest means."

"Charlotte," I hissed, wondering what she was referring to, what she might inadvertently reveal to him in her anger.

A strange mixture of fear and disbelief crossed Brom's face briefly before his bravado returned. "Oh, no?" he said. He looped an arm possessively around my waist and drew me against him. "And yet I am married to the object of my affections, while you, it seems, are not."

"Not yet."

"Brom, they are betrothed," I said, willing him to calm himself.

"And does he know the truth about you, Crane's cousin?" Brom demanded. "This Giles Carpenter?"

"He knows the vile rumors you spread about me, yes," Charlotte said calmly. "He knows, and thinks more of me and less of you for it."

"You besmirch me to a stranger, you witch?" he shouted.

"I speak only the truth."

"Why, I'll have you—"

"Enough!" I cried, stepping between them. "Not in front of Anneke. And not in front of me, preferably." I scooped my daughter up again and made to carry her inside. "Charlotte, will you help me put her down for a nap? Brom," I added over my shoulder as Charlotte followed me inside, "please act the gentleman before a guest, won't you?"

Brom looked abashed and regretful, and followed us. "Charlotte," he said, his tone subdued, "I am sorry. I should not speak to you in such a way."

She looked surprised. "I had liked to think you might change with age, Brom Van Brunt."

"Perhaps I may yet," he said. I could still see a hint of fear in his eyes as he beheld her, but I could not believe the civility and sincerity in his voice.

She smiled, but I could tell it was forced. "You should," she said. "For what, in truth, have I ever done to you?"

He had no answer, and with that she left.

55

Impotent

"Damn it. God damn you, Katrina. God *damn* you!"

I wrenched myself away from Brom. Once more, he found himself unable to perform the marriage act, his member slack against his legs, and no amount of vigorous stroking on his part or mine could rouse it to action. "You blame me for this?" I burst out. That was new.

"You and that witch have cursed me," he growled. "I know it. You must have. I have never had this problem before, not with any other woman. Only you."

"How dare you." I was truly hurt. After the tenderness that had sprung up between us of late, he would now seek to blame me? "You have done a fine enough job on your own with drink this evening, I think. I have no idea how to do such a thing, nor does Charlotte." A lie well told. "You have long accused my best friend of being a witch; now you accuse me, too? Your wife?" I demanded.

"How else to explain this?" he asked, gesturing down. "You must have cursed me, or poisoned me, or ill-wished me. Or she did. Or you both together."

I leapt from the bed, angrily grabbing my shift from the floor, where Brom has tossed it in the hope that tearing my clothes from my body would suitably arouse him. "You are a fool," I said. "And if you ever repeat such vile accusations in anyone else's hearing, about either me or Charlotte, being unmanned will be the least of your problems, that I can promise you." With that I left to sleep in the guest room.

"Katrina, wait . . . I am sorry, of course it is not your fault. I am frustrated, that is all . . ."

I slammed the door behind me.

The rest of the summer passed, and Charlotte continued to live in a blissful haze over her upcoming nuptials, though a date had yet to be set. Giles was still finalizing the sale of his tavern, and was unfortunately faced with the prospect that he would likely need to build his own home for himself and Charlotte, further delaying the wedding. But none of this dampened Charlotte's good spirits, though she longed to make wedding plans, and every once in a while her frustration showed.

I continued to warm to Brom further, though we still argued at times. It was to be expected when we had been at loggerheads for so long. Besides, we had the rest of our lives to continue smoothing out our relationship—a prospect that once made me despair, yet now brought me a feeling of contentment.

But I was not content with everything. Soon it was time for the harvest again. Two years had passed since Ichabod's disappearance, and I had let his fate remain a mystery. I was ashamed of my failure in a way I could not have explained to anyone else. Though I was happier in my life than I had been, it was still not the one I would have chosen. My visions all continued to be of the clearing in the forest—nothing more and nothing less. But why? Why on earth had Ichabod been there? Why had he been riding through the forest at all? After two years I still only had some of the pieces, but not enough to put it all together, the whole shattered picture.

The clearing was the key, though I had not known it on that winter day when Charlotte, Nox, and I trekked through the snow and frost to get there.

My desperation to know the truth grew to a height only matched by those days immediately following Ichabod's disappearance. Again the flighty birds of my thoughts returned, relentlessly hopping from one branch to the next and giving me no peace, except in sleep. Every time I looked at Anneke I saw reproach in her face, that I did not yet know what had happened to her true father. It was all in my head, of course, but it did not stop the feelings of anguish and guilt.

And so I decided what I must do, in the days leading up to All Hallows' Eve, when the veil between this world and the next is the thinnest.

October 30th dawned bright and warm, the latter perfect for what I had in mind. I kept an eye on the Jansen cottage all morning. After noon, I saw Charlotte leave the house, and after waiting to make sure she was not coming back, I acted.

I went up to the cottage and knocked. Mevrouw Jansen answered, as I had anticipated. "Katrina," she said warmly. "How nice to see you."

"Good day," I said pleasantly. "Is Charlotte home?"

"No, she just went off to see Mr. Carpenter," Mevrouw Jansen said. "I'm sure you know he is in town."

"Yes, indeed. Well, I believe she left some herbs for me in the stillroom. She said if she was out I could pop in and grab them."

Mevrouw Jansen studied me for a beat too long, then stepped aside. "Very well, then," she said. "Do you need any help?"

"No, thank you," I said, moving toward the stillroom door. "She told me what I need to know."

Once I was certain Mevrouw Jansen had no plans to follow me, I acted quickly. Pulling a scrap of paper from my pocket, I read it quickly, then pulled the appropriate jars from the shelves. I took just a bit more of each than what Charlotte had given me the last time. I placed them in a small glass bottle I'd brought with me and stuffed both the bottle and the paper deep into the pocket of my

THE SPELLBOOK OF KATRINA VAN TASSEL 371

cloak. Please forgive me, Charlotte, I thought. She would find out what I had done eventually, and I could only hope that she would understand.

I went home, tossing the scrap of paper into the kitchen fire when Nancy was not looking, and went and locked the bottle of herbs into the same drawer as my notebook. Now all I needed was for night to fall.

Then I would have my answers, once and for all.

56

The Fate of Ichabod Crane

As dark began to fall that night, I went to find Nancy in her room, Anneke in tow. Brom was out drinking with friends, celebrating the harvest and the end of all their hard work. "Nancy, can you do me a favor?" I asked brightly.

She eyed me warily for a moment, and I knew she'd seen right through me. "Of course, Katrina," she said. "What is it?"

I squeezed Anneke's hand. "Will you put Anneke to bed for me tonight? I am off to visit with Charlotte."

There was no reason at all for Nancy to doubt my explanation or to think anything of it whatsoever. Anneke enjoyed being put to bed by Nancy just as much as she did by me; Nancy, I knew from personal experience, was also an excellent teller of bedtime stories. Anneke, as if on cue, reached out for Nancy. "Nancy!" she cried.

Nancy smiled and rose from her chair, picking up Anneke. "A bath for you, angel, and then bed," she said. She glanced up at me, searching my eyes and finding something she did not like. "Katrina . . ." She sighed. "I wish you wouldn't do this."

"I have to." I gestured to my daughter. "For her as much as for me."

"I don't know that I believe that. You remember what I told you about the price to be paid?"

I nodded unwillingly.

"Don't forget it. And if you must do this—if you *really* feel you must—then be careful." She kissed Anneke on the top of her head. "This little one cannot lose you. And neither can I."

Tears threatened behind my eyes, but I blinked them away. "I do not know what you think will happen, Nancy, but—"

"You are playing with forces outside your control," she said. "Anything could happen."

"I have to know, Nancy," I said softly. "I have to know what happened to him."

"And there may be some things you are better off not knowing, Katrina Van Tassel."

Afterward, a part of me would always wonder if everything would have been better if I'd listened to her that night. "I'm sorry, Nancy. I know we disagree about this. But I will not turn back now. I cannot."

Both she and Anneke regarded me in silence. "Be careful," she said at last. "Please be careful."

"I will," I assured her. "I promise." I gave Anneke a kiss on her forehead. "I shall leave Nox here as well," I said, turning to leave. I went into the kitchen, swiftly packing a basket of the things I would need, and donned my cloak against the nighttime chill. Nox was waiting by the door, whining, as if he, too, knew where I was going and what I was going to do, and wished that I would not.

"It'll be okay, boy," I whispered. I bent down to kiss his head, then headed out into the eerie night.

I paused at the edge of the churchyard and looked up at the plain, brick-and-clapboard building. I said a silent prayer that I might be protected from evil that night, and might find what I sought and escape unscathed. Even then, I was not sure what I meant by *unscathed*. And I wondered if God or his angels would hear my prayers, if they granted the prayers of witches. For I was certainly as much of a witch as Charlotte, now.

What would Ichabod think of me if he could see me, dabbling in such arts as he had always feared and mistrusted? Would he even know me? Would he recognize who I had become?

Would he fear me?

But it did not matter. He was gone, and I had become who I needed to be in his absence. And tonight I would find out why.

I headed into the woods behind the churchyard, taking the same path Charlotte and I had that January day, one I had not walked since. I shivered in the nighttime air, remembering all those nights I had gone into the woods to meet Ichabod, and the things I had feared and fancied I'd seen and heard. I tried to clear my mind of all the things I'd written in the book now resting in the basket I carried: the Woman in White of Raven Rock; Major Andre's ghost; the ghostly rower on the Hudson, and so many more. And, of course, the one story I still had yet to write down, the one that haunted my entire life: the legend of the Headless Horseman.

Yet the more I thought about the Horseman, the more my fear faded, and the more I almost—almost—wished he would appear. He might as well save me some time and show himself.

I made my way purposefully along the path; my feet somehow knowing the way despite having only walked there once. Is this where Ichabod rode that night? I wondered. Is Ichabod guiding me to the truth at last? Or is it someone—or something—else?

My ears stayed perked for the sound of hooves, for a horse's whinny, and my eyes peered into the dark shadows for a glint of orange and flame through the branches. But there was nothing but the wind in the trees, scattering dry leaves as I walked.

When at last I stepped into the clearing, I could not resist a shiver.

The moon—nearly full—floated directly above the clearing, bathing the circle of grass and dirt in a silvery light. It created a spooky scene, with the pale glow casting the shadows of gnarled and bare tree branches against the ground like so many grasping and twisted claws, but I told myself to be glad of the moonlight. It would be easier to see as I went about my task.

I set my basket near the center of the clearing and gathered a bundle of dry twigs and leaves to use as kindling, then dragged over larger branches and logs. I began to sweat slightly beneath my midnight blue dress and cloak.

Fog started to creep in, blanketing the ground as I worked, a remnant of the unseasonably warm day. I shivered again, trying to ignore the feeling of foreboding as I returned to the center of the clearing, having gathered enough firewood.

I withdrew the flint and steel from my basket. I struck it once, twice, three times and got a spark, which quickly caught on the kindling. As the flames grew, I added a few larger branches, and then finally one of the logs.

I waited as the fire blazed higher and higher, shrugging my cloak off and letting it fall to the ground as the heat grew more intense. Next, I withdrew from my basket a bottle of red wine, a silver goblet, and the bottle of herbs I'd taken from the Jansens' stillroom. Pulling out my book and opening it to the proper page, I consulted the recipe I'd hastily scribbled down, even though I had it well memorized by then. I poured the wine into the goblet, and then opened the herb bottle. Steeling my resolve, I dumped them all in, swirling the mixture in the goblet. I placed it near the edge of the fire to warm the wine before I drank it.

I glanced around the clearing warily, though what I was expecting to see, I wasn't certain. What *wasn't* I expecting to see, really? Any one of the ghosts that haunted Sleepy Hollow might well have appeared to me, from the Woman in White to Mother Hulda to the Headless Horseman to the devil himself. Yet there was nothing and no one there—that I could see—and so I turned my attention back to the task at hand.

I picked up the goblet and, closing my eyes, drank down the warmed contents in several large swallows. The wine hid much of the bitter taste of the herbs. Once I had consumed it all, I waited a few moments for the potion to take effect, then began the ritual.

Deep breaths, in and out, in and out. Calming my body, quieting my mind, slowing my heartbeat. Once I felt sufficiently calm, I opened my eyes again and gazed with focused intensity into the roaring fire.

"Show me," I said, putting power and breath into my words, forcefully speaking what I had begun to think of as my incantation. "Show me the truth, O flames. Reveal to me the secrets and the truth I seek. Show me, once and for all, what has become of Ichabod Crane."

I stared into the center of the fire, and almost at once it flared up and opened around me, becoming a dark mirror, a window, into which I could see.

It was different this time; everything was different, and I could not say if it was due to using a blazing fire as my divination tool, or the herbs and wine, or the combination of the two. But rather than seeing shadows and flashes of images, I saw everything, as though I were present on that night two years ago, bearing witness to it all.

Gunpowder galloped down the Albany Post Road, Ichabod astride him. I saw his face, at long last, and as he turned to look over his shoulder at something behind him, I almost cried out at the sight of him after so long. I was shocked to realize I had not remembered his face exactly as it was; his features were a bit sharper than in my memory, his ears bigger, his hair just a shade lighter. His eyes, though, I had not forgotten, for I saw them every day on my daughter's face.

Yet then I shifted my attention to what Ichabod looked at so fearfully: a rider, astride a mammoth black horse, directly behind him. Chasing him. I struggled to hold back a gasp, so as not to break the vision, as I beheld the rider: for above the collar of his jacket, where his head should be, was nothing. On the pommel of his horse was a pumpkin, carved with a grimacing face.

It was the Headless Horseman, more real than he had ever appeared in any dream or nightmare I'd had in all my life. I was seeing him; Ichabod was seeing him, too.

Ichabod urged Gunpowder on, though it seemed the old horse was already running as fast as his legs would allow. They sped on, pursued by the ghostly rider, approaching the church and the bridge that spanned the stream near it. Ichabod leaned down closer to

Gunpowder's neck, urging him on ever faster, and his hooves made a hollow sound as they pounded against the wooden planks of the bridge. The Hessian's horse let out a whinny, and it reared up. I watched the Horseman pick up the pumpkin and hurl it straight at Ichabod.

The pumpkin collided with his head, taking off his hat and nearly knocking him from his horse. Somehow he managed to keep his seat, even as his hat and the pumpkin went tumbling into the stream. Gunpowder, panicking, took off through the churchyard. Ichabod tried desperately to guide him back onto the road, but the Horseman followed close behind and Gunpowder, spooked, would only run forward, away, trying to escape.

They plunged onto the path through the woods behind the church. Some of what I now saw I had seen before. I heard the hoof beats, heard the whinny of the black horse.

Suddenly, the Headless Horseman's coat shifted down. He now had a head. His blond hair glinted through the darkness as he leaned forward in his saddle, urging his horse on. As he moved into a shaft of moonlight, I saw his face, and the shock that tore through me was even greater than when I had seen what I thought was the Headless Horseman, for I had been expecting him.

I had not been expecting Brom.

Ichabod did not duck in time to avoid a low tree branch, and he was knocked clean out of his saddle. Gunpowder whinnied in surprise, yet without the burden of his rider he increased his pace, tearing onward through the trees and brush and out of sight.

On foot now, Ichabod ran, running for his life, looking somewhat dazed from the blow he'd suffered, and I wondered if he knew it was Brom Bones chasing him, or if he still thought it was the Headless Horseman, straight out of the legend I'd told him that day as we'd walked back from our sheltered spot by the stream.

As Ichabod ran on, the path through the trees narrowed, and the branches came down too low for a mounted rider. Brom pulled up his horse—whom I now recognized as Daredevil—who whinnied in surprise and protest, rearing up. For a second I thought that was it; that Brom, having had his fun and played his joke and scared off his rival, would cease and turn back. That this was the end; that Ichabod had simply been too desperately frightened to return to Sleepy Hollow.

Yet the terrifying scene was far from over. Brom leaped down from his own saddle and, leaving Daredevil waiting obediently on the path, started after his quarry on foot.

They ran along the path, in another scene I recognized from my very first vision: two men in shadow, one chasing the other through the trees, breathing heavily as they ran. Ichabod let out a wordless shout of fear and panic. The knot of anxiety in my chest was unbearable as they burst out into the clearing, the same one where I now sat in body, watching the scene in the flames.

Ichabod halted, whirling around, looking for another pathway out, and I wondered if he recognized the clearing from the tale I'd told him of the Horseman. Yet whether he did or not, his hesitation proved a grave error, for then Brom was upon him.

Brom seized him from behind, wrapping one beefy arm around his throat, trying to drag him to the ground. The force of Brom's attack proved too much for Ichabod, who dropped to his knees, disturbing the fog that covered the ground. Yet once on the ground Brom's hold must have loosened somewhat, for Ichabod was able to slip away and crawl toward the trees, back to the path, scrambling to get back on his feet. Brom was upon him again, tackling him and knocking him flat. Ichabod struggled, but Brom had hold of his jacket collar and arm, and dragged him to the edge of the clearing, flinging him up against a large tree. "What are you doing, Van Brunt?" Ichabod yelled, the sound of his voice a bullet piercing my heart. "Let me go! What in hell are you—"

Brom silenced him by striking him across the face, hard. It took everything in me not to cry out, not to break the vision, though a part of me wanted to end it here and not see what came next.

Brom hit him again, and Ichabod let out a groan of pain, blood now pouring from his nose. Brom punched him one last time and his lip split, more blood trickling out as he slumped against the tree trunk, no longer able to try to escape.

"How dare you," Brom hissed, breathing heavily. "How dare you come here and take what belongs to me."

Ichabod groaned. "No," he denied sluggishly. "I don't know . . ."

"*Katrina*," Brom said. "Katrina. She was supposed to be mine, and you took her."

Ichabod tried, with a shaky hand, to wipe the blood from his face. "I love her," he said, his voice thick. "And she loves me."

Even more enraged now, Brom reached to his side and, in a near blur, unsheathed a dagger that was strapped there, one I had not seen before. The sound that had haunted me, in both visions and dreams for two years, now rang out. I was vaguely aware of tears streaming down my face.

"No," Ichabod protested, seeing the dagger and seeing what Brom surely meant to do. "No—"

Yet in one swift movement, Brom brought his arm back and plunged the dagger into Ichabod's gut.

I screamed. I screamed so loudly it tore at my throat, and I did not know whether I would ever be able to speak again. I did not care. I could not care about anything else ever again.

Ichabod's eyes snapped to mine, to where I stood watching the macabre, chilling scene play out. His beautiful, wide green eyes, just like his daughter's, widened, and I knew he could see me. Somehow, that night, he had seen me. He opened his mouth, and blood poured from it. "Katrina . . ." he gasped.

This only incensed Brom further, however. He withdrew the dagger and plunged it in again, and then one more time, his head thrown back, as if even he could not bear to watch what he was doing.

I screamed again and again, the vision fading around me. The last thing I saw were Ichabod's eyes, still locked on mine, go dark and empty as he breathed his last, blood still trickling from his mouth.

I was still screaming when the fire spit me back out. My voice echoed back to me from the surrounding trees, the fog. "Ichabod! No! No! *No!*" I collapsed to the ground, sobbing so hard I could not breathe, my hair dragging in the dirt. I screamed and cried and thought that I would never stop.

He is dead. Dead, and Brom killed him. Murdered him. I am married to the murderer of my true love, the father of my child.

And the last word he ever spoke was my name.

I could not bear it. I wanted to die as well, right where I lay, did not want to open my eyes to the sight of the clearing where Ichabod had died, did not want to wonder which tree had absorbed his blood. I prayed, begged, bargained, asking whatever spirits or goblins or demons that could hear me to come take my life right there, so I did not need to face the rest of my life with this truth I now carried within me, heavier than gold or lead or sin or death.

The sharp whinny of a horse shattered the silence like glass.

I sat up, thinking my wish was going to be answered. That the Headless Horseman was coming for me.

I sat up, screaming again as I saw a figure seated on the other side of the fire, opposite me.

But it was not the Headless Horseman.

It was Charlotte.

57

What Charlotte Knew

I tried desperately to regain my breath, Charlotte's eyes and mine locked across the flames crackling between us. She did not look away, silent and still and unflinching as a statue. Her pale skin and red hair glowed in the light of the flames, unearthly and ethereal, like a spirit of the fire. Finally, when I could breathe normally again, she spoke. "You know. You saw."

I stared hard at her. "You knew."

She nodded once, slowly. "Yes."

I felt as if a dagger had been plunged into me as well. "You knew," I repeated, "and you never told me."

She nodded again, not bothering to deny it. "Yes."

"How could you?" I whispered.

She arched an eyebrow at me. "Would you have believed me if I had just told you?"

"*Yes*," I said, in an anguished whisper.

She went on as though I had not spoken. "Would you truly have believed me if I had told you? If you had not seen it yourself? If you had not found out on your own?"

"I . . ." As her words began to penetrate my drugged, grief-fogged haze, I began to wonder.

"You would not have," she said. "I know you, Katrina, better than anyone else on earth. You would have denied it, insisted on finding the truth for yourself. On seeing it for yourself."

I could not deny what she said, yet her betrayal still stung. "How long have you known?" I asked, voice hushed.

"Since that winter day when we came here to investigate."

I remembered that day well, remembered the moment when I had seemed to stir her from a reverie. She had been staring off into the distance, at nothing, seemingly. I had recognized the look on her face, had known it well, yet when she'd brushed my questions aside I had not pushed the matter. *I was merely lost in thought*, she had said, and like a fool—even though I knew better—I had not questioned her further.

"You knew, all this time. The day . . . oh God, the day we heard about the body in the Hudson. You reassured me. *You reassured me* it likely was not Ichabod. But no doubt it was. You knew, and you were giving me false hope."

She shook her head. "What was I supposed to do? You were eight months pregnant. I needed to calm you down, for the good of yourself and the child, so I said what I needed to say."

But they were still lies! I wanted to rage at her. *You knew better, and you lied to me!*

"I had a vision," she said, her words slow and clear. "I was in Giles's bed at the inn, trying to fall asleep, when I saw you here, with your fire and your herbs. And I knew I had to leave my lover's bed to come to you." She looked at me evenly. "You stole the herbs from me." She paused. "What you did was dangerous. Did you think that I would not find out?"

"I had no choice, Charlotte. I couldn't not know any longer. Why did you not let me have them when I asked? Why did you not let me see this so it could all be over?"

"Has it occurred to you yet I *was* trying to help you?" she asked. "Once I knew the truth, I did everything I could to protect you."

"*Protect* me?" I cried. "By hiding the truth, denying that you knew it, and lying to me? By deciding on your own what is best for me?"

"And now that you know?" she inquired, almost conversationally. "Do you feel better now that you know the truth, Katrina Van Tassel? Do you feel at peace?"

I closed my eyes, as if that could block out her words, or the screams of anguish still reverberating inside my head. "You should not have lied to me," was my reply when I finally looked at her. "You should not have made that choice for me."

She bowed her head. "Perhaps you are right."

I rose on unsteady, shaky legs. I gathered my things blindly, tossing them all into my basket.

"Katrina," Charlotte said, reaching out to me, as if now she wanted to offer me comfort.

"Just tell me this," I said, not moving toward her. "You did not knowingly let me marry my lover's murderer, did you?"

"No," Charlotte said at once. "I told you, I did not know until we came here together, after your wedding, and by then there was nothing to be done. I would never have let you marry him had I known the truth. I swear it to you."

I believed her. Donning my cloak, I walked out of the clearing and toward home.

Charlotte let me go. Despite her betrayal, she was a good enough friend to know I was in need of consolation, and a good enough friend to know she could not give it to me just then.

58

The Headless Horseman

I moved slowly, incapable of walking faster, as though it was my body and not my soul that had been injured—and no doubt I was still feeling the aftereffects of the herbs I had taken.

I did not want to go home to face Brom, this man I had married and lived with and begun to trust and, oh God, felt *affection* for. I had reveled in his touch, let him make love to me and pleasure me, and all this time he had been the cause of my greatest sorrow. I almost could not breathe past the pain.

Yet I had nowhere else to go. I could not seek refuge at Charlotte's cottage, not tonight. Nor could I walk to my parents' house. I would never make it there, not in my current state, and even if I could have, I did not want to see those rooms where Ichabod and I had first met and fallen in love.

So I went home, knowing that what would come would come.

When I walked into the house, the clock on the mantelpiece struck three o'clock in the morning. It was All Hallows' Eve again.

I climbed the stairs to my bedchamber and pushed open the door. All I wanted was to collapse into bed and never wake. Yet this was not to be.

Brom was seated in a chair by the window, a single lamp lighting the room. He brought a whiskey bottle to his lips and took a swig. "There you are," he said, though his voice was not as slurred as I would have expected at this hour. "Where have you been?"

I slammed the door behind me, shutting out Nox, who had trailed me anxiously up the stairs. At the sight of Brom, the sound of his voice, my lethargy vanished and was replaced by blinding, crippling rage. I stared at his hands, one draped over the arm of the chair and the other clutching the neck of the bottle. Those hands had been soaked with Ichabod Crane's blood . . . and he had touched me with them, *and I had let him . . .*

With a scream worthy of a banshee, I launched myself across the room at him, wanting to gouge his eyes out with my fingers; rip his hair out; hurt him as much as I possibly could with my bare hands. *Brom Bones, if you knew what was good for you, you would never have come home this night*, I wanted to scream.

Jumping up, he caught my wrists in his strong hands, holding me away from him. I struggled, but I was no match for his brute strength. Just as Ichabod had not been. "Katrina, damn it," he said, his tone a mix of anger and bewilderment. "What in hell has gotten into you?"

I laughed then, laughed so hysterically I knew I sounded like a madwoman. Brom still did not release me, but I could feel him staring at me quizzically. "What the . . ."

I wrenched away from him violently. "You," I hissed, my voice low and venomous. "You monster. You *monster*."

"What the devil are you talking about?" he demanded.

This caused me to laugh maniacally again. "What the devil," I gasped between gales of laughter. "*The devil*, indeed."

"Katrina, have you gone mad?"

"I must have, to have ever married *you*," I cried, shoving against his shoulders hard enough that he stumbled back.

"What the—"

"*I know what you did, Brom Van Brunt!*" I shrieked. "*I know what you did!*"

Fear briefly flickered across his face. "I don't know what you're talking about," he said, but he could not hide the tremor of panic in his voice.

"You do!" I screeched. "*You do!* Or must I tell you? Must I speak the words aloud and accuse you? Have you *forgotten?*"

He went very still.

"*You murdered Ichabod Crane!*" I screamed.

Complete, utter silence fell over the house. Nox did not bark or whimper outside the door; even Anneke, in the next room, did not make a peep, though I did not see how she could have slept through the racket I was making.

I suppose I expected Brom to deny it; expected him to hide behind the haughty, untouchable arrogance that was always his refuge. I had not imagined that he would, or could, do anything else. Yet his shoulders slumped forward. "You know," he said softly.

I was flabbergasted he would admit it. "Yes," I said. "Yes, I know."

He looked back up at me, hatred smoldering in his eyes. "And how is it you came to know, or needn't I ask? I suppose the witch has everything to do with it."

"Not that it makes any difference, but Charlotte told me nothing," I said. Brom could not know how deeply rang the truth of those words, how much they hurt, how much it cost me to say them aloud. "I discovered the truth all on my own." Charlotte was exactly right: being able to speak those words was exactly what I had wanted all along. But I could not admit it yet.

Brom hung his head wearily. "I suppose I always knew you would find out sooner or later. That someone would find out."

"So you do not deny it?" I spat.

"No. What good would that do me?" he asked.

My horror and rage returned in a fresh wave. "You ... you are a monster who murdered an innocent man," I said. "The man I loved! How could you? *How could you?*"

"How could I not?" he burst out. "It didn't seem to me like I had any other choice."

I was speechless, gaping at him.

"I . . . nothing else had worked," he said. "I had challenged him to a duel, had won, even. Wounded him. But he lived, and you wouldn't see him for the weakling he was. I . . . I didn't know what else to do." He curled his hands into fists. "He had taken the woman I loved, the woman I had always loved. The one thing I had ever wanted. I knew he would never leave you of his own free will. I . . . I lost my head. I figured he had asked your father for your hand that night, at the All Hallows' Eve feast, and it seemed your father had said no. I couldn't take the chance that you would run away with him. And so I followed him, meaning to scare him off by making him think I was the Headless Horseman. But then I . . . I got carried away. I was angry, so angry that you loved him and not me. I got angrier and angrier, thinking of him touching you, kissing you. I was drunk, too, and I kept chasing him, and once I got my hands on him I . . . I snapped." He looked up at me, eyes pleading. "I didn't set out to kill him, Katrina. I swear to you."

There was earnestness in his gaze, which perhaps shocked me most of all. That he would tell me this truth, and think his honesty would endear him to me. "Do you think that absolves you of your crime?" I demanded.

"No, obviously it does not!" He took another deep swig from the bottle. "Obviously it does not," he repeated. He laughed harshly, and I could hear the drink beginning to creep into his voice. "For I got what I wanted, did I not? I wed you, as I always wanted, as I always promised you I would. As I always promised *myself* I would. And what has it gotten me? What good has it done me?" He took another long drink and laughed bitterly again. "I cannot look at you without seeing his face. I cannot touch you without feeling his blood on my hands. I cannot get into bed with you without remembering the look on your face the first time I saw you after he disappeared—after I killed him. That look in your eyes when I knew it had all been for naught; that this sin which stained my soul was for nothing, for you would never love another man except for him." He shook his head. "I am like the king in that tale you told us when we were children—the king whose touch turned everything to gold, even his food, so that it was cold and metallic in his mouth and could not nourish him. Why do you think I have been drinking so much?"

I was speechless. Whatever I had expected him to say when I confronted him, it was not this. Instead of the unrepentant sinner I had believed him to be since the moment I learned the truth, I found that he had instead been suffering all along. He had done this horrible thing and it was eating him alive from within. It had made him an impotent drunk.

A fitting punishment, though not all he deserved.

I remembered, pain ripping at my heart anew, that evening months ago when we'd had our picnic in the garden, and he'd confessed his fear that he would lose everything, lose our family. Now I knew why he was afraid. And I knew that what I, too, had wanted to hold on to that night had only ever been a lie.

"And yet you married me," I pointed out. "In spite of this remorse you claim to feel, you married me all the same, and quite happily, too. You married me knowing you had slaughtered the one man I truly loved."

He laughed, a hollow sound. "How could I not, after what I had done to win you? I thought, at first, that it would be worth it. It would become worth it. To the winner went the spoils, I told myself. I would become happy again, once I finally had you. And I was, at moments. But it never lasted." He shook his head. "How wrong I was."

"And you never took my feelings into consideration, obviously," I raged. "How I would feel if—when—I found out. Your supposed guilt, your regret, is all focused on you, and how this horrible thing you did has ruined *your* life. You wish you had not done it so that *you* could be happy again. What of me? What of the happiness and peace I had begun to find? Oh God . . ." I broke off, literally choking on my words. I wanted to vomit.

"I wish I had not done it for every possible reason there is!" Brom protested. "Every minute of every day. But it is done. I cannot go back. Cannot take it back, though God, how I wish I could."

"And what did you do with . . . with his body?" I forced myself to ask. "And Gunpowder? Did you . . . oh, God." I felt the blood drain from my face. "That body they pulled from the Hudson. The man who had been stabbed. That . . . that . . ."

Brom nodded grimly, done keeping any secrets. "Yes. That was him. It must have been, in any case. After he was . . . after, I took his body to the Hudson and dumped it in. I could not think what else to do." He took another deep drink. "The horse I hid in my father's barn until I could sell him off to a man who was passing through. My father never noticed."

"And all of the villagers thought Ichabod had been carried away by the Headless Horseman," I whispered. "No one thought any more of it, except as a frightening tale to tell by the fire on an autumn evening. They all but *gave* you a safeguard."

Brom laughed mockingly. "There is no Headless Horseman. *I* am what haunted those woods on All Hallows' Eve. I am the Headless Horseman."

I see blood in your future, Brom Van Brunt. Blood and death. The Headless Horseman is your fate. The Headless Horseman is your end.

I shivered. It had come true. It had all come true, every word.

"Thank God for this village and its superstitions," he added, putting the bottle again to his mouth.

"I do not think God has anything to do with this endeavor," I said. "And you . . ." I began to laugh, the sound sharp and shrill. "Before I agreed to marry you, I asked if you had done anything to scare off Ichabod Crane. And you swore to me you had not. You liar. You *liar*." It seemed such an inconsequential thing to get angry about, after everything, but for some reason it mattered to me just then.

He grinned, a ghost of his old cocky grin. "I did not lie. I did not scare him off, after all. I did much more than that."

I wanted to fly into a rage at him again, at the ghastly way he played with the definition of truth, but I could not. Suddenly, the wrath drained from me, and I felt tears shoving their way out of my eyes again.

Outside Nox, weary of scratching at the door to be let in, howled.

Ichabod was dead. Murdered. He was dead, really and truly gone.

And I was married to his murderer. I had betrayed him three-fold.

The sobs wracked my body, and I did not think they would ever stop.

Brom, still drinking determinedly from his bottle, did not seem to notice. "I see him every time I look at you," he said again, his voice flat. "I see him every time I look into Anneke's face."

I froze. Did he know? Or had his guilt simply poisoned his love for the child he thought his own?

I wasn't to know.

I drew myself up to my full height, though I couldn't have made much of an imposing sight with my tear-streaked face and swollen eyes and muddy dress. "Get out, Brom," I said. "Get out of this house."

"Where do you expect me to go?"

"I do not know, nor do I *care*!" I shrieked. "Go to hell, where you belong! Just get out, and do not come back!"

I expected him to argue, to protest that this was his house, and I his wife, bought and paid for in blood, and he would not leave. Instead, he staggered out the door on drunken, unsteady legs. I heard him clomp down the stairs, and held my breath until I heard the front door open and slam behind him. Only then did I exhale.

Anneke began to wail in the next room, and Nox started barking, adding to the cacophony. My eyes welled again and, my whole body trembling, I moved, shakily, to the nursery next door. "Mama, Mama!" she cried when she saw me, reaching her little arms up for me. I picked her up out of her crib and sat down in the chair with her, clutching her tightly, shaking. I did not feed or change her. I could do nothing except hold her, with all my might, until her crying, and my own, ceased.

59

The Ambition of Macbeth

Once Anneke was again fast asleep, I went back into my bedroom to find Nancy waiting for me.

"What on God's green earth is all the racket?" she demanded. "Where is Brom? What . . ." Her eyes widened as she caught sight of me, my eyes red, my expression devastated, and with dirt and mud still streaked on my face, in my hair, my clothing. She paled. "Good Lord, Katrina," she whispered. "What has happened?"

I began shaking again. "He . . . he killed him. Brom killed him."

"Who?" Nancy asked, though from the look on her face she already knew.

"Ichabod Crane," I whispered.

She wordlessly vanished from the room, returned later with a basin of warm water. She propelled me to sit on the edge of the bed, and I did so obediently, like a child. She dipped a cloth into the water and began to clean my face, wiping away the dirt as I continued to weep.

Afterward, she put me in a clean shift and tucked me into bed as though I were as small as Anneke. "Sleep now," she said, kissing me on the forehead. "Sleep. The world will look brighter in the morning."

"The world is all darkness," I whispered. If she heard me, she did not respond, only went silently out, closing the door behind her.

Nox, having finally been allowed into the room, jumped onto the bed and, after licking my face, curled up close beside me. It was the first night since Anneke had been born that he had not slept outside her door. He knew, in that strange and uncanny and wonderful way that dogs have, that I needed him more just then.

I wrapped my arms around his warm, furry body, unable to stop trembling. I would not be able to sleep that night.

Now that the noise outside of me had quieted, I could hear Charlotte's voice inside my head, repeating over and over. *Do you feel at peace? Do you feel at peace?*

Peace was the last thing I felt. I recalled, too, Nancy saying to me, before I'd left—a different woman, a lifetime ago—there might be some things I would be better off not knowing. I had scoffed. I had not believed her. I had thought nothing could be worse than not knowing what had happened to Ichabod.

But this was worse. Much worse.

I could never escape this knowledge, never outrun it. I could never forget that the one man I ever loved had been murdered in cold blood *because* I loved him. Because he loved me.

He was dead because of me.

If Ichabod had never come to Sleepy Hollow, if we had never fallen in love . . . if I had denied him, denied my own feelings, refused to act upon them, as a well-brought up young lady ought, then he would still be alive. I had killed him as surely as if it had been my hand that plunged the dagger into his body.

To think there had been a time when I thought Ichabod leaving me was the worst thing that could have happened. What a fool I had been. What I wouldn't have given for that to be the truth I now faced.

And I was bound for life to Ichabod's murderer. Fitting, I suppose, since I was his murderer as well. Brom's lust and ambition had brought us to this, and now we both had blood staining us, a veritable Lord and Lady Macbeth. I would go mad like her, unable to forget the blood on my hands; doomed to wander the halls crying, *Out, spot!*

But the desire for power was what was supposed to bring one to a bad end. Not love. Never love.

It was not fair. It was simply not fair.

I began to cry again, quietly.

For the first time in two years, I thought of Ichabod's last words to me, what he said before he had left the farmhouse on All Hallows' Eve night.

All will be well.

I began to sob harder. How wrong he had been. Nothing had been well since that moment, nor ever would be again.

Do you feel at peace?

To think, that I had ever thought such knowledge could bring me peace.

I must have slept at some point, if only because my body could no longer stay awake. When I awoke, sunlight was peeking through the curtains. It was much later than I usually rose. And there were a few brief, blissful moments in which I did not remember. But all too soon, my hideous new reality invaded my mind once again.

I got out of bed, moving like an old woman, my entire body hurting, and went next door to the nursery. But the crib was empty. Nancy must have gotten Anneke up and dressed and fed, so that I might sleep longer.

I was not about to squander such a gift. I went back to bed and pulled the covers over my head.

"Oh, Ichabod," I whispered into my pillow, tears leaking from my eyes again. "I am sorry. I am sorry. I am sorry. I am so sorry."

And Charlotte. Charlotte had known, and never told me. Yet if there was one blessing the light of day had brought me, it was relief of my anger at her. She had wanted to protect me, she said. And well she might. It had been nice, in hindsight, to have been shielded from the knowledge that Ichabod was dead because of me.

From downstairs, I heard Anneke babble on, and Nancy's approving voice in response.

A voice inside me whispered: *You have your daughter to think of. Ichabod's daughter. And if you would seek to atone, what better way than to care for her as best you can?*

It couldn't be that easy. I turned over and tried to go back to sleep.

60

The Mystery
of Brom Bones

"Katrina. Katrina! Wake up!"

Someone was shaking me, and Nox was barking. I groaned and opened my eyes. "What . . . ?"

As I blinked sleep from my eyes, I saw Charlotte standing over me. And it all came rushing back again. "What is it, Charlotte?" I demanded.

"You must come with me. Quickly," she said, pulling the coverlet off of me. "Get dressed."

I sat up. "What do you mean? What is going on?"

"I know that you are upset with me right now, and rightfully so. But there is something you need to see."

"Oh, *now* you want to show me things?" I spat, but my rage was blunted from what it had been the night before.

She flinched. "I suppose I deserve that. But please, just come."

"What is it?" I asked, getting out of the bed and crossing the room to my wardrobe. "What's happened?"

"I . . . I cannot tell you. You just need to see."

I paused and glanced at her. "You've had a vision?"

"Yes."

I pulled a dress and petticoat from the wardrobe. "Quick, help me dress." Charlotte laced me into my clothes, and we started immediately for the stairs, Nox bounding behind us. "Let me just get Anneke and—"

"No." Charlotte's sharp tone stopped me. "No. Leave her with Nancy. This is not something she should see."

"Charlotte, what . . ."

"Just come." She took my hand and practically dragged me down the stairs and out the door.

She led me down the road toward the church, and when she started toward the path that led to the clearing, I stopped. "No," I said. "I am not going back there."

She shook her head. "Don't worry. He's not there. We needn't go that far."

He?

Soon I realized we were not the only ones coming to see whatever spectacle Charlotte wished to show me. I saw a few people from the village up ahead of us on the path, and soon there were more behind us, as well.

A crowd had gathered in the middle of the narrow path up ahead, and everyone was conversing in low voices. A few women were weeping. Charlotte's steps slowed as we reached them, and I did the same. I still could not see what everyone was looking at.

Then someone saw me. "It is her! Let her through!"

"What is going on?" I asked. As if in answer, the crowd parted. I gasped, the breath freezing in my lungs.

In the middle of the forest path was a body. A corpse. And the cause of death was quite obvious, for his head was gone. Not merely separated from his body, but nowhere to be seen. Gone.

And it was Brom.

I knew in an instant, knew his body—as a wife would—even without his head, his face. He was still dressed in the clothes he'd been wearing last night, when we had screamed at each other.

And he was dead. Beheaded.

I remained stock still, gawping at what remained of him. The gathered villagers were watching me, waiting for me to burst into tears, to sob and tear my hair and scream and wail at the sky, or perhaps to faint.

But I did none of those things. I simply stared down at his headless corpse, silently. Nox cautiously approached the body and sniffed at it, then growled and backed away, hackles raised.

Without a word, I turned and walked away, Charlotte and Nox both following on my heels.

Though it would never bring Ichabod back to me, justice had been served.

They made excuses for my reaction in the village, of course, not that I cared. They said I had been in shock, poor thing, and with such a young child to care for, too. But I was glad he was dead. He deserved it, for what he had done, for killing Ichabod and marrying me anyway and making me, almost, start to love him. And if feeling such a thing was enough to consign me to hell, then I would see Brom Bones there.

The villagers also knew exactly who to blame for Brom's murder. It was obvious; there was only one culprit: the Headless Horseman. Brom had been too brash, too bold for his own good, they said. He had run afoul of the Hessian, and not even Brom Bones could escape *him*.

If Charlotte and I were less certain, it was not by much.

"But you did not see who did it?" I asked her, once we were back in my house, a cup of calming tea in both our hands.

She shook her head. "I saw a sword separating his head from his body," she said calmly, as though discussing the weather. "I did not see who wielded the sword."

We were both silent for a while. "Could it have been a suicide?" I asked. "He was guilty over what he had done. He was eaten up with it. Maybe once I accused him, told him that I knew . . . ?"

Charlotte gave me a hard look. "Is a man really capable of cutting off his *own* head? And even if he somehow did it himself, what then became of his head?"

I shrugged. "Animals, maybe? Stranger things have certainly happened. Who else could it have been, then?"

"I do not know." She glanced up at me. "The ghost of Ichabod Crane, I suppose."

"Aye, perhaps," I said bitterly. "Would that he had killed the wretch before I married him. In that case, he shall be coming for me next, for I killed him just as surely as Brom did."

"Katrina, *no*," Charlotte said vehemently, setting down her tea and taking my hands in hers. "This is part of the reason I did not tell you. I knew you would blame yourself, I *knew* it. But you are not to blame, and that is the truth. It was Brom's hand that wielded the blade, and Brom and Brom alone is the guilty party."

I shook my head, beginning to weep again. "Brom killed him because he loved me and I him," I said, tears dripping onto my skirt. "For that and no other reason. If Ichabod had never come here, had never met me, if we had never fallen in love . . ."

"*No*," Charlotte said, with even more force this time. "Do not spend the rest of your life tearing yourself apart over this, Katrina. Please. I beg of you. Ichabod died because of Brom's hate and jealousy and desire and selfishness. For no other reason. Do you hear me? *You are not to blame.*"

"But I could have . . . I should have saved him, somehow . . . should have made him stay with me that night . . . should have realized . . ."

"There is nothing you could have done, Katrina. Nothing. Brom turned evil, somehow. That little boy who was our closest friend died long before the man met his grisly end in the woods, and none of us noticed until it was too late.

"So this is what you will do," Charlotte went on, tightening her grip. "You will raise your beautiful daughter, your and Ichabod's daughter. For you have not lost him, not truly. A part of him is in Anneke. So you will raise her the best you can, and tell her all about her kind, warm, generous, intelligent, handsome, loving father."

Charlotte's amber eyes filled with tears as well. "And someday, when she is old enough, if you choose to, you can tell her how he met his end—bravely, and with her mother's name on his lips."

By this time, I was sobbing, and Charlotte held me until I was through.

That night, I dreamed of the Horseman for the last time. I saw him sitting atop his horse at the entrance to the forest path behind the church, the one that led to the clearing. He sat there, facing in my direction at some distance, as he always had. The flaming pumpkin was in one hand, and his sword and axe were sheathed at his side, as always. Then, he bowed to me from his saddle, inclining his shoulders to where I stood, before wheeling his horse around and riding away.

61

Let It Die

There was a funeral held for Brom in the church, of course. They buried his headless corpse, for as hard as the men of the village looked, his head could not be found. This surprised precisely none of the old Dutch farmwives. "You'll not find it," Mevrouw Douw was heard to say. "It's not to be found. It was taken by the Headless Horseman. Perhaps now that he has the schoolteacher and Brom Bones, he shall be satisfied and leave us in peace at long last."

As Brom's widow I was in the first pew of the church and first at his graveside. I did not know if anyone noticed the lack of tears beneath my black veil, and I did not care if they did. Nor did I cry during the funeral feast that followed, where I welcomed our close friends and family into my house and served luncheon and the *doot koekjes*, the huge biscuits always prepared for funerals.

I mourned Brom in my own way, though. I mourned the man he might have become, if fear and bitterness and jealousy had not warped that boy who was my friend into what he became. I mourned the life we had been slowly, hesitantly, starting to build together; the genuine love that had been growing between us. His father had much blame to bear, in my mind, for never finding his son good enough or manly enough. Meneer Van Brunt had never had much interest in Anneke, and never sought to see her after his son's death. I was happy to keep it that way.

Yet ultimately Brom had chosen his own path. It had been his hand that plunged the dagger into Ichabod Crane, and none other. And he had suffered for it.

I wondered, sometimes, if the Headless Horseman had somehow heard Brom's boast that night. *There is no Headless Horseman. I am what haunted those woods on All Hallows' Eve. I am the Headless Horseman.* Perhaps the Hessian had taken exception to this, to Brom doing violence in his name. And so he had taken Brom Bones's head. Perhaps that was the price that had needed to be paid. And so Charlotte's prophecy was fulfilled more completely than I had ever thought possible.

I see blood in your future, Brom Van Brunt. Blood and death. The Headless Horseman is your fate. The Headless Horseman is your end.

I thought it had come to pass the night that I confronted him. But it seemed Charlotte's prediction had not been quite done with Brom then, not yet.

Days passed, then weeks turned to months. Autumn gave way to winter, as it always does, and what a dark winter it was. I spent all the time I could with Anneke, and with Charlotte, and with Nancy. For any time I was alone was time spent in sorrow and anguish and rage and bloody memory and regret.

I was not the same woman I had been before I learned the truth, and I knew it. And the women around me knew it as well. But I could not go back to being who I was before I learned of Ichabod's death, before I had *seen* it. And I wondered, every day, why I had thought that knowing the truth would allow me to move on. I had thought that, once I knew, my life would somehow change for the better, would become more satisfying, full of meaning. Why had I not listened to Nancy and Charlotte, who had so warned me?

Do you feel better now that you know the truth, Katrina Van Tassel? Do you feel at peace?

"Ichabod would not want you to go on this way, Katrina,"

Charlotte said to me gently, one day in February. "He would want you to live life to the fullest. He loved you. He would want you to be happy, with or without him."

I knew she was right; knew that happiness was exactly what Ichabod had always wanted for me. His death would not have changed that. But knowing it and living it are two very different things, I found.

Her words did inspire me to do one thing, though. That very day, I went home and pulled out both my old notebook and a new one, one that my father had procured for me in New York at my request.

In the last few remaining pages of the old book, I finally wrote down the first story I had ever told Ichabod: the legend of the Headless Horseman.

When that was done, I opened the new notebook. And I began to write down the story—the true story, in all its passionate and joyous and tragic and bloody detail—of Ichabod Crane and Katrina Van Tassel.

In the early spring of that year, I had a dream.

In it, Ichabod and I were sitting out in the garden of my house, the one I had shared with Brom and now lived in with Anneke and Nancy. We were on a blanket spread out on the grass, his arm around my shoulders as I nestled against him. The sun was warm on my skin, a soft, sensual caress. We sat quietly, peacefully, not speaking; then Anneke came running out into the garden.

"Mama! Papa!" she cried, tumbling onto the blanket between us.

Ichabod smiled down at her and ruffled her curls. Then he turned to look at me. "She is beautiful, our daughter," he said.

I returned his smile. "Yes, she is. And so you will have to beat the suitors away with a stick someday, after all."

"I once promised that I would, did I not?" he said, squeezing me to him, and we both laughed.

Then his face sobered. "We will not have another, Katrina."

My smile faded as I looked up into his eyes.

"No," I said slowly. "We will not."

He turned to me and took my face in his hands, his forehead resting against mine. "Take care of her for me," he said softly. "Take care of her, and teach her all you know, with that powerful mind of yours. It has always been what I love best about you." He paused. "And teach her how to be happy."

Tears were streaming down my face. "Yes," I said, my voice thick. "I will. I promise."

He kissed me once on the lips, gently at first, then with more passion. "Love her for me," he whispered. "And know your love was the greatest gift of my life. Never forget that I love you. Always."

I was still crying when I woke up. And I thanked God and whatever powers existed that I lived in Sleepy Hollow, where such magic was possible.

That day turned out to be marvelous and sunny, the first truly warm day of the spring. After I had broken my fast, I asked Nancy if she would watch Anneke for a time. "I am going to go for a walk."

Nancy smiled encouragingly. "You do that, Katrina. It is a fine day."

"I will take Anneke out into the garden with me when I return," I said, donning my cloak and stepping outside.

I walked past the Jansen cottage, not seeking Charlotte's company that day. She was likely not home, anyway. Giles had bought a plot of land along the Albany Post Road, and construction had just started on their new house. It would be modest to start with, but they could always add on to it later, if and when his new tavern became as successful as he predicted. They planned to marry in the fall, once construction was finished.

Charlotte had asked my permission to tell Giles the truth of Ichabod's fate, and I had granted it. We would leave it to him how, and whether, Ichabod's mother should be told. Furthermore, with Brom dead, there was no reason Giles should not also know that

Anneke was Ichabod's daughter, so long as he kept the matter to himself. She was, after all, his cousin by blood. And so Charlotte and I would soon be related, in a fashion.

I walked down the Albany Post Road, seeing a few people I knew but not stopping to greet them. When I reached the Van Tassel property, I turned left and walked down the path through the forest toward what had once been my favorite spot to read, and then my and Ichabod's lovers' nest.

Before I set foot in that small clearing by the stream, I froze, my breath catching in my throat. I had not been here for years now. But nothing had changed. It seemed no one else had discovered this spot and sought to claim it as their own, and for that I was glad.

I lowered myself onto the bank of the stream, spreading my skirts around me. I listened to the water trickling over rocks and branches, reminding me of Ichabod's guitar playing. I listened to the birds in the trees above me, exultant at the coming of another spring, and to the light breeze rustling the leaves of the trees, finally feeling the first measure of true peace I had known in a long time.

I thought about how, just last month, John Adams had been sworn in as the second president of the United States of America, the same man who was a longtime patriot and revolutionary and had been George Washington's vice president. A man who knew how the government worked, and what to expect, and what we as a country needed. The nation was, in fact, moving on. And perhaps so must I. Perhaps it was time to move ahead with my life, to revisit those dreams I had as a carefree girl, of seeing more of the world than just my ghostly little corner of it, of sailing to London and seeing a play in Master Shakespeare's theatre. I could take Anneke. Charlotte would be happy to accompany us.

I would never cease to be sad or enraged at Ichabod's death, nor the manner of it. I would never rest easy with it. But I could accept it, and lay the past to rest. I could let it die.

I began to hum, softly at first, then louder. It was the song about the willow tree and the lotus flower and the lovers, the one I was sure Ichabod had written for me. For us. Then I began to sing aloud, at full voice. But unlike the time I had sung it here before, when I had tried to bid goodbye to my memories, my voice was full of joy and hope, not sorrow. The lovers in the song were star-crossed, and separated, but it was not forever. I had my memories, and I would no longer try to push them away. I would cherish them. And someday Ichabod and I would meet again, on the other side.

As I finished singing, a white crane rose from behind a tree along the bank and soared up into the sky. And I smiled.

Author's Note

Washington Irving's short story "The Legend of Sleepy Hollow" is one of the best-known works in the American literary canon. His characters—Katrina Van Tassel, Ichabod Crane, Brom Bones, and perhaps especially, the Headless Horseman—have traveled down through the centuries, and still make appearances in today's popular culture, through movies, TV shows, cartoons, and more.

And, now, this novel.

I suppose I should have been intimidated when I sat down to write a feminist retelling of one of America's most famous literary works—and I was, later on—but when I first started writing, all that mattered was Katrina's voice and the story that she was urgently telling me. As a lover of all things spooky and creepy, especially Halloween, "The Legend of Sleepy Hollow" has always been one of my favorite stories. Yet Katrina, the one significant female character, is portrayed in a rather flat and, frankly, sexist way. There is a line where Irving's narrator even laments, "Oh, these women, these *women*!" And so I wondered what Katrina's side of the story was. And boy, did she tell me.

I have, of course, departed from Irving's original tale in many ways; I have incorporated some aspects of the story while leaving out others, and added in much of my own invention. A retelling, to me, should be built on the bones of the original tale while bringing in something new and different to become a fulfilling story all its own. It is my hope that Katrina's story will resonate with both those who love the original legend, as I do, and those who have not encountered it before.

One of my goals in this novel was to bring historical context to Irving's tale; nowhere in the story is the year definitively stated, though it is certainly after the American Revolution. So I chose a span of a few years that seemed to suit the story best. I wanted to add historical texture and detail to the life of the people in the Hudson River Valley at that time and further flesh out Irving's tale. So while historical accuracy was, of course, extremely important to me, my editor and I agreed early on that of equal importance was establishing Sleepy Hollow as something of an otherworldly place, much as Irving does in the original story. As such, I have taken a few liberties in creating this story and its world.

The area that I refer to as Sleepy Hollow in the novel includes what is today the actual village of Sleepy Hollow (yes, it is a real place), as well as parts of Tarrytown and Irvington. I chose to refer to the entire area that my characters inhabit as Sleepy Hollow, both to simplify things for the reader, and to help create the impression of Katrina's Sleepy Hollow as a little world unto itself. I hope the residents of this portion of the Hudson River Valley, both past and present, will forgive me. The Albany Post Road, which connected Albany with New York City, did indeed run through this area as I have described; today Route 9 runs where this road once was.

The people of the Hudson River Valley in the late 1700s would not have carved jack-o'-lanterns as decorative pieces in the way that I describe the Van Tassels having done for their harvest feast; the first jack-o'-lantern as we know it today was still many years in the future. However, I could not resist adding in this anachronistic detail as a nod to the original legend's association with and impact upon our modern holiday of Halloween. Indeed, in Irving's original story, he does not state that the Horseman's pumpkin is carved with a jack-o'-lantern face. Yet that has become the familiar image of the Headless Horseman, so of course in my version he had to carry a jack-o'-lantern.

I did a lot of research on herbal remedies over the course of my work on this novel as well, and those described within are remedies made with herbs that would likely have been available to Charlotte and her mother in this time and place. The exception, though, is the mixture Katrina takes to assist her with her visions. This is a potion completely of my own invention (though some of the herbs I included in it, including nutmeg, do have hallucinogenic properties), and I have no idea what its effect would be should it be ingested. This is the standard disclaimer not to try to make it at home!

While writing the scene in which the Death card is drawn, Katrina and I realized at the same time that the figure of Death is, in fact, a horseman. I'm honestly not certain if there were decks at that time that utilized this image—perhaps there were, as the imagery of "death on a pale horse" comes from the Book of Revelation in the Christian bible—but it was such a cool and perfect coincidence that I had to include it in that scene. The tarot deck I referenced while writing this novel is the famous Rider-Waite deck, perhaps one of the most well-known and recognizable tarot decks. That deck dates to the early 1900s, so Charlotte's cards certainly would not have had that exact artwork. I did base my descriptions of her cards on this deck, though, to keep consistent with the Death card image, and since that is the deck and imagery likely most familiar to readers.

I based the Van Tassel farmhouse upon Washington Irving's home of Sunnyside, nestled in a gorgeous spot on the banks of the Hudson (and open to the public!). Irving did not live in this house until many years after the writing of "The Legend of Sleepy Hollow," but the description of the Van Tassel farmhouse's location in the original story seemed to fit with Sunnyside. And, furthermore, a woman named Eleanor Van Tassel—whom some have speculated was a possible model for Katrina Van Tassel—lived in that very house before Irving bought and remodeled it.

Dutch was indeed still heavily spoken in the Hudson River Valley into the 1800s, and remained the primary language for many, which I have reflected here, as well as the increasing influence of the English language and culture on the area.

In bringing this era to life, I have tried to be as accurate as possible, though I am certain I have made errors. I am so grateful to the wonderful staff, tour guides, and docents at Sunnyside, the Old Dutch Church, Philipsburg Manor, and the Sleepy Hollow Cemetery for the treasure trove of information they impart to visitors, for their commitment to keeping history alive, and for the wonderful local lore and legends they share. My visits to these sites and others really impressed upon me—as does Irving's original tale—that the people of the Hudson River Valley are and always have been storytellers, and so assisted in my development of Katrina's character as a writer and storyteller herself. I learned so much in the time I spent in Sleepy Hollow and the surrounding area while researching this novel, and I did my best to use this knowledge to bring the novel's characters and setting to life.

I am indebted to two books in particular that were invaluable to me while writing this novel: *Food, Drink, and Celebrations of the Hudson Valley Dutch* by Peter G. Rose and *Legends and Lore of Sleepy Hollow and the Hudson River Valley* by Jonathan Kruk. The former helped me accurately portray what my characters would have been eating and drinking—something that Irving himself is rather concerned with in the original story—as well as providing me with great insight into the Dutch culture of the area. The latter provided me with the wonderful stories that Katrina tells to Ichabod and later writes down in her spellbook. I am extremely grateful to both authors for sharing their knowledge in these works.

For further reading, below are just some of the sources I consulted while writing the novel:

Benjamin, Vernon. *The History of the Hudson River Valley from Wilderness to the Civil War.* New York: The Overlook Press, 2014.

Chernow, Ron. *Alexander Hamilton*. New York: Penguin Books, 2004.

Ehrenreich, Barbara, and English, Deirdre. *Witches, Midwives, & Nurses: A History of Women Healers*. 2nd ed. New York: The Feminist Press at the City University of New York, 2010.

Irving, Washington. *The Legend of Sleepy Hollow*. Ed. Henry John Steiner. 1820. Sleepy Hollow: Millstone Productions, 2014.

Kruk, Jonathan. *Legends and Lore of Sleepy Hollow and the Hudson River Valley*. Charleston: The History Press, 2011.

Lewis, Tom. *The Hudson: A History*. New Haven: Yale University Press, 2005.

Ott, Cindy. *Pumpkin: The Curious History of an American Icon*. Seattle: University of Washington Press, 2012.

Rose, Peter G. *Food, Drink, and Celebrations of the Hudson Valley Dutch*. Charleston: The History Press, 2009.

White, Deborah Gray. *Ar'n't I A Woman?: Female Slaves in the Plantation South*. New York: W.W. Norton & Company, 1985.

Acknowledgments

This novel is very much a book of my heart. So much love and hard work and inspiration went into it, and as such there are a lot of people whose own love, hard work, and ability to inspire allowed me to make this book what it is.

First I must thank Washington Irving, for giving our young country some of its first great literature and one of my very favorite stories. Obviously, this novel would never have come to be without his work. If his ghost is out there somewhere, I hope he likes Katrina's story.

Enormous thanks and my boundless gratitude, as always, to Lindsay Fowler, the kind of friend who would ride out with you at dawn to break up a duel if you asked her. As always, your notes and critiques have made this book better than it was before you read it. I don't know what I'd do without your close reads and your patience with me when I get excited about a new project and can't stop talking about it. Life is easier, and more fun, knowing you're always just a text away.

This is a book very much about friendship, particularly female friendship, and so I must thank—forever and always—my dear circle of friends. I am so, so fortunate to count among my friends some strong, resilient, and amazing women, whose love and support inspired me to try to fully depict the power of female friendship on the page. To my Pumas: Amanda Beck, Andrea Heuer Bieniek,

Alex Dockstader, and Jen Hark-Hameister, I love you all and am so incredibly lucky to have you. I'd face down a headless ghost for you all any day, and I know you'd do the same for me. I can't wait for all of our crazy adventures to come.

Special thanks to Jen and Amanda for road-tripping to Sleepy Hollow with me and letting me drag them to all the historical sites. I think that road trip has become our own personal legend! And thank you for all the Halloweens past, present, and future.

Extra thanks to Jen for taking my author photo for this book, and for creating AMAZING promotional graphics for this novel. You are so talented I can't even handle it. And if anyone loves this book as much as I do, I know it's you.

My eternal gratitude to my agent, Brianne Johnson, who is so wonderful I'm pretty sure she is magic, and whom you all can blame for letting me write books where people's heads are chopped off! Thank you for loving this witchy book so much, for your unflagging support of me and my work, and for your excellent notes and inspiring advice. I am such a better writer now than when we first started working together, and much of that is due to your guidance.

All of the thanks to that most fabulous of editors, Vicki Lame. I am so, so lucky to get to work with you. This is our best book yet! Thanks for all of your tireless work, for answering my email questions at the speed of light, and for all the Tom Mison GIFs!

Thank you to the art department at St. Martin's Griffin for creating a cover that perfectly captures the vibe of this book. I love it and will never be tired of looking at it!

Thank you to the publicity and marketing teams at St. Martin's for the great job they do spreading the word about my books, especially Staci Burt and Jordan Hanley. Thanks to the foreign rights team for getting my books into the hands of readers all over the world.

My deepest gratitude to my fellow authors who have lent their words of support to this novel: Greer Macallister, Erin Lindsay McCabe, Cat Winters, and Gwendolyn Womack. I am so incred-

ibly honored by your kind words about my work, especially as I am
such a fan of each and every one of you!

Thanks to my Canisius Alumni Writers for reading various
parts of this manuscript. You guys always make me see my work
from a new angle, usually while making me laugh as well.

Thanks to my Wednesday night writing group, in whose presence much of this novel was written. Thanks as well to Public
Espresso, my favorite coffee shop, where much of this novel was also
written (and revised, and revised again).

My sincerest thanks and appreciation to the Canisius College
Creative Writing department for their continued support of me
and my work. A special thanks to Dr. Jennifer Desidero, profes-
sor of American literature at Canisius, for letting me write a ten-
page paper on Washington Irving's famous short story as well as
Tim Burton's version. To this day, that's my favorite college paper.

All my gratitude to Talking Leaves Books, for all you've done
for me and my books and for all you do for so many authors and
for our community as a whole. Buffalo is lucky to have you.

Music is what fuels my writing (and revising, and editing) day
in and day out, so thanks as always to the musicians whose work
inspired me as I wrote this novel: Delain, Nightwish, Autumn, La-
cuna Coil, Kamelot, Xandria, Sirenia, Garbage, Stream of Passion, The Murder of My Sweet, Auri, and Danny Elfman. Special
thanks and shout-out to Phantasma, whose album *The Deviant
Hearts* very much became the soundtrack of this novel.

Thank you to Lin-Manuel Miranda, for writing *Hamilton* and
making me fall back in love with the history of my country.

All my gratitude and love to my family, Mike and Kathy Zimmerman, and Tom and Mary Zimmerman, for your support and
relentless promotion of my books! I am so lucky to have you all.

Thanks and love to my brother, Matt Palombo, for being so
proud of me. And, hey! This book has a duel! FINALLY!! See, I
told you I'd get there eventually!

Thanks to Fenway the silky terrier, for inspiring me to add a dog to this novel. You may be a lot smaller than Nox, but you are no less ferocious.

I have the best, most supportive parents anyone could ask for. Thank you to my dad, Tony Palombo, fellow Headless Horseman aficionado, who loves Halloween as much as I do. Thanks for always encouraging my love of all things dark, creepy, and spooky. And for encouraging my love of history. It all came together in this book! Thank you to my mom, Debbie Palombo, who loves me even with my Goth side, and who is, I think, better at selling my books than I am. I love you both and could do none of this without you.

To all the friends and family members I haven't mentioned by name, thank you for your continued support and love and enthusiasm.

Last but certainly not least, thank you to my readers. It still surprises and thrills me that people read my books, love my books, connect with my books, and want to read more of my books. It means the world to me that my books mean something to others. It is because of you that I am able to continue doing what I love. I am so, so fortunate to have my dreams come true.

1. Were you familiar with Washington Irving's short story "The Legend of Sleepy Hollow" before reading this novel? How did your familiarity with the story—or lack thereof—influence your reading of *The Spellbook of Katrina Van Tassel?*

2. Though much of the novel focuses on Katrina and Ichabod's romance, in many ways Katrina and Charlotte's friendship is the true focal point of the story. Discuss how their friendship changes the course of the story and both of their lives. In what ways is their relationship similar to or different from your own friendships?

3. In what ways might Katrina and Charlotte be viewed as feminist characters despite the restrictions on women of their time?

4. Charlotte knew what truly happened to Ichabod long before Katrina discovered it for herself. Do you think she made the right choice in keeping it from her friend? What would you have done in her position?

5. When Ichabod disappears and Katrina is left alone and pregnant, she makes a difficult decision to protect her child, without knowing whether or not Ichabod will ever return. Did you understand why she did what she did? Would you have made the same choice in her place, or would you have acted differently?

6. If Ichabod hadn't disappeared, what do you think might have happened to Katrina, Ichabod, and their unborn child?

7. Discuss the character of Brom Van Brunt. How did you feel about him over the course of the novel?

St. Martin's Griffin

Did your feelings towards him change at any point? Are there any ways in which redemption could have been possible for his character?

8. What do you think happened to Brom Van Brunt? Do you think the outcome of his story is deserved, or was he—much like Katrina—a victim of his time period and circumstances?

9. What role does grief play in the novel and how does it consume Katrina? Do you think she dealt with it constructively? Or did her obsession with the truth prevent her from finding her way to peace sooner?

10. Stories and legends are very much at the heart of this novel. Are there any stories told about the place where you live? Do you have any family stories that have been handed down over the years? What are the ways in which stories connect the characters in this novel, and how do stories function in our own world to bring us together?